THE MOST WONDERFUL TIME OF THE YEAR

BETH MORAN

First published in Great Britain in 2025 by Boldwood Books Ltd.

Copyright © Beth Moran, 2025

Cover Design by Alice Moore Design

Cover Images: Shutterstock

The moral right of Beth Moran to be identified as the author of this work has been asserted in accordance with the Copyright, Designs and Patents Act 1988.

All rights reserved. No part of this book may be reproduced in any form or by any electronic or mechanical means, including information storage and retrieval systems, without written permission from the author, except for the use of brief quotations in a book review. This book is a work of fiction and, except in the case of historical fact, any resemblance to actual persons, living or dead, is purely coincidental.

Every effort has been made to obtain the necessary permissions with reference to copyright material, both illustrative and quoted. We apologise for any omissions in this respect and will be pleased to make the appropriate acknowledgements in any future edition.

A CIP catalogue record for this book is available from the British Library.

Paperback ISBN 978-1-83633-473-6

Large Print ISBN 978-1-83633-472-9

Hardback ISBN 978-1-83633-471-2

Ebook ISBN 978-1-83633-474-3

Kindle ISBN 978-1-83633-475-0

Audio CD ISBN 978-1-83633-466-8

MP3 CD ISBN 978-1-83633-467-5

Digital audio download ISBN 978-1-83633-468-2

This book is printed on certified sustainable paper. Boldwood Books is dedicated to putting sustainability at the heart of our business. For more information please visit https://www.boldwoodbooks.com/about-us/sustainability/

Boldwood Books Ltd, 23 Bowerdean Street, London, SW6 3TN

www.boldwoodbooks.com

For Sarah Ritherdon
with all my love and huge thanks for your
unfailing support, encouragement and all those nudges in the right direction
I wouldn't have made it to book 14 without you

1

MARY

I'd spent the past few hours trying to convince myself that this couldn't be happening. I mean – obviously I knew it was going to happen. Someone said that the only things you can be sure of in life are death and taxes, but I'd like to add that a pregnant woman with a bump big enough to contain a small hippo is going to give birth at some point.

But it was always going to be *then*. At some future moment in time that was far enough away I could pretend I didn't have to worry about it yet. It was still October.

And while, yes, three weeks before my due date was probably close enough that I should have been starting to get ready, I'd had some other stuff going on. You know, minor distractions like mourning the loss of my career, home, friends who I'd considered more like family, and, most of all, the marriage that was supposed to make all my dreams come true, until everything tumbled into a nightmare.

Plus, the cottage I'd rented without bothering to view in person first was a bleak shell that however many times I vacuumed still stank of a sad, lonely loserness. I had plans about how I was going to make it fit for a new baby. Well, less *plans*, more vague notions when I happened to notice another patch of mould on the bathroom ceiling or spot an indeterminate stain on a scrubby carpet.

And now, after months of floundering around in my grief, no idea who I even was any more, trying to eat something reasonably healthy in between drifting from my bed to the sofa and back again, I couldn't ignore the increasingly distracting pains gripping my humungous uterus. My head was in denial, but my body knew.

I was having a baby, in a house right in the middle of Sherwood Forest, snow falling, and not a clue who I could call on to help me do whatever I needed to do now. I scanned the leaflet that the midwife had handed me at my last appointment, listing useful items to bring to hospital. I couldn't focus on the words, instead stuffing a few random clothes, a bag of basic toiletries and my phone charger into a bag.

Would I need anything else? I added a water bottle and a cereal bar, my purse, and then remembered the free sample pack of maternity pads I'd picked up at some point.

Given it was past nine o'clock, I added a dressing gown in dire need of a wash and a hairbrush.

What about a book? Labour took hours. I wondered whether I'd need something to fill the time, until the next contraction hit, and I decided that giving birth was probably enough to be getting on with.

Okay, bag packed, next step was to order a taxi. The Sherwood Taxis app calmly informed me that, due to high demand, a car would be with me in ninety minutes.

Stress levels building in sync with the pains, making it

increasingly difficult to think clearly, I tried another firm. They wouldn't even accept my booking due to the increasingly bad weather, and because they didn't normally operate this far into the middle of nowhere. The third one I tried was horribly expensive.

I went back to Sherwood Taxis and found their number, hoping that if I could speak to an actual human being, I might persuade them to let me jump the queue.

By the time my phone pinged to tell me the taxi was here, I'd given up sitting and was completing another cumbersome circuit of my tiny living room, mumbling and grumbling under my breath. The twenty minutes since I'd told the taxi-firm dispatcher that I was a pregnant woman, alone in the middle of nowhere, needing to get to the hospital, and she'd promised to send someone over, had felt more like hours. I'd timed two more contractions before I stopped caring, the sensations merely blending into ouch, and oof and the need to get to the chuffing hospital, because my brain had abandoned clear, rational thought about the same time my body merged into one, singular agonising spasm.

I dragged my bag across the floor after the latest contraction eased and opened the front door to find a man-bear looming on the other side.

My attempt at a scream emerged as more of a strangled moan, which didn't really matter seeing as there was no one within a quarter of a mile to hear me.

'Are you all right?' the bear rumbled, sounding even more alarmed than I felt.

He stepped forwards into the light from the hallway behind me and morphed into simply a very tall, broad man in a heavy sweatshirt, snowflakes melting into jaw-length, straggly dark hair as he peered at me with even darker eyes, creased with concern.

'Most taxi drivers wait in the car,' I gasped, one hand still pressed against my pounding heart.

'You're pregnant,' he said, stating the more than obvious. 'I didn't want you to slip.'

He glanced back at the snow settling on the driveway and then at my flip-flops. 'Shoes?'

'I'm pregnant.' I shrugged. 'Nothing else fits.'

He picked up my bag before I had a chance to ask, and held out a hand to take mine.

I hadn't told the dispatcher on the phone that I might actually be in labour, scared it might send any taxi driver heading in the opposite direction. After all, having fallen asleep on the sofa and missed my antenatal class, and not got past the introduction of the book the midwife had begged me to read, who knew if this was, in fact, a bad case of pepperoni-induced indigestion thanks to the pizza I'd eaten for dinner?

So, I did my best to look like a woman who wouldn't be pushing out a baby for at least another three weeks, and, aware that I was completely out of alternatives, gripped the bear-man's hand and followed him into the blizzard.

* * *

The driver hadn't said a word since questioning my footwear – a sensible query, given how cold and wet my feet were – but as we turned onto the main road leading into Nottingham, he kept glancing in the rear-view mirror, the furrows between his eyebrows deepening every time.

'Are you okay?' he asked, giving up on the furtive glances and taking advantage of the current queue of traffic to twist around and look directly at me.

'Yep,' I squeaked, keeping my gaze firmly out of the window, despite there being nothing to see but snowflakes splatting onto the glass and the darkness beyond. A sudden wave of nausea sent my head reeling once he'd turned back to advance the car a few inches forwards.

'Do you know what, I'm actually quite hot. Can I open the window?'

'Not in this weather,' the man replied. 'Try taking your coat off.'

I looked down at the puffy black jacket that had refused to zip closed since September, which I had completely forgotten I was wearing, and started wrestling it off. I now felt less worried about revealing my potential situation and more concerned that I was going to throw up in his car.

'I'm fine,' I gasped, in a futile attempt to convince at least myself, if not him. 'It's fine. I'm just really, really hot.'

And what was going on with my hair? Coat half off, I flicked the long strands of light brown that wouldn't stop falling into my eyes back over my shoulder. Since when was hair this heavy? It was unbearable. I felt a disturbing urge to rip it out.

'Oh. No.' *Here we go again.* 'Not fine. Nope. *Really not fine!*'

I wasn't normally a sharer. Definitely not the type of person to chat to a taxi driver. Yet, I now continued jabbering incoherently about how I was 'not fine', ensuring this stranger had no option to politely ignore the emergency on his back seat.

As the pain peaked, I finally stopped talking, instead gripping the headrest in front, screwing my eyes shut, jacket still hanging off one arm, and let out the kind of groan that would have been mortifying in any other situation. Once the torture had passed, I flopped back, shoulders dropping as I tried to control my breathing.

'You're in labour.' It wasn't a question.

Still, I glanced at his frown, debating whether to finally admit it – to him, and myself – before deciding that he wasn't going to throw me out of his cab into a snowstorm. If anything, he'd find a way to get me to the hospital a bit faster, reducing the risk of things getting messy in his car.

'I'm starting to think so, yes.'

'When did it start?'

'Um, a few hours ago.' I leant my head against the window. The cool glass felt like heaven. 'I'm only thirty-seven weeks, so it could be false labour or something like that.'

He looked at me, impassive. 'Waters broken? It might be a trickle, not a gush like you see on TV.'

I shook my head. 'No.'

'First time?'

'Yes.' I remembered to finally shrug out of the jacket sleeve. 'Is it yours?'

'I've never given birth myself.'

That caught my attention. Had this sombre bear-man made a joke? His mouth gave a tiny twitch.

'Hah. Funny.' I screwed up my face again, doubling over with a moan as everything disappeared into the force of another seemingly endless contraction. I didn't want to tell him, but they were getting a lot more intense. Once it was over, I leant sideways to look at the maps app on the phone stuck to his dashboard. The further we went, the journey time only got longer.

My fear ramped up another few notches.

'I have a medical degree.'

'You're a doctor?'

He shifted uncomfortably on the seat. 'I qualified as a doctor. I don't practise as one.'

'Why not?' I asked, genuinely curious.

'Life had other plans.'

'Ugh.' I slumped lower. 'Tell me about it.'

'Do you want me to call anyone?'

'Believe me, if I had anyone else I wouldn't have called you.'

For the next half an hour we crept along the main – and only – road leading towards Nottingham. In clear traffic, the hospital was about another ten minutes away. At this rate it would be… well, my body was screaming that it would be too late. The driver had turned up the radio, tuned into some easy-listening station, and while focusing on it helped a tiny bit, I concluded that I'd never be able to hear Ed Sheeran without reliving this nauseating, sweaty and scared journey again.

'What's up, Shona?' It took a second to realise he was speaking into his headset. 'Yeah. We're still stuck on the A60. By that new pub, The Jolly Farmer.'

A brief pause. His dark eyes darted to the mirror.

'Thanks for the heads-up.'

'What?' I asked from my current position, sort of crouched along the seat on my hands and knees. While this might not be the safest way to travel, it helped me feel less as if I were going to split in two, and seeing as the fastest we'd managed in the past forty-five minutes was five miles per hour, I wasn't too bothered. 'What's the heads-up?'

He gave a small sigh.

'Not telling me is only making me panic.'

I waited another half a minute. 'Now I'm really worried.'

'The traffic jam is caused by a major accident up ahead, completely closing the road off. We could try heading back out of the city and in through Hucknall, but a lot of the roads that way are impassable.'

'What are we going to do?'

What I really meant was, 'What are *you* going to do, random stranger who I'm assigning the role of hero?' I would have been twice as anxious if it weren't for the impassive solidity of the man in front of me. He seemed capable of handling anything. He knew these streets inside out so he could find another way. Failing that, he was a doctor. What were the chances of my driver being trained in obstetrics?

'Hang on, I have to take this.'

Unlike the two previous ignored calls that I'd nosily noticed were from somebody called Tanya, this time he answered her.

'Hey. I'm sorry... I'm stuck in traffic... I have a woman in the car in labour... Shona tried, they said an ambulance would be hours. Suggested we call the fire brigade. I know, Tanya. I know I promised this wouldn't happen again. Is everything okay, though?... Yes. The last time. I know. Can I bring you back anything – wine, chocolate?... Okay. Thank you. You know how much I appreciate you. Yep. Action not words. I'll see you soon. Bye.'

He leant his head back with a weary sigh.

'I'm sorry. I've got you into trouble.'

'Not your fault.'

'Will Tanya be really mad?'

'Not your problem.' He turned and raised his eyebrows at me. 'Besides, we've got bigger things to worry about right now. Like—'

He was interrupted by a deep-bellied, primal groan.

Later, I might be embarrassed about swaying on the back seat, head hanging low like a cow about to birth a calf. Right now, as the man said, I had far bigger problems that were only getting bigger.

'What's your name?' I ground out through a clenched jaw.

'What?' he asked, as if that was the last thing he expected me to say.

'This all might feel slightly less undignified if I knew your name,' I panted, moving back into a sitting position.

'Oh. It's Beckett.'

'Hey, Beckett, very nice to meet you. I'm Mary.'

'Okay, so – Mary – we aren't going to make it to the hospital.'

I said nothing, too stricken to form a sentence.

'You asked what we're going to do. I'm thinking... this.'

And then he suddenly U-turned into the opposite side of the road, which was empty thanks to the road closure ahead, accelerated about thirty metres back the way we'd come, slowed for a sharp turn into a small side road, then skidded to a stop in front of a large, boxy building.

We sat for a moment. The windscreen wipers on high swished in time with my hammering heart.

Lights in the ground-floor windows shimmered through the twirling flakes, and the small area of tarmac contained about half a dozen cars, already covered in a couple of inches of snow. I glanced at the clock – ten-thirty.

'What is this place?'

'Apart from somewhere dry, and hopefully warm, and with a lot more space than my back seat?' Beckett peered through the windscreen. 'New Life Community Church.'

'What?'

'Everyone welcome.'

'I can't give birth in a church,' I groaned. 'What am I going to do, spread out along a pew?'

'It's literally called New Life.' He undid his seat belt. 'Wait here and I'll check it out.'

'No!'

Beckett quickly reclosed the car door. 'They'll have an office or something. You can get comfortable until an ambulance arrives.'

'*Comfortable?*' I shook my head, grimacing. 'I meant, no, I'm not waiting here. Help me out.'

'Mary, it's a blizzard. You'll freeze, and there might not even be anyone there.'

'Then we'll break in! Besides, look at me.' I waved vaguely at my sweat-soaked top. 'I could do with cooling down. Help me out or I'll climb out myself and probably slip over.'

His eyes met mine for a second, and he must have seen the fear behind my determined stare because he gave a small sigh before getting out of the car and opening the back door.

'You need your coat on,' he said, hair already glistening.

Ignoring him, I heaved myself out before the next contraction hit, leaving Beckett to grab the coat and hold it over my head as he used his free arm to grip what used to be my waist, edging us around the worst drifts towards a pair of double doors.

Everyone welcome, I reminded myself after Beckett tried the door, then rang the bell when it wouldn't open.

It didn't take long for the blurred outline of a person to appear on the other side of the fogged-up glass. It seemed a bold move to me, opening a locked door in a side-street off what wasn't the most reputable area of the city, without ascertaining who was on the other side.

Maybe they were serious about the sign.

'Hang on, hang on…' The door flew open. 'Oh. Can I help you? I thought you were Moses with our pizzas.'

A tiny, older woman wearing a rainbow-coloured jumper beamed at me, a millisecond before I fell against Beckett's damp hoodie, clinging on to his upper arms as I buried my head in his chest and brayed like a donkey.

I wasn't listening to whatever exchange happened between Beckett and the woman, but as soon as the pain eased they hustled me inside, down a corridor and through a side door into a small room with a kitchenette and living space with a large sofa.

My heart began to race, head swimming as the reality of what was happening briefly penetrated the fog of labour. I scanned the room, desperate for something to get me out of this.

Beckett immediately knelt in front of me. The woman had already disappeared.

'Take some slow breaths.' He took my hands, dark brown eyes fixed on mine, voice soft and steady. 'Here, with me.'

For the next few moments, I did my best to suppress the rabid panic as I tried to copy Beckett's slow, steady in and out.

Once I'd stopped whimpering, he gave a gentle nod. 'It's okay. I've got you. You're going to be all right.'

I nodded back, because right then I'd have crawled after him over the edge of a cliff.

'Promise you won't leave me.'

'I promise. We're going to do this.'

'I don't want to,' I whispered.

He gave a wry smile, transforming his craggy features. 'I don't especially, either. But we will. Pretty soon you're going to be holding your baby, feeling like a complete warrior.'

'Warriors die.'

'Not this one. Not this time. I won't let you.'

I let out a pathetic, non-warrior-like sob. 'Am I going to have to take off my knickers? Because I don't think I can reach them at the moment.'

He burst out laughing then, his whole face lighting up.

And then the next contraction came, and everything changed.

It was brute force, and I was grunting for breath.

Squeezing someone's hand.

The hair smoothed off my brow, which felt so lovely I sobbed.

Someone helped me onto the floor. The rug rough against my now bare knees.

Beckett's voice, making no sense but a soothing burble like the brook behind my cottage.

I pressed my cheek into the sofa cushion and surrendered.

2

BECKETT

To everyone's relief, Mary's baby boy slithered into the world with a face scrunched in determination and no apparent issues or anything to worry about. Patty, the woman who'd opened the door, had immediately fetched another woman, Yara, who she assured Beckett was a medical professional, and Yara had handled the actual birth while Beckett held Mary's hand and tried to find something helpful to say. He only felt grateful that Yara waited until she was wrapping the baby in a towel to reveal that her specialism was large animal dentistry.

'I can handle a haemorrhage, help avoid infection. Hooves, trotters, paws. The basics don't change.' She shrugged, while Patty rushed off to let in an on-call midwife who, it turned out, lived only four streets away.

Beckett had witnessed births during his obstetrics training, but had still been mesmerised at seeing how Mary transformed as soon as the midwife helped her into a sitting position and placed the squirming baby onto her chest. Any trace of fear and agony melted into pure wonder as her son blinked a few times, then gazed solemnly into his mother's blue-grey eyes. Beckett turned towards the window, almost overcome at witnessing such an intimate, yet monumental moment.

He was swallowing hard, willing himself back under control, when the midwife appeared at his shoulder.

'Here you go, Daddy, introduce yourself to your son while I help Mum with the placenta.'

Before Beckett could protest, the bundle wrapped up in a small towel was pressed into his arms. He was too dumbfounded by the past hour to figure out if it would be worse to correct her about who he was, and therefore probably have to leave, when he'd promised Mary he wouldn't, or risk the mistaken identity escalating into something that came across far worse in the long run.

He went with his default life-strategy, turned away to give Mary some privacy, and kept quiet. The baby felt as light as the dwarf lop rabbit he'd had as a boy, the feel of tiny bones making him nervous he'd break something.

It was startling – mind-blowing – that here he was cradling a whole new person. Someone with their own individual personality and unique set of DNA. A whole uncharted life ahead of them.

'Here we go.' Patty brought him back to earth by bustling in with a tray of mugs. 'Plenty of milk and sugar for Mummy. I've been in your shoes, love – six times, would you believe it? – and this'll be the best cup of tea of your life.'

Yara took a drink and left them to it, then once Mary was back on the sofa, a bath towel draped over her like a blanket, the midwife settled on a footstool to get started on the admin.

'I don't suppose there's anywhere Mary can clean up before she leaves?' the midwife asked.

Patty beamed. 'There's a shower room right on the other side of that door.'

'Is it normal for a church to have a shower?' The midwife glanced up from her laptop.

'It's our brand-new church apartment. Here in case of emergency. This is our first one!'

'Brilliant. Mary, if your partner fetches your things from the car, he can help you get freshened up.'

'Yeah, I'm not her...' Beckett said, cheeks hotting up.

'We aren't together,' Mary added, half hiding behind her mug. 'Just friends.'

Patty's eyes swivelled between them, looking interested.

'Don't look so worried!' The midwife laughed. 'You're not the first, by a long shot. Whatever works for you. Either way, Mary needs a change of clothes and her toiletries, and this little man definitely needs a nappy and something snuggly to wear.'

'Is it okay if I fetch your bag?' Beckett asked Mary, because he wasn't going anywhere unless she said she didn't mind.

'Maybe leave him here?' she said, smiling as she nodded at her son, to show she was fine about it.

Even so, after gingerly handing the baby to his mother, Beckett had to restrain himself from running down the corridor, across the small car park and back again. He was nothing to this tiny new family, yet felt startlingly protective of them.

While Patty dug through the bag for whatever Mary would need, she discovered a problem.

'There's nothing for baby. Did you leave another bag in the car, or at home?'

Mary leant back onto the sofa with a wince. 'No... I...' She glanced at the midwife. 'I was in such a panic I must have forgotten it.'

'No problem,' Patty said. 'I'm sure we'll have some spares in the toddler-group cupboard. Let me ask Moses.'

She returned a few minutes later with a clean sleepsuit that was only a few inches too big, a nappy and a soft woollen blanket. She also brought Moses, a Jamaican man who introduced himself as the co-pastor of New Life Church. He bore a takeaway pizza box emitting a smell that had Beckett's stomach gurgling with anticipation.

'Shall we leave the experts to it for a few minutes?' he asked Beckett, winking as he placed the pizza on the kitchenette worktop. 'I've got plenty more where this came from.'

'Um. Sure.' Beckett again looked at Mary to check whether she was okay for him to leave. As she nodded and smiled, despite the dazed exhaustion on her face and strand of hair plastered to one cheek, he couldn't remember ever seeing anything more beautiful. Except, perhaps, for the baby in her arms.

He wanted to stay with them. Indefinitely, if possible. But he was already treading a fine line between hero and creep. He sent Tanya a quick text and followed Moses out of the room.

* * *

'So, big night,' the pastor said once he'd collected a fresh pizza box from a room where a handful of people were sitting on leather sofas. They'd burst into applause when Beckett had walked in, standing up to shake his hand or hug him, before Moses led him into an office, where they sat down on either side of a cluttered desk.

'My most heartfelt congratulations.'

Beckett was too hungry not to cram in half a slice before answering.

'Thank you. But I should say, I didn't meet Mary until this evening.'

Moses sat back, warm eyes gleaming with curiosity as Beckett explained what had happened.

'Well,' he said after a considered moment of silence, 'I'd say that accompanying the safe arrival of a new baby warrants congratulations, whatever the circumstances. Besides, from the brief interaction I witnessed between you, I'd be bold enough to suggest your story doesn't end tonight.' He furrowed his brow. 'A woman with no one to call on in an emergency like this is probably in need of a friend.'

'I plan on being that for her. If she doesn't mind.'

'Son, she just squeezed your hand through one of the toughest moments of her life. She's not going to mind.'

Beckett, who when it came down to it could probably do with a couple of friends himself, was starting to like this Pastor Moses.

'Is it normal for a church to have takeaway pizza at almost midnight on a Sunday evening?'

Moses smiled. 'It is not. I've got to get five kids up and out for school tomorrow while my wife hosts a women's prayer breakfast. Believe me, I needed to be asleep hours ago for that to feel like a blessing. But some of us stayed behind for a quick meeting after the evening service, and by the time we'd cleared up, the blizzard was in full force. We decided to wait until it had passed, or at least the main road was open again, before venturing out.'

'You have five kids? Maybe you'd have been better off as impromptu birth-partner.' Not that Beckett would have given up that role for anything.

'All adopted.' Moses grinned. 'Hearing it through the wall was enough to make my insides coil up like a corn snake. Happy to let you take all the glory on that one, my friend.'

Moses carried on while they finished the pizza, asking how Beckett had ended up stopping at the New Life building, the wider impact of the weather, the church, nothing too serious. Beckett tried to respond as if making conversation, rather than enduring a job interview, and his genuine interest prompted him to ask a few questions. However, it had been too long since he'd sat with someone and simply talked, and he felt painfully out of practice, even if Moses' easy manner did help the adrenaline of the past couple of hours to subside.

Eventually, Patty knocked on the door and poked her head in.

'Mary's ready to get going. Bill still has a car seat from when his grandson was staying with him, so he's given it to her.'

'Leant it,' Mary called from somewhere in the corridor. Hearing her voice, Beckett quickly downed the rest of his squash and got up to join her.

'Sorry,' a strong Scottish accent, which Beckett assumed belonged to Bill, replied. 'That's not how we do things here. I'll be downright offended if you give me that car seat back. When you're finished with it, pass it on to someone else.'

As Beckett moved into the corridor, he saw Mary standing a couple of metres away, a bright orange car seat with the baby strapped in on the floor beside her. The people from the meeting room were lining the corridor like a send-off committee.

As he reached her, she whispered, 'I can't pass it on. I don't know anyone else.'

Beckett's chest tightened. 'You know me.'

'Any chance you might need a car seat in a year or so?'

He shrugged. 'Might be useful the next time someone tries to give birth in my taxi.'

She gave him a mock-offended nudge with her elbow, ducking her head to hide a smile, and Beckett felt a strange glow inside his chest that he realised was happiness.

'Come on. Let's get you to the hospital,' he said as yet another message pinged on his phone. He didn't need to check the sender. He was in so much trouble with Tanya, dropping Mary off at the hospital couldn't make it any worse.

'Oh, no. I'm going home.'

'What?' Beckett looked at the midwife, expecting her to challenge this. While he knew that sometimes new mums stayed only a few hours in hospital, and others opted for home births, this was surely different. Mary had given birth in a church emergency apartment. She didn't have a nappy with her. She had a scarily tiny baby to take care of, and no one to look after her. She'd been so distressed, she'd thrown herself at Beckett. Literally, at his chest, and clung onto him for dear life. What if Simon had picked her up instead, or Razza? The prospect of how they'd have handled it made Beckett's fists clench.

'It's Mary's choice,' the midwife said with a shrug, clearly itching to get home herself. 'She'll have a visit from the community team tomorrow, and then the follow-up appointments will be at home too, given that she doesn't have a car.'

'You don't have a car?' Beckett was gobsmacked. Mary lived in the absolute middle of nowhere. There were several inches of snow on the ground.

'Well, if I did I wouldn't have called a taxi, would I?'

Not for the first time that evening, he felt the urge to shout very loudly at whoever should have been helping her. Parents. A best friend. *The baby's father.* What the hell were they playing at?

'Mary's family will be coming straight over now this one's made an early appearance. To be honest, she'll be far better taken care of by them than on a busy ward.'

Mary caught his eye, and he saw the flash of desperation.

She didn't have any family to take care of her.

But for now, she did have him. Tanya would have to wait.

* * *

The storm had blown over, but Beckett wanted all his concentration on the snow-covered roads, so he let Mary doze undisturbed in the car, despite his concerns. Once back at the cottage, he left her bag in the porch before gently nudging her awake and helping her inside, the car seat in the crook of his free arm.

He stood in the living room as she unstrapped the baby and slowly lowered herself onto the sofa, eyes drifting closed. She looked so fragile, yet Beckett was in awe of the strength she'd displayed earlier.

He shuffled, reduced to his standard social awkwardness now the urgency was over, and Mary's eyes sprang open.

'Oh, I'm sorry,' she said after a moment of confusion at why this man was still in her living room. 'How much do I owe you?'

Beckett jerked his head back, startled. That hadn't even entered his mind.

'Nothing! I'm not charging you for this. I'd refund you for the other journey if it wasn't locked on the system.'

'What then? You look like you've been sent to the headmaster's office for a crime you didn't commit.'

Beckett cleared his throat, shuffled a bit more, then accepted that neither of them had the time or energy to faff about.

'Your family aren't coming, are they?'

Mary dropped her eyes to the carpet, cheeks reddening. 'My parents are living in Chicago. For various reasons, I haven't actually told them about this yet. And my brother... he's very busy promoting his latest book, *How To Be Perfect Like Me,* or something like that. His idea of help would be to send me his latest podcast.'

'What do you need?'

This seemed like a relatively straightforward question to Beckett, but after an initial stunned silence, Mary crumpled. Tears began streaming down her face at an alarming rate as she clutched her baby, rocking back and forth and gasping for air.

Beckett carefully took the infant and strapped him back into the car seat, then did what he'd been wanting to do since Mary had opened her front door, several hours ago. He gathered her into his arms and held her while she sobbed.

* * *

'I'm sorry,' Mary said for about the hundredth time as she used the last of the box of tissues on the chipped coffee table to blow her nose. 'I guess it's the hormones. I've cried more in these past few months than the rest of my life put together.'

Beckett suspected there were other reasons for that apart from hormones, but what did he know? He waited while she sat back, straightened her T-shirt and tucked her long hair behind her ears.

'I just... I can't remember the last time someone asked me what I needed. And, to be honest, the answer to that is so terrifyingly overwhelming, I wouldn't know where to start.'

'Okay. Let's start with the essentials.' Beckett nodded at the car seat, then got out his phone and pulled up an NHS list of newborn-baby equipment. 'What on this list do you have, and what do you need that I can find at 1 a.m. in the middle of Sherwood Forest?'

It turned out Mary had nothing on the list apart from some blankets. However, after managing a sort of breastfeed while he'd been eating pizza with Pastor Moses, she'd decided that all she needed urgently was more nappies, cotton wool or non-scented baby wipes and maybe a spare sleepsuit.

'What about a cot?'

'I was going to order one online, but, you know, there are so many to choose from. All these options. They're so expensive I was worried about getting it wrong.'

Beckett got off the sofa and pulled a drawer out of a cabinet on the other side of the tiny living room. He was going to empty it out, but there was nothing in it. 'Apparently this was good enough for me. So, I'm sure that, for now, it can be good enough for... Does he have a name yet?'

Mary looked as though she was going to start crying again.

'It doesn't matter. You have weeks, don't you, to decide?'

She nodded, mutely.

'Had you narrowed it down to a shortlist?'

'I didn't know if I was having a girl or a boy. So when I talked to them, I called them Blob.'

'Yeah. Probably best not to go with that in front of the midwife.'

They looked at baby Blob for a few moments.

'Could do Bob? As a temporary thing while you decide?'

Mary glanced up. 'That would work. Thank you. For this, and everything else. I can't even imagine what would have happened without you. And I'm sorry I'm being so useless and pathetic. I'm not normally like this. Well. Until last March I wasn't. The last few months have been a lot. I think I'm still in shock. That, and totally knackered.'

'Mary, you just pushed a human being, who you grew yourself, out of your body. With no pain relief and only a horse vet to help. I think that's as far from useless as it gets.' He put the drawer down on the coffee table. 'Let's see if this works, then I'm going to find some nappies.'

Mary fetched her baby blankets from upstairs, and they fashioned a bed in the drawer using a thick towel as a mattress, then Beckett left her to it, wondering whether Mary's life wasn't the only one that had changed for good that night.

3

MARY

Now that I was alone in my cottage again – well, obviously not alone, I reminded myself as Bob gave an unexpectedly loud sigh from the drawer-cot – I found it impossible to even think about sleeping. The enormity of what had happened reverberated through my system like the after-buzz from an electric shock. I had a baby. He was here. I was completely unprepared, practically, mentally and emotionally. Both besotted and utterly terrified. The past few hours were mostly a jumbled haze, yet the reality of the present moment filled my vision like ultra-high definition.

I had been a capable, confident person, not so long ago. A company director, managing both a team of other people and my own life. Every day an exhilarating juggle of meetings, deadlines and social events, around which I occasionally squeezed in luxuries like the gym or a hair appointment.

The past few months had been filled with empty time, and no clue what to do with it, even if I had summoned up either the motivation or the mental energy.

And now, everything was him. This seven pounds one ounce of snoozing, snuffling, wondrous life was it.

Time to get my crap together. Once I'd figured out how the hell to do that, of course.

But first, who was Beckett, and what on earth was I thinking, inviting a man into my house, and then blubbering all over him?

My head was blaring a warning siren that a taxi driver claiming to be rather coincidentally trained as a doctor had somehow inserted himself into my highly vulnerable situation. Surely the safe, sensible thing to do was to lock my door and hope he never showed up at the cottage, which was starting to seem like the perfect setting for a horror movie.

My shattered heart, however, had trusted him the second I'd looked into those mahogany eyes and seen something there it recognised. Loneliness. Suffering. Desolation. I don't know. I supposed stalkers and serial killers felt lonely and sad as much as anyone.

Yet... he wasn't alone. Tanya was waiting for him. I didn't think any reasonable person could mind him getting delayed by a childbirth emergency, even if he'd 'promised this wouldn't happen again', presumably 'this' referring to coming home late. Then again, maybe Tanya was a horrible person and he regularly found excuses to stay out, hence the offer to go shopping now. Either way, I didn't feel at all comfortable about him going out of his way to help me, a stranger, if it meant upsetting his wife or girlfriend.

Having said that, I didn't feel especially comfortable with fashioning nappies for my newborn baby out of a chopped-up tea towel and Sellotape, which was what I'd be doing if Beckett had no intention of coming back.

After a few more minutes of going around and around in circles, I decided the prudent thing to do was gratefully accept the supplies if he came back, politely make it clear that our unconventional interaction would end there, and pray he wasn't a psychopath while checking all the doors and windows were properly secured.

If he never returned, then the bigger problem was solved, and the smaller problem was solvable. I'd helped create a successful fashion business. I could certainly channel some of this current restlessness into creating a nappy.

It was almost three in the morning. Bob was still sleeping and I was unable to do much more than shift about uncomfortably on the sofa and stare aimlessly at episodes of *This Is Us* that I'd watched a disgraceful number of times over the past few months. I'd have dismissed the soft tap on the door as one of the random sounds that accompanied living in an old house if I'd not seen the sweep of headlights across the living-room window a moment earlier. By the time I'd carefully clambered off the sofa and shuffled to the front door, Beckett was already halfway back to his car.

'Thank you!' I called, the boost at seeing another human being overruling my decision to shut down any future contact.

He turned around, hesitating as if equally unsure about whether to nurture this microscopic seed of a friendship. When I waited, door wide open – despite my rational mind yelling at me to close it immediately – he strode back over.

'I didn't want to risk waking you, if Bob was still sleeping.'

Oh, boy. There was probably some proper psychological terminology for this – helpless victim attaching themselves to a rescuer, developing disproportionate feelings of dependency beyond all common sense or appropriateness.

Whatever it was, the non-rational, baby-hormone-addled,

wired-with-exhaustion part of my brain scrambled to find something – anything – to say that would make him stay a bit longer.

'He's not stirred since you left. Apparently that's normal the first night. Unfortunately, I'm currently facing the existential crisis of suddenly being completely responsible for a whole other person, which as you know I'm woefully unprepared for. That, alongside soreness in places I won't mention, means I'm about as awake as I've ever been.'

Beckett nodded, the creases between his eyebrows back. 'Can I make you a hot chocolate?'

'Um. This being my house means I'm the one supposed to be offering you a drink. Plus, I don't have any hot chocolate. Or milk. I probably don't have a clean mug.'

'When it comes to new mothers, convention dictates that visitors make the drinks. Which is why I brought this.' He delved into the shopping bag he'd left on my doorstep and produced a tin of expensive-looking hot chocolate. 'And these.'

When he followed that with squirty cream and a bag of chocolate buttons, it was all I could do not to drag him over the doorstep.

'Are you sure this is okay?' I asked once he'd brought our mugs, topped with three inches of cream, over to where I was perched on a cushion at the kitchen table. 'I mean... I wouldn't want to cause upset with you and Tanya. It's pretty late.'

Beckett sat down and took a sip of his drink, face a blank mask. 'Yeah. Tanya hit maximum upset about three hours ago. Right now, she's crashed out on my sofa.'

'I'm sorry. The last thing I'd have wanted is to cause trouble.'

'No. The last thing you wanted is to give birth here, alone.' He grimaced. 'Or in the back of Razza's taxi. That car is a biohazard on wheels.'

He did a swift scan of my kitchen, no doubt taking in the

dried pasta sauce on the hob, the dirty floor and crumbs on the worktops. I liked to think of my current living standards as *relaxed*. Seeing the lines appear on Beckett's forehead made me wonder if I'd taken the midwife's advice to 'get plenty of rest, don't worry about a bit of mess' too seriously.

'Do you have any children?' I asked. The way he'd held Bob as if carrying an unexploded bomb strongly suggested otherwise, but I was attempting to distract him from the dirty pots scattered around the sink. 'When I asked if you'd been at a birth before, you said about training as a doctor, but not whether you have your own kids.'

'No,' Beckett said in a tone that suggested he'd much rather focus on the dust webs trailing across the ceiling.

'Well, an even bigger thank you for being there today, then. It must have totally freaked you out.' I used a chocolate button to scoop up the last blob of cream in my mug. 'The only thing preventing me from deleting my Sherwood Taxis app in humiliation is knowing you'll have probably seen far worse at medical school.'

'Glad I mentioned it, then.' Beckett kept his eyes on a scorch mark on the table. 'But I was holding your hand the whole time. Yara dealt with anything potentially... personal. And like I already said, that was the least humiliating thing I've ever seen.' He scratched the blue-black stubble on his cheek. 'People can assume being six-foot three and fourteen stone makes me powerful. But today – I've never seen power like it. You, Mary. Fierce and strong and... awesome.'

I shook my head, even as I couldn't stop smiling. 'I did feel quite badass at the end, there. Like, "I am woman, hear me roar".'

'Everyone in a three-mile radius heard you roar.'

I started laughing then, a semi-hysterical release of pent-up emotion that segued into a giant yawn as the weariness suddenly caught up with me.

'Come on. Time to sleep.'

Beckett offered to carry Bob's drawer upstairs, but I didn't want to put it on the draughty floor and there was nowhere else safe to position it, so we left it on the living-room coffee table and he fetched my duvet from upstairs. Probably sensing my prickle of panic at the prospect of him leaving, he picked *Lessons in Chemistry* off my small shelf of books, took a seat in the armchair and, in the dim glow of my dusty lamp, started to read.

Finding it impossible to convince myself that I was safer with this man out of my house than sitting two metres away, I used a couple of cushions to find the least-uncomfortable position I could under the duvet, put the momentous events of the past few hours to one side, and succumbed to much-needed oblivion.

Given my new status, perhaps it was to be expected that I dreamed about my parents.

* * *

While I hadn't always been the pathetic loser of the past few months, I had spent most of my childhood feeling pitifully ordinary. Which, in my family, kept me in a solid last place. Mum and Dad would always believe they were exceptional parents. My brother, Cameron, was conclusive evidence that they'd achieved their goal of raising a Good Person. One dedicated to leaving the world in a better state than if he'd never existed. My choice to pursue what they considered far less noble goals meant *I* failed, not them.

Of course, the fame and fortune that accompanied Cameron's self-help empire was purely a happy by-product, rather than the reason for his viral TED talk, 'Why You Keep Making Stupid Choices and How to Stop.'

Mum was a barrister when I was young. The year I started secondary school she retired from the law, becoming a women's rights activist. Dad spent twenty-three years as a local politician in Sheffield, the South Yorkshire city where we'd lived, his crowning glory being a revolutionary scheme that drastically reduced ex-prisoner reoffending rates.

So, fulfilling the left-wing, liberal stereotype, we ate a lot of home-grown, organic vegetables in our house. Mostly cooked by me, because everyone else was far too busy fighting for social justice alongside election campaigns, protest marches and general world-saving.

Efforts to redress the imbalance of our privilege included second-hand clothes, recycled everything, no car, and a tiny television. I had to wait until sixteen for my first phone, and computers were for educational purposes only. I was expected to spend my very limited spare time on edifying pursuits such as reading, playing the piano and tending our raised beds.

I was mostly okay about all that – I was genuinely proud of my parents and knew their work was important and brilliant. I just wished they could think I was important, or a tiny bit brilliant, sometimes. I'd longed for a weekend slouching about doing nothing much, not hunched in the corner of a refuge pretending to do homework while Mum doled out advice, helped traumatised women fill in vital forms or handed them tissues while they cried.

Of course, I never had the audacity to cry, having been given everything I could possibly want in life.

Everything, that was, apart from being allowed to worry about my own problems, like the shame of being forced to give Daniella

Button a book about the suffragette movement at her twelfth birthday party.

I spent two bearable years at the perfectly decent secondary school a couple of miles from our shabby town house. However, after a standoff with the head teacher about what they considered institutional sexism in the home-economics curriculum, my parents smugly enrolled me in a failing inner-city comprehensive. This was mainly to prove some point I never quite understood, but also included the expectation that I would waltz in there like a teen white-saviour and enlighten all my peers in the playground, or at the very least share my home-made oat bars.

Instead, I met Shay and Kieran. Who, the truth was, saved me.

4

BECKETT

Beckett didn't think of himself as a nosy person. One of the reasons he'd probably have not been the best doctor was his lack of curiosity. It wasn't that he didn't care, more the courtesy of not wanting to impose on other people the same discomfort he felt when pressed to share personal details.

And yes, he understood that this reluctance to open up and partake in the healthy exchange of information that friendships thrive on only increased his isolation. His resulting shame at having no social life or much life at all to speak of perpetuated the problem indefinitely.

Yet. In the hours since he'd first stood on Mary's doorstep, he couldn't stop wondering about her. Once she'd fallen asleep on the sofa, he'd finished the chapter of the book he was reading and then made to leave. However, something had compelled him back into her kitchen first. When fetching her duvet from upstairs, he'd not been able to help noticing that the bedroom was stark. There was a small pile of clothes on a wooden chair in one corner, a clutch of toiletries on a chest of drawers, but no photographs, artwork or ornaments. He'd never been in a woman's house that didn't have a candle or a throw.

There was nothing to suggest this place was a home. He suspected Mary had not been here very long, but also that she'd no intention to stay. In which case, why was she holed up in a remote cottage that was, to be blunt, a dump?

The kitchen cupboards had made his stomach clench. He'd found pasta, a box of crackers, teabags and a few tins. The fridge wasn't much better – some soggy salad leaves, half a packet of cheese and enough milk for maybe one cup of tea. The freezer held a couple of ready meals and some peas.

After quickly washing up, wiping down the surfaces and sweeping the floor, he'd headed home, relieved to see that the snow was already melting, but the thought of Mary sitting alone, eating one of those grim excuses for a pasta bake, wouldn't stop bothering him.

Everything about her situation pointed to her having run for her life. The only thing that made him hesitate in concluding that Mary had fled domestic violence was that while she seemed sad, even depressed, she didn't appear watchful or scared. She might be hiding, but he didn't think it was from anything dangerous.

He'd snatched three hours' sleep before his alarm went off. Gramps was still sleeping, which confirmed that he'd been unsettled by the change in routine the night before, and Beckett was downing some much-needed caffeine when Tanya shuffled into the kitchen with a face like concrete.

'Coffee?' he asked. A pathetic peace offering, but she looked as though she might need it before he said any more.

She banged a travel mug onto the worktop. 'To go.'

'Thank you for being here.' Beckett ran a hand through his hair, about two years overdue a cut. He forced himself to find the words to explain. 'A woman was literally giving birth on the back seat, and, with the road being closed, I had to stop at the nearest building I could see...'

'I stayed for him, not you.' Tanya leant against the table, arms folded. It was a decent-sized kitchen, but Beckett felt as though there wasn't enough room as he filled her mug from the jug of freshly ground filter coffee.

'Yeah. I know. We're very grateful to have you...'

'You don't have me, Beckett. I meant what I said last night. I'm done with being treated like this. We have boundaries for a reason, and I won't keep letting you disrespect them, and me.'

'I understand. It's not okay, and I'm sorry. I'll pay you overtime for being here all night, and can finish early today to make up for it. It won't happen again.'

He handed Tanya the travel mug, and she shoved it into her giant shoulder bag, clearly not appeased.

'No. It won't happen again because I'm resigning. I told you, I'm done.'

Beckett's heart dropped to the kitchen floor.

'Say bye to Marvin for me. I don't want to disturb him.' Tanya's voice cracked on the last few words, and Beckett knew she was serious.

'Please.' He had to try, anyway. 'Can we talk about it properly, when we aren't both exhausted? Give me one more chance. Please.'

'I gave you one more chance the last time.'

'Last time I had that seventeen-year-old, passed out drunk on the back seat. If I'd not stepped in, the guy would have—'

'I know, Beckett! You had to help. You *always* have to help. That's the problem. You aren't going to change, so this isn't going to work.'

'What will we do without you?'

She let out a noisy huff. However livid she was with Beckett,

Tanya loved his grandpa. 'You're going to go online and find another care agency, and this time you'll stick to the contract and not treat them like their own family or plans aren't as important as yours.'

Swiping angrily at a tear, she pushed her trainers on. 'It was my wedding anniversary last night, Beckett. Ian was waiting up for me. Instead I was here, on another man's sofa.'

Tanya stalked over to the kitchen door. 'Good luck. I wish you both the best.'

* * *

So now, here he was, facing the nightmare of trying to find another care assistant prepared to spend ten hours a day looking after an eighty-two-year-old man with multiple health issues and a foul temper. He'd taken the day off to take care of Gramps himself, and although Gramps struggled to keep track of which day it was, on some level the disruption to his schedule had caused anxiety, which displayed itself in rudeness, exhausting demands and generally being a grouch. The main reason Beckett drove a taxi was the flexible hours, because all too often a care assistant would call in sick at the last minute, quit with no notice or simply fail to show up, and, quite frankly, he couldn't blame them. However, from her first day, Tanya had been a godsend. She'd taken Gramps' difficulties in her stride and seemed instinctively to know how best to handle them. Beckett tried not to dwell on the irony that, this time, it was his unreliability that ended up being the problem.

He did call Sonali, who sometimes stood in when Tanya was on holiday or otherwise unavailable, but Sonali was in high demand and uninterested in working regular long shifts.

'I'm available this afternoon, if you're desperate. The fellow I was meant to be with died, so I've got a few spare shifts this week if you want to pencil something in. No ten-hour marathons, though. As much as I respect your grandfather's unbreakable will and Houdini-like ability to place himself in life-threatening situations, it's a lot easier to admire in small doses.'

They agreed that she'd come in at four, in time for a game of cards and a meal before Beckett came back at eight to start the evening routine.

Beckett didn't mention that he wouldn't be spending those four hours earning much-needed income.

After making a sandwich, then coaxing Gramps into eating three bites of it while surreptitiously trying to look up home-care agencies on his phone, he settled him in his armchair, turned on one of the quiz shows Gramps enjoyed shouting at and, for reasons he couldn't admit to himself yet, quickly showered and pulled on a clean sweatshirt and jeans. He even tried putting his hair in a ponytail, but that made him feel like an oversized member of a nineties' boyband, so he ditched that idea.

He opened the door for Sonali, and she did her usual playing with fire, scurrying in and planting a kiss on the top of his grandfather's bald head.

'It's the witch!' Marvin shrieked, and Sonali gave Beckett a triumphant thumbs up at being immediately recognised. He ignored how his guts twisted in response to the person his dignified grandfather had become.

'Feeling well today, are we, Marvin? As full of your indomitable spirit as ever?'

'I was until you turned up and assaulted me. Where's the other one?'

'Tanya is unable to come today. She's very disappointed to miss out on whatever fabulously creative insults you come up with, but I've promised to record them for her, so don't hold back just because I'm your favourite.'

'Shut up and die.'

'How about I put the kettle on, instead?'

* * *

Beckett left Gramps in Sonali's capable hands, feeling guilty that he got to benefit from someone else passing away, but he couldn't in all good conscience leave Mary and Bob to fend for themselves out there in the forest, with next to nothing.

He did have a last-minute wobble as he pulled into the driveway almost an hour later, loaded up with food, more baby stuff and a supermarket bouquet, because surely every woman giving birth should get flowers. What if he'd misread things last night, and right now Mary was being taken care of by a best friend, or even a partner? He'd not seen her notify anyone about Bob's arrival, but she could have done it while he was talking with Pastor Moses. Maybe she had a whole gang of help who had simply happened to be too far away last night, or working. Looking after an elderly, sick relative.

But she'd told him she had no one to call, and the type of friends who might turn up to help the day after a baby was born would have made sure she had a cot, or at the very least a pack of nappies, before reaching this point.

Resolve strengthened, Beckett grabbed the bags of food and went to find out.

He almost left the shopping in the porch, concluding that Mary was either out or sleeping after she failed to answer his knocks, but then he heard a faint wail and decided she probably hadn't heard him.

He walked around the side of the house and peered through

glass doors leading into the back of the living room, where the cries were a lot louder. Seeing the shadow of Mary cut across the dim glow of a lamp, doing the unmistakable carrying-a-baby-bounce-up-and-down, he rapped on the glass without thinking about it.

She spun around, Bob clutched to her chest, her squeal blending with the baby's, and Beckett realised a moment too late how stupid he'd been to bang on the patio door in the pitch-black darkness.

'It's me,' he called, holding up the bags, as if the intruder being last night's taxi driver would make it any less terrifying.

Mary stood there, frozen, so he chose the least awful of the limited options flashing through his mind and hurried back to the front of the house, trying the front door, which was unlocked, and stepping inside.

'I'm sorry,' he called, still breathless as Mary came to the open living-room doorway. 'I brought some food, and other baby stuff. That was stupid, banging on the window like a scene from a slasher movie. I'll drop these in the kitchen and go. Or, here. I can just put them here. There's more in the car, but I'll leave them on the porch.'

He put the bags down and turned to go, but, to his shock, Mary reached out and took his arm.

'Please, don't.'

'Don't leave the bags?' Beckett really wanted her to have the supplies, but right now he'd do whatever she asked.

Mary shook her head, swinging her torso from side to side as Bob still cried. 'Don't go. He's not stopped crying in so long, I don't even know what day it is any more. I'm desperate for a wee and a hot drink, but I don't know if it's okay to put him in the drawer while he's screaming.' Her voice dropped to a hoarse whisper, prompting Beckett to lean closer. 'I have no idea how to do this.'

'Okay. Right. Um. Here.' He gently took the baby, startled at how something so light could bristle with strength. 'Do what you need to do. I'll put the kettle on.'

In what felt like a previous life, Beckett had spent enough time with babies to know that they liked hearing your heartbeat and being held securely, so they felt safe. Bob was so tiny that Beckett could cradle him against his chest with one arm while making the tea.

By the time Mary came back, a couple of minutes later, the cries had eased to a pitiful snuffle.

'I knew it,' she said, face creasing in despair. 'It's me. He knows I'm clueless and is distraught at the thought of me being his mother.'

'Milk?'

She shook her head.

'You've provided everything he's needed for the last nine months. He knows you're not clueless. But babies can pick up on emotions like anxiety or upset.'

'Or a total freaking breakdown?' Mary sank into a chair, head dropping onto her hands.

'What time did he start crying?'

'Which time?' she groaned. 'He woke up just after five this morning, so I tried to feed him and put on a clean nappy, which made him scream. I managed to calm him back down to sleep, when he pooed – who poos in their sleep? – so I had to change him again, cue more screaming. It's been on and off like that ever since. He slept for about an hour at one point, but when I tried to put him in the drawer he started crying again. I mean, who can blame him – what self-respecting person wants to sleep in a drawer? The book said he'd be worn out for the first two or three days. I think it was a typo. It should have said the *mother* would be so exhausted it feels as though her bloodstream has turned to tar.'

'Have you eaten?'

Her lip began to wobble, causing her to grip her jaw with one hand. It made Beckett's heart constrict, seeing her trying to hold it together. 'I had some crackers.'

'Right. I don't know much about babies either, but people have been doing this without books or Bluetooth baby monitors for a long time. Every single one of our ancestors managed it, so it's in our genes. We can figure it out, one step at a time.'

'I'm guessing my ancestors didn't live alone in the middle of a wood.' Mary sounded sceptical, but she sat up and took a sip of tea, so Beckett thought he might be doing okay.

'Maybe not, but you're not alone right now.'

'Are you moving in?'

'I have to get back home in a couple of hours, but I can come back another day. Unless, of course, you'd rather not have a strange, unnervingly overfamiliar man insert himself into your life. I could be anyone.'

'Or you're Dr Beckett Bywater, graduate of Lancaster University, one-time champion of the medics rowing team, devotee of JustGiving appeals and life and soul of the party.'

Beckett leant back against the worktop, stunned.

'Including your own engagement bash, to fellow medical student Rebecca Atkins.'

'Are you some sort of spy? Is this a safe house? Are you fine about me being here because you could kill me with your little toe?'

Mary smiled, and Beckett's life mission instantly became to make her do that again. 'Or, your full name is on your taxi ID card, and I took the sensible precaution of looking you up and finding your Facebook account.'

Beckett grimaced. 'Is that still there? I haven't been on it in years.'

'Since you graduated. When "life had other plans", as you put it.'

'Yeah, well. I'm guessing you didn't plan to end up here, either. Life happens to all of us.'

'Life, death, and a whole lot of fun and games in between.'

'That's one way of looking at it.'

The doorbell rang, catching them both off guard, and Beckett had to do a few seconds of readjusting and shushing before Bob settled back against his chest with a sigh that made Beckett's throat ache.

'The midwife!' Mary whispered, eyes darting around the room in panic. 'Look at this place. Look at me! What the hell am I going to do?'

5

MARY

By the time Beckett left, two hours after scaring the life out of me, I'd have more easily believed he was a bona fide angel than any sort of danger. While I wouldn't go so far as to call him charming, he'd certainly won the community midwife over as he'd hauled in more bags from the car, made her a drink and told the story of how Bob had almost been delivered in the back seat of his car, making me out to be some sort of superwoman, and him the bumbling best friend. Because, yes, in this version Beckett was my bestie. Which I initially felt guilty about, until I realised that at this point in my life it was the genuine truth.

He made a vague excuse about why some equipment had only arrived today while unwrapping a Moses basket and setting it up, then proceeded to convert a small chest of drawers into a nappy changing station. Following that, he unpacked more tiny clothes, muslin cloths, breast pads and a papoose.

'Is there anything else we've forgotten?' he asked with a nonchalance implying everything was under control and always had been.

'I spotted the car seat,' the midwife said, ignoring Beckett and speaking directly to me. 'Are you getting a pram?'

'Yes, absolutely,' I stammered.

'Well, as far as I'm concerned anything else is simply over-expensive clutter. I mean, I was bathed in the sink, my mum used an old shawl as a makeshift sling. I slept in a drawer, for pity's sake! Can you imagine? They'd want a referral to social services if I found that happening these days.'

After she'd completed all the basic checks and declared everything 'tickety boo', which had me fighting back the tears because, honestly, if this was tickety boo then motherhood sucked, Bob started wailing again. The midwife offered to check how feeding was going, which apparently turned out to be 'beautiful!', so in this alternate reality I'd stepped into, 'beautiful' now had a whole different meaning, too.

I did start crying then. Woeful, silent tears that dripped onto Bob's head as I rubbed his back in the hope of producing a burp.

'I'm sorry,' I whimpered. 'It's all been a bit of a shock.'

'Darling, if he'd been a planned C-section two weeks after your due date, this would still be a *lot* of a shock. Don't worry. You're doing great. It's the mums who don't cry that make me nervous. Besides, this fella clearly has you well looked after. You'll be fine.'

I briefly imagined how it would go if I told her I'd met this fella less than twenty-four hours earlier, which threatened to turn my sobs into a bout of hysterical laughter, so I instead asked her a nonsense question about the umbilical cord.

As soon as she'd left, Beckett ushered me upstairs to where he'd run a bath, which I only dozed off in once, and when I came back down, he handed me an omelette stuffed full of bacon, mushrooms and tomatoes, which was quite possibly the best meal of my life.

Even if he did have to go before I'd finished eating.

'I'm sorry, I have to get back.'

'Of course. I wouldn't want Tanya upset with you again.'

He gave a sheepish shrug. 'Tanya's gone. It's Sonali this evening.'

'Okay. Wow.' Nothing about Beckett so far had made him seem like the type of man who had multiple women waiting about for him. But, then again, my track record proved that I was about as hapless at sussing out men as I was at parenting.

'Yeah.' He ducked his head. 'It's really not wow.'

His phone rang, preventing him from saying any more. 'Sonali. I'll be there in fifteen minutes... Okay. Twenty at the most.'

Giving me an apologetic wave, he backed out of the room, before running back in thirty seconds later and handing me a scrap of paper with a mobile number on, his own phone still held to his ear.

'Call if you need anything,' he mouthed, then left us to it.

* * *

I didn't call, however much I longed to over the next few weeks, where feeding, wailing and pacing up and down in exhausted desperation blended together in what appeared to be my life now. I laughed pitifully at the thought that I'd viewed living alone as a negative thing, back in the days when no one demanded to gnaw at my nipples or peed in my face the second I took their nappy off.

I waited almost a month, until I'd started to get the hang of the baby bath and sleepsuit poppers, how to make toast and tea one-handed and navigate the aisles in the local farm shop with a sling on my chest. I began to know this tiny person, what his cries were telling me, how best to soothe or stimulate him, when to panic – which, after a few false alarms, I discovered was pretty much never. In our newborn bubble in the forest, I relearned how to get up, even when every muscle begged me for five more minutes of sleep, and keep on plodding through the next twenty-four hours. As I fell more fiercely in love with my son – even as, during a few dark and desperate hours, I felt like I couldn't stand the sight of him – my broken heart continued to mend.

I didn't know whether to feel relieved or disappointed at, apart from pale-blue eyes, how little he looked like his father.

Eventually, on a Friday evening towards the end of November, I showered, put on a relatively clean pair of pre-pregnancy yoga pants and brushed my hair before sending a message I should have sent weeks earlier, but simply didn't have the mental energy to muster up the courage.

> MARY
>
> Hi, this is Mary – the woman who went into labour in the back of your taxi
>
> I wanted to say thanks so much for the food and baby things
>
> I don't know how we'd have got through that first week without it

I waited an anxious few minutes, but there was no reply, so I sent another one.

> MARY
>
> I'm so sorry it's taken me this long to say thank you, I hope you understand things have been full-on

I spent a fretful couple of hours still waiting to hear back, imagining Beckett was far too distracted with Sonali, or whoever it was this evening, to read it. He was probably right this moment showing his gorgeous date the messages arriving from the hopeless woman who'd been so abysmally unprepared he'd felt compelled to help her. They'd be in a lovely restaurant somewhere, or cosied up on his sofa with a takeaway, shaking their heads in sympathy at this sad single mother who didn't realise that Beckett had been simply doing the decent thing for a stranger in distress, and of course he'd never meant for her to actually contact him.

Bristling with indignation, I picked up my phone the second Bob dropped off again. Yes, it had taken childbirth to force me into acknowledging to what extent I'd dropped the ball this year, but I was a strong, independent, capable woman. I didn't need Beckett, or anyone else.

It only took me about half an hour to come up with the perfect message to convey that I was, in fact, a thoroughly competent human being who was smashing new motherhood.

MARY

> If you let me know your bank details, and whether there were any other receipts apart from the ones you left on the coffee table, I'll sort the money for all the stuff

> Sorry again for the delay in getting around to this – like I said, I've been rather busy, ha ha!!

It was almost eleven when a reply pinged through.

BECKETT

> Genuinely pleased I could help. Don't worry about the stuff.

Okay, so now I was even more irritated. That message was verging on dismissive and the full stop downright snarky. Plus, I wasn't *worrying about the stuff*, I was a successful businesswoman who paid her debts.

MARY

> The receipts add up to £315. If you don't want me to have your details, I'll round it up to £400 to cover anything else and leave cash at the Sherwood Taxis office.

Dr Beckett Bywater wasn't the only person around here who could do snark.

This time, I didn't have to wait for a reply.

BECKETT

> Please don't do that. The office is in Bigley. You can't get there without a car.

MARY

> I can hire a taxi!

I did a quick maps search.

MARY

> Or walk – It's only seven miles

BECKETT

> With a pram?

Well, no, seeing as I was too busy sending petty messages to a random taxi driver to order one.

MARY

> I can use the papoose

The Most Wonderful Time of the Year

BECKETT

> You had a baby a month ago. I'm guessing you're even more shattered now than you were then. Besides, there's more snow forecast. Please don't even think about walking to Bigley with a tiny baby.

MARY

> Do you always use perfect punctuation in your messages?

There was a two-minute wait this time, which felt like twenty. The last comment was supposed to be more light-hearted banter than a reaction to him implying I was being stubborn and foolish, but during the past few months of isolation I'd lost all perspective on these things. I reread the conversation about fifteen times, wondering if instead I came across as slightly unhinged.

When the next message contained only his bank details, I shrivelled up in embarrassment and dismay.

After an agonising few seconds, there were two more pings.

BECKETT

> I only want £265. The Moses basket is a gift. For Bob, not you (if that's still what you're calling him?). If you pay me any more I'll drive over and post the extra through your letterbox.

> And yes, I always use punctuation, due to being a thirty-two-year-old doctor speaking to a friend, not a teenage boy sending offensive memes to his mates.

Oh, boy. He even spelled out his age.

But I hadn't messed things up between us, and £265 felt like small change considering what he'd done for me was priceless.

Were we going to make it more than a few hours in this house without someone crying, ever again?

To my surprise, we ended up chatting for a few more minutes about Bob, how I was doing, whether the forecast was right about more snow, and then, emboldened by the combination of Beckett calling me a friend and sleep-deprived semi-delirium, I took a risk.

MARY

> I really want to take the car seat back and bring a bunch of flowers or something for Yara and Patty

> Fancy coming with me?

BECKETT

> Do you mean, would I fancy giving you a lift?

MARY

> Excuse me, I'll pay you the standard fare. Not even 'friend' rates. Just thought you might like to say hi, too!

BECKETT

> So, you'd be the one doing ME a favour? Paying me to take you to the church so I could say hello?

MARY

> Well, if you put it like that...

BECKETT

> For future reference, saying hello to people is my least favourite thing to do.

> However, I'm exceedingly grateful that a horse vet was prepared to take on the business end of things.

> Of course we'll go together.

MARY

> 'The business end of things?' Am I a horse, or what?

The Most Wonderful Time of the Year

BECKETT

Sorry. I'm woefully out of practice at making conversation with people of sound mind. I'll try again.

I'm grateful Yara was there to tackle what was going on in your nether regions.

Or is this any better...?

I'm relived an equine expert was prepared to assist you in your personal matter.

MARY

STOP NOW

BECKETT

If you refuse to use basic punctuation it's impossible for me to tell whether you're disgusted or amused by my ex-medic sense of humour.

MARY

STOP NOW!!!!!!

BECKETT

I'm going to go with impressed.

I sent him a row of alternating cry-laughing and eye-rolling emojis, because while under any other circumstances a man I barely knew making flippant comments about what had actually happened regarding my nether regions (nakedness for a start...) would have resulted in me instantly blocking him, he had been my saviour on that terrifying, unimaginable, beautiful and what ended up as most tender of nights. After sharing a moment so raw, this fundamental of human experiences, when nothing can be toned down, filtered or politely ignored, joking about the state I'd been in, how people I'd never met before had seen things that would otherwise have horrified me, was the best possible way to deal with it.

Besides, it was probably the first time I'd heard anyone use the term nether regions in real life, and I was laughing hard enough to make my pelvic floor beg for mercy.

Although, my mental haze did briefly wonder what he meant about not speaking to people of 'sound mind'. Was he making a nasty remark about Tanya, or Sonali? Given the complete lack of disrespect in anything he'd said so far, I decided to let that thought float back into the haze and sent another message.

MARY

Are you free tomorrow?

It might have been too short notice, but the truth was, I felt so lonely and lost that even tomorrow wasn't soon enough.

BECKETT

The church is more likely to be open on Sunday. I could pick you up at about twelve?

MARY

Perfect, see you then x

The kiss might have been a step too far, but slouched on the sofa, breasts swollen, nether regions still faintly sore, eyelids rough as sandpaper, listening to my son gruntle awake again, meeting Beckett suddenly felt like the most perfect thing to have happened to me in a very long time.

* * *

I'd noticed Shay and Kieran from my first day at the new secondary school. Honestly, everyone had, they were impossible to ignore. However, due to their being the kind of kids who existed in an alternate universe to shy, deeply uncool and slightly posh girls, I never for one second dreamed they'd notice me.

That was until they plonked themselves down either side of me on the isolated bench I'd specifically selected to ensure the minimum number of people would see that I had no one to eat lunch with.

'That science teacher was bang out of order.' Shay Obasi rolled her eyes, lids heavy with purple fake lashes, and crossed her dark brown legs in a brisk motion that made me flinch. 'You should complain to the head.'

'I'm used to it,' I said meekly. The teacher had made a joke during our physics lesson, comparing my politician dad to gamma radiation. It wasn't the first time someone had made a derogatory remark about one of my parents. It certainly wouldn't be the last – or the worst. 'It didn't even make sense.'

'Still though. You shouldn't tolerate your family being disrespected,' Kieran said in his thick South Yorkshire accent. 'If other kids sense weakness, they'll chew you up and spit you out, just so they can chew you up again tomorrow.'

His ice-blue eyes met mine, and for a horrible moment I thought I was going to get *chewed up*, whatever that meant, there on that bench, on only my fourth day.

'This is the crucial time,' Shay added, turning to face me with a look of concern that made me dare to hope they were here to help, not hurt me. She folded her arms before uncrossing them to adjust an earring, pat one of her thick bunches, and fiddle with the cuff of her non-regulation blazer. In the years to come, Shay always made me think of a fish, her body in constant motion. Fluid and confident, like everything she did.

'New school year, packs are reforming. It's kill or be killed. Hunt or be hunted. Especially for the new girl.'

'I don't want to be in a pack,' I stuttered.

'Lone wolves won't last 'til half-term,' Shay said, as solemnly as a thirteen-year-old girl with Mis-Teeq nail stickers could. If I'd worn anything on my nails, let alone the lashes, lip gloss and skirt several inches above knee-length, I'd get a detention. In a school where teachers were resigned to choosing their battles, Shay was one of those girls who won far more than most.

'You need us,' Kieran said, raising white-blond eyebrows ominously. His appearance was equally rebellious for the first week of year nine. Hair bordering on a mohawk, stud in one earlobe, a red belt with silver studs holding up his skin-tight trousers.

'And, luckily, we like the look of you,' Shay added, staring me straight in the eye. 'Forgetting that weird salad you're eating, you seem like one of us. Plus, the joke you made in maths was so good Kieran almost wet himself. So, want to join our pack?'

'Okay,' I said, face flushing. I'd mumbled the joke, not intending anyone to hear, but it *had* been funny, and knowing that these mavericks liked the look of me was both bewildering and unbelievably awesome.

So from then on, we were a pack of three. While being the newest member of the group, and one with a very different home-life from the others, meant that I would often feel slightly on the edge, I could live with it.

My smug parents assumed that exposing these new friends to our enlightened lifestyle would provide the route out of their downtrodden, ignorant existence.

Kieran and Shay gave this notion the contempt it deserved.

They didn't need anyone to tell them how to overcome the disadvantages of where they'd started from. By the time I joined their shambolic secondary school, life had already taken plenty from them. They were determined to take it back.

6

BECKETT

After caring for Marvin a couple of times a week since Tanya left, Sonali point-blank refused to come on Sunday, even for a few hours.

'It's a holy day of rest, my friend.'

'You told me you're not religious any more.'

'Well, I'm beginning to see the light after spending yesterday with your grandfather. When he accused me of "feeling him up" when I tried to mop up the coffee he'd tipped down his shirt, I suddenly felt the urge to pray I didn't face a sexual harassment investigation.'

'Is he getting worse?'

Sonali carefully folded the tea towel in her hand before looking up at him. 'Yes.'

Beckett could only nod. It wasn't as if he hadn't noticed himself, but hearing it from a professional felt like a punch in the abs.

'You should take the day off, too. Try having some fun together while you still can.'

He gave a wry grimace. Gramps had never been fun, even

before he'd got ill. Well, that might not be true. He might have been the life and soul of the party, prior to the pain of losing his daughter, when everything became about trying to keep their tiny family afloat, and then eventually helping support Beckett through five years of medical school. This included working well past the usual retirement age, barely scraping above minimum wage after being made redundant from his office job the day after his sixty-fifth birthday. He'd endured gruelling cleaning shifts, unsafe working conditions in a factory, useless co-workers at the local petrol station and a vindictive boss at the corner shop. He was probably too tired and miserable to remember fun existed.

Beckett knew how he felt.

'Try taking him out.' Sonali shrugged as if she hadn't declared, after an aborted trip to the health centre two weeks ago, that from now on she would only be caring for Marvin within the home. 'The fresh air will do you both some good.'

'I hate fresh air!' Marvin shouted from the living room. 'And I don't want any good.'

Imagining the effort it would take to persuade Gramps to leave the house made Beckett's head hurt, but he'd made a commitment with Mary. He wasn't going to let her down.

He ignored the tiny voice suggesting that Mary would be fine waiting a day or two, or even using a different taxi driver. Beckett hadn't hung out with anyone except Gramps for longer than he cared to think about. He wasn't ashamed about looking forward to seeing her and Bob again. Besides, Sonali was right. He should try to do more with Gramps.

The thought that this would include taking him to a church made him laugh out loud for the first time in longer than he could remember.

* * *

The Most Wonderful Time of the Year

'I'm not going,' Gramps said for the hundredth time since Beckett had started trying to wrestle shoes onto his grandfather's feet fifteen teeth-grinding minutes earlier. 'I told you I'm too tired. You go out.'

'Come on,' Beckett said, kneeling on the living-room floor, holding one shoe. The other one had been hurled somewhere behind the sofa. 'You haven't been anywhere apart from the surgery in weeks. Remember the doctor said it would help you feel better, if you managed to get out of the house?'

'I don't care what that brain-dead doctor said!' Gramps tipped up a bony chin, covered in straggles of white stubble, but the tremor in his voice was painful to hear. 'All he's interested in is filling in his stupid forms. Prodding at me and talking to me like I'm a child. I'm a grown man, and I'll decide what I do!'

'We're going to see a friend of mine.' Beckett picked up Gramps' foot, massaging the arch a couple of times before slowly, gently, sliding on the fabric loafer.

'You don't have any friends.' He sniffed.

Beckett paused. Was Gramps simply making a jibe, or was he more perceptive than he'd appreciated?

'This one has just had a baby.'

That caught the older man's attention. Gramps had always loved babies.

'Is it yours?'

'No.' Beckett took the opportunity while Gramps was distracted to look behind the sofa, pulling the shoe out from where it had wedged itself against the radiator. 'I would have told you if you were a great-grandad.'

'Good. I don't trust that Rebecca. She's far too nice. All smiles and everything's "so lovely, Marvin,".' Gramps put on a high voice with an Essex accent that was an alarmingly accurate imitation of Beckett's ex-fiancée. 'I don't trust a woman who won't speak her mind. How can you deal with problems if you're pretending there aren't any? Besides, she'd make an unbearable mother. Boring us with endless photos and bragging about every little thing. I don't know how you can stand the thought of spending the rest of your life with her.'

'We aren't going to see Rebecca.' It wasn't the first time Gramps had expressed his disdain for Rebecca since a stroke had decimated his inhibitions. However, the confusion was fairly new. Beckett would have to ask about it at Gramps' next hospital appointment, in a few weeks. It terrified him, because he knew what the likely answer would be.

'I said I don't want to go.' Gramps jerked his foot away as Beckett had just about wriggled the other shoe on. 'Why won't you people ever leave me in peace?'

A merciless forty minutes later, Beckett helped Gramps out to the car, strapped him in, turned on a podcast about the First World War so he'd be too distracted to try to climb out while they were moving, and set off.

For the millionth time in the past few days, he wondered whether taking care of a baby could be any harder than this.

* * *

'Who is she?' Gramps scowled. Usually, he struggled to get himself out of the car, but he was like one of those Weeping Angels from *Doctor Who*. The second Beckett had turned his back, the older man had somehow managed to clamber out and hobble after him. 'Her face is grey. Has she got a parasite?'

Mary's eyebrows shot up into her fringe, but to Beckett's relief she appeared more amused than offended as she stood in the doorway holding the baby.

'I'm Mary,' she said. 'And this is Bob. He's doing a good job of draining me of all energy and nutrients, but I don't think most parasites look this cute when they burp, so I'm going with a baby.'

'I like babies.' Marvin held out his hands, wobbling like a Bobblehead. 'I want to hold him.'

'No, Gramps,' Beckett said, taking his arm. 'Bob and Mary are coming in the car with us. He needs to ride in his baby seat.'

'Here.' Before he could stop her, Mary handed her tiny, helpless baby to his confused, aggressive, frail old grandfather. 'Have a quick cuddle while I grab my coat.'

Beckett didn't breathe for the full two minutes it took Mary to get her coat, boots and hat on, and fetch the car seat.

'Chill out, Beckett.' She threw him an amused glance. 'Didn't medical school teach you that babies are made of muscle, bone and a never-ending stream of poo, not glass? He won't break.'

Beckett dared not tell her that, a few hours ago, the man now holding the most precious person in the universe had needed help eating breakfast. He did have to admit that his grandfather looked happier inspecting Bob's fingers than he'd seen him in months.

'I like babies,' he repeated, watching Mary place Bob into his seat, then squeezing past her to do up the straps. 'I wanted lots of children. Only my witch-wife ran off with a van of hippies when Margo was still small. I didn't have the time or energy to think about another woman until my girl was grown. Then after she got cancer, I had another baby to look after. The married RAF rat had scarpered as soon as he heard she was pregnant.' He stood back, scowling at Beckett, as if it were his fault his dad was a cheating rat and his mum had passed away.

Then Gramps made one of those comments that caught Beckett so off guard it rendered him speechless. 'It got us through the grief, having each other to take care of. It was an honour, to raise my grandson on Margo's behalf. Young Beckett is worth a dozen other babies I never got to have. I've messed up a lot of different jobs in my time. But not this one. This one made all the others worth it. Your mother would be proud.'

Beckett had to blink back tears as he undid the knot Gramps had tied with the car-seat straps and clicked them in properly. Not because his grandfather had said something nice. All those years it was only the two of them, he'd consistently conveyed how much his grandson meant. No, it was because of all the times he couldn't say it any more, thanks to the damage in his brain.

Because, Beckett realised with a jolt, he missed who his grandfather had been with an ache that made it hard to breathe.

'Sorry about Gramps,' he said, waiting in the doorway when Mary nipped back into the house to fetch a carrier bag of nappy things because he'd not thought about buying her a changing bag, and it seemed as if she'd not got around to it, either. 'I wouldn't have brought him, only with Tanya quitting...'

'Is that what people call it around here?' Mary squinted at him. 'Quitting? It makes it sound as if she worked for you.'

'She did work for me,' Beckett said, eyebrows furrowing as he automatically took the bag off her. 'What would you call it?'

'I think you'd better explain, because I'd call it moving out, or breaking up with you. Ending the relationship. A good old-fashioned dumping. But I've no frame of reference for someone who sees being your girlfriend, wife, whatever, as work. And what about Sonali? Is this a bigamist, weird-religious-sect thing?'

Beckett stopped dead halfway to the car.

'Tanya was Gramps' carer. She had enough of me coming back late. Sonali, our stand-in carer who's been filling in, has a day off today. They're both married.' He grimaced. 'And decades older than me.'

Mary looked at him, her mouth gaping, cheeks flushed. After a drawn-out few seconds, she hurried over to the car.

'Okay, so I thought you seeing me writhing about honking like a dying goose was as bad as it could get, but now I'm genuinely mortified. My only excuse is being so tired my mouth has held a referendum and chosen independence from my brain.'

'I don't know whether it's worse that you thought I was in a bigamist cult or paying women to be in a relationship with me.'

Beckett stopped then, and grinned.

'What?' Mary peered at him suspiciously.

'You did sound like a goose.'

7

MARY

As we set off back towards New Life Community Church, I mulled over the major revelations about Beckett. He lived with his gramps, who was too unwell to be left alone. Tanya and Sonali were carers, not girlfriends or partners. His mum had died when he was young, so his grandfather had brought him up single-handed.

And while on the subject of single parents, his gramps had been like me, raising a tiny baby by himself. Now I understood why Beckett had felt so compelled to help me. He was doing it for his gramps. Or even for Margo, who hadn't had the chance to take care of her son.

Gramps refused to tell me his name when I asked, but Beckett calmly explained that it was Marvin.

'He had a stroke, amongst other things. It still affects him mentally and physically.'

'Who did?' Marvin gave his grandson a sharp look. 'I don't think you should be sharing information about your patients with strangers.'

'It's okay if I keep it anonymous, Gramps.'

'Hmph.' He closed his eyes, head slumping onto his bony chest a few seconds later as he began snoring.

'When did it happen?' I whispered.

'Six years ago. Two weeks after I started working as a junior doctor.'

Woah. Beckett had told me he was thirty-two. Dealing with that when still in his twenties must have been awful. And Gramps was his only family.

'Is that why you gave it up?'

He glanced over at the passenger seat, but Marvin was still wheezing softly. 'It was why I stopped then. But to be honest, I'd had my doubts for a while. Some of the training was far tougher than I envisioned.'

'Like what?'

'The patients.'

I wasn't expecting that. 'You don't strike me as the kind of person who doesn't like helping people.'

He waited until turning out of the country lane onto the busy main road before answering.

'It's not that I don't like people. I don't love being forced to interact with them.' He frowned. 'That's not quite true. I didn't mind the difficult conversations, breaking bad news, discussing treatment options. What I found excruciating was the hours of having to reassure patients with small talk. A surprising number of people find it uncomfortable or even frightening to have someone examining them in silence. They'd prefer me to be prattling on about sport, or roadworks, rather than concentrating on what I'm supposed to be doing. It felt more exhausting than an A & E night shift.'

'So you thought a job famously involving waffling about nothing was a better option?'

'I find that most people prefer their taxi driver to remain

quiet. The rest are happy to do the chatting while I nod occasionally. What was a better option, in order for me to be able to look after Gramps, was a job where I could pick and choose my hours, clock off early or cancel a shift as and when I needed to, with the bonus of driving between clients with nothing but my own thoughts for company.'

'But if Marvin hadn't got ill, you'd have carried on as a doctor?'

'I was looking into specialising as a pathologist. Their patients aren't so bothered by silence.'

'Why did you keep going if it didn't suit you?'

'A five-year slog to get there, a hideously sized student loan, and the dream of being able to provide for Gramps. I took a year out to earn as much as I could before starting uni, but I could have kept working, or at least chosen a degree that allowed time for a part-time job, so Gramps didn't have to be subbing my rent when I was twenty-four. He was so proud, said it was all worth it. If I dropped out, then his sacrifice was for nothing.'

'That must have been really tough.'

He was quiet for a moment.

'Yeah. This is tougher.'

* * *

'You don't seem to have much problem talking to me,' I observed a mile or so later.

Beckett kept his eyes on the road. 'I don't remember us having much time for idle chit-chat. I told you, I don't have a problem talking about things that matter, or hold some interest.'

'I hold some interest?'

He flashed a glance in the rear-view mirror this time. 'If you think what happened last month was boring, I'm definitely interested in what the rest of your life is like.'

I shook my head. 'The rest of my life is desperately trying to grab more than ninety minutes' sleep, hours wrangling Bob's feet into separate legs of his sleepsuit, only for one of them to wriggle out again the second I've done all the poppers, and crying. So. Much. Crying. Probably more me than him. It's agonisingly mundane. I had cream cheese on my toast for breakfast, and that felt like a wild decision.'

I cleared my throat, and again the filter on my mouth seemed to have taken a leave of absence, because I never would normally admit something like this to anyone apart from Shay or Kieran.

'The only people I've spoken to this week are you and Gramps, Bob and a woman in the farm shop who stopped to admire his hat. Except she was talking to him, not me, so that doesn't count.'

'That's three more people than I speak to on the average weekend.'

'So, compared to you, my life is fascinating?'

'My one friend is my grandpa. Maybe I'm curious about how someone else ended up as alone as me.'

I might have told him, something at least, but then Marvin woke up, opened the car door and tried throwing himself out. Thankfully, he couldn't undo the seat belt, so Beckett was able to pull over before any harm was done.

It was well past midday by the time we arrived at the church. The car park was full, so Beckett found a space on a nearby street. I tucked Bob into his papoose, picked up the flowers I'd bought that morning at the farm shop down the road, and Beckett carried the car seat. A group of people were leaving as we walked up, and a couple of vehicles were now pulling out, so I felt hopeful that we were in time to see at least someone who'd been there when Bob was born.

'What is this place?' Marvin asked, leaning heavily on his grandson. 'It smells.'

'It really doesn't,' Beckett said firmly, but there was a definite waft of spices coming from somewhere.

'I don't want to be here. Take me home.'

'We won't stay long. Mary just needs to give these flowers to someone.'

'Who the hell is Mary?'

Before Beckett could reply, a woman bounced up to us from the church doorway.

'Hey, hello!' she said with enough energy to make my exhausted bones wince. 'I didn't spot you guys in the service.'

She wore a baggy blue boilersuit covered in daisies, and had a giant crocheted daisy at the end of each of her long brown plaits. A little girl was clinging to her middle like a baby koala, chewing solemnly on the end of one plait as she stared up at Beckett's giant frame.

'We just got here,' I said with an awkward smile.

'Oh, okay! Well, the service finished about half an hour ago, but you're welcome to a drink and a chat. I'm Sofia, by the way. I help run New Life with my husband, Moses.'

Beckett visibly cringed at the offer of a chat, but when Sofia mentioned Moses, his shoulders dropped slightly.

'Is Moses here?'

Sofia took a few seconds to answer him, having been distracted by noticing the baby on my chest. 'Um... yes, he's inside somewhere. Oh, my days, this one is *teensy*! How are you here? You're wearing make-up! Why aren't you at home, lying on the sofa while someone—' she gave Beckett a sharp look '—tends to your every need and want?'

'We met Moses last month,' Beckett pressed on, while I tried to process Sofia's questions. 'When Bob was born.'

'Really?' Sofia glanced at him, then back at me, the realisation dawning on her face. 'You're Mary! This is the baby born in our flat! I can't believe you came back. This is amazing. Wait, let me get Moses. Oh, and Yara. Who else was asking about you? Patty! Has anyone seen Patty?'

'She talks too fast,' Marvin pronounced. 'And says too much.'

'I'm normally quite chilled,' Sofia said, scanning the car park. 'But it's not every day that someone gives birth in our building. It's *no day*, apart from that Sunday. I'm very excited right now. Luke, have you seen Patty or Yara?'

The whole time she was talking and twisting her head about, she had a hand on Bob's foot. The girl she was carrying, who I guessed was three, dropped the plait.

'You're very old,' she said, dark eyebrows beetling at Marvin.

'You're rude,' he shot back.

'You're ruderer!' the girl shouted, and who knew how things would have escalated if Moses hadn't appeared at that point?

'Mimi, it's actually rude to call someone rude.'

'Well, then, you're rude, Dad, because you called Mimi rude,' a boy holding Moses' hand said. 'And now I'm rude, because I called you rude.'

'Mimi might have said something rude, but that doesn't make her a rude person, Micah,' Sofia said, thankfully letting go of Bob and bending down to talk to the boy. 'Remember we had a conversation about this? Who you are isn't defined by your worst actions.'

'Tell that to someone on death row,' Marvin snorted.

'Okay, so what's really rude is ignoring visitors at church,' Moses said with a desperate grin, before suddenly realising who we were. 'Mary! Beckett, my friend. And the star of the show!' He leant closer to look at Bob, but could only make out the top of his head thanks to him currently headbutting my chest, baby talk for 'feed me!'.

'I'm calling him Bob, for now,' I said with a nervous smile. 'Although, to be honest, I'm so knackered I'll probably be too tired to think of anything else, so he'll end up Bob by default.'

'As good a way to choose a name as any.' Moses laughed. 'We spent days agonising over what to call our youngest – she was the only one we had as a baby – but in the end our eldest daughter, Adina, chose Mimi because it's the name of her Auntie Emma's cat.'

'How are you doing?' Sofia asked. 'Is Bob all right after his dramatic arrival? Did you make it home through the snow okay? Have you recovered from the trauma of your baby being delivered by an equine dentist?' She stopped then, hitching Mimi up higher on her hip. 'Sorry, I'm bombarding you again. Look, we're having a lunch here, to kick off plans for the Christmas carol service. Why don't you join us, and we can talk properly?'

'No, we really couldn't...' I said, although part of me wondered why, precisely, I couldn't stay for lunch, given we'd been invited by very friendly seeming people, and I'd been living off mainly crackers and toast. I glanced at Beckett, who shifted uncomfortably.

'Thank you, but I really need to get my grandpa back. It's a big deal for him to be out of the house these days.'

'All the more reason?' Sofia said, looking bemused while still beaming.

'Come on, you're here to give us an update, you might as well enjoy a bowlful of tagine and a comfy chair while you fill us in,' Moses said.

Beckett bit his lip, resolve cracking.

'We only came to give Yara these and say thank you. Oh, and to return the car seat. I'm sorry, I can't remember the name of the man who leant it to us.'

'Gave it!' A brogue I instantly recognised boomed back. 'It's Bill, and I told you I'd be offended if you tried to give it back.'

He wagged a faux-angry finger as he slipped through the gathering crowd of interested onlookers to join us. 'I've made my speciality carrot cake for pudding. I'd be genuinely insulted if you rejected that as well as the car seat.'

'I like carrot cake,' Marvin announced. 'I'm staying for lunch.'

'What?' Beckett turned to his gramps, looking the most stressed I'd seen him, and that was saying something considering how we'd met. 'No, we're going to give Bill the car seat back, and then go.'

'Then where will the baby sit on the way home?' Marvin retorted. 'Are you giving this Bill the baby, too? I wouldn't,' he said to me. 'He looks shifty.'

I turned to Beckett. 'Whoops.'

Beckett took a moment to catch up. 'You didn't bring another car seat to take Bob home.'

'I don't *have* another one, yet. I completely forgot.'

Beckett looked at me. I thought I spotted a twitch of amusement at the corner of his mouth, but his overriding expression was one of discomfort. He leant close enough for no one else to hear. 'What do you want to do?'

I shrugged. After my hermithood of the past few months, it was overwhelming enough being in this busy car park, with random curious people clustering around, and now we'd turned up with a car seat that we had to take back again.

But. I had a baby now. I had to break out of my self-imposed incubation and start living again. For Bob's sake, if not mine. Bob shouldn't have to miss out on one bright, beautiful day this world had to offer because of his mother's broken heart. I might as well give it a go when I had Beckett here to provide moral support. Although, Beckett looked as though this was as big a step beyond his comfort zone for him as for me. All the more reason to try. It wasn't as though we were going to see any of these people again.

8

BECKETT

Once Mary had accepted the invitation, they were sort of swept into the building like geese in the middle of a small gaggle, ending up in the room where people had been eating pizza on the night of the snowstorm.

With lots of 'here we go', and 'make yourselves at home', 'let me take your coat' and other chatter that made Beckett's head swim, he found himself sitting at a large table, while three extra places were hastily set and a mug of tea thrust into his hand. He turned to Gramps, who was being helped into the chair beside him.

'Okay?' Beckett braced himself for the inevitable onslaught of verbal venom that accompanied his grandfather feeling harried, confused or in any way expected to do something he didn't feel like.

'I'm famished. When do we get food?'

Beckett tried to feel reassured that Gramps seemed reasonably content for now, but it was hard not to feel anxious, knowing this could change in an instant.

'Can you wait ten minutes while we round up the stragglers?' Sofia asked, appearing at Gramps' shoulder and gently handing him a mug. 'Coffee with milk and four sugars, as requested.'

To Beckett's growing astonishment, Gramps not only said thank you, but he *winked*.

'Four sugars?' Beckett asked him.

'And?' Gramps huffed. 'I've taken coffee like this since rationing ended. Are you going to start policing this now, along with everything else I find remotely pleasurable?'

Gramps had stopped taking sugar in his hot drinks after being diagnosed with type 2 diabetes, almost a decade ago, but Beckett merely sat back and decided to try to enjoy their first joint social outing in at least that long.

'Is Mary okay?' She wasn't amongst the dozen or so people now milling around or taking their places at the table.

'She's gone to feed Bob,' Sofia said. 'Obviously it's totally fine for her to do it wherever, but she preferred somewhere quieter.'

'She said enough people here have seen her never reasons, she didn't want to risk flashing them her blistering nipples, too,' Sofia's boy, Micah, said, with enough relish for everyone to stop talking and turn to look.

'She should show them to my grandson,' Marvin said, taking a loud slurp of coffee and smacking his lips. 'He'd know what to do with a blistered nipple.'

Once the smatter of shocked laughter had faded into loaded silence, Beckett then felt compelled to clumsily explain to a bunch of strangers that he'd qualified in medicine, although he was no longer practising as a doctor. He hated telling people this. It came across as trying to impress them, as if he considered his current job to be lesser, while at the same time inviting questions that he never felt like answering. Mercifully, as soon as he'd stumbled to a stop, a hatch opened at the back of the room and Moses announced that once he'd said a prayer of thanks, it was time to eat.

* * *

'What is this?' Gramps asked the older teenager sitting on the other side of him. 'It looks like something my old mutt threw up.'

Before Beckett had time to apologise, Gramps carried on. 'But it tastes delicious. My compliments to the chef.'

To Beckett's relief, his grandfather then hunched over his bowl and proceeded to determinedly finish the whole lot without feeling the need to make any further comment. Beckett was so relieved, he managed to join in with some of the other conversation.

Mary slid into the empty seat a while later.

'All sorted?' he asked.

She nodded across the table to where a woman with silvery hair was cuddling Bob, his head resting on her shoulder. 'He's drunk his fill. Which means he'll probably throw half of it up on her any second.'

'Here.' Sofia placed a bowl loaded with tagine, rice and salad in front of Mary. 'You must be ready for this.'

'It smells heavenly, thank you.' Once Sofia had returned to sit with her younger two children on the opposite end of the table, Mary ate a huge spoonful, closing her eyes as she swallowed. 'Oh, it tastes even better. I think this is just... it's the most... I'd started to forget what proper food tastes like. Oh, crap,' she murmured, face screwing up and rapidly turning blotchy. 'Here I go again. Every single time someone is nice to me!'

She turned towards Beckett, holding one hand up to shield her face from the rest of the table and mouthing, 'Help!' as a fat tear leaked out.

'Gramps told Sofia's eldest son – Eli, sat next to him – that the food looks like dog sick.'

She gasped, the glisten in her eyes switching to a sparkle, until she suddenly dropped her hand from her face, resting it on Beckett's hand. 'I'm sorry. It's not funny. What's happened to him is horrific, and it must break your heart to hear him say those kinds of things.'

Beckett's mouth twitched up. 'Yeah. It's terrible. Only...' He found it impossible to stop the twitch spreading to a full-on smile. He honestly didn't know if it was being here, or being with her. Being the one to turn her tears into laughter. Most probably it was the warmth of her hand on his – he was more than a little starved of human affection.

'If I didn't find the funny side of a rude comment, I don't think I could bear the straight-up meanness when I'm cleaning him up in the middle of night or he refuses to take his medication, and there's no one to share the wretchedness with.'

She nodded, understanding. 'Would he have found this funny, maybe? Did he have a good sense of humour, before the stroke?'

Beckett shook his head. 'He didn't even have a bad one. I reckon he was born a dour old man.'

'Well, I'm glad you don't take after him in that respect, at least.'

It was a slight dent to his ego that Mary might think he took after Gramps in other ways. Not the Gramps she knew, anyway.

* * *

Once slices of either carrot or coffee cake had been passed around, and drinks topped up, Moses called for everyone's attention.

The Most Wonderful Time of the Year

'Now you're all in that post-lunch state of bliss, it's time to get those amazing brains working and creative juices flowing. We aren't here just because we love Ali's cooking.'

'Speak for yourself!' someone said.

'I'm only here to get a look at the baby,' another person added. 'I'm not at all sure I want to help at the carol concert this year. Why add to all the Christmas stress if you can help it?'

'What was that, Auntie?' Moses raised his eyebrows innocently. 'How very kind of you to volunteer to organise the flyers before the meeting's even properly started.'

'You might be my pastor, but you're still my nephew. Just remember, boy, I changed your nappies once upon a time,' his auntie replied archly. 'And yes, put me down for that, and I'll help with set design. As long as we aren't using that high-wire harness again. My blood pressure can't take it.'

'That's wonderful, but before we run away with ourselves, I'm going to hand over to this year's carol-concert organisers.'

'Um, before you start, we should probably get going.' Beckett stood up, because the last thing he wanted to do was sit in on a meeting that was nothing to do with him. He had a million things to catch up on at home, thanks to having no carer. Not least of which was to find a replacement.

'Mary hasn't had any cake,' Bill said, perturbed.

'No, but we don't want to gatecrash your meeting. She could take some home with her.' He turned to Mary. 'Do you want to take a piece home?'

'No,' Mary said, causing Beckett to frown in confusion. 'I want to eat my cake here, please. With my new friends.'

'Okay, but I really think that Gramps...'

'Can someone bring me a second slice?' Gramps called. 'To eat in. I don't do takeaway. And another coffee. Four sugars and full-fat milk.'

'Fine. Okay. Fine. Sorry for interrupting.' Beckett sat down again. 'But he doesn't take sugar. And only a small piece of cake.'

'Are you fat-shaming your grandpa?' Eli asked, leaning back and rubbing a languid hand over his cornrows. 'Because to me he looks like he needs all the calories he can get.'

'He's always trying to control me. When I get up. What I say. What I eat. It's worse than the army.'

'He's diabetic!'

This was why Beckett didn't go out anywhere. Least of all with Gramps.

'Anyway, while someone fetches a large piece of cake for Mary, and a smaller one for Marvin, I will leave you in the capable hands of our carol-concert maestros, Carolyn Dennis and Cheris Gray!'

The room suddenly erupted with the sound of Noddy Holder shouting, 'It's Chriiistmaaaas!', leading straight into Slade's enduring festive hit, 'Merry Xmas Everybody', as two women sprang out from behind floor-to-ceiling-length curtains at one side of the room.

'What?' Gramps yelled, loud enough for those nearest to him to hear over the blare of music. 'Please no. It can't be blummin' Christmas already!'

'Have they been hiding there the whole time we were eating?' Mary asked, collapsing into giggles.

Both women were wearing garish Christmas jumpers, one composed of green and red tinsel and the other with a knitted Rudolph complete with flashing red nose. One of them balanced a foot-high Christmas-tree hat on her head, the other one a top hat decorated like a chimney, with Father Christmas's feet sticking out of the top. They were both shaking sleighbells and lip-syncing along to the song until, at the end of the first chorus, someone dashed over to the sound system in the corner of the room and pressed stop.

'Sorry,' the woman said. 'I have to be finished here in time to pick up Kasey from a birthday party. But I think we've got the gist.'

'What was this meeting about again?' Eli asked, with an impressively straight face.

'It's Chriiiiistmaaaas!' both the women shouted, shaking the bells vigorously above their heads. To be fair, at least four people in the room joined in. Including Mary.

'Have I had another stroke? Is this hell?' Gramps looked so affronted, even Beckett had to smile. 'Because if not, somebody kill me now.'

'Right, let's get down to business,' the first woman said, beaming. 'Or Chris-ness, as we like to call it.'

'Doesn't even rhyme properly,' Eli mumbled, slumping lower in his seat.

'Let us start by introducing ourselves.'

'Carolyn, we all know who you are,' Bill said, sighing.

'Well, this very lovely man doesn't!' Carolyn replied, beam unwavering, as she pointed her bells at Beckett and rattled them vigorously. 'Seasonal greetings!'

Mary snorted in her attempt to contain her laughter. *This can't be hell,* Beckett thought. Seeing her fizzing with mirth felt more like heaven.

'My name is Carolyn Dennis. I'm forty-four years old, and, like my birthday twin bezzie, Chezza, was born on Chri-istmas Daaaay.' She sang the last phrase to the tune of the Boney M cover, 'Mary's Boy Child'. 'Over to you, Chezza.'

'Hey!' Cheris waved as though greeting a crowd at Wembley rather than a small group of people sitting around a table.

'Thanks, Chezza.' She blew a round of kisses at Carolyn, who enthusiastically caught each one. 'Cheris Gray, at your service. I'm thirty-three years old, but, miraculously, I am also born on Chri-ist-mas Daaaaaay. And, after several years of prayerful petitions, followed by a paper petition with a grand total of twenty-seven signatures, Pastor Moses has finally granted us *full creative control* of this year's legendary masterpiece that is the New Life Community Church Christmas Carol Concert!'

'NLCCCCC for short!' Carolyn added, with another flourish of her bells.

'They aren't related,' Mary whispered to Beckett, her face glowing with delight. 'How are they not sisters?'

He had to agree; the 'bezzies' looked remarkably similar. They both had tufts of ginger hair sticking out from underneath their hats, round cheeks full of freckles and huge green eyes. Chezza appeared to be no more than five feet in height, her friend a few inches taller, but both had the kind of stocky physique that made Beckett think about hobbits. Their wacky energy brought a lightness to the room that he could imagine was generally well received – in limited doses, at least. He did wonder how things had gone for them at school, where tolerance of children who were a little different could be harder to come by.

'Not quite full creative control, Cheris. We did discuss this,' Moses said firmly. 'Several times. You will run anything major or requiring a risk assessment past me.'

'Yes, yes, we know. You get to decide the boring bits.' Cheris dismissed this with a flap of her hand. 'Shall we get on, Chezza? Ali needs to collect Kasey from a birthday party.'

'Why, certainly, Chezza. Unleash the sheet!'

Cheris flipped over the top page of a flipchart, to reveal what Beckett thought, in less bonkers circumstances, might be classed as a mood board. The paper was covered in various images, scraps of paper and fabric. Mostly, it was covered in different pictures of Santa Claus.

Cheris gave three overexaggerated nods, as if counting them in, then the friends both shouted, 'Everyone's a Santa!'

'Picture the scene...' Carolyn said, leaning forwards and spreading her hands out dramatically. 'It's Christmas Eve. The year is 3024.'

'No!' Moses, Sofia and a few other people groaned.

'Okay.' Carolyn did a small huff, then resumed the theatrical pose, with accompanying suspenseful voice. 'The year is unspecified. The place is Sherwood Forest. The people are you, me, whoever else we can rope in to help us, because a lot of New Life Church seem unable to commit to 22 December. The spotlights are low, fog machines set to maximum. Enter, from stage right...'

'Are you planning on narrating the whole concert?' Ali asked. 'I thought we were here to discuss who's doing what, and when we need to get it done by.'

'Well, yes,' Carolyn said, straightening up. 'We thought it would be helpful to share our creative vision.'

'Whatever's living in your two brains is a vision I can do without,' Bill said. 'No offence, ladies. All I need to know is: what's the budget, what cake do you want for refreshments and do you need to borrow my Shelby's donkey again, because she gets a lot of requests this time of year, so it's best to get in there quick.'

'Eight hundred pounds,' Cheris chirruped. 'Mince pies, mini chocolate logs and a bucketload of mulled wine. Absolute yes to the donkey and if she's still got the sheep, we'll have five or six, please.'

'I am here, in the room,' Moses said.

Cheris darted her eyes over to her pastor and back to Bill.

'Five hundred. Non-alcoholic wine and no sheep. Unless she's got a lamb. You promised to let us include a lamb if we found one, Moses!'

'Shelby only breeds spring lambs,' Bill said.

'Oh, that's a shame.' Moses smiled, with enough hint of sarcasm to earn a hard stare from Sofia.

'So what setting do you need, apart from a load of trees?' Moses' auntie asked. 'If we're going to need stairs or anything else above floor level I need to speak to Jimmy asap.'

While Cheris was answering that, Gramps stood up and announced that he needed the toilet, so Bill offered to take him, whispering indiscreetly that he was a nurse and happy to handle any 'mishaps'. When they came back, Bill helped Marvin into one of the armchairs in the seating area, where he promptly dozed off. Beckett soon zoned out, as more people asked Cheris and Carolyn practical questions relating to the individual committee roles, which were mostly answered with cryptic references to yet more farm animals, hula hoops, and the main character being a baby Santa version of Baby Yoda.

Beckett was on the brink of dropping off himself when he felt a nudge. The past few days had wiped him out even more than usual. Mary nodded her head in the direction of the Christmas carol concert organisers, eyes glinting.

'What do you think, Beckett?' she asked.

'Um.'

'Come on, why not give it a go?'

Beckett could have bowed to the expectant, hopeful faces and simply said yes, but when there were hula hoops and Baby Yodas involved, he wasn't signing up to anything without checking the small print.

'I know you're really busy with work, and Gramps, and finding a new Tanya, but it might be fun, the two of us working on a project together. Plus, it'd be so much easier if I could team up with someone with a car.'

Working on a project with Mary? Forget the small print.

'Okay.'

Mary's eyebrows shot up. 'Wow. Really? That's... incredible.'

Beckett had to wait until the rest of the room were distracted by Cheris and Carolyn breaking out into what they called 'Santa-day Night', which seemed to simply be Whigfield's nineties' hit, 'Saturday Night', only a lot faster and with the lyrics changed from 'party time' to 'Christmas time', and various other cheesily obvious replacements.

'What have I agreed to, and will it mean killing off our friendship a month after it started?' he muttered out of the side of his mouth.

'Don't worry, it's nothing humiliating. Once I saw you'd stopped listening, I was tempted to try hoodwinking you into playing Boyband Santa, but I wouldn't ruin the NLCCCCC for my own amusement. I love the Christmas Day Twins far too much for that.'

'I don't think it's too late for me to suddenly remember an important commitment on 22 December.'

'Yeah, this isn't a part in the actual concert, so it won't be a disaster if you miss the big night.'

'Ah, so what about that big holiday I've got booked?'

Beckett kept his eyes on 'Santa-day Night' the whole time they were talking, because once upon a time, he'd known how to flirt with a woman, and this felt dangerously close to it. Mary had a month-old baby. She had a past that led to her being stuck in the middle of nowhere, with no car, no friends or family who knew she'd been pregnant, let alone an outfit for her new son. Not even a mention of Bob's father. The last thing Mary needed right now was a lonely loser developing feelings for her.

Wind it back, Beckett. Man up, here.

'Honestly, Beckett. Have you taken *any* holidays in the past six years? Even a day out somewhere?'

Well, that would do it. This lunch was the most adventurous thing he'd done in months. Years, more like. He had nothing to offer Mary beyond friendship. Beckett checked his phone. It was almost three. Definitely time to head home. He'd been playing Gramps Rude-Comment Roulette for long enough.

'I've offered to oversee all the costume design for the concert,' Mary said softly, as if realising how hard the holiday comment had hit him. 'I don't expect you to do any dressmaking, but a second opinion is always helpful, as is someone to pass me pins, stand in as dressmaker's dummy and help me transport all the materials. Sofia said I can borrow her sewing machine, but there'll be some back and forth getting people to try them on, see what tweaks are needed at the dress rehearsal. If our dramatic bonding experience last month means I can qualify for mates' rates on the taxi every now and then, it'd help.'

'By mates' rates, do you mean for free?'

'I don't have any other mates right now, let alone ones who drive taxis. You tell me.'

'Yes, I will drive you where you need to go. I can hold a crying baby while you create Santa costumes, and pass you pins. I can also do the basics like buttons and hems.'

'You can sew?' Beckett sensed Mary's head twist towards him.

'What, apart from human flesh? Are you surprised because I'm male? There was no room for traditional gender roles growing up with Gramps.'

'I've worked with plenty of men who can sew. I just... I don't know. You seemed... Okay. I made a sweeping judgement based on you clearly being a man of logic, rather than creativity. I apologise.'

'Apology accepted, if you tell me what qualifies you to head up the costume department of an illustrious production like the NLCCCCC?'

Mary shrugged, looking uncomfortable for the first time since she'd sat down for lunch. 'I used to work in a fashion company.' She stopped, blinked for a long second, then steeled her shoulders, opened her mouth and closed it again.

'You don't have to tell me, if it's private.'

She shook her head, lips pressed together. 'Not private. Just a bit sensitive these days. I co-founded, and used to be a director of, an ethical fashion accessory company.'

'Will I have heard of it?'

Before she could answer, the room broke out in muted applause as the Santa-day Night dance came to its jazz-handed conclusion, and Gramps slowly stood up.

'Well, it could have been worse. I once spent an afternoon having a boil lanced. If the show's over, I want to go home now, Tanya.' He looked around the room, panic flashing across his face when he couldn't find his carer. 'Tanya?'

Beckett jumped up, striding over to put an arm on his grandfather's shoulder, which only made him flinch away. 'Don't touch me!'

'Gramps, it's me,' Beckett said, voice tender, heart aching. 'Let's go home now, shall we?'

Gramps searched Beckett's face, nodding anxiously as his tired, old eyes watered. 'Yes, please. I want to go home.'

'Here.' Sofia followed them out to the main entrance, pressing a flyer in Beckett's hand. He briefly caught the words 'Lunch Club', before stuffing it into his pocket. He might look at it later. He might not. Today had been mostly okay, but his head was frazzled with the effort of meeting a load of strangers, in an unfamiliar place. Santa-day Night. These people were A Lot. A lot of kindness, fun, generosity, genuine interest. But, still, it was *a lot* compared to a ham sandwich on a tray, watching the same old quiz show.

All Beckett wanted to do was get Gramps home, without incident, and try to figure out what to do next.

9

MARY

I spent the journey home in rapt silence. I had set off in Beckett's car that morning feeling pitiful. I had only one maybe-friend in the whole world, nothing meaningful to do apart from try not to mess up being a mum as badly as I had the rest of my life, and no hope of feeling anything other than a complete wreck for the foreseeable future. I returned home with a stomach full of good food, a head bursting with a festive project to get stuck into – with my definite-friend, who was turning out to be much more fun than I'd supposed, and an invitation to have coffee with Sofia – a real-life, interesting and lovely-seeming person.

I'd forgotten what it felt like, spending time with other human beings. Camaraderie and the buzz of conversation. Witnessing the joy of sharing stories, jokes and problems with people who cared.

It felt invigorating. Overwhelming. Thrilling. Hopeful.

As if a bucketload of raw, rampant grief had been tipped over my head.

I had known that kind of friendship. The lightness that came from not having to explain, or fill in the gaps, or worry about a reaction. Losing it had broken me.

Today, as I sat in Beckett's car and watched buildings give way to field and forest, amongst the agony that had taken root in my soul nestled the tiny green shoots of a new beginning.

* * *

After a massive thank you to Beckett, who had been railroaded into doing far more than he'd originally agreed to, I hurried inside my cottage, left a sleeping baby in the car seat on the living-room floor, and, propelled by all the unleashed feelings, opened up my laptop and got browsing.

By the time Bob let me know he needed another feed, and a nappy change, and a long, fretful cuddle, I'd ordered a pram, changing bag, some proper nursing bras and various other bits I'd chucked in my online shopping basket that my midwife would no doubt consider fripperies, but which to me were the lifeline pulling me a wobbly step out of the bog I'd been wallowing in.

I also searched for local fabric suppliers. I wasn't about to order any materials for the carol concert without being able to inspect them first.

I briefly wondered whether it was time to look at buying a car. Having my own transport would make everything so much easier. But until I had a reliable source of income – and how could that happen, with a baby? – I wasn't comfortable blowing that amount of savings.

The plus side of having no transport was the excuse to spend more time with Beckett, until our friendship was secure enough to no longer need one. I did feel an appropriate pang of guilt that this would take up both time and petrol, but I would find ways to repay him if he didn't want money, and it was pretty obvious that Beckett needed more enjoyable things to do with his time.

The answer came to me during a 2 a.m. feed.

MARY

> I have the perfect way to pay you back for driving me about and everything else

To my surprise, he answered almost instantly.

BECKETT

> I told you. I don't want paying back.

MARY

> Why are you still up at this time? Have you and Gramps been out partying?

BECKETT

> Why do you find it so difficult to accept help?

MARY

> I asked first

BECKETT

> Yes, we've been out partying. If 'partying' includes lighting a bonfire in the garden while wearing only long johns and slippers.

MARY

> Sounds like my kind of party. I didn't take you for the kind of guy to wear long johns

As soon as I'd sent that message I regretted being flippant about something so horrible. It was the middle of the night, and my head was full of fuzz, but that didn't make it okay.

Before I could think about it, I called him.

'Hi.'

'That was really insensitive. I'm sorry. You said the middle-of-the-night stuff was the worst. I shouldn't have made a joke.'

'I told you, laughing about it keeps me sane.'

'Are you okay to talk? Is Gramps back in bed?'

Beckett sighed. 'Yeah. For now. I'm only grateful that him banging about looking for matches woke me up.'

'Is there any way you can stop him getting into the garden, like hide the door key?'

'I'll sort something out.'

'So, you normally work during the day and are up at night putting out fires?'

'I usually worked the evening shift because it fitted with Tanya's hours.'

'How do you cope? When do you ever get time to relax or have fun?'

'I find driving relaxing. Right now fun is not a priority. Or a possibility.'

'Hello, Santa-day Night?'

'Right now, fun is not a poss—'

'But it should be. It *has* to be. If you carry on like this, taking no time to look after yourself, you'll end up ill, and what will happen to Gramps then?'

'Well, thanks for that. Just the pick-me-up I needed to hear right now.' Beckett's voice had noticeably sharpened. I pressed on before he grew really annoyed.

'I want to help. Please. Not instead of you paying for a professional carer. On top of that, as a friend. If you're going to be working on the carol concert with me, it's the least I can do.'

There was a brief pause.

'You have Bob to take care of.'

'Gramps loves Bob. Having a baby to coo over will stop him getting into mischief.'

'Gramps can be really unpleasant. Today was a good day because he had his own way.'

'Yesterday Bob peed in my eye. I can handle offensive comments.' I didn't mention all the times I'd listened to people pouring their frustration out to my mum, far too distressed to tone it down because there was a teenager sitting in the corner.

'It's a bit more than that.'

'Beckett, a few minutes ago you asked why I find it so hard to accept help. Can you answer the same question? I'm offering to sit with your grandpa for a few hours, I don't know, a couple of times a week. In exchange for you doing me a massive favour that will take loads of your time. You can go for a walk, or enjoy a coffee in a bougie café, sit and read. Join a club. Go on a date! Find *something* that makes you laugh, or simply forget for a while.'

He was silent in response to this, so I kept going.

'I have virtually nothing to do.'

'Apart from Bob.'

I dismissed that with an irritated tut. 'Other mums look after babies while caring for older kids, running their own business, or at the very least having a basic social life. Sofia and Moses have five kids!'

'Sofia and Moses have each other.'

'Look, just stop, okay? I'm going to do this. I need to do this. Otherwise I... I can't be friends with you.'

'You're giving me an ultimatum?'

'No.' I sighed. That wasn't it at all. When was my brain going to start functioning again? 'It's a fact. Despite current circumstances, I know how to be a good friend, and that includes not wasting your days watching *Grey's Anatomy* ignoring a friend who's struggling. I literally can't do it. I hate myself enough already at the moment.'

Woah, Mary. That was way too much information.

I spent a few moments mentally beating myself over the head while waiting for Beckett to reply. When he did speak, it was hesitant, as if he was far more competent than me at thinking before blurting out humiliating opinions about himself.

'If you're going to be coming around to my house, then I'd consider it more relaxing and... fun...' he stumbled over the word as if it were in a foreign language '...if I stayed, rather than went to some coffee shop. I spend enough time in my taxi trying to ignore the strangers sitting behind me.'

'Then how does that give you a break?' I tried to hide how high my spirits leapt at being invited to hang out more with Beckett.

'Maybe having someone to offer moral support will help more than trying to find something productive to do by myself, while stressing about what's happening at home.'

'Okay. I take your point. So, let's do both. Build it up slowly while I get to know Gramps and you remember what it is you like doing. Go to the gym, do a food shop, whatever. I don't believe you can't think of something. Then when you're back, we can work on costumes together.'

'Okay.'

'Okay?'

'I mean, I think Bob would miss me if you insisted we stopped being friends.'

'And you can't do that to Bob.'

I hovered for a moment, enjoying the easy warmth that accompanied an amicable conclusion. Still bewildered about how a random taxi driver had suddenly become one of the most important people in my new life.

'Tuesday morning?'

'Perfect. I won't have had the costume list from Cheris and Carolyn yet, but I could help you look for a new home carer?'

'Perfect. We'll pick you up about nine. Gramps wakes up with the sun, and I'm guessing Bob isn't one for lie-ins. Now, get some sleep while it's all quiet.'

'You, too.'

Perfect.

* * *

Up until becoming friends with Kieran and Shay, I'd thought about clothes far less than the average thirteen-year-old. My parents considered focusing on outward appearance to be a shallow, selfish waste of money. I grew up wearing whatever they could grab in the local charity shop, with no one to help me appreciate that the way we presented ourselves to the world could matter – both to how we felt about ourselves, and how people saw us. My parents' couldn't-care-less dowdiness sent as strong a message as the person with a five-figure handbag.

I started year nine with a shapeless pair of jeans, saggy leggings, a few scruffy tops and two hand-knitted jumpers that my mum had bought from a fair-trade stall, both of which were lopsided, unfashionable whatever the decade, and downright ugly. Even if I was vaguely aware how for some kids, clothes were a form of self-expression, denoting what 'pack' they belonged to, it had never crossed my mind that this was something I might have any control over when it came to my own wardrobe. My pocket money was paltry, earned tramping the streets delivering Dad's campaign flyers or putting together care packages for the women's refuge. Once I'd bought a bar of chocolate or paid for the bus into town, there was nothing left to spend on clothes, even if I could be bothered or knew what I wanted to buy.

Shay was simply stunned by this revelation.

'Mary, being skint is even more reason to look good! It's about self-respect, int it?'

Um, was it?

My friends had the same philosophy about having fun. Whereas my 'educated' upbringing had drummed into me that spare time was for bettering either oneself, or others, the viewpoint of the kind of 'youths' that my parents funded programmes for was that they worked hard enough on surviving. They were going to make the damn most of whatever entertainment they could find. Like a big two fingers to all the crappiness they had to deal with the rest of the time.

'Yeah, we have no money,' Kieran drawled one Saturday afternoon when I went to hang out at the burnt-out skate park near their block of flats. 'People dismiss us like we're nowt. Teachers have no idea how hard it is to figure out maths problems when all you've eaten is dry cereal and your uniform's damp because the flat's freezing and there's nowhere to dry it. Who cares about rich blokes' ancient battles when you've been kept awake all night listening to non-stop fighting through the walls? I've had six detentions this year because when the lift's broken, Mum can't do the stairs, and taking Angel to school makes me late.'

'But don't you dare feel sorry for us,' Shay added, with a sidelong glance. 'We won't moan about our problems or reveal our weaknesses. We have to work harder, dream bigger, fight stronger, so we will. The greater our challenges, the smarter, fiercer, braver, more determined we get.'

These were not the helpless, hopeless victims my parents talked about. They were warriors. More importantly, they knew it.

Their entrepreneurialism, their capacity for finding joy in the smallest things, the certainty in who they were and all they were going to be and do, were irresistible.

Their wild, fabulous, unashamed declaration of all this to the world via clothing and accessories, accompanied by the way they strutted and sashayed through the estate they were so proud to have come from, was downright magnificent.

Guided by Shay, I chopped my unflattering jeans into cut-off shorts, which I wore over tights or the least-terrible of my leggings. Kieran used his growing textile skills to crop my sweaters, and they rifled through the years of hoarded tat in my bedroom to find ribbons, badges, scraps and other random things to give basic tops an emo twist. They tucked, hemmed, mixed, matched and loaned, and overall performed wonders until my sorry collection of outfits felt like something the person I was starting to dare to be might wear.

I used the money my grandparents gave me for my fourteenth birthday to buy hair-dye, eyeliner and a bag and boots from the local army surplus store. Shay and Kieran made me a set of leather bracelets.

For the first time, when out with my self-assured family on that spring's campaign trail, I no longer felt invisible. To my parents' chagrin. They were both irritated and beyond irritating about my 'little rebellious phase', but, with the general election coming up, were too distracted to do much about it.

I didn't care. I was spending as much time as possible at Shay's flat, jam-packed with brothers and sisters, wizened great-nannan, an uncle battling alcoholism and parents who laughed loud and loved each other with a rambunctious enthusiasm that was dazzling, compared to my own mum and dad's cordial partnership.

Heavy work schedules, parliamentary commitments and a serious snoring issue meant my parents rarely slept in the same room. Shay's dad would order all the kids out of the house, grab her mum's backside and declare 'afternoon-nap time' as he chased her into the bedroom, accompanied by giggles and squeals.

It was chaotic, cramped, noisy and never failed to offer me a warm welcome. I learned that Kieran and his little sister spent at least as much time there as they did in their one-bedroom flat on the thirty-third floor. A mum with myriad health problems, one dad who'd left when Kieran was a toddler, and another who remained anonymous, meant there was never enough, of anything. Let alone the capacity to properly care for two children.

Two or three times a year, Kieran would decamp to London to stay with his dad's new family, where at least he was fed and could have a hot shower. He never spoke about these weeks, though. Kieran talked to Shay about everything, but the rare times she asked about his London trips, his face would shut down and he'd change the subject. It always took a few days of Obasi affection to become himself again. As the years passed, the visits reduced to once a year, then the odd weekend or day trip. It helped me feel better about hanging around Shay's home, knowing that Kieran needed it even more than I did.

Seeing the near-miracle of my style transformation, other girls at school started asking Shay and Kieran to customise items for them. As we reached the summer holiday, the three of us no longer had time for balmy evenings on the rundown park or weekends window shopping; instead, we became obsessed with scouring the market and junk sales for trinkets or clothing items to modify or chop up for something else. One of Shay's aunties gave her an old sewing machine, and the three of us spent hours at my largely unused dining room table practising different techniques and learning what worked and what didn't via trial and error. As summer rolled into the start of our GCSE years, we settled into our different skill sets. Shay was constantly sketching, hunting through magazines and on the family's battered computer for new inspiration. Kieran made the designs come to life, and I handled everything else: pricing, packaging, running to

Poundland for more buttons, arguing with customers about whether they could pay in instalments (no chance, unless they wanted to wait until the last payment to get the goods).

My parents were initially happy for us to hang out doing 'something constructive' at their house. They even stopped dragging me around with them, now I'd apparently found my own worthy cause, and were providing my friends with the opportunity to spend time in an 'aspirational environment'.

They were less pleased when they suspected I was putting more effort into sourcing velvet than I was on schoolwork. When my woeful exam results came in, they preferred to blame my grievously misspent use of time, rather than any chance I'd failed to inherit the family's brainy genes.

Either way, I felt in no way a failure when by that summer, aged sixteen, we had tenaciously built up a thriving little business, gradually homing in on bags, hats and other accessories. Kieran had been able to pay his flat's heating bill for the whole of the previous winter and buy his mum and sister warm coats and boots. Shay bought a brand-new Singer sewing machine, and we cleared out the empty bedroom opposite mine and set up an official workshop.

I used what little family brains I had to compose a pitch asking Mum and Dad for a start-up grant to open a market stall. Once they'd got over their dismay that instead of resitting my exams and continuing on the treadmill to university, I was selling out to the evils of capitalism, they accepted that, like my short-lived stint as an emo, this was yet another phase, and they might as well help me get something out of it, while simultaneously supporting my two disadvantaged friends. The caveat was that we also studied part-time at college. I focused on business, and Kieran and Shay enrolled on a textiles and fashion course.

Our recycled-fashion empire, ShayKi, was born.

Kieran came up with the name. None of us liked it particularly, but we were sixteen and couldn't think of anything better. Also, my parents were strenuously opposed to my name being included in the branding. I think they thought it would make it harder for me to leave, once I regained my senses.

It didn't. After walking – limping – away, I discovered that as swiftly as I'd joined their trio twenty years earlier, Shay and Kieran had wiped all trace of me from their online presence, seamlessly reforming as a power-pair. That young girl who'd lingered inside me, knowing I was something of a third wheel, regretted not making a fuss about being included. It wouldn't have made it harder to leave – nothing could have made that any worse. But they might have tried harder to convince me to stay.

10

MARY

On Monday, I faced down the ongoing, internal whine of anxiety and mental paralysis that would prefer me to remain hiding in the forest forever, donned my stretchiest pair of jeans and a gorgeous pale-pink cashmere sweater that was large enough to hide my deflated-balloon belly, and braved an outing to Sofia's house. Apart from walking to the farm shop down the road a few times, and an appointment at the baby clinic, this was my first proper solo trip as a mum. As tempting as it was to use Sherwood Taxis in the hope Beckett was somewhere nearby waiting for his next job, I knew it was important for me to manage this alone. The pram hadn't arrived yet, so I carried Bob in the papoose on my front and a rucksack crammed with baby supplies on my back. The balance of weight sort of worked, as long as I didn't have to negotiate any narrow spaces.

It was a twenty-minute walk to the bus stop on the outskirts of the nearest village, Hatherstone. I could count on one hand the number of times I'd made it as far as the village since moving here, thanks to online deliveries and a local takeaway.

This morning, the promised snow had never appeared, but

there was a thick frost on the ground, and, allowing my post-birth body to take it slowly, for the first time I bothered to notice my surroundings.

I'd spent the whole of my old life living in a city, considering a jog in one of the parks or watching a fox rootling through my bins to be experiencing nature. This was like stepping into an alternate reality.

The forest was eerily quiet, the only sound my boots crunching along a path littered with crisp leaves, acorns and pine cones, and the occasional scuffle of a bird in the undergrowth. I'd grown shamefully unfit, so soon grew breathless, sucking in lungfuls of exhilaratingly fresh November air, ripe with earthy decomposition. Tendrils of morning mist weaved amongst the tree trunks, in contrast to the occasional dapple of sunbeams that breached the canopy of scantily clad branches above my head.

I felt as captivated as Lucy Pevensie, finding herself in Narnia. Strolling through the dancing shadows, all my senses alive for what felt like the first time in forever, ideas for new fabrics, textures and embellishments cascading through my head. I had to remind myself that the days of bringing my creative concepts to the collaborative table were over. Well, unless the Christmas Day Twins had written some sort of Forest or Nature Santa into their script.

Before I knew it, I could see the kissing gate leading to the edge of the village up ahead. In just under a mile, it was as if the anxiety and apprehension about not only today, but tomorrow and the next day, and a lifetime of days stretching out after that had somehow dissolved with the last wisps of mist.

I turned a slow circle, wobbling slightly due to the weights on my chest and back, head tipped up to scan the tops of the oak trees, the pastel sky beyond.

Who knew that a change in scenery, twenty minutes of

forward motion, getting lost in the moment instead of wrestling with the past or panicking about the future, could shift something inside that felt somehow deeply significant?

Once I'd found a seat on the almost empty bus, angling sideways to make room for the rucksack, I pondered what that shift might be.

Perspective, maybe? That morning, something had started to become a little unstuck.

And the *something*, I realised as we rattled along the main road into Nottingham, was me.

* * *

After getting off the bus at the stop nearest to the church, I walked for another fifteen minutes through the city suburb before arriving at Sofia's address. The street reminded me of the estate where Shay and Kieran had grown up. A couple of the terraced houses had boarded-up windows; lots of them projected that aura of neglect that accompanied poverty. Ill-fitting, yellowing net curtains in random windows, a pile of scrap metal in a front yard, chipped paintwork and rusty gates.

Then I arrived at the last house before the road came to a dead end, the only one with a proper front garden. This house was Victorian brick like the rest of the street, but detached, with three storeys and a garage.

I climbed three wide stone steps up to the traditional front door and banged twice using a brass knocker in the shape of an owl. Waiting for someone to open it, the peace of Sherwood Forest far behind me, I couldn't help wishing I'd stayed stuck. Stuck on my sofa, in my pyjamas, by myself, with no one to ask me uncomfortable questions about the current state of my non-life, or how I'd ended up living it.

After I knocked again, someone eventually opened the sunflower-yellow door.

'Hello?' It was a young woman, maybe late twenties, with auburn hair even more bedraggled than mine and a smear of what looked like mushed-up banana down her purple hoodie.

'Is this Sofia's? She invited me for coffee.'

The woman's face lit up. 'Yes, of course. I was confused because everyone just walks straight in. I was going to the toilet when I heard the knock. But I'm guessing you're Mary, so you wouldn't know that, and this is Bob.'

She paused to offer a coo to the back of his head. I'm sure he'd have appreciated it, had he been awake.

'Come in, before all the good cake's gone. We're dying to hear everything. You are literally our heroine. Oh, I'm Rina.'

I tentatively stepped into a beautiful hallway with sanded floors and dark red walls covered in a mix of family photographs and kids' drawings in colourful frames. Slipping off my rucksack, shoes and the coat I'd put on over the top of the papoose, I shuffled after her, trying not to panic at who 'we' consisted of, and what precisely they wanted to hear.

'Hey, everyone. She's here! The living legend that is… Mary!'

There were three other women sitting in Sofia's family room, so it could have been worse. Although, it should have been better seeing as Sofia never mentioned inviting anyone else along, and we'd only arranged it the night before.

There were also two babies and two toddlers, plus Mimi, Sofia's three-year-old. She was currently offering a plastic teacup to a golden retriever, who gazed back at her adoringly. The room was beautifully cosy; woollen throws lay across the women's knees, a wood-burning stove crackled and the scent of candles glowing on a high shelf mingled with the fragrance of freshly brewed coffee and pumpkin spice.

'Mary!' Sofia clambered up, adjusting the baby in her arms as she came over to give me a hug. 'Did you find us okay? You know one of us would have been happy to pick you up, save you trekking in on the bus.'

'It's fine. Bob and I enjoyed the journey, and we had the whole morning to kill.'

'Yeah,' a worryingly slender woman with a drawn face, breast-feeding a baby not much bigger than Bob, said, with more than a twinge of bitterness. 'It's not as if there's anything else to do, apart from feed, change nappies, clean up sick and all the other mess, make a cup of tea so it can sit there going cold, then start another feed just to stop the chuffin' crying for a few blessed minutes.'

'Mary, this is Rosie,' Sofia said. 'Oh, and Amber, who is three months old today.'

I nodded hello. Rosie wore a beige crop-top and crumpled khaki pants, and her lank blonde hair had, at a guess, about four months' worth of dark roots.

'Amber's started teething, so Rosie's feeling quite tired.'

'Rosie's wondering why none of her older, wiser, supposed "friends" didn't lock her in a cupboard until she'd got over this insane notion about having a baby,' Rosie said, with a groan.

'We must have been jealous of your carefree life, and relished the thought of you sharing our misery,' Rina replied, rolling her eyes. 'We know it's tough, Rosie, but can I remind you of the New Life Coffee Mum rules? One good moan each to let off steam, then we move on. No wallowing à la Jane and her never-ending pustule.'

'Thanks for the reminder, Rina. Maybe you can also remember when your clean-freak mum invited herself to stay when Mitch was tiny, and whether there was any leeway about the rules, then,' Sofia added, not unkindly, before turning back to me. 'Rina's boys are Jock and Mitch, over there with the fire engine, and this scrummy ball of joy is Kimmy, who belongs to Li.'

Li waved hello. She was, in contrast to the rest of the group, dressed in tailored trousers and a silky cream blouse. Her bobbed hair was glossy and she wore a tasteful shimmer of make-up to complement her perfectly manicured nails.

'Li has a dream husband who works part-time,' Rina said, noticing me noticing Li. 'He sends her off on spa days, treats her to shopping trips and freakishly enjoys housework. She's a genius scientist, and we secretly suspect she created him in her lab. We would all hate her for it, except she's the kindest person you'll ever meet, and has been through more crap than any woman should have to, so deserves all the treats.'

I nervously perched on the edge of Sofia's giant corner sofa while she hurried off to fetch me a drink. I had no idea if it was considered acceptable to mix caffeine with breastfeeding, but assumed these seasoned mums would know and have offered me decaf, if so. It appeared to be a coffee group, after all.

'How are you finding being a mum?' Rina asked. 'It's impressive that you're out and about with a month-old baby. I still hadn't got dressed a month after Jock was born.'

I didn't know what to think about that. It hadn't felt impressive, dragging myself out to ensure there were still normal, functional humans in existence, going about their day-to-day lives. What was I supposed to be doing all day?

'Jock is three and you still don't bother to get dressed most of the time,' Li said, with a teasing smile.

'That's one benefit of working at home.' Rina shrugged. 'Alongside being able to skive off and eat cake with you.'

They carried on chatting about how they'd coped with the initial weeks of parenthood, forgetting Rina had asked me a question. It didn't stop me mulling on it while sipping on deliciously smooth coffee and eating a slice of cinnamon fruit loaf.

How was I finding being a mum?

As if I'd fallen asleep on a plane and woken up, jet-lagged and disoriented, on a whole different continent.

Lost, scared, and yet somehow cautiously optimistic.

I simply listened for most of the morning as the women chatted about what they'd been up to, how, no, none of them had started getting ready for Christmas yet. They discussed problems in a strictly non-moaning manner and shared advice and anecdotes. I learned that Rina was wrangling her way through a nasty divorce. Rosie was married to Rina's brother, Jay, a local club DJ who was currently on a week-long stag-do in Ibiza with a guy from school he'd not seen in years.

'This is stating facts, not moaning,' she insisted. 'But I've been fantasising about setting fire to his decks. He left his filthy football kit on the bathroom floor and no milk in the fridge.'

'He'd better let you have a break once he's back.' Rina shook her head in disgust. 'I can only apologise for my big brother's pathetic lack of maturity when someone waves a nightclub ticket under his nose.'

'Come to Birkland Hall with me!' Li said, her face lighting up.

'Babe, you know I can't afford to get my roots done, let alone visit your super-posh spa.'

Li's slender eyebrows arched. 'I'm not going to invite you to spa with me and expect you to pay!'

'Did I ever mention that I'm raising five adopted kids on a pastor's salary?' Sofia tapped her chin thoughtfully.

'Isn't rule-number-something that coffee mums are too damn tired for subtle hints, straight talking only?' Li responded.

'Please can I go to the spa with you one day?' Sofia asked, scooping up Mimi, who'd dipped the dog's tail in her cup of orange squash and was about to use it to paint the sofa. 'I'll babysit in return. Or get Emma to bake you a cake.'

'Her sister runs a celebration cake company,' Rina said, filling me in.

'You can all come,' Li said. 'It's my birthday the second week of December. I'll have a fudge cake with extra fudge, please. No candles.'

'Mary, you in?' Rosie asked me.

'Um... I can't leave Bob.'

That was an odd realisation. Knowing, from now on, my life was not my own.

I looked around at this group of women, phones out as they messaged their partners and family members, trying to figure out a date.

Okay, so my life was no longer my own, but I would be able to go for a spa day once Bob was older and I could hire a babysitter or book him into a nursery.

Who wanted a life all to their own, anyway? I'd been doing that for the past six months, and it sucked.

'Let us have a think about it.' Sofia narrowed her eyes in thought. 'See if we can come up with something.'

'It's fine, you really don't have to.'

Coming here was more than enough. I feared a day at a fancy spa with these women would be neither restorative nor relaxing.

'We know. But we will, anyway.'

After an hour or so, Bob had started the headbutting thing again, doing his best to latch onto Li's arm, where she'd been sitting beside me having a cuddle. She handed him over, and I felt about ready to die as I fumbled with the nursing bra I'd remembered to wear and tried to hold in my wince as he latched on, then slipped off again, milk spurting in his eye. Rosie casually feeding as if she barely noticed it made my clumsy attempt appear even worse.

'You're doing great,' Li said quietly.

'I'm really not,' I said, forcing the words past the shame in my throat.

'When Kimmy was a month old, I still sobbed through every feed. I tried expressing instead, so we could give her bottles, but I couldn't get the hang of that either. I felt like a total failure. As if the whole world had ended. Honestly, you are doing *great*.'

'Please tell me it gets easier, and one day I'll not feel like I'm wandering about in a maze, blindfolded, with my hands tied behind my back.'

Li's raucous laugh made Bob, now drifting off, spring awake with a start.

Sofia, who'd come to squat by the sofa, gave me a sideways look. 'Raising my seventeen-year-old still feels like that. You've been a mum for just over a month and you've already worked out how it's going to go.'

'I'm not sure that's reassuring.'

She bent her head closer as I shuffled Bob around to rub his back. 'Feel free to head off once Bob's ready. I'll have to strong-arm Rina and Rosie out of the door or they'll still be here when Moses comes home for lunch, and he's been conducting a funeral so won't be in the mood for coffee-mum conversation.'

'Thank you.' It might have seemed weird feeling grateful for someone basically telling me to leave, but, as nice as these women were, I was sorely out of social practice, had stuff going on with my post-birth body that I preferred not to be happening in public, and I would fall asleep on the bus if I didn't get back for a nap soon.

'I'll change Bob's nappy and then go.'

'Let me get your bag. You can use the mat behind the

armchair.' Sofia popped into the hallway, and then returned holding up a white square-shaped bag with black trim. 'Is this yours?'

My whole body froze. It was. But not in the way she meant.

'That's mine,' Rina said. 'I found it in that new charity shop on Mansfield Road. Only five quid, and I reckon it's one of Shay-Ki's exclusive lines.'

She was right. While most ShayKi products were deliberately kept at high street prices – our best-selling bags cost around thirty pounds – every year the company also released a limited-edition range, which all three directors worked on together. This bag was from 2021 and had been made from recycled plastic bottles. I'd designed the zebra-print buckle and strap. It had cost nearly a thousand pounds and sold out almost instantly.

'Oh, it's a literal work of art,' Rosie breathed, standing up to come and take the bag off Sofia, opening it up to inspect the lining fabric printed in soft shades of blue, green and brown inspired by Shay's safari holiday in the Serengeti. 'I'll give you twenty for it. It can be Jay's apology present when he gets back.'

A wave of nausea rolled through my stomach.

This abrupt intrusion of my old life, while sitting here still suffering with the whiplash from being thrust into my new one, was too much. The room suddenly felt stifling, as if I couldn't breathe properly. I lurched to my feet, Bob clutched to my chest, and weaved past the scattered trucks, plastic tea-set and dozing dog, practically flinging myself out of the door into the mercifully chilly hallway.

'Are you okay?' Sofia asked as I wriggled into the papoose, naturally having followed me out.

'Yeah, just a bit of a hot flush. Is that a thing? I know the midwife said my hormones will still be all over the place.'

Sofia handed me my boots.

'Honestly? I wouldn't know,' she said, with an apologetic smile. 'But it certainly sounds plausible.'

There was a click as the front door swung open, and Moses walked in, shaking rain off his Afro.

'Oops. I'd better start shooing the others out. It was *amazing* to have you here. Please promise you'll come next week. Or before. I mean, things are pretty full-on most days, but if you message first I can always meet you somewhere. Oh, and can I add you to the chat? That way, you'll see if any of the others are hanging out. Sometimes they take the babies swimming, or go to a soft-play centre. The church toddler group is Friday mornings, but you might find that a bit much to start with.'

'Okay, yes. Thank you.' I ducked past Moses to the door.

'If you need anything, a lift, baby stuff, advice, more cake, just let us know, yes? Promise? Okay, fabulous. Oh, and rehearsals start for the carol concert next week, straight after casting, so you can come and start measuring up, and I'll need to hand over the sewing machine. One way or another, I'll being seeing you soon! Yay!'

Phew.

By the time I'd reached the end of Sofia's street, the mizzle had intensified to a downpour and continued for the seventeen minutes I stood at the bus stop, using both hands to try to stretch my non-maternity raincoat around Bob, while praying his snow-suit lived up to its water-resistant promise. I spent the whole bus journey, and the mile squelching back through the forest, weeping pitifully, while trying to hide inside my hood.

All I wanted was a bowl of soup, a bath and to collapse into bed in my fleecy pyjamas.

That wasn't true. What I wanted was to rewind the past year and do everything differently.

I wanted to go back and force myself to open my eyes, stop

drifting along on some stupid, loved-up cloud, ignoring the warning signs flashing at me from every direction.

I didn't want to undo Bob. I'd never wish for that. But, with a grief so sharp it ripped through my guts, I wanted his dad to have been honest. For my *friends* to have tried harder to pop my bubble of blissful ignorance.

I wanted to turn back the clock and act sooner, so I could have kept my job, my home, the friends who were my family. *My husband.*

More than anything, in that moment I ached, burned, raged, with how fervently I wanted him.

I managed a handful of crackers, a three-minute shower and a half-hour snooze on the sofa.

It was better than nothing.

11

BECKETT

After spending most of Monday in a foul mood, Beckett woke up at five-thirty on Tuesday to hear Gramps clattering about in the kitchen. With a resigned sigh, he slid out of bed, threw on joggers and a jumper and went to start breakfast.

By the time he'd chugged down his first coffee and plate of scrambled eggs, the weariness had been replaced with a welcome prickle of anticipation, given how the day before had worn him down. Gramps had been especially cantankerous, feeling drained by Sunday's exertion, and after barely any time to search for a stand-in carer, Beckett had endured a five-hour shift in the pouring rain, chugging through roadwork jams and rush-hour snarls. He'd had a middle-aged woman stumble into the front passenger seat, and then proceed to put her hand on his thigh every few seconds, despite him swatting if off every time. At a set of traffic lights, she'd leant over and blown tequila fumes in his ear before telling him that her destination had changed to a five-star hotel ten minutes away, if he'd like to join her.

He'd declined her invitation and dropped her off at her original destination, where she'd promptly thrown up on the pavement the second she'd got out of the car. It wasn't Beckett's responsibility to clean up his client's vomit, but it had been right outside a primary school, and no one else had been going to do it. He'd half carried, half dragged her inside her huge house, borrowed a bucket and a brush and then, instead of accepting her continued offer of 'fun times', he'd left her sprawled on the sofa with a glass of water, now eight precarious minutes late to get back to relieve Sonali.

There'd been scarcely a second to form a coherent thought before he'd collapsed into bed, let alone a plan.

Although, the truth was, every one of those spare seconds had been spent thinking about one thing. One person.

And it wasn't a new carer.

* * *

By the time they'd set off to pick up Mary, stopping at a supermarket on the way because they'd run out of milk, and Beckett was worried Mary had run out of everything, the flutter in his stomach was something he hadn't felt in years.

Not because of Mary, specifically, he kept reassuring himself. It was only natural to look forward to hanging out with a friend, especially after such a long time. Especially when it was a friend who made him feel so positive. Unburdened. As if he wasn't a pathetic failure.

Even Gramps behaved less contrary about another outing, as if he could remember how his previous adventure with Mary and Bob had lifted his spirits.

They pulled up outside her cottage at five minutes to nine, and Beckett quickly grabbed the shopping bags from the back seat and went to knock on the door, which whipped open the second he reached the porch.

The Most Wonderful Time of the Year

'Hey,' Mary said, with a slightly manic smile.

'Bad morning?'

'That obvious?' she said, her eyes dropping to her torso, seeming to realise her shirt was buttoned up wrong and a tiny nappy dangled off her hip. 'Oh. I stuck that there because I was changing Bob and needed more cotton wool, and... I can't remember why.'

She gave a half-hearted laugh. 'It's clean.'

Beckett leant forwards and gently plucked a large crumb of toast from her matted hair.

Mary's eyes widened. 'I'm a wreck.'

'Hey, I tried to microwave my wallet this morning. My barely lucid grandfather had to intervene.'

'Do two knackered, floundering, possibly inept people make one half-competent one?'

'I guess we're about to find out.'

Beckett put the shopping away while Mary got Bob ready, and he felt a ridiculously warm twinge at seeing she'd eaten the food he'd bought last month. Gramps wandered around the house pointing out its more obvious defects, and promising Mary that next time he'd bring his tools over and get them sorted.

Beckett did wonder for a moment if this might not be a terrible idea – Gramps had been employed as a handyman a few times over the years and had used to complete their own DIY with skill and diligence. He then saw his grandfather's hand trembling as he poked at a patch of crumbling plaster, and stopped wondering.

* * *

'Are we going back to the café with the lunatic women?' Gramps asked, once they were back in the car.

'We're going home,' Beckett said. 'And that's really not a nice thing to call someone.'

'If they don't want to be insulted, then they shouldn't behave like imbeciles.'

'Also not an okay word.'

'Why are the woman and the baby here? Have we kidnapped them?'

'We invited them over for the morning.'

'What, to our house?' Gramps sounded incredulous, and then he did something Beckett hadn't heard in, well, hardly ever. Gramps started to laugh. Not the reluctant chuckle Beckett had occasionally heard in the past. A full-on, belly-shaking, rip-roaring guffaw.

'Um, why is that so funny?' Mary asked from the back seat.

'I have no idea,' Beckett answered, knowing Gramps would lose control of his bladder if he didn't calm down.

'You finally meet a woman worth impressing, and you bring her to our hovel to hang out with a grumpy old codger.' Gramps wheezed. 'I thought doctors were supposed to be smart.'

'Okay, so since we've brought up kidnapping, am I allowed to know where we're going? Or do I need to memorise landmarks en route, because, due to barely going out since I moved, I've no clue where we are?'

'We're in Bigley,' Beckett said, nodding at the sign up ahead. Gramps' house was on one of the more respectable streets of a large village that had long been the butt of local jokes thanks to the unfortunate name of Bigley Bottom. This scorn had the advantage of meaning that, back in the golden years of the housing market, Gramps had been able to afford a mortgage for a 1950s semi with two reasonable-sized bedrooms and a boxroom, plus a kitchen-diner and living room on the ground floor.

Beckett had always considered it to be modest, yet adequate.

It was only now, as he stopped the car beside their rickety fence, that he saw it through Mary's eyes.

It was a hovel.

As she followed him inside, it only got worse.

'Now this makes me feel better about the toast in my hair.'

How had Beckett not appreciated the level to which a house could fall into a complete state without Tanya? Although, while the grotty mess was recent, the mounds of clutter and random junk had been building up for years. It was the total opposite of Mary's sparse cottage. The kind of house that, when he'd been shadowing an occupational therapist as a student, had made him feel appalled at the conditions some people allowed their elderly, ill relatives to live in.

'Yeah. It's been...' He had no excuse.

'It's been impossible,' Mary said, firmly. 'Trying to keep earning, taking care of Gramps, sourcing Tanya's replacement... it's been *impossible* not to drop some balls under those circumstances. Most people wouldn't have made it this far without cracking under the strain of it all.'

She looked at Beckett, shaking her head as if baffled. 'And you found the time to stop and buy me groceries. You found the energy to even *care* that I might need some.'

'You can see why I'd find a trip to Tesco more appealing than trying to tackle this.' Beckett gripped the back of his neck. Any lingering shame Mary might have felt after the birth had to be eclipsed by this disgrace. 'I'll take us back to your house.'

'What? Why? My house is hardly any better.'

Beckett simply looked at her.

'Okay, it is better, but the whole point of me being here is to help.' Her face softened as she leant in to whisper, 'Beckett, I've spent only a few hours with Gramps, but it's enough to understand how all-consuming that must be.'

'This isn't a fit place for a baby.'

Mary rolled her eyes. 'Really? Then how did our ancestors survive slums, and shacks, and caves?'

'I'm not sure many of them did...'

'He'll be fine in his car seat. Germs can't crawl that fast. I don't think.'

Gramps, who'd wandered into the living room, stomped back into the corridor. 'Where's the baby? I want to hold him.'

'There you go. Looks like Gramps is cleaner than me. Bob'll be fine with him.'

Beckett didn't want reminding of the wrangling it had required to get Gramps presentable. Mary unclipped Bob while Gramps shuffled into the living room, where he happily collapsed into his recliner, arms outstretched for the baby.

'You'll have to hand him back when I bring you a cup of tea, mind.'

He gave an absent-minded nod, already engrossed in tenderly stroking the black wisps on Bob's crown with a gnarly finger.

'Are you sure?' Beckett asked, the apprehension clear in his voice.

'Stay with him if you're worried. I'll make you both a drink.' Mary grinned as she waltzed out of the room.

'Once I've decontaminated the kitchen,' she called a couple of seconds later, prompting Beckett to trust Gramps for a few seconds and hurry after her.

'Mary, you said yourself you've had a rough morning. There's no way I'm going to be the ass who lets you clean my kitchen.'

'Um, what, like you cleaned mine?' She twisted around from where she was already running the hot tap.

The kitchen was a dump. Pots piled up everywhere because the slimline dishwasher was full. Empty food cartons, the lingering smell of eggs from breakfast. Sticky worktops, hob, tiles. He could only bear a split-second glance at the floor.

'I've had no one to take care of but myself for a long time.'

'You've got Bob.'

'That's different. I would happily die for Bob. I'm biologically programmed to look after him. I haven't been able to do anything nice for anyone in months.'

Beckett didn't ask if this was because of lack of opportunity, or because she'd not been up to it.

'I've been pickling in my own problems for far too long. Being able to do this for you isn't a chore, it's a pleasure. I'm actually being quite selfish. So, how many sugars is Gramps allowed?'

* * *

Beckett jerked awake to hear Mary singing in the kitchen, Gramps and Bob both gently snoring in their respective seats. He quickly checked the time and, to his chagrin, had been asleep for almost an hour. His plan had been to drink his tea, respecting Mary's insistence upon cleaning the kitchen, and then go and help her as soon as he thought he could get away with it.

Stretching the kinks out of his neck – honestly, he'd never have dreamt that waking up to the sound of 'Christmas Every Day' being sung out of tune could be so un-annoying – he quickly went to find her.

'Wow.'

'Looks better, doesn't it?'

Mary had washed up, cleared all the worktops, sorted the mess on the table into orderly piles and was sweeping the floor. Loose tendrils of hair curled around flushed cheeks as she smiled, and an image of her as Cinderella flashed through his head.

In which case, he was obviously Buttons. And he hoped Prince Charming, whoever he might be, ended up with an ugly sister.

'I can't remember it being so spacious.'

'Opening the blinds properly helps.'

'Gramps gets annoyed if he sees the neighbour's cats.' Annoyed, as in he would throw saucepans at them. 'Have you had a drink?'

'I'll have one once the floor's done. Then we could look at domiciliary care companies? Unless you'd rather I clean the fridge, or start on the living room.'

'No. I definitely wouldn't rather you did that. Please sit down. Do you want tea or coffee?'

'Now I've wiped down the machine, I'll have coffee.'

They had almost another hour before either of their dependants woke up. The atmosphere was so comfortable they could have known each other for eons. At the same time, Beckett had to work hard at quashing the spark of joy that in the past he'd have described as attraction, but in this case spelled inevitable disaster.

Mary was happy to chat about her childhood, which offered some explanation regarding the disconnection with her family, but whenever the conversation strayed to more recent years, she would redirect it back onto him.

He found himself describing how when he gave up on a medical career, his fiancée, another doctor who he'd been with since the first week of university, made it clear she wasn't prepared to share Beckett with his grandpa, or marry someone with such altered ambitions from hers.

'Wow. That sucks.'

'She spent all her working life with ill people, why would she sacrifice her precious spare time caring for a sick old man, too?'

'Because he's family, and he hasn't got anyone else? Because whatever challenges he has now, he sacrificed so much for you? Because it's the right thing to do?' Mary found it hard to hide her distaste, and in that moment Beckett felt as if he loved her a little bit for it.

'We spent weeks discussing it while he was in hospital. Then, one night I overheard her on the phone to a friend, saying that hopefully he wouldn't hang on much longer, so maybe she should persuade me to stick him in a home and take the financial hit, ride it out. Once I'd got over the grief, I could go back to medicine.'

'I'm so sorry.'

'Yeah. At least I found out before we got married. You saw my old Facebook account. We were too busy out socialising for loads of deep discussions about taking care of Gramps in his old age, but, even if we had talked about it, I think she'd have given me all the right answers until facing it for real.'

'It's impossible to know how we'll truly respond when everything falls apart, until it does.'

Mary shook her head, her gaze focused on something a long way from the kitchen. Beckett wondered if now was the time to ask how she'd ended up in Sherwood Forest, but then Bob started wailing, which woke up Gramps, and for the next couple of hours they barely had a spare minute.

'Well, not the productive day we intended,' Mary said, screwing up her nose in apology when Beckett carried Bob back into her house later that afternoon. He'd have been happy for her to stay longer, but didn't want either her or Bob to witness Gramps letting rip when his favourite quiz show came on.

They'd kept getting so distracted with talking, and making sure everyone was fed, jigging the baby up and down and playing a three-way game of cards where Gramps managed to wipe the floor with them, that they'd only managed to send off a couple of enquiries to home-care agencies.

'I disagree,' Beckett said, resisting the urge to tuck a stray strand of hair off her face. 'I haven't talked, or laughed, that much in literally years. You cleaned my kitchen and kept Gramps out of trouble. Time well wasted, in my opinion.'

'Fair enough.' Mary ducked her head. Beckett wondered for a thrilling moment if she was *blushing*. 'Would you like to waste some more time with me another day?'

Every day?

'Sonali's coming in tomorrow, and if I don't get a replacement soon I'll be taking Gramps out in the taxi with me.'

Mary burst out laughing. 'Oh, that'll get you some interesting tips. How about Thursday? We'll be more disciplined this time, so you can make some proper progress.'

Beckett replied before his brain could stop him.

'Okay, Thursday. It's a date.'

Date? He didn't stop cringing the whole way back to Bigley.

12

MARY

I messaged Beckett on Wednesday night.

> **MARY**
>
> Any chance we can pop over to the church tomorrow morning? Sofia's found a box of old costumes and leftover fabric and she's going to bring her sewing machine for me to pick up
>
> If not, we can collect it another day, but Cheris sent over the cast list this afternoon and I'm starting to panic about making eighteen costumes in three weeks
>
> Especially given that one of them is a goblin shark Santa

Waiting almost two hours for a reply shouldn't have felt so torturous, except, of course, that I'd not spoken to another adult the entire day.

Then he phoned me, which more than made up for the wait.

'Sorry, Gramps only just settled down. He kept fussing about not being able to find the electric drill. The truth is, it broke a couple of years ago and I never got around to buying a new one.

He kept insisting he needed to replace a curtain pole. Curtain poles are one of the few things in our house that don't need fixing.' Beckett sounded grim. 'Anyway, what time do you want me to pick you up?'

'Sofia said around eleven is best for her. But, Beckett, the pole in my dining room fell off a few weeks ago, taking a hole out of the plaster. It's propped up against the wall.'

He released a long sigh.

'I thought he'd dreamt it up out of nowhere. Or had got lost in the past somewhere.'

'I'm so sorry you're having to go through this.' My voice was thick with sadness for them. 'Both of you.'

There were a few beats of silence before he replied. When he did, I had to press my phone against my ear to catch the words.

'Having someone to talk to about it makes all the difference.'

'Okay, I've nowhere else to be. Let's talk.'

So, we did. All the way through Bob's first feed of the night, a mug of tea and two rounds of buttery toast for me, three for Beckett. He told me how Gramps had been worsening as I transferred wet clothes to the cranky drier, then described more about the man Gramps had been as I rocked an even crankier baby back and forth in front of the curtainless window, as the moon became gradually obscured by the next lot of snow clouds.

I read out the cast list for the carol concert, and we brainstormed ideas for how to create Shrek Santa and Taylor Swift Santa, until tea snorted out of my nose.

Oh my. Even as we laughed, and jabbered on, and both of us cried a couple of times, the truth of how achingly lonely I had been engulfed me, swiftly followed by the realisation of how precious this friendship had already become.

Eventually, as midnight rolled in, both of us now in our respective beds, we admitted that we were beyond coherent conversation and had to get some sleep if we had any hope of surviving tomorrow.

'Goodnight, Mary,' Beckett murmured.

'One of the best,' I mumbled back, my befuddled head misinterpreting what he'd said.

'Really?' He suddenly sounded a lot more alert.

'Yes. Thank you for such a good night. Goodnight.' I hung up before I could say anything else that I might regret in the morning.

Drifting off to sleep, I replayed one of the last times I'd spent an evening talking for hours, mask off and filter down, emotions meandering as we shared stories and opinions, and, along with them, our hearts. As always, it triggered a stab of pain. Although maybe less deep than usual.

That time, the other person had kept a big, fat filter up. One that hid from me the most important thing I needed to know.

Despite how, that time, I was talking to my husband. Not a brand-new friend who had no obligation whatsoever to tell me his biggest secrets.

This time, I was the one with a past I wasn't ready to share.

* * *

Beckett flashed me a conspiratorial glance in the rear-view mirror as he stifled yet another yawn. The other passengers were, naturally, snoozing, and I gave Bob an exaggeratedly jealous glare.

'You can sleep if you want.' Beckett shrugged.

'That hardly seems fair, given we are equally to blame for the foolishly late night. I insist on staying awake, in the name of solidarity.'

Twenty minutes later, I came to in the New Life car park with a stiff neck and a patch of drool on my scarf.

Beckett said nothing, but I caught the smug gleam in his eye.

* * *

'Hi, guys!' I'm not sure Moses could have seemed more pleased if Jesus had appeared in his church foyer. 'You're a few minutes early, but I guess that's got something to do with the boxes in Sofia's office.'

'Um, yes. We're here to pick up stuff for the carol-concert costumes.'

'You don't sound too sure.' Moses started leading us towards the back of the building.

What I wasn't sure about was his comment about being early, implying that there was another reason to be here.

Sofia's office was empty, but there were three large, clearly labelled boxes, a sewing machine in its case and a closed basket containing threads, scissors, a tape measure and other essentials.

'Why don't Beckett and I load up the car while you and Gramps find Sofia? She'll be in the small hall,' Moses said.

Bob's pram had arrived that morning, which Gramps now insisted upon pushing, so it took a few unsteady rams of the front wheel against the double doors and a polite-yet-assertive insistence upon me helping him before we made it into the small hall.

The room had been rearranged since Sunday's lunch. The sofas were pushed up against a back wall, and the rest of the space was now filled with different-sized tables. A stack of board games covered a smaller one, another had neat rows of plant pots and seed packets. A third held various materials that, judging by the predominance of red, green and gold, were probably for Christmas decorations. Bill and another person were laying the empty tables with cutlery, napkins, glasses and tiny vases of autumn foliage.

The Most Wonderful Time of the Year 121

Were we being corralled into yet another lunch? Because we really didn't have time for board games and crafts.

Sofia appeared from the door into the kitchen, greeting us with a delight completely out of proportion considering we'd arranged for me to come only the night before.

'We've got fish pie, with smoky baked beans or cabbage, then blackberry cobbler.'

'I hate cabbage,' Gramps announced.

'Perfect, you can have beans,' Sofia said, utterly unfazed. 'Do you want a drink first? Why don't we find you a comfy seat, then when some of the others arrive I'll introduce you.'

'I don't like new people.'

Sofia linked her arm through his and began steering him over to a sofa. 'Well, once I introduce you they won't be new any more, will they? They'll be Jan, Inga, Derek and Baljit.'

'Um, we can't stay,' I said, scanning behind me for any sign of Beckett.

'Absolutely. Even if you wanted to. We sometimes allow a companion for the first week, if needed, but strictly speaking that should be agreed in advance because of catering. The funding won't budget for extras. It was all on the leaflet. You can pick him up around two-thirty. Have you decided on that drink yet, Marvin?'

'The usual please.'

* * *

I had to hurry after Sofia back towards the kitchen. 'I don't understand. You're offering Gramps lunch, but you said we can't stay?'

'Well, yes, because he's over seventy. I presume. He must be over seventy? Oh my goodness, don't tell him if I've made a boobie.'

'He's eighty-two.'

'Phew! I thought so. Anyway, you and Bob, definitely being under seventy, are not invited.'

'Okay. So this is some sort of older people's thing?'

'Yes. It's our Long-Life Lunch Club. I gave Beckett a leaflet.'

'He didn't mention it.'

'Oh.' Sofia looked slightly crestfallen. 'Marvin can join us, though?'

At that point, Beckett arrived. 'What's happening?'

'An over-seventies' lunch club. Gramps is having beans but no cabbage.'

'What?'

'No youngsters allowed, so we'll pick him up at two-thirty.'

'No.' Beckett shook his head, disconcerted. 'We can't leave him here.'

'Yeah, you can.' Sofia grinned, reappearing with a mug of tea. 'He'll have a great time. I reckon Doreen could out-insult him any day of the week. Especially when it's fish pie.'

'No, he's not safe.'

'Which is why we have trained, experienced volunteers.'

'He has significant cognitive impairment, some apraxia, other issues...'

'Did you fill in the form online?'

'No, because I had no intention of him coming here.'

'Hang on.' She called across the room. 'Bill? Can you come and help Beckett sort a form for Marvin, please?'

Sofia nipped past us and went to give Gramps his tea.

'Sorry,' Beckett said, face creased with anxiety as Bill approached. 'He can't stay without someone who can manage his needs. I'll let him finish his drink and then we'll go.'

Bill gave Beckett a patient stare. 'I worked as a geriatric nurse for thirty-six years. In the seven years since retiring, I've volunteered with a dementia charity, a stroke support group, in five different nursing homes and here. I can manage his needs.'

'Sometimes... he can't feed himself properly.'

Bill nodded at a woman in a wheelchair, her limbs and neck painfully contorted. 'That's what we're here for.'

'We can't afford this,' Beckett said. 'I'm in between home carers at the moment, so barely managing to work... I... Thanks for the offer.'

Bill grinned. 'There's no charge, pal.'

'What?' Beckett frowned as he scanned the room, which was now filling up with more elderly and in some cases very infirm people. 'You do this for free?'

Bill put a hand on Beckett's shoulder as his tone grew serious. 'I've spent enough time with families going through what you're facing to know what a lifeline a few hours off a week can be. Take your lovely friend here out for a nice wee lunch, aye?' He held out a twenty-pound note, which was a sweet gesture, but would definitely limit us to a 'wee' lunch. 'Marvin will be in safe hands with us. I'll see to it personally.'

Beckett looked at me, as if hoping I'd be able to come up with a better excuse.

'Gramps loves it here. What's the worst that can happen?'

'If I answer that, they'll definitely not let him stay.' He shook his head, the corner of his mouth twitching. 'Okay. We can try it, I suppose. Thank you.'

They spent a couple of minutes completing the necessary information online, then Beckett politely declined the money Bill was still trying to thrust into his hand.

'Call me, if there's the slightest bit of trouble. He can be really—'

'Offensive, ornery, shaky, confused, incontinent... I know, buddy. So, no, I won't call unless it's a full-on emergency. What happens at Long-Life Lunch Club stays at lunch club. Now get out of here – it'll be two-thirty before you know it.'

***

'Why don't we find a café with free Wi-Fi nearby?' I asked as Beckett hovered in the car park, as if staring hard enough would enable him to see through the church walls.

We quickly checked Google Maps but Beckett rejected the few places within walking distance.

'If we're treating ourselves to lunch, let's do it properly. I'm not wasting almost three hours just anywhere.'

'Where, then?'

'Can you take a pram on the tram?'

'I've got the papoose in my bag. I can switch.'

Fifteen minutes later, we'd hopped off the tram in Nottingham city centre, at a large open area that Beckett informed me was the Old Market Square. Today, it was transformed into a 'Winter Wonderland', with rows of fake log cabins, some selling Christmas gifts and goods, others with roast turkey sandwiches, spicy German sausages or hot chestnuts. There was a large 'ice bar' with outdoor seating beside a towering Christmas tree. As well as the Nottingham Wheel and a toboggan ride, at the centre of it all was an ice-rink. Everywhere was flashing lights, cheesy Christmas music and seasonal hustle and bustle. Part of me felt in total sensory overload – the contrast to my secluded cottage was dazzling, making me squint as if a torch were being shined in my face. At the same time, the all-too-familiar seasonal sights and sounds triggered a cascade of memories that threatened to knock me to my knees.

I took a deep breath, did my best to shake off the ghosts and forced myself to focus on the here and now.

'I love this smell.' I paused to savour the scent of fried onions, doughnuts, and cinnamon.

'Which one?' Beckett asked, tugging his scarf tighter.

'All of them!'

We ambled around the stalls before finding a seat in an alpine-themed bar and ordered wedges topped with pulled beef, melted cheese and slaw.

'Okay, how about an hour looking at care agencies, then we can do another loop before heading back?' I suggested, warming my hands on a mug of gingerbread hot chocolate.

After calls with three agencies who could offer a two-hour slot, but no one available for much more than that, the fourth one asked why Beckett didn't just try a residential home.

'Because he's happy in his own home?' he seethed, abruptly ending the call.

I raised my eyebrows. *Happy?*

'Okay, not the best choice of words. But why move him to an unfamiliar place, with minimal control over routines or even what he eats, cared for by strangers? At home he's comfortable, surrounded by a lifetime of memories. He's loved.'

'Maybe someone at the lunch club can recommend an agency?'

Beckett nodded. 'Do you think Bill would consider coming out of retirement?'

'To care for Gramps? How could he resist?'

* * *

Finally managing to arrange interviews with two different companies, we had another wander, toasting marshmallows and eating them while watching the ice skaters looping in time to 'Holly Jolly Christmas' jangling from the overhead speakers.

'I hadn't even thought about Christmas until last Sunday,' I admitted once we'd started to make our way back to the tram stop.

'Other things on your mind?' Beckett nodded at Bob.

'Yeah, I'd been so preoccupied with getting ready for a baby,' I said, rolling my eyes at my disgraceful lack of preparation. 'There aren't many reminders of Christmas in the forest. Although, the farm shop put some decorations out last week, along with a big display of parsnips and Brussels sprouts.' We reached the stop, huddling into our coats as a few tentative snowflakes began to fall.

'The supermarkets have been bombarding us since September. Hatherstone market must be almost as bad with the tourist stalls.'

I pulled my hat down another inch, instinctively stepping closer to Beckett's huge frame in the hope it provided some shelter.

'I haven't really been to a supermarket in the past few months.'

He waited for me to share more.

'I haven't really been anywhere, apart from the farm shop and midwife appointments. Until I got into a Sherwood Taxi a few weeks ago.'

The tram arrived, and we found a seat in a half-empty carriage.

'How long have you been living in Sherwood Forest?'

I took a deep breath. 'Since May.'

Beckett lowered his head so he could talk quietly.

'I would love to ask what happened, but I'm assuming now isn't the time or the place.'

'You're also assuming something happened worth telling.'

'The pregnant director of a fashion company moves to a neglected cottage in the absolute middle of nowhere and lives like a hermit for six months. Doesn't even go to a supermarket.' He furrowed his brow, as if pained to even contemplate it. 'You don't have to tell me. I understand there may be a good reason why you *can't* tell me, but, given your prolonged isolation, it might help to finally tell someone.'

'Why wouldn't I be able to tell you?' I asked, picking up on the one statement that didn't feel like swallowing a rock. 'What, like I'm a spy or something?'

He shrugged. 'Witness protection. Or you're running from the law, accused of a terrible crime you didn't commit. Or did commit.' He dropped his head, expression turning serious. 'Escaping a situation that wasn't safe.'

'None of the above,' I said, able to sort of smile because he wasn't even close to the truth. 'Anyway, you don't strike me as someone who's got all their presents bought and gift-wrapped by Bonfire Night. It's hardly shocking that I'm not in the Christmas zone yet. It's still November.'

Beckett grimaced. 'Gramps always insisted we waited until the twenty-first before putting a tree up. And I'd love to know who all those presents I'm supposedly buying are for. You know full well it's just me and Gramps.'

'Um, hello?' I gave him a shocked glance, covering up Bob's ears despite them being tucked underneath a Christmas pudding bobble hat bought from one of the stalls. 'You don't think Bob deserves a present? Sonali, or the person manning the phones at Sherwood Taxis? Bill has spent three hours keeping an eye on Gramps. Never mind the Christmas Day Twins.'

'I'm sorry. It's not just me and Gramps. I'm not allowed to get

Sonali anything, but meeting you and Bob has tripled the number of presents I'll be buying.'

'If only we'd met after Christmas, dang it.'

He pretended to consider this. 'Yes, but this way, I might actually get a present that isn't the Lynx toiletry set Tanya arranged for Gramps to give me the past two years.'

'Lynx?' I smothered a smile. 'Does she think you're fourteen?'

'Hey, it's better than the plastic keyring stamped with "Becker" I got one year.'

I stopped hiding my smile. 'Oh, now I'm going to have to go gift shopping with Gramps and see if we can top that.'

'So, do you like Christmas, when you remember?'

'As a kid, Christmas was mostly an opportunity for my parents to feel superior and self-righteous. The run-up to it was packaging toiletries for the refuge Mum supported, or Dad dragging us along to light switch-ons and endless community events where I had to behave impeccably and avoid the weirdos wanting me to pass on their gripes about the government. On the day itself, we would be out doing yet more good deeds for local poor unfortunates, enduring Mum's annual lecture about how domestic violence, sexual assault and countless other terrible things all increase over Christmas, ho ho ho. For a few years, we gifted a Christmas food hamper to someone and then ate cold sandwiches, supposedly to allow a deprived family the chance for a proper Christmas dinner, as if we couldn't afford two turkeys. Everything was a home-made, recycled point to prove. One year our tree was a branch dragged from the local park, stuck in a bucket and decorated with paper baubles depicting the faces of murdered women.'

'I'm guessing you did something different once you got older?' Beckett did an impressive job at not looking horrified.

I rested my head against the back of the seat, a warm, slow

smile breaking across my face. 'I left home at eighteen. Now, *that* was when Christmas really became something worth celebrating.'

* * *

The year I turned eighteen, when most of our peers from school were spending their minimum-wage pay cheques on WKD-fuelled weekend blowouts, the founders of ShayKi moved into our first terraced house. Kieran had the ground-floor bedroom complete with his own tiny en suite bathroom, while Shay and I had a room each on the first floor. There was also a galley kitchen and a living room large enough for one sofa, a beanbag, flatscreen television and a sound system that cost more than the company car we all shared.

Most importantly, there was a whole attic floor with large dormer windows that became our new workspace. We added two huge tables, a desk for me and rows of shelving to house all our materials. Cork boards and easels were covered in fabric samples, images torn out of magazines and other random things to spark our creativity.

The bathroom was mouldy, the carpets smelled like stale cigarettes and we were constantly battling mice invasions.

We thought it was paradise.

I wondered if most entrepreneurs considered those early days the golden years of their business. Fuelled by the passion of youth, alongside the arrogance that came from pleasing no one but ourselves, we lived, breathed, argued about and celebrated nothing but ShayKi.

We stuck to the market stall for longer than others might have done, but, because we were ahead of the curve with online shopping, we continued to build a steady brand. It was around the same time that YouTubers and bloggers were first becoming popular, and when a couple of the bigger names showcased one of our bags and a belt, things started to get exciting.

That first year, we spent most of December working eighteen-hour days to meet the surge in festive orders, even with Shay's aunt and two cousins helping us produce and package them all. It took everything we'd got to reach the magic day, 20 December, the last postal date before Christmas.

Shay arrived back from the post office that afternoon with an armful of champagne, and once we'd toasted the temporary staff, asked the new employees if they wanted to come back in the new year, and devoured a feast from the local Indian takeaway before sending them all home, we lolled in a heap on the floor of the workshop and vowed to make this the Best Christmas Ever.

We just needed about a full twenty-four hours of sleep, first.

By Christmas Eve, we'd covered the tiny house from top to bottom in tacky decorations. Shay considered it a waste to pay for any, given our natural talents, but I reminded her of the depressing home-made tat I'd been forced to grow up with, so she conceded that this was a form of therapy for me. We'd spent a morning buying gifts at Meadowhall, Sheffield's giant shopping centre, driven out to Chatsworth House in the Peak District for the garden light trail and giggled our way through Shay's sister's school nativity. We'd gorged on mince pies, chocolate, and pigs in blankets, had ourselves a ShayKi directors' Christmas brunch, as well as a fancy-dress party, with karaoke and a proper buffet. Kieran had almost ruined that by inviting his new girlfriend, one in a steady stream of shallow, short-term relationships he miraculously squeezed in between the incessant work hours. Thankfully, this latest 'try-too-hard', as Shay had deemed her, only stayed for an hour when we refused to let her smoke weed.

Personally, I'd always secretly presumed Kieran was hopelessly in love with Shay, but she only had eyes for the business, and when I'd dropped the tiniest of hints after a second glass of vodka and lemonade one night, she'd made gagging noises and accused me of accusing Kieran of incest, seeing as they were practically brother and sister.

Now, on Christmas Eve, we were hosting the highlight of our Best Christmas Ever – a family party. By family, we meant Kieran's mum and sister, and a bunch of Shay's relatives. The ShayKi family, as we'd started to call it.

Our house was far too small to squeeze everyone in, so we built a bonfire in the tiny back garden and prayed for good weather. Everyone brought their own drinks, which we supplemented with bottles of prosecco because we were fancy these days, and served steaming bowls of Auntie Ada's lamb curry followed by toffee trifle. We drank, ate, bickered and bantered and danced like wild men and women in the glow of the bonfire. When the neighbours came around to complain about the noise, we offered them a glass of mulled cider and they proceeded to teach us how to do a traditional polka.

The children lit sparklers, hunted for chocolate coins and fell asleep in a heap of blankets on the living-room floor.

At one minute past midnight, we linked arms and sang 'We Wish You a Merry Christmas' at the top of our voices, before Shay promptly kicked everyone out.

I lay in bed that night, in the brief moment before tumbling into post-party sleep, and thought about how my parents and Cameron would have spent the evening. Reading, probably. Or if they were feeling particularly wild, playing Trivial Pursuit. Not that there was anything wrong with reading, or playing a knowledge-based board game. I liked both those things. But when there was no warmth, no merriment or good cheer? When that was as close to celebrating as it got?

I'd choose my new ShayKi family every time.

Christmas Day, I did wrench myself away from Shay's parents' flat to have dinner at my grandparents' austere house in Grindleford. They made clipped conversation about roadworks, fuel prices and the neighbour's new conservatory. Grilled Cameron about his degree and plans for the next year.

Nobody asked what I'd been up to. I wolfed down a bowl of bland, dry Christmas pudding with thin white custard, and headed back to a home brimming with love.

13

BECKETT

'Hey, how was the lunch date?'

Beckett stopped dead. He hadn't intentionally overheard Sofia's surreptitious comment to Mary from the other side of a pillar, but he absolutely waited to earwig the answer.

Was that what it was? A date? Under most circumstances, going to a Christmas market and having lunch with a woman – a woman who had eyes that made him feel genuinely seen, whose voice on the phone soothed the tension in his neck, whose smile made him feel invincible, who he wanted to take care of, fight for, cherish – would 100 per cent constitute a date.

Mary had a tiny baby. Who had a father somewhere. Whatever had happened to her, it couldn't have been good. The last thing she needed was a date.

'Are you joking? The last thing I need right now is a date.'

He released a breath he hadn't realised he'd been holding, nodding in agreement, even while his heart sagged with disappointment.

Although, depending upon Mary's circumstances in the future, it didn't mean there couldn't *ever* be a date. In the meantime, Beckett was more grateful than he would have thought possible to have her as a friend.

'Oh, you know what I mean. Did you enjoy the market?'

He really should move away.

'Oh. Oh, Mary. I'm sorry. Come here.'

He did move, then, at the same moment Sofia started ushering Mary to one of the sofas, so their paths crossed anyway.

'Hey,' he stammered, resisting the urge to flick Sofia's arm off Mary's shoulder and replace it with his. 'Is everything okay?'

Clearly not, but it would have been wrong to ignore the tears on his friend's face.

'Yes, honestly. Yes. I cried earlier this week when Bob's umbilical cord fell off. I've become a person who gets emotional about a dried-up scab.' Mary gave a weak laugh. 'I don't even know if I'm crying because I had such a nice lunch, or, well, because...'

'Because I made a tactless comment?' Sofia shook her head. 'I'm so sorry. I shouldn't joke about things that are none of my business. Sometimes my natural curiosity bulldozes through the line into intrusive. I'm sorry.'

'No, it's fine. Like I said, I'm overreacting.'

Beckett's glow at Mary's lunch comment was severely tempered by how upset she was at the thought of it being a date. Irritated, he could deal with. Incredulous, even. But *upset*? He couldn't begin to process what that meant. Apart from that he'd never ask her out, ever.

At that moment, Gramps called from one of the other sofas, asking if they'd finished yakking and could they take him home before he missed *Tipping Point*, causing Mary to briskly wipe her face, stick on a smile and give Sofia a quick hug before turning to Gramps.

'Have you enjoyed yourself?' she asked.

Beckett braced himself for the answer.

'He had a whale of a time!' Bill said, pausing as he strolled past.

Gramps huffed. 'Maybe a small fish of a time. A minnow. Or a sea slug.'

'Okay, so next week shall we aim for a seal, or a small walrus?' Bill asked, his grave tone betrayed by the glint in his eyes.

'I have to do this again?'

'Excuse me?' Bill pulled his head back, affronted. 'You promised me a rematch.'

Gramps looked smug. 'Sucker for punishment, this one. Fair enough. Same time next week. No cabbage.'

As Gramps insisted on heaving himself up, then started shuffling with Mary towards the foyer, Beckett waited behind in a daze. He'd tried a day centre, back when Gramps first came home from the rehabilitation place. The plan that the healthcare team had come up with included Gramps attending various groups on top of his physiotherapy. He had either refused to go back after one visit, or made sure he wasn't welcome.

'I don't suppose you do any home-care work?' Beckett asked Bill, before he could move on.

Bill raised his eyebrows. 'Only at my own. Our lass has moved in with three kiddies while her sailor's on deployment. Believe it or not, I've come here for a break.'

'Do you think anyone here could recommend someone?'

He looked thoughtful. 'I'll ask around, let you know.'

'Thank you. I'd appreciate it.'

Since the initial support from the recovery healthcare team had tailed off, Beckett had been navigating the social-care system alone, an organisation he'd come to view as a behemoth as frail and infirm as most of its older service users. Endless waiting for appointments with people who simply shunted them onto another waiting list. Wrangling with forms and files, policies and procedures. Trying to get his grandfather seen as a person, not a problem. Tanya had been an ally of sorts, at least before she'd grown sick and tired of Beckett taking her for granted. She at least knew the system and in the initial days had offered sympathy and the occasional word of advice. Now, he was forced to yet again entrust Gramps to a stranger, and he'd seen how badly that could turn out enough times to be losing sleep over it. To have something as simple as a recommendation, to *know someone* who could offer one. Beckett appreciated that in the way only a man with no friends or family could.

* * *

Once back in Bigley, Gramps immediately fell asleep in front of the television, so Beckett made coffee and Mary started to wade through the boxes of material and costumes. This rapidly became a game of 'guess the plot' as they pulled out increasingly baffling outfits.

'Okay, so this banana hates Christmas. He's fed up with it being all about the clementines and sultanas, the cranberries rubbing their big moment in all the other fruits' faces. Barnie's being rude and – yes, obviously that's the banana's name, what would you call him?'

Beckett pulled an impressively serious face. 'It's not about me. What would the Christmas Day Twins call him?'

'Barnie, actually.' Mary gave a smug nod, dropping the banana costume and holding another one up against her. 'So, he's sulking in the bowl when everyone else's gone carolling, and suddenly the magical Christmas Eve toad appears.'

'A magical Christmas toad?'

'*The* magical Christmas Eve toad!' Mary's eyes, looking more grey than blue today, became round. 'Please don't tell me Gramps never told you about her?'

'It's a her?' Beckett furrowed his eyebrows. 'Toads are always male.'

'Then how do we get toad tadpoles?'

'In stories, I mean.'

'Not to the millions of children who have grown up enthralled by tales of the magical Christmas Eve toad. Susan, to her friends, of course.'

'Of course.'

'So, anyway, Sue gives the old pep talk, Christmas spirit, let poor Russell the Brussel enjoy his chance to shine, everyone hates him the rest of the year, blah blah blah, when suddenly, up pops the evil Boxing Day... um, let's call it a saxophone?'

* * *

Once Bob's cries interrupted the silliness, Beckett sorted the costumes and fabrics by colour and packed them back up while Mary fed him. Beckett had to work hard at not grinning like a chump the whole time. He wanted to ask if they'd stay for dinner, but that felt too much, on top of lunch and everything else. The 'date' comment was still ringing in his ears. Besides, Gramps had woken from his nap extra antagonistic and foul-mouthed. As understanding as Mary might be, Beckett didn't want to risk Gramps ruining what had been the best day – for both him and Gramps – in such a long time.

He arranged to pick her up on Sunday for the first carol-concert rehearsal, where Mary could measure the cast for costume sizes, and by which time she'd hopefully have come up with some basic ideas so she knew what to measure for (three days felt like an age away). Beckett then called a taxi, seeing as getting Gramps back in the car would take more time and effort than any of them had the energy for.

'Thank you,' Mary said, giving his wrist a quick squeeze as Jakob, probably the only other Sherwood Taxis driver he'd trust, pulled up. Her thumb skimmed the bare skin at the edge of his hoodie sleeve, sparking a cascade of memories from the day they'd met, swiftly followed by that almost primal urge to protect her. 'I haven't laughed that much in... well, since moving here, for sure.'

'I'm still crushed at how mercilessly you mocked Monsieur Peppercorn. Please don't bring it up again.'

'Oh. But I will. It's my new favourite festive tradition. From now on, Christmas won't be Christmas until I've seen you squeezed into those peachy bloomers.'

Beckett ducked his head, his arm feeling bereft as she let go and grabbed the pram handle. His heart fizzing like a Catherine wheel. If he unzipped his hoodie, she'd be able to see it glowing through his T-shirt.

From now on. He couldn't quite believe Mary was here this Christmas, let alone dare to imagine she might be part of his future.

He'd wear those damn bloomers every day if it meant he got to see her smile.

* * *

On Friday afternoon, Beckett met with the registered manager from a local domiciliary care company. He wasn't sure whether them being available at such short notice was a good sign or not.

It didn't take long to find out.

'Howdy! Meryl Maverick at your service, sir.' The fortyish woman standing on his doorstep looked as though she'd been rifling through the New Life Christmas costume boxes. Wearing jeans that were more rip than denim, a paisley shirt and tan suede waistcoat covered in fringes that swayed distractingly as she talked, she tipped back a black felt hat and winked, only a couple of inches smaller than him in her high-heeled boots.

'Let's get this show on the road,' she added, in a broad West Country accent.

They initially sat in the kitchen, so they could chat without Gramps interrupting.

'So, how many carers do you have?' Beckett asked once he'd made them both a drink and Meryl had removed her hat to reveal what was surely one of Dolly Parton's retired wigs.

'Currently, it's me and Tiger. Had a little issue with our sub-team. Those two were health and safety mad! Always droning on about risk assessments and "following correct procedures".' She screwed up her face and used a sneery voice while mimicking the sub-team.

'What a waste of blinking time that could and should be spent cheering up the poor biddies we're here to help. Honestly! Health and safety. Boring and boringer, I call it. What happened to plain old common sense, I ask you? Didn't have all this nonsense when my gran was around, and she lived to be seventy-seven! Imagine if some NHS boffin had insisted upon risk assessments back when the Wild West was being won. They'd still be stuck in the east, arguing about slips, trips and falls.'

Beckett managed a polite smile.

'How do you cover holidays and time off sick, with only two of you? I'll be out working, so it has to be reliable.'

'Oh, that's not a problem. My Barry'll step in if we're desperate.'

'He's trained in domiciliary care?'

'Well, he helped out with Gran often enough, and I've already told you how long she hung on in there for.' She did a laugh-snort that sounded so like a horse Beckett almost choked on his coffee.

'So, he isn't trained?'

'To be honest, I wouldn't worry about it. Tiger usually covers my hols.'

'How many service users do you have at the moment? I did explain on the phone that I'm looking for at least thirty hours a week.'

'That's not a problemo, Mr Beckett.'

'Dr Bywater.' Beckett couldn't remember playing the doctor card before, but this felt like as good a moment as any to start.

'Right. Apologies.'

'Service users?'

'Look, I can cover as many hours as you like. Well. Obviously we all have to sleep at some point! I wouldn't mind the odd trip to the saloon for a little line dance.' More snorting.

'Are you saying that currently you don't have any other clients?'

'Well, like I said. We had a whole thing with the sub-team. Spreading misinformation. Fearmongering. All cleared up now, of course. The police have said they want nothing more to do with it.'

'Yeah. I think that's all I need to know for now. Thanks, Meryl.'

'Er, that'll be Dr Mav to you,' she said, firmly sticking her hat back on.

'You're a doctor?'

'I can be anything you want me to be, sunshine.' This would have sounded alarmingly inappropriate, except that she growled it, as if pretending to be a baddie from an old western.

Beckett stood up. If Gramps woke up before she left, he dreaded to think what would happen.

'No, seriously, though. It's probably best if I meet the old fella before we agree on a start date.'

Beckett opened the kitchen door. 'This way.'

He then led her straight to the front door and opened that one, too.

'Bye, Dr Mav.'

'But... what? I haven't met your grandpa yet.'

'That won't be happening. Today, or ever.' He moved forward, forcing her to step backwards over the doorstep. 'Putting it bluntly, Ms Maverick, this ain't my first rodeo. No way on earth I'm letting a cowboy like you near my grandfather. Whose name, by the way, is Mr Bywater.'

Beckett slammed the door so hard Gramps woke up.

When he retold the meeting to Mary, later that evening, she laughed so much she snorted louder than Dr Mav had. Something else Beckett had forgotten from his medical, sociable days – sharing a dreadful story with a safe person will usually reveal the humour hidden below the horror. Panning for gold, as not-doctor Meryl Maverick might say.

14

MARY

On Friday afternoon, while I was cleaning mud off the pram wheels after taking it for a test-drive through the forest, Sofia sent three messages in quick-fire succession.

SOFIA

> Hey, Rina's picking you up at 11 tomorrow
>
> Coffee mums meet-up
>
> That ok?

MARY

> Am I really so sad and boring you've assumed I'm not already busy?

SOFIA

> Mary, you had a baby like a month ago. You've no family here and we're your only friends
>
> Of course you're not busy

MARY

> I could be doing something with Beckett and Marvin!

SOFIA

Nah, Moses already checked for me

But I take the point that you do have 2 other friends

* * *

Despite being awake since six, I was nowhere near ready to go when Rina pulled up in a grey estate car.

'I'm sorry,' I said, opening the door in the hope I could deter her from entering into the mess that had accumulated over the past few days. 'I'll be with you in a minute.'

I was hurriedly hunting for baby wipes when Rina appeared in my living-room doorway, seemingly unfazed by either the baby shrieking as if being tortured, or the chaos.

'What can I do?' she asked, scooping Bob out of his new bouncy chair. 'How about I take that, and you sort your hair out?'

She gently prised the changing bag out of my hand.

'It needs restocking. I'll do it if you can hold Bob.'

'Mary, I have two small children. I can do up a bra, bake brownies and certainly shove nappies into a bag while holding a baby. Don't worry,' she added, noticing my perplexed expression. 'It took a lot of practice. When Jock was this tiny, I couldn't even drink a glass of water without putting him down. Then my husband went AWOL, and I had to learn. Make use of my hard-won expertise, and go and brush your hair.'

'That's the second time you've mentioned my hair. Is it really that bad?'

Rina's hair had been a mess when we met at Sofia's the week before, so either she was a hypocrite, and slightly rude to boot, or there was more toast stuck in there. She did look a lot less dishevelled this morning.

'It's really not. Forget I said anything. There's a brush in my bag if you change your mind.'

Feeling a prickle of apprehension about this irregular coffee-mum meet-up, I went upstairs and swapped my leggings for a slouchy, cream knit-dress I'd worn earlier on in my pregnancy, that wasn't too unflattering to my deflating bump and had buttons so I could breastfeed, and thick tights. Instead of brushing my hair, I twisted it up into a bun and even added a dab of concealer under my bloodshot eyes before grabbing a jade fake-fur coat left over from an advertising shoot.

'Wow. You do not dress like a woman who lives in a place like this,' Rina said when I met her in the hallway.

'I've had the clothes since way before a baby decimated my housework schedule.'

'Oh, gosh, no, I don't mean the mess,' she scoffed, carrying Bob to the car. 'But I'm surprised that someone who clearly has impeccable taste and values aesthetics would choose an interior as beige as an Aldi buffet. Plus, that outfit is pure city chic.'

I opened the back door, finding Jock and Mitch snoozing in their car seats.

'I'm renting the cottage and haven't had the energy to do much with it yet.'

'Where were you living before?' Rina asked once she'd jammed Bob's seat between the other two and strapped him in. 'And, more to the point, how did you end up in this place?'

'I was in Sheffield. Not having a car meant it was hard to view places in person, and it looked a lot better online.'

As Rina reversed out of my drive and started heading down the lane towards the main road, I didn't add why I'd left Sheffield, or how, when frantically searching for a place to live, the cottage was the first place I stumbled across that was affordable, fully furnished and immediately available. Crucially, it was also far away from anyone else, but not so far I couldn't afford a taxi to get me there.

'What brought you to Sherwood Forest?'

I shrugged. 'I came this way with work a couple of times, and to a wedding at Hatherstone Hall. It seemed as nice a place as any, and a lot cheaper than the Peak District, which was my other option.'

Rina gave me a shrewd glance. 'Escape to the country?'

She didn't add the obvious: *while pregnant, and alone.*

I wanted to reply with something light-hearted, make a reference to the fresh air or peace and quiet, but I'd heard these coffee mums sharing, witnessed the depths of their friendship, and I'd missed that so fiercely I ached. I might not be ready to reveal everything, but I wasn't going to deny that she was right.

'I'd left the business I helped run, under difficult circumstances, but also happened to share an apartment with the CEO.'

'Awkward.'

'Yeah. Sheffield has always been home, so I thought a new start was the best option. Or a break, at least.'

'Right.'

'How long have you lived here?' I asked, redirecting the conversation to avoid her next question, which was surely about Bob's father.

'I grew up in Middlebeck, a tiny village a few miles from here. When I married Alex, he wanted to live in the city so we rented a place not far from the church, which is how I met Sofia. When everything imploded, I moved back to Middlebeck. Mitch was about six months.'

'That must have been tough.'

'Yeah. Thankfully, I have family right around the corner who I only want to throttle half the time. Also, Sofia and the others were ridiculously good at bringing around meals and helping out, making sure I didn't lose it altogether.' She glanced at me, eyes serious. 'It's been close, a couple of times. I couldn't have got through it without them.'

'Yet you still manage to work, even with two small boys?'

'Do you know the *Enduring Life* series?'

'The anime?' Kieran used to watch the show about a girl travelling through time, trying to find each generation of her family and save them, or something like that.

'It's also a set of manga books.'

'You're not the author?'

She grinned. 'Best-selling author and illustrator, these days, thanks to Netflix.'

'That's very cool.' I'd met enough celebrities through ShayKi not to be starstruck by this, but I had learned to value creativity – especially when people found a way to earn a living from it.

'I mean, it's not quite brought fame and fortune, but I don't have to rely on my ex for anything, and I'm saving nicely for a house deposit. I also get to attend some very fun Comic-Con events.'

We chatted a bit more about her job, the boys, some tips about how to manage as a single mum. I grilled her about the Christmas carol concert, and to my relief she was clear that it was an amateur production that nobody took too seriously.

'Honestly, I think most people come for the bloopers. No one will care how well made the costumes are. It won't really matter whether we can tell *what* they are, because usually the storyline makes no sense anyway.'

A couple of minutes later we turned off into a long driveway, just inside the Nottingham city boundary.

'This is it. Don't be intimidated. When we met Li, she lived in a dingy bedsit above a kebab shop.'

I wasn't intimidated. Li's home was stunning, but it was startlingly similar to where I'd been living for the past eight years. The house was a modern design made up of blocky shapes and lots of glass, all on one floor. Li welcomed us into a wide hallway, with light oak floors and gleaming white walls.

She led us into a kitchen about the same size as my entire cottage, one half of which contained a seating area with sofas, a fireplace and what appeared to be a lot of Not Coffee Mums.

'Surprise!' everyone chorused.

I turned to Rina, assuming the surprise was on her. She was beaming at me, green eyes expectant.

'Smile,' she said, without moving her lips. 'Pretend you're happy about this, even if you hate surprise parties and people so much that you moved to a hovel in the middle of the forest to avoid them.'

'Happy about what?' I replied, forcing an anxious smile. 'What's happening?'

'Welcome to your baby shower!' Li cried, giving me a tight hug. 'We guessed you hadn't had one before Bob was born, seeing as you had absolutely no baby things, and New Life Coffee Mums always throw each other a shower. It's one of our rules.'

'Besides,' Sofia added, nudging Li out of the way so she could hug me next, 'even if you have had one, no one's going to complain about two baby showers, are they?'

'I can't believe this,' I said, genuinely flabbergasted as I looked around. Rosie was there of course, but also Patty and Yara. I spotted two pairs of antler horns bobbing on top of ginger heads, and Cheris and Carolyn gave me an enthusiastic double thumbs up. There were a couple of women who'd also been at the carol-concert lunch, and maybe three more who I was pretty sure I'd never seen before.

All the coffee mums' children were there, as well as a few older ones.

I noticed then the huge vases of pastel-coloured flowers, the white and gold banner over one of the bi-fold doors spelling out 'welcome baby Bob', confetti-filled balloons and paper pompoms, napkins and a tower of white cupcakes with gold B's on them, as well as a table in the corner containing a pile of wrapped presents.

While still taking this in, I was ushered over to a giant white armchair, and someone swapped Bob for a pink mocktail in a martini glass, pinning a badge on my chest saying, 'New Mummy'.

I glanced at Rina, giving her a nod of thanks for the heads-up about not arriving looking as wrecked as I felt.

'Okay?' Sofia asked discreetly, perching on the arm of my chair. 'Is this too much? We'd deduced from your coat and boots that pre-pregnancy you were used to a bit of sophistication, so Li's level of hosting seemed ideal.'

I tried to unhunch my shoulders, not sure whether to be touched that these near strangers had bothered to spot the clues to my other life, or feel creeped out by their brazen nosiness.

Was it okay? Was *I* okay?

'It is a lot,' I said quietly once everyone else had gone back to their conversations, and I was sure only Sofia could hear. 'I've spent so much time by myself lately, and I'm still readjusting to doing things outside my cottage. Have you ever noticed how loud people are? They ask questions and notice things like an expensive coat. You have to manage your facial expressions and eat with your mouth closed.

'On the flip side, your deductions were right. I didn't have a baby shower, but I've been to plenty of them in the past few years, some unnervingly similar to this. It's like a weird flashback to my old life, and it might take a few minutes for my brain to place itself, if that makes sense.'

'Totally. How about I sit here and act as security guard? If you start to get overwhelmed, send me the secret signal and I'll spring into action.'

'Is there a coffee mum secret signal? Because I haven't been through the full initiation ceremony yet.'

Sofia gave me a conspiring glance, eyes narrowed. 'This is even more secret than the coffee mums. If you... um... ask me where I got my necklace from, I'll shoo away whoever's bothering you.'

'What if you're the one bothering me?' I asked, attempting a joke. Even that felt clunky, as though I'd forgotten how they worked.

'Oh, tell me straight out to go and talk to someone else if I start getting annoying. I've got five kids and work for a church, I'm pretty much impenetrable when it comes to being insulted.' She sat up straighter as someone approached the chair. 'First, though, can I introduce you to my biggest sister, Emma? She lives not far from you, on the other side of Hatherstone.'

I ended up chatting to Emma for longer than I'd have expected. She also lived by herself, and enjoyed the solitude of the forest, having moved out from the city a few years earlier.

'You don't get lonely?' I asked.

Emma laughed. 'I've got four very loud sisters, a dozen nieces and nephews, an interfering mother right down the road, *and* I run my own hectic business, which includes regular meetings and calls with some particularly monstrous brides. Having my own space where everything's quiet and organised, and just how I like it – that's my idea of bliss.'

'I've never lived on my own until this year. Honestly, not much in my cottage is organised, or how I like it. It's a lot less quiet these days, too.'

'I don't suppose now's the time to be thinking about sorting your house out,' Emma said. 'But the day will come.'

'In about eighteen years?'

'I think nurseries accept children a bit younger than that. In the meantime, how about we do a walk?'

We arranged for her to come over and show me one of her favourite forest routes, and I sat back with a second drink, absorbing the fact that I'd potentially made another new friend.

My hand itched to message Beckett and tell him where I was and how well I was doing, but even if I was going to be rude enough to get my phone out in the middle of my own party, that would have been way too overfamiliar.

I chatted to a few more people, someone brought me a plate of delicate sandwiches and a mini scone, then Cheris and Carolyn homed in on me from both sides like lions hunting the weakest antelope in the herd. They were both wearing red pinafores embroidered with mistletoe over green polo necks, with sprigs of holly pinned to their chests.

'Congrats on the baby, Mary,' Cheris said. 'He's gorgeous.'

'Is he a crier?' Carolyn asked.

'Um, he does cry, yes. Being a baby.'

'Yes, but does he cry a lot?' Cheris squinted at him, currently being cuddled by Patty over by a window. 'Can he be trusted not to cry, if he's fed and changed and what have you?'

'I have no idea what a lot is,' I confessed. 'I don't have any other babies to compare him to. Sometimes he does cry for seemingly no reason, but I'm sure there is one, I just haven't figured it out.'

The Christmas Day Twins looked at each other. 'He is still very small,' Carolyn said. 'We've got twenty-two days until the concert. Babies can change a lot in that time.'

The Most Wonderful Time of the Year

'Yes, but is that a good or a bad thing?' Cheris replied. 'Will he get better or worse by then?'

'Excuse me, but can I ask where this is heading?' I asked, although having seen the NLCCCCC cast list, I had a good idea. 'Because there's no way Bob is going to play Baby Yoda Santa. He won't even be able to hold up his own head by Christmas.'

They turned back to me, eyes glinting.

'Don't be a sausage, my dad's going to play Baby Yoda Santa. He was born for the role!' Cheris chortled. 'However, if you're familiar with the nativity story, you may remember that another baby usually features quite prominently.'

'You want Bob to be Jesus?'

'That would be Crimbo-tastic! Thank you so much.'

'We promise to take care of him. He'll have a lovely time.'

'No misplacing him right before the dress rehearsal, like last year.'

'Last year Jesus was played by a doll,' Sofia said, returning to her position on the chair arm with a plate of food. 'No one is leaving a human baby in a cardboard box under the stage.'

'Um. Okay, then, I suppose. Maybe have a stand-in doll in case he does start crying? And I'd like to see the script before I confirm.'

I didn't trust these women not to strap him onto the donkey or launch him into the audience from a cannon.

I did have a few questions about the costumes, but they refused to answer while 'civilians' were in earshot, and at that point Li called everyone together so I could open the presents.

I couldn't think of anything more awkward than opening gifts from people I'd never met before, but thankfully they must have found the idea of giving someone they'd never met a present just as bad, as most people had clubbed together to give me a voucher, and the actual presents were from Patty, Yara and the coffee mums, which I could handle.

They gave me a gorgeous baby blanket, embroidered with 'Bob', which I decided probably sealed the deal with sticking to that name, some tiny clothes that were originally meant to be for Mitch, only he'd been too chonky to fit into them, and some very expensive toiletries with which to pamper myself.

Best of all, Sofia handed me a sign-up sheet with names and meals on.

'Another thing we always do is a meal train. We're embarrassingly late, but one of us is bringing you dinner every day for the next few days. If you're going out or something, you can freeze it. Let me know if there's any food you hate, or love, and I'll pass it on.'

What I hated was living off crackers and cereal.

What I loved was the very thought of these women cooking and driving over a hot meal.

So there I was blubbering again, but this time it was for good reasons.

Then I went and thought about Shay, and Kieran, and all the chances to love me that had been taken from us. They'd have been feeding me creamy pasta and my favourite burritos, adding extra dollops of sour cream because they knew how much I liked it. They'd have run me baths, then tucked me up in the blanket Shay's mum knitted for me when we first moved into the tiny terrace, taking Bob out for a walk so I could sleep.

They'd have let me cry, and mourn, and feel scared and lost and angry.

Then they'd have made me laugh so hard my poor post-birth bladder couldn't take it.

'I r... really like your necklace...' I sobbed, confusing everyone apart from Sofia. 'Wh... where d... did you get it f... from?'

'I have no idea,' she said, squeezing my arm, before bundling me and Bob out of the door and driving us back to our blissfully quiet, dreadfully empty cottage.

15

BECKETT

Beckett had just dropped off a couple at Nottingham railway station when he got a message from Moses.

> **MOSES**
>
> Guys' games night 7.30 at mine if you're interested
>
> We take both the cake and the competition seriously

It was not long after five. Sonali was with Gramps until nine, but Beckett had only been working since three. He really ought to do more than a four-hour shift.

Or, he thought, he really ought to do something other than work or take care of his grandfather for once.

Well, for twice, he corrected himself, thinking about the Christmas market.

He messaged Sonali.

The Most Wonderful Time of the Year

BECKETT
> I've been invited to a games night. Any chance you could stay an extra half-hour or so?

The replies were so fast it was hard to believe she'd had time to type them out.

SONALI
> Be home at 11 and not a minute earlier.

> Will your new friend be at this game?

> Gramps told me all about the 'pretty lass' who came and cleaned your kitchen. I would have dismissed it as another one of his fantasies, but those countertops didn't wipe themselves and you're hardly in a position right now to hire a cleaner.

BECKETT
> This is a guys' night. Staying out until 11 will ruin me. I'll be back by 10.

Beckett allowed himself a moderate glow of satisfaction at having more than one friend. He replied yes to Moses, arranged to bring some snacks, and headed to his next fare, humming along to the radio's power-rock ballads the whole way there.

* * *

There were four men sitting at Moses' kitchen table when Beckett arrived bearing bags of tortilla chips and salsa dip, only fifteen minutes late after the elderly woman he'd driven home had realised she'd misplaced her housekeys.

Moses placed the largest chocolate marble cake Beckett had ever seen in the centre of the table and introduced Sofia's brother-in-law, Sam, who gave a quick nod before going back to sorting out game cards, a guy called Angus who had been hiding at Moses' house while his wife hosted a baby shower, and a couple of others whose names Beckett immediately forgot. They all looked to be around his age, were drinking Pepsi or tea, because Moses' adopted son Eli was currently working through some alcohol issues, and to be honest they looked about as knackered as Beckett felt.

He'd readied himself for the usual questions. What do you do? Where do you live? Any kids...?

But they never came. Moses had been correct about them taking the evening seriously. There was as much small talk as you'd expect at a professional competition as they set up and dived straight into a strategy game involving surviving on an uninhabited planet. It was almost as complex as performing surgery, and the stakes could have been as high, judging by how focused they all were. He'd not have believed these men even liked each other if it hadn't been for the quips that accompanied every decision, and the grins and hugs offered to Sam once he'd won.

Beckett loved it. He came a very respectable third, considering it was his first time. Once they'd finished, he again steeled himself for conversation, but the only topic mentioned was what game they'd play next time and who was giving Moses' cousin, Dante, a lift home.

'Was that normal?' he asked when Moses showed him out. 'You said it was serious, but, well...'

Moses nodded, picking up on what he meant. 'Yeah, the whole point is we find the most complicated games we can, so we have to forget about work, family, everything else, for a few hours. It's a safe space, no pressure to put on a front or talk about the hard stuff. We have other times when we ask the uncomfortable questions and get real with each other about how we're doing. Our Wednesday night group, Bravehearts, is strictly BS free, if you're interested.'

'Maybe another time.'

Like, never.

He would come to next month's games night, though. He had to have found another carer by then.

* * *

Sunday, Gramps was up and out with miraculously minimal fuss, so they arrived at Mary's house a few minutes early. Beckett did his best to temper his happiness at seeing her again to a reasonable level. She seemed as tired as ever, even dozing in the car for a few minutes, but somehow lighter at the same time.

'Good weekend?' he asked once she'd jerked awake and taken a few minutes to orientate herself.

'I went to a baby shower,' she said, running a hand through her hair, which despite the snooze looked tidier than he'd ever seen it.

'At Li's house? For someone from the mums' group you went to?'

'Yes but no.' Mary shook her head, as if as bemused as he was. 'They threw one for me. Then someone gave me a Tupperware full of beef stew to take home.'

She went on to describe the party, and how they'd organised something called a meal train. Beckett was pleased, but couldn't deny the prickle of jealousy that other people were helping Mary and Bob.

For pity's sake, it wasn't as though she couldn't do with all the help she could get.

He was able to shake it off once he told her about his own

unexpected invite, able to demonstrate that he didn't completely rely on this woman he'd met mere weeks ago for any hope of a social life.

* * *

They arrived at the New Life building a good twenty minutes early, due to light traffic, Gramps being engrossed in a podcast about the Boer War and a free parking space right outside. Unlike the previous week, the car park was empty of people milling about, so while Mary and Beckett were fighting with the pram, Gramps wobbled straight inside.

Hurrying behind, they found him already engaged in conversation with a young man in the foyer.

'We've booked a table for lunch,' Gramps said, forcefully. 'Let us through.'

'I already said, lunch isn't on this week,' the man, wearing a 'New Life' T-shirt, said, relief flooding his face when he saw Beckett and Mary approaching. 'Maybe you got the date wrong?'

'Hey, Gramps. We're not here for lunch today,' Beckett said, gently taking hold of his arm.

'What? I came for lunch. No cabbage! The Scottish man promised me a rematch.' He shook Beckett's hand off with an angry huff. 'Why are you always spoiling my fun?'

Beckett took a deep breath. The tiniest of wrong moves here, and things could turn sour.

'We're here for the rehearsal,' he said quietly, trying to convey his apology.

'Ah, right.' The man nodded. 'It's in the small hall, but not for another half-hour. You could catch the last few minutes of the service, if you want.'

'I do not want!' Gramps said, his voice rising. 'What I want is for this pipsqueak to stop trying to steal my lunch.'

'It's not lunchtime yet,' Beckett said, sounding impossibly calm considering the stress flooding into his system. 'Why don't we go and listen to the music while we're waiting?'

'Because it's terrible music,' Gramps scoffed. 'Is that a tone-deaf woman, or a cat being strangled? Take me to the dining hall. I'll wait there.'

'I said, it's—'

'I don't care what you said! I'm an old man and I need to sit down and have my lunch.'

'Hey.' Mary slipped her arm through Gramps' and leant in close to him. 'I would really love to hear the end of this song first, if that's okay? Who doesn't love a bit of music before dinner? Let's find a comfy seat, so the lunch staff can get everything ready without us getting in the way and you can introduce Bob to the joy of live music.'

Mary carried on chattering in a soothing voice that Beckett suspected she used to get Bob to stop crying, and as she patted his hand and rested a shoulder against his arm, Gramps gradually began to soften, his jaw unclenching, posture easing back.

All Beckett could do was mutely follow with the pram as Mary cajoled Gramps down the corridor and through double doors into a large meeting room.

The hall was about three quarters full of chairs, most of which were occupied. A band played on a large stage at the front, and everyone was clapping as the guitar, drums and trumpet came to a final, triumphant crescendo.

The man who'd been in the foyer showed them to empty seats in the second-to-last row, which Gramps promptly declared to be about as comfortable as a haemorrhoid, and everyone sat down.

'Them!' Gramps growled as two familiar figures in dresses

shaped like Christmas trees bounced onto the stage. 'Please tell me they aren't going to sing again. The other one was bad enough.'

All Beckett could think of to do was hand him the baby.

'Does anybody know what day it is?' Cheris called into a microphone, in the style of a pantomime dame.

A few people called out that it was 1 December.

'She said,' Carolyn bellowed, 'does anybody know what day it is? Come on, all together! Make sure Santa Claus can hear you!'

There must have been a couple of hundred people in the room, at least a third of them children, and the response rattled the windowpanes.

'Twenty-one sleeps to go!' the Christmas Day Twins cried.

'Um, no,' Moses said, hovering near the edge of the stage. 'Twenty-four.'

'What are you talking about?' Carolyn asked, as if perplexed. 'What is he talking about? I think Pastor Moses has forgotten how to count!'

'No, Chezza!' Cheris said, waving her arms about vigorously. 'What Pastor Moses is talking about is piddling old Christmas Day.'

'The day billions of people mark the birth of our Lord and saviour, Jesus, with family gatherings, gifts and food, while basically the whole country comes to a stop?' Moses asked. '*That* piddling old day?'

'Meh.' Carolyn pulled a face. 'It's something, I suppose, but anyone would agree it's not a patch on the New Life Community Church Christmas Carol Concert! Am I right?'

The room erupted in a mix of whoops, whistles and laughter.

'Is she right?' Cheris shouted over the noise.

'No, she isn't right!' Moses said, and it was difficult to tell if his exasperation was real or for show. 'But it is a fabulous occasion, and we hope you'll invite your friends, family and neighbours along. All the details are on the website, or there's a pile of flyers in the foyer. Now, ladies, what were you supposed to be talking about in these closing minutes?'

'Oh, yes.' Carolyn pretended to look sheepish. 'This is 1 December, which is the first Sunday in advent, and this week the theme is hope.'

'What does hope mean to you?' Cheris asked, looking more serious. 'What are you hoping for this season? Apart from getting to see the best carol concert since the angels sang over that stable. Take a few seconds to think about it.'

Beckett couldn't help asking himself this question as the hall fell silent. Last year the answer might have been that he'd hope taxiing would bring in enough money to stop him lying awake at night panicking. That he and Gramps would find the strength, the courage, the patience, to keep on going even knowing things were only getting tougher.

That hope would have felt more like folly. Genuine hope had been a stranger to the Bywater house for a long time.

Now – now hope was springing up faster than the hairs in Gramps' ears.

For the first time, Beckett was hopeful that he might have found a friend or two to help him bear this burden. He dared hope for good things up ahead, not simply misery and struggle and emptiness. He hoped that for Gramps, as well as himself.

If he dug deep, and was really, brutally honest, for the first time in maybe a year, he hoped his grandfather, the man who'd basically been his father, wouldn't slip away in his sleep sooner rather than later.

Even more marvellous, for the first time in forever he had hopes for someone else beyond him and Gramps. His hopes for Mary and Bob were so strong and wide and deep that he wondered how they didn't consume him, sitting here in this moderately uncomfortable hall surrounded by strangers.

He decided that, for now, he simply hoped to make Mary smile again.

'Hope?' Gramps announced suddenly, causing most of the two rows in front to jump in surprise. 'What's the point of hoping at my age, in this state? I hope I bloomin' well die before I lose my marbles altogether. Did you hear that, God? Oh, and I hope that someone will hurry up and get my lunch. No cabbage.'

The service ended with Moses praying about hope, and faith, and some other things that Beckett couldn't concentrate on. Everyone stood up and sang another song on similar lines, and then Moses wrapped things up and people started milling towards the back of the room where tables were laid out with coffee machines, tea and plates of flapjacks and other traybakes.

Bill came over and started talking to Gramps, which could have caused the lunch demands to resurface, but Beckett decided to leave them to it, and went to get a drink. When someone on the other side of the aisle had shouted 'Amen!' to Gramps' outburst, causing a ripple of laughter, Beckett had realised that nobody here seemed to mind that much, and he might as well stop worrying about what he couldn't control anyway.

'So, what do you hope for?' Mary asked once they'd both helped themselves to coffee and found a spare space to stand.

Beckett paused, eyes firmly on his cup. 'Um...'

'Honestly, mostly all I could think was that I hope I don't bodge these costumes up.'

Beckett changed gears, scrambling for a similarly light-hearted answer.

'I was hoping Gramps wouldn't feel the need to share whatever dropped into his head.' He shrugged.

'Wow. I would not have guessed that Dr Beckett Bywater was such a hopeless optimist.'

He shifted, glancing around. 'You really shouldn't call me that.'

'What, an optimist? Given that you were clearly hoping in vain...'

'Doctor.'

'What? Why? You earned it.'

'It only invites questions I don't want to answer.'

Mary's face softened. 'Ah. I understand.'

'Like, can I show you the boil in my armpit?'

Mary laughed so suddenly she almost spilled her coffee.

Not such a hopeless optimist after all.

16

MARY

The end of the advent service was still buzzing in my head as one by one I met the cast, whipping my tape measure around waists and up inside legs while my capable assistant recorded the numbers I called out.

I hadn't been completely honest with Beckett about my hopes. I did hope that I didn't make a hash of the costumes. Cheris and Carolyn were so delightfully invested in producing the best show on earth, and it had been a good few years since I'd sewn outfits from scratch.

But at the end of the day, I had far bigger dreams at stake. What I had determined to hope in those quiet few minutes, deep in the marrow of my bones, was that I'd not mess up being a mother. I'd find my way through this maze of old wounds, do my utmost to figure out who I was now, and where Bob and I were meant to be heading. I'd stop wallowing, and even as I unboxed my creativity for the first time since I'd moved, I'd commit to designing and crafting a life Bob deserved. One where he never felt unimpressive, or a let-down, or as if he didn't really belong.

I also hoped that the men sitting beside me would be a part of that. Bob would need a good role model, and my dad or my brother weren't getting that position, even if they were remotely interested in applying for it. Beckett, on the other hand?

I'd known him for five weeks, but I'd trust him with my life. Of course, when I thought about it, I remembered that I already had.

* * *

Some godsend had found Gramps a sandwich and crisps, which he was happy enough to sit and eat while I got the numbers I needed, but once he'd finished, we were all more than ready to leave the cast busy learning the 'Everyone's a Santa' theme song.

I was disappointed when Beckett turned down my offer to have lunch at my house, but when he explained that another care manager was coming to discuss their service, I solved that by inviting myself to his.

I offered the pasta bake Patty had given me for that day's meal train, but Beckett insisted I saved that for later. Instead, we stopped at a café in Bigley to pick up cheese toasties and pots of curried parsnip soup, eating them in companionable silence while Gramps and Bob slept.

Things might have gone better had the care manager not arrived seven minutes early. However, at the point Beckett opened the door, I happened to be in the middle of changing a ghastly nappy on the hall floor, due to it being a lot cleaner than the living-room carpet.

'Oh my... oh my good grief!' the man who marched into the hallway exclaimed, whipping out a handkerchief from his black blazer and pressing it over his face. He was around fifty, with a bald head and beady eyes that were currently squinched into tiny black raisins. 'What is that?'

'Sorry, we had something of a volcanic eruption,' I said, with an apologetic wince. It didn't even smell that bad. Although I had already used half a packet of wipes, and Bob's sleepsuit and cloth nappy lay discarded in a browny-yellow heap about three inches from the manager's polished brogues.

'Have you deliberately left exposed human faeces in a public thoroughfare?' the man barked through the hanky. 'Are you not aware that this constitutes a significant health and safety hazard?'

'It's not a public thoroughfare,' Beckett said, furrowing his forehead. 'It's a private residence.'

'One where an elderly, vulnerable male with multiple serious health conditions lives?'

'Well, yes.'

'And presumably he uses this corridor to access other...' The man paused to gag. 'Other essential areas in the home, such as the kitchen or bathroom facilities?'

'Not while I'm changing a nappy,' I said, doing my best to secure a fresh one around an increasingly disgruntled Bob.

'But if he experienced the urgent need to empty his bladder, he has to run the risk of slipping in or tripping over a pile of human waste, resulting in potential cross-contamination, injury or at the very least an attack on his dignity.'

'Please, come through to the kitchen,' Beckett said, although his heart clearly wasn't in it. 'We can talk properly there. Mary doesn't live here. This is a one-off situation. She would usually use the bathroom, but I've got a new bathchair in there waiting to be set up, so there isn't space.'

'I'll remain here until the area has been disinfected.'

I did my best to hastily double bag the clothes and nappy, dispose of the wipes and then one-handedly clean the floor, side of the stairs and everywhere else I could think of with anti-bacterial spray while holding Bob, who wailed as though he'd been the one to slip in human waste and break his hip. Beckett stood helplessly watching, because this stranger now standing in his hallway and jabbing at a phone insisted they wait by the front door until the hazard had been correctly dealt with.

Needless to say, I was mortified, realising I could have ruined Beckett's chance to secure another carer.

'Right. After that delay, we'd better get straight to it.' The man marched into the kitchen, where he carefully inspected a chair before sitting down.

Beckett gave me a surreptitious smile. My having cleaned the kitchen at least went some way to assuage my guilt for the nappy.

'My name is Kenton Cumberworth the Third. Time of meeting, fourteen twelve. Present, Kenton Cumberworth the Third, Mr Beckett Bywater—'

'Doctor,' I added, equally businesslike, keeping my eyes firmly away from Beckett.

'You're a medical professional?' Kenton Cumberworth asked, mouth curling up in distaste as he glanced back at the hallway.

'He is.'

'And you are?'

'Mary Whittington.'

'The baby?'

'What?' I couldn't help laughing. 'You want to record the baby's name in your meeting minutes?'

'Unless you want to resituate him in another room. Which would be preferable.'

'He doesn't have an official registered name yet.'

'Infant Whittington.' Kenton Cumberworth rolled his eyes as if to say, 'of course a woman with such appalling hygiene habits would leave it until the last minute to register her child's birth'.

'Now, may I stress, *Dr* Bywater, that my agency upholds the most stringent of standards at all times. If I'm sending my team into an alien working environment, I must be able to guarantee that it is sanitary. For example, food waste is securely disposed of, not left breeding bacteria on a worktop.'

'That's my lunch. I hadn't finished eating it yet,' I said. Because, of course, I was the culprit.

He ignored me. 'All I'm asking is that the premises are clean. Is that achievable?'

Beckett sat back, arms folded. 'Previous carers have incorporated cleaning tasks into their role. Washing up, vacuuming. It does state on your website that this is *achievable*.'

'That would depend on the service user. Are you able to confirm that Mr Bywater is safe to be left unattended while my team member is cleaning up your mess, or are you paying for a two-person package?'

'Mr Bywater will be sleeping for prolonged lengths of time. Usually the carer does some tidying up then.'

'Do you have a copy of his daily schedule?'

'Excuse me?' The lines between Beckett's eyebrows grew even deeper than his growl.

'A detailed itinerary, describing what he does and when. I prefer it to be broken down into fifteen-minute slots, but we can work with thirty to start with.'

'He likes to watch quiz shows in the afternoon. Apart from that, your guess is as good as mine.'

'No, Dr Bywater. A guess is not good. We don't care for vulnerable people using guesswork. My team members will follow the schedule to the minute, unless an incident arises requiring them to implement emergency procedures. This way, we can ensure consistency of care.'

'To start with, you could try asking my grandfather what he

wants. He's quite capable of expressing his needs. Once the carer's got to know him, they can settle into their own routine, surely?'

'No.'

'What do you mean, no?' Beckett pushed his chair back. This meeting was about to be over.

'No. I operate with a broad team of carers. That way, no unhelpful attachments develop. In my experience, a personal relationship, friendship, affection, whatever you call it, risks decision-making that may not be in the objective best interest of the service user. The schedule removes the need for such decisions.'

'You do realise that this is a human being we're talking about?' I bristled, unable to keep quiet. 'The number-one thing Marvin needs is friendship, and some control over what decisions he's still able to make. Like any of us.' I couldn't help glancing at Beckett. 'Someone who knows and cares about him, not a stupid schedule.'

'I apologise, I've been remiss.' Kenton Cumberworth gave me a hard stare. 'I forgot to record your relation to Mr Bywater.'

'I'm his friend.' I gave myself a mental kick for allowing my voice to tremble.

'So, Mary Whittington has no agency when it comes to planning care,' Kenton said slowly, typing it up as he spoke.

'We're done here.' Beckett stood up.

'I haven't finished asking questions.'

'Yes, you have.' Beckett opened the kitchen door.

'Or logged photographs of the house.'

'That won't be happening.'

The force of Beckett's presence was enough to propel the care manager up and into the hallway, which now smelled of disinfectant along with a faint whiff of dirty nappy, and right out of the door.

* * *

'Have you really not registered Bob's birth yet?' Beckett asked once we'd finished going over our mutual abhorrence of Kenton Cumberworth.

'Yeah, the midwife said something about that. I think I've still got ages.'

Beckett did a quick search on his phone. 'It's six weeks. So that's what – next Sunday?'

'Oh. Whoops.' While on the one hand life before Bob felt lost to the mists of time, I couldn't believe it had been that long. I used to co-run a business employing a whole load of people. I thrived on deadlines and appointments, targets and Getting It Done. I couldn't even blame this on the sleep deprivation, or the utter disruption a baby had brought. My capacity to manage myself had been left behind in Sheffield. I was a mother now, though. I had to get it together for my son's sake.

I found a list of local register offices on the Nottinghamshire County Council website.

'This one isn't far from a fabric place I wanted to look at. Would you be up for combining the two, if I came and sat with Gramps for you afterwards? You could get in some taxiing, or take a break.'

Beckett checked the address. 'If you can book an appointment for Thursday lunchtime, we could go when Gramps is at the lunch club. It's only a ten-minute drive away.'

I scanned the slots. 'Twelve-fifteen?'

'Perfect.'

* * *

I waited until I got home before looking up how to register a birth when the father was no longer around. It turned out that in Bob's situation, it wasn't an issue, so I dug out the relevant paperwork and then allowed myself a long cry on the sofa, followed by a shorter cry in the bath, then another one in bed. Once Bob woke up, I decided that was enough for one day. My new rule – only one of us were allowed to cry at any one time. I didn't know if all these sadness chemicals would end up in my breastmilk, but Bob would surely be disturbed by some of the noises I'd been making.

* * *

Monday morning, I went back to Sofia's to meet the coffee mums.

Since the week before, the house had been transformed. A wreath constructed from mistletoe and pine cones hung on the door, and, inside, the hallway ceiling was covered in brightly coloured paper chains that Sofia told me the kids had made out of old wrapping paper. More wound around the banister, and there were candles, lights and glittery ornaments decorating every surface.

The family room was equally festive, with more candles and greenery filling the mantlepiece, silver stars dangling above our heads, and a real Christmas tree that seemed way out of proportion given the size of the room.

'This is what happens when you entrust my husband and kids with buying a tree,' Sofia said, rolling her eyes. 'I've had to move the bookcase into the dining room to fit it in, and it's still sticking in front of the TV, so I've got a month of arguments about who gets to sit where so they can see the whole screen.'

We drank from Christmas mugs and ate stollen and mini chocolate yule logs, Fair Isle-style throws over our knees. The scent was heavenly, and the atmosphere so cosy I had to chip in to the conversation to avoid falling asleep. Then they started discussing Christmas in earnest, and the inevitable questions followed.

'What are your plans for Christmas, Mary?' Li asked, either failing to notice or deliberately ignoring how I was trying to shrivel under my snowflake blanket.

'I'm not sure yet. Bob wasn't due until November, so I was going to wait until after that to start thinking about it, but now I can barely focus on tomorrow, let alone a few weeks away.'

'You won't be seeing family?' Rosie asked.

'You don't have to talk about that,' Sofia added quickly, giving Rosie a fierce glare.

'No, it's fine,' I said, because this was one thing I could talk about. 'My parents are working in the States at the moment. My brother will probably go and join them, but obviously that's too much of a trek for me this year.'

'They won't come to spend Christmas with their new grandson?' Rina said, pretending not to hear Sofia's tuts.

I took a deep breath.

'To be honest, I'd prefer it if they didn't. I haven't spent Christmas with them in years, and I don't think this one is the time to start.' I paused, glancing at the expectant faces and finding nothing but kindness there. 'They aren't terrible people; we just don't see eye to eye on a lot of things. They're rubbish at pretending not to disapprove of my choices, and I can't be done with all their thinly veiled digs about what coffee I buy or why I haven't done something more worthwhile with my life. Especially at Christmas. I usually spend it with my best friends and their family, instead.'

'No judgement here, babe,' Rosie said with a sympathetic grimace. 'If I had the choice not to spend Christmas with my brother and his stroppy, stuck-up wife, I'd jump at it. Family ain't always all it's cracked up to be.'

'I'd invite you here,' Sofia said, 'but I'll be at my sister's with the rest of my giant, bonkers clan and no one could survive a Donovan Christmas without years of slow acclimatisation to the chaos.'

'No, it's fine,' I said, doing my best to smile. 'Like I said, I'm always with my friends. If I decide to stop at home and have a quiet day just me and Bob, it'll be because I've chosen to.'

'I wonder what Beckett and Marvin will be doing?' Rina asked, so ridiculously innocently that Li threw a cushion at her.

'Time to change the subject,' Sofia said, in a tone that brooked no arguments. 'Are we doing secret Santa this year, or not?'

* * *

I left not long after that, having picked Li in the secret Santa, which was potentially not the best, considering that she clearly had expensive taste, so it would be tricky finding something she'd like for ten pounds, but on the other hand, I was sure she'd be kind about it. I could imagine Rosie dissing my present in front of everyone before she'd figured out it was from the new girl, who was now dying inside at having got her something rubbish.

All the way home on the bus, another meal – this time from Rina – in my bag, I couldn't stop thinking about my family. What I'd told the others was true, but it was by no means the whole truth. If my parents knew what I'd been through in the past year, where I was now – that I'd lost everything, yet in the process had gained a son, who was now more than everything – would it be another opportunity to lecture me about how if I'd grown out of my stubborn teenage rebellion, like most people, none of it would have happened?

Or would they get on the next available flight? Offer me the same degree of non-judgemental compassion that they'd been handing out to struggling strangers for decades? No recrimination, only love.

I didn't know whether I wanted them to.

I wasn't sure I could bear to find out.

17

MARY

It was when I started thinking about a name that I decided it was time to tell my parents. I couldn't think of Bob as anything else at this point, but I did want something a little more formal. However, I vaguely remembered my great-grandfather had been called Robin, which could work. Picturing Dad's eager face as he described how various ancestors had championed social justice, including a great something uncle who helped found one of the first orphanages back in the nineteenth century, and someone else who'd been a suffragette, I accepted that where we came from mattered. Bob might never know his father's family, but it wasn't fair to deny him the chance to know mine. The later I left things with my parents, the harder it would be.

That evening, I dithered until Bob had fallen soundly asleep, poured a small enough glass of wine for the NHS website not to disapprove, and picked up my phone.

'Mary?' Mum sounded brisk, as if in the middle of something. Who was I kidding? The only time she wasn't in the middle of something was when she was rushing to get to the middle of something else.

'Hi, Mum.'

'Oh, thank goodness you called. Did you know your email isn't working?'

Since leaving ShayKi I'd reverted to my old Gmail account from years ago. I'd not thought to tell Mum and Dad not to contact my work email, as they'd never used it before.

'Yeah, I'll send you my current one. Why did you try to email me?'

'We wanted to discuss Christmas. You never remember details on the phone so I thought it would be easier to have it all written down.'

Less than thirty seconds for criticism number one.

'You could have sent me a WhatsApp after the email bounced back.'

'Yes, we would have got around to it, but things have been rather busy here.'

She then spent the next five minutes describing the highly important people they'd met with, the lectures, lunches and various other impressive things they'd been doing.

'So anyway. Christmas. You remember the fantastic little charity we've been offering free consultancy advice to? They have an outreach during the week before Christmas, handing out gifts to children with a parent in prison, and we hoped you would consider a donation. Hats, or bags or something. I know they're a big thing at the moment. The teen girls would be thrilled to have a ShayKi, rather than one of our usual fuddy-duddy brands.'

'Wow.' I sat back, wishing I'd poured another centimetre of wine. This was the first time my parents had mentioned my company in a remotely positive light. I had no idea they even knew how well ShayKi was doing, or how in the past few years our teenage market had boomed.

The Most Wonderful Time of the Year

'And then, well, we felt that seeing as Cameron is also visiting with Daytona...'

Who is Daytona? I would never ask, but would no doubt find out in great detail on social media as soon as the call had ended.

'And given you were unable to join us last year...'

Because I'd been informed they were far too busy to take any time out to see me, even if I'd wanted to come.

'We've decided to take off the day itself. A contact has offered the use of a beach house. It's rather ostentatious for our taste, but you'd probably love it. All designer whatever and impossibly complicated gadgets. Anyway, we can light a fire, order in food, walk on the beach, hope it snows and have a jolly old time for once.' Mum paused to let this bombshell sink in, and when she spoke again her voice was stilted. If I hadn't known better I'd think she was almost nervous.

'What do you think? I know your business keeps you dreadfully busy, but would you be able to squeeze us in? We can have the house for three nights.'

I took a deep breath, determined not to reveal how emotional I was. Furious that she was talking as though it were down to me that we'd not seen each other for almost eighteen months, and spoken less than a handful of times. Unable to help how my heart cracked in two at my mother requesting to spend time with me.

If Shay and Kieran had been there, I'd have assertively told her what I thought about a last-minute invitation to take a nine-hour flight across the ocean and spend three whole nights battling with jet lag and parental passive aggression.

Now, here, if it hadn't been for the logistics of travelling with a passport-less Bob, I'd have been tempted.

'Anyway, think about it as flights are horrendous that time of year, and you'll need to hire a car to get to the house. How do we move forward on a ShayKi donation? Are you able to expedite the request, or do an email introduction to the right person? We don't have time to waste on people with no authority to give the go-ahead. Do you have someone who oversees social impact?'

'Yes, Mum. For thirteen years, that was me.'

Contrary to my parents' belief that all our business cared about was conning women on TikTok to spend money they didn't have on things they didn't need, all three founders were adamant our business would be a positive force in our city. We had rigorous policies about social value, sustainability and ethics. I'd created a fashion and business scholarship for Sheffield University and we partnered with women's and youth charities to provide apprenticeships, training and flexible employment.

'Ah, marvellous. Shall I send you the details?'

'No.'

We'd been on the phone for long enough for a headache to start pounding at the back of my skull. She was never going to ask how I was, or what I'd been up to. I could hear her gearing up to end the call and move on to the next task on her list.

'I'm sure Shay or Kieran will be able to sort you out with a donation, but I'm not with ShayKi any more. I resigned.'

A brief silence while she processed this.

'Why? What are you doing instead?'

I could almost hear her holding her breath, praying I'd moved on to something more in line with the family values.

'I had a baby.'

Mum released her breath with a brittle laugh. 'Oh, my goodness. For a moment there I thought you said you'd had a baby.'

'His name is Robin Timothy Whittington. He was born 27 October.'

'Mary,' Mum gasped. 'Why didn't you tell us?'

'Honestly? I'm an unemployed single mother living in a cottage with a leaky roof in the middle of nowhere. I've had a lot to deal with lately and couldn't face yet more of your disapproval on top of everything else.'

'We could have... I don't know. We could have helped.'

'What, got one of your charities to send a care package?'

I was possibly being unfair, but if my parents had taken any interest in my life, had asked how I was, what I'd been up to, at any point in this past year, I would have told them. Mum clearly had no clue how to respond to such brutal honesty from her daughter. Truthfully, *I* didn't know how to handle it – I was alarming myself. It appeared as though motherhood had opened the door to a heap of ugly feelings previously locked safely away in my brain's deepest basement.

'Are you both all right? I mean, healthy? Are... are you coping? Shay and Kieran must be supporting you.'

'I haven't seen Shay and Kieran since I left ShayKi. But we're doing fine.'

I realised, with a flicker of surprise, that, for the first time in almost a year, this was mostly true.

'Right. Okay. That's good. Obviously, I have questions, but I won't bombard you now. I've a meeting in two minutes. Can we talk properly, another time? How about we fly back to Sheffield for New Year, and you come and join us? Both of you?'

'Both of us? As opposed to leaving my baby by himself?'

'Mary.' A hint of steel broke through Mum's fluster. 'You've dropped a monumental bombshell. You can't blame me for requiring a moment to rally my thoughts.'

'Sorry.' I hated sounding like a bitter teenager. This was supposed to be a calm, composed conversation. If only the very sound of Mum's voice didn't make my nerves screech in protest. I took a deep breath and tried again.

'I don't want to come to Sheffield for New Year. Please don't change your plans. Not... not because I don't want to see you.' Or rather, not *only* because of that. 'A lot happened there before I left. I want Bob's first Christmas to be about making new, happy memories, not confronting old, painful ones. I hope that makes sense.'

Mum sighed. 'Yes. It does. And to be honest, cancelling everything now would mean letting down a lot of people. Let me speak to your dad and see if we can work out some other dates. We've a lot to get done, with never enough time to do it, but no one can begrudge us rejigging the schedule to meet our grandson. Robert, did you say?'

'Robin, but I'm calling him Bob.'

'Your great-grandfather was Robin. He did some excellent work on behalf of ex-servicemen after the war.'

'Yes, I know.'

'Of course you do. Right, well. I'll be in touch. Oh – and you said Shay would be the best person to speak to about the donation? If you send me her number I can take it from there.'

No request for a photo of their grandson, or an address. Whether there was anything Bob needed, or ideas for a gift.

Shay and Kieran had spent a long time convincing me that my dysfunctional family was not my fault. I'd been the child, and as parents it was up to them to love me unconditionally, support my perfectly acceptable choices and champion my not insignificant successes. When they consistently – and, even worse, intentionally – led me to believe I wasn't good enough, dismissed my choices as selfish and my success as shallow, the only way to protect myself from being crushed by the weight of their criticism was to establish firm boundaries.

Today, with no friends insisting I remembered this, it was impossible not to feel the sting of guilt about the distance I'd deliberately created between us.

Even worse, as I spent yet another night pacing the floor with my fractious son, I couldn't help wondering that if I'd listened to them more, maybe I wouldn't have found myself living in the disaster zone of my own making.

* * *

For the five years the ShayKi founders lived in that first, terraced house, we ploughed almost everything into the business, setting aside a modest amount on top of living expenses for our sacrosanct fun-fund. While I worked in the background, crunching numbers, dealing with suppliers, keeping us legal, Shay and Kieran networked, charmed and were downright pushy, until an influencer took a shine to our bags, and things exploded. We soon learned that hiring more staff meant rethinking our entire way of operating, as we brought in a branding expert, created marketing and sales teams, logistics and HR, and eventually opened up a trendy office and flagship store in the city centre.

We made a ton of mistakes, almost lost everything one year, then scraped it back again. Yet, through it all we stuck together. Shay and Kieran revelled in the kind of blazing rows that involved drinks tossed in faces and sample fabrics ripped in two, but I was always there to broker the peace deal and bring some much-needed perspective.

I continued to wonder if behind this passion lay more than a lifelong friendship. However, Shay remained resolutely determined to stay single. She would go on dates, but the moment things started to turn serious, she'd end it, citing her commitment to the business as the reason. Kieran carried on with a string of relationships, mostly lasting a few months, the longest ending up with two years living together while Shay and I bought our own newbuild apartment with amazing views across the city. The one thing Kieran's girlfriends had in common was that they were the kind of women Shay couldn't stand – fawning, opinionless, requiring minimal effort. There were days I dreamed about holding the two of them hostage in a register office until they'd signed the marriage papers and put all three of us out of our misery, but as the years went by and we crossed into our thirties, I eventually let it go.

Meanwhile, my parents didn't try especially hard to hide their consternation that their daughter was continuing in a commercial career. Our recycled products, ethical suppliers and generous employment packages couldn't outweigh me dedicating myself to making money from people, rather than helping them.

'Lifestyle porn', they called it. Not to my face, but in a message meant for my brother but accidentally sent to our family group chat, shortly before I removed myself from it. One year, I persuaded them along to our annual awards evening, where we showcased our partnerships with local charities and our latest innovations to achieve sustainability. They stood stiff limbed amongst the unashamed shimmer of a room of people who loved expressing themselves through fashion, and any hope that they might finally realise what we'd achieved was crushed beneath their disdain.

I told myself that I didn't need them to feel proud of me. I was proud of myself, and how my input into ShayKi was not only making it into something my parents should have been proud of, but causing ripples across the whole industry.

I was lying. My whole life I'd failed to impress my impressive family, and it still hurt.

So I dealt with it by not talking about my work, and they handled the shame of a daughter who'd sold her soul to capitalism by not asking. All of us were constantly busy, so it was easy to let weeks go by without talking, months without meeting up, and when they accepted a contract to replicate the prisoner rehabilitation project in Chicago, I made a vague promise to book a trip to visit them at some point, and got on without them.

I didn't miss my family, if I was honest. I didn't miss feeling inadequate, their impossible standards or the very idea that happiness was a frivolity, and how dare we waste an evening laughing our hearts out when other people were suffering?

After all, I had the ShayKi family now, who thought I was fabulous, and the feeling was mutual. Christmas, Easter, summer barbecues and other celebrations were mostly spent in the gorgeous house that Shay's parents had bought, thanks to tiny investments near the beginning paying off.

Mum and Dad were also consistently lacklustre about my romantic life, which was far less exciting than my job. I had three semi-serious boyfriends in my twenties – an economics student, an engineer and a commercial solicitor – followed by a string of first dates, before accepting that most of the time I'd rather be at home with my friends, instead.

And then I met Leo.

18

BECKETT

Thursday morning, Beckett knew he shouldn't be looking forward this much to browsing reams of fabric and sitting in a register office. He tried to play it down – of course he'd relish three free hours while Gramps was being happily entertained. He'd spent the last few days trying to chip away at the rubbish in the living room – fighting Gramps over every item, ranging from long-completed puzzle books to dusty cassette tapes and a bottle containing a finger of sherry (Gramps solved that argument by downing it). He'd managed to book Sonali for one more shift before she started with a new service user, and spent hours on the increasingly dismal search for a care provider.

The truth was, he couldn't think of a single thing that would seem preferable to a day with Mary. What he was really looking forward to was watching her whole face grow animated as she teased him about something. Hearing more about her life, and sharing more of his. He couldn't wait for Gramps to melt under her powers of persuasion yet again. He'd missed seeing her with Bob, how her confidence was slowly increasing as she felt more at ease with being a mum.

He was again a few minutes early, having allowed plenty of leeway for how stubborn Gramps might be feeling that morning, but Mary was already waiting for them.

'Shall we go and finally make this boy an official human being?' Beckett said as she wound a knitted scarf around her neck.

He waited for the glint of enthusiasm, but her only response was a tight nod.

'Rough night?' he asked, more quietly.

Mary shrugged. 'No worse than all the others.'

'What can I do to help?'

She glanced around, as if unsure. 'Um, can you sort Bob while I check I've got everything?'

He ducked into the living room, where Bob was sleeping in his Moses basket, struck yet again by how dreary the cottage was. Even with the signs of new life – a stuffed toy and heap of tiny clothes on the sofa, baby-shower cards lining up on the bookcase, a bunch of flowers in the empty fireplace – it was still so lifeless. So un-Mary-like.

She'd run a fashion company. Surely that meant she valued things like art and beauty.

Beckett guessed that spending most of her time surrounded by cracked beige walls, tatty carpets and cheap, ugly furniture wouldn't be great for her mindset. He made a quick mental note to maybe do something about that, and got on with helping her get through today.

* * *

'Good morning,' an older woman wearing a lilac trouser suit chirruped, her narrow face creasing up in an eager smile. 'Ms Whittington?'

Mary nodded, offering a weak flick of her mouth in return. After she'd given a couple of monosyllabic replies to his questions on the drive over, and the briefest of hellos to Gramps, Beckett had taken the hint and kept quiet. She'd stayed in the car while he dropped Gramps at lunch club.

'You've got an appointment to register this gorgeous little man!' The registrar clasped her hands in delight, her tall frame swaying back and forth.

'Yes.'

Bob currently appeared far from gorgeous. Since arriving in the register office waiting room, he'd been fretting and fussing. As Mary had increasingly struggled to remain calm, Beckett had picked him up, and Bob was now scrunching up his purple face as he whinged, batting himself in the eye with a dribbly fist, increasing his distress.

'It's lovely to meet you, and many congratulations on your son. I'm Delilah Bond, licensed to marry, but not kill.' Delilah put her hands together and pointed them at the ceiling as if pretending they were a gun. 'Shall we go on through?'

Mary looked at Beckett. 'Are you okay with him for a bit?'

'Oh, it's fine for Daddy to bring him in. We're used to noisy babies in here, I can promise you that.' Delilah patted her silver pixie cut, expression thoughtful for a moment. 'I did object to the parrot. Anyway, if you're not married, then, Daddy, you'll need to come in so we can pop you on the birth certificate. If you do have the joy of being espoused, then your presence is not required. Although, I can't imagine why you'd choose to miss it!'

Mary, who had been listening to this, her face frozen, lips in a thin line, suddenly pressed both hands against her face and let out a cross between a wail and a groan that made Beckett's heart crack in two.

'I'm sorry,' she sobbed, hunching over in the chair. 'I'm so sorry.'

Delilah looked aghast as Beckett quickly sat beside Mary and put his hand on her shoulder, causing Bob to start noisily protesting at no longer being jigged about.

'I'm a friend,' Beckett said, wishing he didn't have to speak so loudly to be heard above both people crying. 'Not the father, or husband.'

'Oh!' Delilah's mouth dropped open as her eyes went round. 'I'm so very sorry. The golden rule of births, marriages and deaths is never assume *anything*. A man once came here trying to register a piglet. Said she was more of a daughter to him than any of his biological children had been. Um. Hang on, I have a thing.' She pulled a crumpled piece of paper out of her breast-pocket, clearly reading from it as she carried on. 'I cannot apologise enough for all and any offence or distress caused by my words, actions or facial expression. I deeply regret upsetting you and your loved ones during such an important, meaningful occasion. If you would like to make a formal complaint, please use the form provided.'

She stopped then, looking up, eyes darting in panic. 'Please don't use the form. If I get another one, they'll fire me. This job is my life. It's all I ever dreamed of doing. I just get a bit carried away sometimes.'

'It's fine,' Beckett said, although Mary was clearly far from fine. He suspected she'd not heard a word Delilah had said. 'Here.'

He stood up, handing Bob to the registrar, who confessed she wasn't allowed to hold the babies any more, so Beckett had to promise not to tell anyone. Then he did all he could think of to do, sitting beside Mary and wrapping his arms around her until she finally stopped shuddering and straightened up.

'I'm sorry,' she said again.

'No!' Delilah exclaimed, quickly handing a now settled baby back to Beckett. '*I'm* sorry!'

'I'm ready now, if I've not missed the appointment?'

Mary had stopped sobbing, but tears still trickled out of her eyes as she followed Delilah through a wooden door, head ducked, avoiding Beckett's gaze. When she emerged with the certificate a short while later, her face was pale, yet composed, and her determined smile clearly told him she wanted to move on.

Beckett was longing to ask what had happened with Bob's father. Even if it was just so he could hunt him down and refresh his bowel-surgery skills using no anaesthetic.

Beckett wasn't ignorant to the complicated circumstances around which women had babies alone. However, he also knew a broken heart when he saw one. It was obvious something major had gone on between Mary and whoever the loser was who'd left her alone, in that dump in the forest, to raise their child.

If he'd been in that position, with Mary, or anyone else, he'd have done everything he could to be there for them. Ruefully, Beckett realised that even though he was, at this point, no more than a bit player in Mary's story, with no claim on her or her baby, he still would.

* * *

They had a quick stop in a café for lunch, then Beckett pushed the pram around a warehouse while Mary ruthlessly sifted through endless rolls and swatches of fabric, making lightning-quick decisions about what she wanted to buy, discarding the rest without a second thought.

She pretended to consult her costume assistant on a few

options, but when Beckett offered his honest opinion, she almost always dismissed it outright.

'Are you asking me with the intention of choosing the one I don't like?' he asked, when yet again after he'd pointed out his preference between two colours, she selected the other one.

She looked up, fingers still rubbing a sheet of gold lace, and for the first time that day her eyes sparkled. 'What?'

'Is my taste really that bad?'

Mary laughed, and instantly the whole world seemed brighter again. 'My main inspiration for this carol concert is "bad taste". No, I'm honestly not. When I'm asking you, it's really thinking out loud. Hearing your answer helps confirm the decision I would have ended up with.'

'So you might as well be asking Bob, really?'

She raised her eyebrows. 'Who do you think I consult about things when you're not around? The only reason I'm asking you, not him, now is because I'm going to be bartering for a heavy discount in a few minutes, and I want that shop assistant to take me seriously.'

Once she'd chosen about a dozen different fabrics, and the retailer had chopped the required amounts of each, Beckett met a completely different Mary. The one, he supposed, who'd been a company director.

After hearing the total price, Mary halved it, took a few more pounds off and made that her counter-offer.

The man looked at her, eyebrows raised in surprise, before accepting the negotiation challenge with relish.

'Look,' Mary said, leaning on the counter with her forearms, eyes narrowed as if sharing a morsel of gossip with a close friend. 'This is for a community carol service. A *Christmas* carol service.'

'Unlike all the other, not-Christmassy ones?' the man shot back.

Mary ignored him. 'It's being put on free of charge, to cheer the hearts of local people. Children. The elderly. Those struggling with loneliness or seasonal stress.'

'Does that include the stress of trying to keep a business afloat, despite customers coming out with yet another sob story, demanding a discount that won't even cover the cost price?'

'Do you have children, Stanislaus?' Mary asked with a subtle glance at his name badge.

'Four sons,' Stanislaus said, sticking out his barrel chest. 'All of whom require shoes, endless food and the latest iPhone gadgetry under the tree. Are you suggesting I tell them that this year it's a second-hand Nokia instead, because I'm cheering local community hearts?'

'Would they like front-row seats at a fabulous Christmas carol concert?'

'They also have six cousins. And three grandparents. My wife also very much enjoys a good show.'

'It can't be front row, then. In the general front-ish area? This deal's a lot cheaper than taking them all to the pantomime.'

Stanislaus grinned. 'Are you guaranteeing a pantomime-quality performance?'

'Are you questioning it? We've got Santa-day Night, performed by the Christmas Day Twins.'

He narrowed his eyes. 'Will my children have heard of them?'

'Maybe.' Mary gave a nonchalant shrug. 'Either way, the concert's called "Everyone's a Santa". This is your chance to start the ball rolling, Santa Stanislaus. Which means, of course, our appreciation for the brilliant Stan's Fabric Merchants will be clearly displayed in the programme, including a half-page advert.'

He upped another twenty pounds to her offer, and the deal was sealed.

'You've done a lot of that before,' Beckett said as they walked back to the car, his admiration clear.

'I have. Usually brokering contracts for things that would otherwise be thrown away, but in far larger quantities. I never dreamed I'd be haggling over lime-green netting.'

* * *

When they arrived back at the church building, Mary went to tell Sofia about the deal she'd made with Stanislaus, so Beckett ended up chatting with Bill for a few minutes.

'Has he been okay?' Beckett asked as someone helped Gramps zip his coat up.

'An absolute pleasure. He smashed me at chess and draughts.'

Beckett frowned. 'Please be honest with me if he was rude, or upset anyone.'

'Not at all.' Bill dismissed this with a shake of his head. 'The guys loved trying to puzzle out his riddles.'

'Okay.' Gramps had been a pleasure? Beckett was still absorbing this riddle when Bill handed him a slip of paper. 'You asked about care agencies? Here's a few that've been recommended.'

'Thank you.' Beckett scanned the list. 'Do you know if any of them provide care to people with dementia?'

Bill gave him a sideways look. 'I don't. But, Beckett, Marvin remembered the name of half the people here, which is about the same as me on a good day, and I've known some of them forever. He's sharper than a steak knife. What on earth would make you think he has dementia?'

Beckett shrugged. 'Oh, you know. He's not been formally diagnosed yet, but the signs are starting to show. Forgetfulness, confusion. A couple of days ago I found him digging up a plant with a dessert spoon in the middle of the night, wearing only pyjama bottoms and a vest.'

Bill's eyes studied him. 'Did he say why?'

'Nothing that made sense.'

'Aye, well. No harm in a chat with his doctor. I'd wager decades of experience that he knows exactly what he's doing.'

Then how come he walked straight past the taxi Beckett had been driving for six years and tried rattling the handle of a strange car?

* * *

Once back in Bigley, Mary helped clear out the remaining clutter in the living room, before insisting Beckett went out for an hour. He tried to protest that, having already been out, he was perfectly fine staying in, but Mary was still in boss-mode, and before he knew it he found himself bundled out of the front door.

'It's not about what you need today,' she insisted. 'We're getting Gramps and me used to each other, remember? So you can leave him with me when you really need it.'

With no excuse other than the truth, that he preferred hanging out at home with Mary than going out by himself, which he didn't know how to express without sounding worryingly stalkerish, he checked the time and headed off into the village, planning to return an hour later, and not a minute more.

When he did come back, almost two hours later, the living room was virtually unrecognisable.

Mary had taken down the net curtains hanging at the large window overlooking the back garden and draped a throw she'd found in a cupboard over the back of the tired sofa. She'd rearranged the smaller furniture and added a couple of lamps, which Beckett vaguely remembered seeing somewhere lying around. The swirly rug had gone, every surface gleamed and she'd done something with the remaining photographs and other bits and pieces so that the overall effect was cosy, yet so much calmer. The room appeared about twice the size.

'How did you do all this?'

Mary smiled. 'Gramps helped.'

'What?'

'Not with moving the furniture! He dusted, and vacuumed. Helped unhook that filthy net monstrosity. Another time, I'll wash the curtains and bring a few cushions, and it'll be perfect.' Her eyes shone. 'You might even have room to squeeze in a Christmas tree.'

'It's already perfect.' Beckett didn't ask why, when she'd been able to transform this room in two hours, her own house still looked so drab after months.

'So, the living room's not been this afternoon's only transformation.'

Mary reached up and ran a hand over Beckett's newly cut hair, which now sat just below his cheekbones. Her expression was playful, but the way Beckett's body responded was deadly serious. He had to turn away, fighting the urge to grab her hand and press it against his face.

'It looks lovely.' She spoke more gently, perhaps assuming Beckett's awkwardness was down to feeling self-conscious, rather than his nervous system going into overdrive after being touched tenderly for the first time in forever. 'It's made me realise I've not been to a hairdresser since I moved.'

'Next time, leave Bob with me and you go.'

Beckett took his time after offering to make them both tea, so when he turned around he could at least pretend he'd yanked himself back together. 'Goateez down the road will do you a snazzy short back and sides.'

'What else did you do, then?' Mary sat down at the table. 'It's a great cut, but can't have taken two hours.'

'I had to wait in the queue for twenty minutes. Then, afterwards I walked around for a bit, worried about Gramps. Worried more about why he's been so uncooperative with me since the stroke, so determined to sit at home and feel miserable, and now he's happily hobbling into church to charm everyone. Then I come back and he's cleaning! Yesterday I couldn't persuade him to throw out an old VHS remote.'

'Surely that's a good thing?'

Beckett rubbed his eyes. 'Except it shows how badly I've been letting him down all this time.'

'What? Beckett, you gave up a medical career to take care of him! You lost your fiancée. Until Tanya quit, you've been working all day, looking after Gramps the rest of the time. You get hardly any sleep, handle his insults and unreasonableness, keep an eye out constantly. You've given time, energy, patience. *Everything.* You told me he wasn't interested in clubs and day centres before. Maybe he's simply ready for them now. Maybe Tanya leaving was the catalyst he needed.'

Beckett shook his head. He needed to get this out before it ate him alive.

'I didn't try hard enough. I know I didn't. For the first few months, getting him out of bed felt like an achievement. Then, I don't know, there was so much to figure out. It was easier to stay at home and let him watch quiz shows than think about the next week, let alone what the next few years would be like. I was completely out of my depth. Relying on random care-agency staff who didn't even know him, weren't going to care about finding a way to get beyond survival and start living again. Why would they, when his own grandson didn't?'

'You were mourning.'

'For six years?'

'Beckett, you were so young. It's a miracle you managed to do any of it alone. Most people would have found him a care home and got on with their lives ages ago.'

Beckett's jaw clenched at the thought of it. 'I promised him I wouldn't do that. And still, I wasn't good enough. This past couple of weeks have proven how different things could have been. Should have been.'

Mary screwed her nose up. 'When you're already at breaking point, sometimes all you can do is choose the option that seems safest. You did your best.'

'He's so old. He's getting worse every week. How much precious time have I wasted? How can I begin to make that up to him?'

She reached across the table and took his hand. 'You don't squander the time you have left. You do better from now on.' She gave a rueful smile. 'We both do.'

19

MARY

I woke up on Friday to a moody morning. A blanket of gunmetal-grey stretched above the treetops, and it was one of those wintry days when it never seemed to get fully light. I'd been intending to knuckle straight down to cutting out patterns, but, after the busyness of the day before, decided to be kind to myself with a slower start. I turned on the two lamps in the living room, settled Bob back into his Moses basket and tucked myself up with a blanket, mug of tea, raisin toast and a notepad, sketching out the finer details of the costumes I was hoping to create. The only thing missing was a fire in the grate. I'd tried a couple of times to get one going, using a starter kit from the farm shop, but had got nowhere past a few embers and a lot of smoke.

Not long after eleven, I was startled out of my creative zone by the doorbell. Quickly pulling on an oversized cardigan to hide the roll of flesh sagging above the pre-pregnancy joggers I'd squeezed into, I hurried to answer it.

Someone had already dropped off a generous portion of lasagne, so it wasn't the meal-train calling. I paused in the doorway between the living room and the hall, caught off guard by how my assumption that it was probably Beckett sent a flutter of anticipation through my insides. Quickly dismissing it as the natural reaction to an unexpected visit from a friend, given how the only people ringing my doorbell for months had been delivery drivers, I told myself that I'd be equally pleased if it was Sofia or Rina. Okay, so almost as pleased. I knew Beckett better than the coffee mums. I was allowed to like him more.

I'd not reached the point where I could even begin to consider someone as becoming more than platonic. I knew I'd not get there for a very long time. If ever.

Although, when I saw the unmistakable shadow of a six-foot-three man through my front-door window, the swoop in my belly felt like a long-lost friend. With a flash of shock, I had to wonder if my feelings might have other ideas.

'Hi.' Beckett stuck his hands in his pockets, his eyes shifting to the side and then back again. 'This seemed like a great idea when I was up convincing Gramps that three in the morning wasn't the best time to start dismantling kitchen cupboards. Now I'm here I'm thinking I might have overstepped.'

'In coming to see me? I mean, you could have messaged first, but I'm not busy.'

'No.' Beckett looked sheepish. 'In bringing you this.'

He stepped back to reveal Gramps and, beside him, leaning against the side of the porch, a tree. It was maybe four feet tall, with branches so perfectly even I'd have guessed it was fake if it weren't for the heavenly fragrance.

'You got me a Christmas tree?'

A sudden rush of heat prickled the backs of my eyes. I'd been extra aware, since sprucing up Beckett and Gramps' house the day before, of how unhomely my cottage was. I could blame the lack of effort on being too tired, or too busy, but I couldn't fool myself into believing it. I'd not even tried to make it look nice because, firstly, I was still resisting it being my home. On too many levels I still grieved the gorgeous apartment I'd run away from. Secondly, for the past few months, this miserable, forlorn ambience had suited me perfectly. Thirdly, it was too depressing to even start, knowing that any token improvements I made would be like sticking a bow on a lump of concrete. Which took me back to the first point. Why bother, when I had never wanted to come here, didn't want to be here now, and had no intention of staying once I'd found the mental energy to start figuring out what I did want?

Making this place my own meant accepting my old life was over.

So Beckett wasn't the only one surprised when I stepped out onto the freezing cold stoop in my bare feet and flung my arms around his neck.

As well as the fir tree – Beckett said it would be silly to have got an artificial one, given how I lived in the middle of a forest – he'd picked up a load of decorations, including a random mix of tree ornaments, wicker forest animals covered in tiny lights, and a stack of beautifully crafted three-dimensional snowflakes. There was a red and white throw and blue and silver cushions. None of it matched, some were genuinely ugly, but I didn't care. Especially when I found Gramps hanging a tiny stocking embroidered with 'Merry Christmas Bob' on the mantlepiece.

'You don't have to use all of them,' Beckett said, holding a glittery ornament in the shape of an angel. 'I didn't know what you'd like, so grabbed a couple of everything.'

'Nope, I'm using all of them.'

'You could divide it up by colours, or style, and put some of them in the dining room and kitchen.'

'I don't ever go in the dining room. The radiator in there doesn't work. I want them all in here.'

'You're sure?'

Beckett rubbed his jaw, not at all convinced.

I pinned the last snowflake to the ceiling and walked over to him, taking his hands in mine.

'Beckett. Every single one of these decorations will remind me of quite possibly the kindest thing anyone's ever done for me. Six weeks ago, I was utterly alone. Now I have the type of friend who turns up on my doorstep with a Christmas tree. When I'm pacing up and down in the middle of the night, a baby screaming in my earhole, or sitting here wallowing in the mess I've made of my life, I will see that deranged-looking sheep and remember that this friend genuinely cares about me. A friend who's probably also up at whatever unearthly hour it is, taking care of someone they love. This is so magical, so precious, I don't know how to begin to thank you enough.'

I had to stop, because I'd done more than enough crying in front of this man for one lifetime.

Beckett pulled his hands, still clasped in mine, and bumped them against his chest.

'You just did.'

'Are you two lovebirds planning on mooning at each other until Boxing Day, or is someone going to make me a drink after all that work?' Gramps barked before slumping onto the sofa.

Beckett dropped my hands as if they'd given him an electric shock, turning to one side as he crossed his arms, then unfolded them and jammed his hands in his pockets before pulling one out and running it over his head, mussing up his new haircut.

I gabbled something incomprehensible about the kettle, and bumbled my way out of the room before Beckett could see that I was even more flustered than him.

* * *

While we were drinking tea, discussing the tweaks to my costume designs with such businesslike intensity it wouldn't have fooled Bob, let alone Gramps, a wonderful distraction happened.

'Look!' I got up and walked to the glass doors at the back of the room. It had started snowing. A few light flurries at first, but as I watched, they rapidly intensified to swirls of huge, fluffy flakes.

'Let's go for a walk,' I said, unable to contain my enthusiasm.

'What?' Beckett looked bemused as he came to have a closer look. 'Going out in the snow is fine, once the snow has stopped falling. Walking in a blizzard is not a fun activity.'

'What, you didn't like going out in falling snow when you were little? Tipping your head up and catching a snowflake on your tongue?'

'Okay, being in a blizzard is not fun, unless you're an eight-year-old.'

'Or a woman who has lived in a city her whole life, where snow turns to grey slush the second it hits the ground.' I nudged him with my elbow. 'Come on, it's so-o-o-o pretty. Gramps, you'll come with me, won't you? You don't mind being outdoors in the cold.'

'Gramps might not mind the cold, but he will mind slipping over and breaking his leg.'

'I'll get my coat,' Gramps said, his chuckle sounding not dissimilar to an eight-year-old's.

'Remember, we make up for lost time by not squandering what we have now,' I said softly, placing a hand on Beckett's arm.

'Not squandering it by stumbling about, getting freezing cold and sopping wet? Making up for lost time by staying inside, where it's warm, and we can watch the snow through the window?'

He blew out a sigh, then went to find his boots.

***

With Bob safely ensconced in his snowsuit and tucked under the pram's rain cover, Gramps with one hand gripping the pram, the other firmly held by his son, we slowly set off into the forest.

Beckett was right, the snowflakes felt like tiny needles against our exposed skin. The icy wind made it impossible to look up for more than a millisecond, so for most of the way we trudged on, heads down, eyes squinting, concentrating on our feet not sliding out from under us.

The forest probably looked beautiful, if we could see past the whirling blizzard into the gloom.

After about ten minutes, even I had to agree that Beckett was right, and it was time to head back. However, as we carefully turned around, the snowflakes suddenly faded as rapidly as they'd begun.

We all stopped, transfixed, as a beam of sunlight broke through a chink in the canopy above, and the world was transformed into a shimmering, sparkling wonderland.

'Oh,' I breathed.

'Not bad,' Gramps agreed.

Every leaf and branch was painted with a topcoat of pure white. The air was heavy, sounds muffled as the forest lay still beneath the winter blanket.

A robin appeared on a nearby holly bush, sending a smattering of snow tumbling to the ground.

Suddenly, I felt a thud against my back.

Twisting around, I found Beckett dusting the remains of the snowball from his gloves.

'Didn't think you'd want me to squander the opportunity,' he said, grinning.

Still shaking my head in disbelief, I quickly bent down,

grabbed some snow and shot one back at him. Of course, I didn't have the advantage of surprise, so he dodged it, easily.

What he didn't see coming was Gramps, only a couple of steps away, carefully scooping a handful from the tree stump bedside him and shoving it down Beckett's collar. His shriek scared off the robin, but had Gramps leaning on the stump as he laughed.

'Okay. Ceasefire!' Beckett said, jiggling about as he tried to dislodge the snow now sliding down his back.

'Only if you admit to being soundly beaten.' I giggled.

'By an enfeebled old man,' Gramps added.

'I'm ending this now before someone other than me winds up injured,' Beckett said primly, taking hold of the pram handle. 'We all know there's no question about whether I could destroy you if I tried.'

'Whatever you say. If that makes you feel better, then, yes, of course you could,' I said, moving over to give him a patronising pat on the shoulder.

Our journey back was equally slow, but this was much more of a pleasant amble through the inch of snowfall, rather than a torturous battle against the elements.

'Go on. I know you're dying to say it,' I groaned, catching the knowing smirk on Beckett's face as I stopped to admire a particularly beautiful-looking clearing. 'We should have waited until the snow stopped.'

'I guess some people need to find things out for themselves, rather than listening to someone who knows better.'

'Well, thank you for coming with me.' I linked my arm through his. 'Even though you knew it was a bad idea.'

'If Gramps had slipped, you'd have needed me.' He glanced at Marvin, who had pushed the pram over to where a fungus the size of a dinner plate protruded from a tree trunk.

'But doesn't this seem even more beautiful, having experienced the brunt of the blizzard?'

'Are you turning your stubborn insistence on dragging an old man and a baby out in a snowstorm into a valuable life lesson?'

I grinned at him, feeling that disconcerting belly-swoop again when he gave a resigned eyeroll and smiled back.

Moments like this, it was as though the first rays of sun were breaking through. And yes, they shone all the brighter in contrast to the dark clouds of the past few months.

* * *

Beckett had one more treat for me before they left. After we'd warmed up with the meal-train lasagne, he called me into the living room and guided me through building a fire. What meant the most to me was how he didn't light it while I was preparing lunch, like some caveman showing off his skills. He didn't even show me how to do it. He sat back and patiently taught me how to do it myself, letting me make mistakes and get things not quite right.

'Oh my gosh, I love you,' I blurted the second I was sure enough of the larger chunks of wood had taken.

I immediately froze, gripping the poker as if I were considering bludgeoning someone with it. The someone being me.

'You're welcome.'

'I mean,' I said, sliding my eyes to see where Beckett also sat unnaturally still, staring hard at the fire, 'obviously by I love you, I don't mean that I, well, I'm not saying that I don't love you as a friend. If that's... Is it okay to say that? You don't strike me as the kind of guy who tells his mates he loves them. But me and my friends, we would do it all the time. You know, "love you!" if we made each other a cup of tea, or were off out somewhere, or one of us made a snappy comment. I know we've not known each other that long, but you got me through childbirth. I will love you forever for that. Oh, no. I really need to stop talking now. Please stop me before I keep making it worse. I should have made a joke and moved on. Now this brilliant day will forever be the time I made everything awkward...'

'I love you, too,' Beckett said firmly, his voice impossibly deep, before leaning over and kissing the top of my head in an unmistakably friend-like manner. 'But I do need to get home. I have to tidy up before the care agency Bill recommended come over tomorrow.'

He stood up, sending a snowflake decoration spinning as he stretched his arms above his head. 'Enjoy your fire.'

'Oh, I will. And the tree, the decorations, the freaky-looking elf. When can I come over and make it up to you?'

'If you were able to spend some time with Gramps on Tuesday, that would be great. But he wants to go back to the church on Sunday. If you fancy coming too, let me know.'

'Okay. I'll check my diary.' I pretended to open and scan through an imaginary book. 'I'm free, would you believe it? If the roads are clear, then me and Bob will come. He enjoyed the carols last time, and hopefully I'll have a couple of costumes ready for people to try on, check my rusty dressmaking skills are up to the Christmas Twins' standards.'

Beckett woke Gramps up, took a protracted ten minutes encouraging him into his coat, boots, hat and gloves, and then left, calling out, 'Love you!' as the front door swung shut.

'Look at all this,' I said, turning on the star lights draped across the window frames and picking up Bob to show him. 'Of all the taxi drivers to come and pick me up on your birthday, I think we got a Christmas angel.'

20

MARY

I had no idea who Leo was when I met him. It was ShayKi's summer party. This was a grand affair held in a large hotel just outside the city, and in addition to our employees, we invited key contacts from our suppliers, retailers and various other people who we had working relationships with, ranging from fashion bloggers to charity workers. That year, almost three hundred people wined, dined and celebrated another year of stomping success at our award ceremony.

I was in full-on work mode. This type of event came naturally to Shay and Kieran, but I had to make a concerted effort to work my way around our guests. As per the ShayKi way, this meant taking the time to greet those who probably considered themselves the least deserving in the room, leaving the bigwigs to chat amongst themselves.

I'd been outside in the hotel garden, talking to a group of women who had come through our apprenticeship scheme, when I spotted a man standing in a similar cluster a few feet away. Ordinarily, I wouldn't have thought anything of it. We had a lot of stylish, confident men at our parties. Even when he lifted his glass towards me and gave a playful nod, I merely adjusted my position so he was no longer in my eyeline and continued listening to how one woman had recently regained partial custody of her young children, helped by ShayKi's decent income and flexible hours.

At an appropriate pause in the conversation, I wished them all the best and went to find another drink. Before I'd taken three steps, a full champagne flute was pressed into my hand.

'You looked like you needed a top-up,' the man said in a faint London accent, giving an impish smirk.

'Not at all creepy, to have a stranger watching me from the shrubbery shadows,' I retorted, making to move past him.

'What can I say? I'm a people watcher.'

Supposing that this was better than the many guests who were solely interested in themselves being watched, when I reached a bench and sat down, I decided not to object when he took a seat next to me, leaving a reassuring distance between us.

'I've heard you do things differently here, but it still intrigued me, seeing the big boss hobnobbing with the common workers, rather than schmoozing with the chair of the British Fashion Council, who happens to be standing by the fountain over there, with an editor from *Glamour* magazine.'

'I leave all that to my co-directors.' I took a sip of champagne. It was a gorgeous evening, the air light, the breeze carrying the scent of cut grass and meat sizzling on the barbecues.

'It doesn't make you sound any less creepy, by the way, knowing who I am.'

'Even if I know who Shay and Kieran are? And that the guy standing over there is your head of branding? Now, the woman next to him I'm less sure of. I'd guess by the outfit, those stiff shoulders, that she's something to do with finance. Accountant?'

'She cleans our office.'

'Ah. Okay. Close, then.'

That made me smile. 'You still haven't told me why you know all this. I know you don't work for us.' I would definitely have remembered those slanting electric-blue eyes, the smile that crinkled up his whole face. 'Are you from a rival brand, sent here to spy?'

He laughed. 'I've been swotting up because I'm hoping to join the ShayKi family. I've an interview next week, which is why I got the invite.'

'Ah, okay.'

'Although, now I've met you, I'm wondering if that's such a good idea.'

'Excuse me?'

'Well, things could get awkward if I'm ridiculously attracted to the big boss.'

I jerked my head around to look at him, too surprised to play it cool.

'Although,' he mused, 'I imagine it's a common enough problem.'

He leant forwards, elbows braced on his knees, looking sideways at me from under a floppy blond fringe. 'So I don't suppose it would be an issue, unless the feelings happened to be reciprocated.'

'Are you asking if I'm ridiculously attracted to you?' I said, regaining a little of my composure.

To my chagrin, the truthful answer at that point would have been *quite possibly, yes*.

I didn't fall for charmers. Especially not ones wearing loafers with no socks and a dangly earring. When I had dated, it had been with steady, solid men. Shay and Kieran referred to them as Future Football Dads. The kind of men who preferred an Indian and an action movie to swanning about a fancy party nibbling on miniature artisan hotdogs.

He squinted into the sun, which was hovering above the Peak District hills.

'Actually... no,' he said, drawing it out, as if thinking out loud. 'Seeing as I haven't had the interview yet, I can't see a problem with us hanging around now. I might not even get the job.'

'Could you foresee there being a *problem* with me interviewing a man who told me only a week earlier that he finds me attractive?' I asked in my no-nonsense boss-voice.

'Ah. I can see that could be an issue.' He swivelled around to face me on the bench as we each took another long sip of our drinks. 'How about I retract that inappropriate statement immediately? After all, I never said that I *was* completely, utterly captivated by your dazzling smile, only that it could be a problem if feelings like that were to develop, in the future. I guess all I was saying is I can't rule it out.'

'I'm very relieved to hear that you never said that, seeing as I have no interest in wasting time with smooth talkers.'

'Good. I think I've just proven I'm not one of those.'

'However, your extensive research will have revealed how highly ShayKi values integrity. Can you honestly say that this conversation hasn't constituted flirting?' I dared to glance over at him. Ugh. He was still annoyingly gorgeous. 'Because if you agree that it has crossed that line, then I won't be able to interview you. If you don't consider this to be flirtatious, then you're not going to be the right fit for a company employing 75 per cent female staff.'

'Are you directly involved with hiring new designers?'

'No, but Shay runs any potential names past me before offering them the job.'

'Okay. So I don't tell you my name.'

'Now we're back to you being creepy.'

'Creepy... or mysterious?'

'Mysterious, or dangerous, in a creepy way?'

He laughed. It was a beautiful, full-bellied laugh. The least creepy laugh I'd ever heard.

'Dangerous, or sexy?'

'Sexy, or downright foolish?' I held up one hand. 'That's not actually a question. I've got a lot of people to say hello to this evening. I'm not hanging about with a man who won't tell me his name.'

'I'm Leo,' he said, gently clasping the brandished hand and shaking it. 'Very pleased to meet you.'

We spent the next hour sitting on the bench, talking. As the sky melted into a kaleidoscope of pinks, oranges and gold, we asked questions and shared stories – steering clear of anything to do with work – swiping more drinks from a waiter as he wandered past, ignoring the other guests milling around the grounds.

When it was time for the awards, I took my place on the stage in the function room, although more than once I succumbed to the temptation to allow my gaze to drift to the man standing at the back.

The third time, he lifted his glass, as he had done in the garden, and from that night on, it became our signal: 'I see you, I'm thinking about you. I'm ridiculously attracted to you, and utterly captivated by your smile.'

I spent another half an hour networking, then, as the crowd began to thin, I once again slipped out to the garden bench. It was fully dark now, and it was only instinct that told me Leo would follow.

When he appeared out of the shadows, once again taking a seat a respectable few inches away, it was me who slid close enough for our shoulders to touch, for it to seem natural when his hand slipped around mine. After a minute, he took off his jacket and carefully draped it across my shoulders, and I breathed in the scent of bergamot, my senses on fire.

When our voices were growing hoarse, our skin numb from the night chill, as the hotel staff cleared away the last of the night's debris, I finally replied to the messages pinging through from Shay and Kieran, asking me where the hell I was, had I been kidnapped and did I want to get a nightcap with them in the bar before they headed up?

I sent the only reply that would have made them leave me alone:

MARY

I'm talking to a guy. Do Not Disturb!

When I slipped my phone back into my bag, Leo took a deep breath.

'You don't strike me as a woman who kisses random men at parties.'

I ducked my head, allowing my hair to fall over my face.

'Not since snogging Jason Candy in year twelve.' I grimaced. 'Didn't turn out well.'

'Especially ones who are interviewing with your company in six days.'

I glanced up at this man who had listened to every word I'd said as if eager to know more, not merely trying to win me over.

The truth was, I'd not kissed any man, random or otherwise, in years. I'd had three too many glasses of champagne, and, for the first time in far too long, I was enjoying feeling reckless.

'Ah, stuff it. It's a party.'

I put my glass down, flung my arms around his neck, and as my heart pounded, electricity whizzing through my nervous system, I pressed my lips against his.

21

BECKETT

On Saturday afternoon, Beckett welcomed yet another care manager into his kitchen. He'd been offered an airport run that morning, and was feeling broke enough to risk sticking on a podcast about Frederick the Great and taking Gramps with him.

Following that two-hour debacle, this meeting had to go well.

Which it did, for the first half-hour. Jaden, the care manager, was clearly passionate about ensuring her service users got the best possible care.

'Health and safety, turning up on time, having carers who know you, that's all essential, but we don't settle for being caring and competent.'

Beckett was listening.

'Our aim is that the people we work with look forward to our carers coming. It's one of the highlights of their week, day, whatever. I'm rigorous about only hiring and keeping staff who love their job and treat these precious men and women as if they were their own family. Our staff receive the level of respect we expect them to show the service users, and everyone's happy. We're a non-profit, so we can keep wages fair without working our team like pack mules.'

The reviews that Beckett had found online certainly backed up what she was saying. One man wrote that he'd pretended to be ill in the hope his wife's carer kept coming even after his wife died.

'Is it okay if I meet Marvin?' Jaden asked once Beckett was itching to sign the contract. 'I won't do an assessment or anything this time, but I'd love to say hi.'

Beckett really wanted to say no. Later on, he wished he'd made up some excuse, pretended Gramps was in bed.

Unfortunately, the second Beckett walked into the living room, Gramps jolted awake.

'What?'

Jaden came to stand beside Beckett, politely waiting to be introduced.

Gramps had no such qualms.

'Why is a woman watching me sleep like a psychopath?'

'This is Jaden, from a care agency. She literally just walked in.' Every muscle in Beckett's body was tense.

'She looks like a crow.'

'I'm so sorry.' Beckett turned towards Jaden, his hopes starting to crumble. 'He's sometimes confused when he first wakes up.'

'I am not confused. I don't need looking after. I certainly don't want to be looked after by a fat old crow.'

And then he mumbled a racist expletive that Beckett knew Jaden heard because she flinched.

Before Beckett could usher her out of the room, Gramps stood up, grabbed his coffee mug and hurled it at the mantlepiece. A large photo frame flew off, shattering into pieces.

Jaden swore, diving back into the hallway.

Gramps and Beckett simply stood there, staring at each other.

Beckett couldn't have told you what damage hurt the most. His relationship with the man who'd raised him, or the picture of his mother, now lying in the hearth.

* * *

Beckett found Jaden in the kitchen, gathering up her things.

'I'm so sorry. He's never said anything like that before.' Beckett rubbed a hand through his hair. He couldn't believe this was happening. 'The carer who's been helping tide us over is Sri Lankan.'

She glanced up, a tight smile on her face. 'Beckett, my team are trained in caring for people who exhibit challenging behaviours relating to their condition. We can work around that. However, I will need you to be honest if we're going to provide the level of care that he needs and keep everyone safe.'

'I don't know what to say. This is the first time he's been violent like that.'

She picked up her bag. 'I must stress that we are a person-centred organisation. Unless he's been assessed as lacking the competency to provide consent, Marvin must agree to our care plan. I recommend you have a conversation with him, because we can't move forwards if he's not on board.'

Her tone softened slightly, which said a lot, considering the situation. 'Reassure him that the crow is merely the manager, she won't be doing the day-to-day fun stuff. I'm also going to request that you make a GP appointment to discuss possible dementia, and assess for other signs of deterioration in his condition. Once you've done that, if Marvin is up for it, we can try again.'

'Thank you.'

'You're welcome. I know this is incredibly difficult for you.'

She squeezed his shoulder as she left the room. 'Go and see to your grandfather. I'll let myself out.'

* * *

Beckett swept up the shards of glass, then vacuumed for good measure. His hands shook as he placed the now bare photo back on the mantlepiece. Gramps stared at his quiz show and said nothing.

At a loss for what to do next, Beckett made them both a hot drink and turned the television off before sitting down.

He wanted to yell and curse. Spew out the frustration and pain of the past few years. Make Gramps feel terrible. However, Beckett saw the glint of fear in his grandfather's eyes, even as he took a defiant slurp of tea, and knew that he already did.

'What was that?' he asked instead, as gently as possible.

Gramps turned his head away.

'I know you aren't racist. You've never thrown anything like that before. You scared me, Gramps.' Beckett paused, trying to get a grip on the tremor in his voice. 'I'm afraid something's going on with you, you're struggling, and if you won't tell me about it, I can't help.'

The only indication Gramps had heard was his lips turning white as he pressed them together.

'I understand if you don't know what happened or why, but if that's the case, can you at least tell me?'

'I'm missing the final round.'

'Okay.' Beckett stood up. He couldn't stay here watching television as if everything were fine. 'I get that you're scared, too. We still need to talk about this care agency, though. I have to get back to earning some money and at the moment there's no other option. Please. I need your cooperation on this.'

Gramps stared stubbornly at the blank screen, until Beckett gave in, turning it on and leaving him to it.

He'd see if Mary could get him to open up, or Bill. Because today had made clearer than ever that Beckett was clueless.

* * *

When Mary messaged him that evening, it was like ointment on his emotional bruises.

MARY
> How did the meeting go?

Rather than type the whole story, he called. Pouring it all out felt better than he could have imagined. Mary agreed that a GP appointment was a good idea, and offered at least some comfort in Jaden not shutting the door completely.

'Even if he'd just woken up, I think he knew full well who Jaden was,' she mused.

'Agreed. But that doesn't explain his behaviour.'

'Is it frustration at needing looking after? You said he can be difficult with Sonali. Perhaps it's deliberate sabotage. He could be trying to ensure no care agency will take him on, so you're forced to leave him by himself. Is that what he wants?'

Beckett had considered this. 'He did say he doesn't need taking care of. But he knows he needs help with bathing and getting dressed. He can't make a drink safely, let alone prepare a meal. He can't expect me to work and do everything else. Gramps can be rude, and mean since the stroke, but that's a whole new level of selfish. Unless he simply doesn't grasp how badly we'd struggle without an income.'

'On top of the all the night-time wanderings, the other stuff, it sounds like you need a professional opinion.' Mary paused. 'A second, impartial professional opinion.'

'Yeah. Which only leaves the more urgent problem of the bills needing to be paid in the meantime.'

'I'm here, Beckett. I can bring the sewing machine over and sit with Gramps while I sew. I'm not quite ready to give him a bath, but I can make lunch and ensure he's not getting into trouble.'

Beckett was quiet for a moment. 'I can't leave you with him if he's not safe.'

'It was one incident. And like I said, I suspect he knew exactly what he was doing. Please don't say I can't come over any more. While I love my Christmassy cottage, Bob has cried non-stop for hours. After such a good day yesterday, I'd made all these constructive plans to go to the shops, do some batch cooking, figure out the wings for racing pigeon Santa and be a proper, functional human again. I haven't made it out of my pyjamas yet, and the closest I came to cooking was sticking the meal-train leftovers in the microwave. I did stare at a pigeon out of the window while my baby screamed in my ear. I have to get out of here and remember I'm not completely useless.'

'I'm sorry you had a bad day.'

'Yeah, well. Nobody threw anything. Now, change of topic before we both drown in our own self-pity. What do I get Li for secret Santa?'

Heartened by Mary wanting to continue the conversation, Beckett opened the fridge and took out the beer he'd hidden at the back of the vegetable tray.

'I thought that tall guy was playing Secret Santa?'

'This isn't for the play! It's an actual secret Santa, with my actual new friends.'

'So you have to actually buy Li an actual present?' He

wandered through to the living room. Gramps was in bed, so he was free to settle back, open the beer and take a blissful swig.

'Yes! Did I just hear you open a bottle of beer?'

'I'm having a beer on a Saturday night, as prescribed by the doctor in the house following a crap day. Who is Li?'

'She was the one playing the violin at the advent service, but that's not relevant here. She's gorgeous and rich and perfect. Plus, to make matters worse, one of the nicest people ever.'

'That is *the* worst. How awful to have to buy a nice person a present.'

'For ten pounds! You can't give someone that rich and that lovely a set of supermarket toiletries, or a bottle of cheap wine. The last secret Santa gift I bought was a cushion printed with Sean Bean's face. I'd known the recipient for fifteen years so had no doubt she'd love it.'

Shay's Auntie Ada had slept with that cushion.

'Do you have anything from your accessory company? Surely a scarf or a bag or something would make a good present? It's secret Santa, no one expects to like what they get.'

'Hang on. I'm putting you on speaker while I get a tonic and gin.'

'I don't want to indulge you by asking why you call it that. Do you also partake in chips and fish, with pepper and salt? Do you eat them with a fork and knife?'

'It's a glass of tonic, with one tiny splash of gin. I won't have to feed Bob for another few hours, but just in case. Wait a sec, I'm getting the reindeer blanket.'

Beckett waited a lot of secs.

'Okay. I'm sorted.'

'Where are you?'

'I've pushed the sofa around so I can see out of the glass

doors. It's snowing again. In the glow of the garden light it's magical. Whereabouts are you?'

'I'm also on the sofa, gazing winsomely at where the yellowing wallpaper is starting to sag off the wall.'

'I have a really cool umbrella.'

'What?' Beckett had completely forgotten what they were talking about. He shouldn't have asked Mary 'where are you?' It sounded like something you'd ask on a phone date. If phone dates had become a thing in the twelve years since he'd casually dated. The beer had seemed a good accompaniment to a chat with a friend. Now the drinks and the blanket, the warmth of Mary's voice, had lit a sparkler in his stomach. The gentle crackle that, if he didn't hold it carefully, could start a wildfire.

'I could give Li an umbrella. Although she'd know that brand costs more than the budget, so I'd have to explain where I used to work. If they decided to google me, and I can't believe those coffee mums wouldn't, they'd find out who I am.'

'Is that a problem?' Beckett couldn't believe he'd never thought to google her. He'd obviously underestimated the scale of the fashion company.

There was a pause before she replied. Would the internet reveal how she'd ended up in Sherwood Forest? Was Mary a fashion celebrity? Would there be images or articles about Bob's father?

And in what universe could Beckett think hunting online was better than simply asking her about it?

'I don't know. Rosie has one of our bags. It'll be a big deal to them. People treat me differently when they think I'm some glamorous, swanky fashionista. I've always felt uncomfortable with it. Now more than ever, because that person, that life, has gone. I want my new friends to accept me as me, without my past swaying their opinion.' She sighed. 'One day, I'll be ready to share all about it. Not yet.'

Beckett made a silent promise not to search for Mary Whittington online, however tempting.

They carried on talking for another half an hour or so, but Mary was clearly exhausted, and so Beckett made the mature move and insisted they ended the call before it got too late.

He sat for a long time on the sofa once they'd both rung off with a jokey 'Love you!'

Beckett loved Mary, that was in no doubt.

What shook him to his core was finally admitting to himself he was falling in love with her.

You idiot, he berated himself, finally dragging himself up to bed. *This is only going to end badly.*

Badly. Or was there the tiniest chance it could be the start of something wonderful?

Either way, he felt helpless to stop it.

22

MARY

It was still snowing when Bob started whimpering at six-thirty on Sunday. Thankfully, after a fretful day he'd only woken once in the night, and this time he settled enough to allow us another couple of hours cuddling in bed before a need for a bathroom trip and a nappy change forced us up. Now fully light, the view out of every window was pure, sparkling white, as far as I could see. I messaged Beckett to say there was no way a car would make it out here, and he replied confirming that he was also snowed in. I settled upon a day of snipping, sewing and strategically adding sequins, with lots of tea and toast, soup and snacks. After my weeks of Christmas-merriment avoidance, I now felt ready for some gentle Christmas songs in the background while I worked. I did skip every track that reminded me of previous years, which meant expanding my repertoire to some very weird and not-so-wonderful festive tunes.

Coffee morning on Monday was also called off, so I spent a second day in solitude. This time, however, having plans that were cancelled, alongside messages asking if I was okay, still had electricity and groceries and plenty of nappies, it felt very different.

The exhaustion felt different these days, too, I realised after waking up from a late-morning nap. For months, I'd been weighed down by a bone-deep listlessness. Once the raw anger and loss had eased, it had been replaced with a numb apathy that would have frightened me, had I the energy to be bothered. Now, while my body was so tired some days it felt like lugging around a bag of wet sand, it was a product of sleep deprivation, as well as, I assumed, recovery from pregnancy. For the first time since spring, I wanted to do things. I had purpose, and motivation, to force my jellied muscles up and about. I'd had days during the summer when I'd wondered if I'd ever feel joy, or hope, or anything much at all, ever again.

Now, I reflected while stitching toadstools onto green felt knickerbockers, my emotions ending their hibernation meant that I had moments when I felt the pain of everything I'd lost so keenly it took my breath away. Yet I accepted it, because I now knew this was the only way to also experience the contentment of a cosy afternoon watching a blackbird hopping through the drifts in my garden, a needle and thread in my hand, my heart-stoppingly beautiful son cooing in his bouncy chair beside me. Allowing my brain to process another chunk of the rage and resentment also made room for the glimmer of anticipation at how perfect the angel wings I'd constructed out of layer upon layer of glittery netting would look under the spotlights.

It was hard, when the hurt reared up out of nowhere and impaled me through the chest (it wasn't out of nowhere, it was the first three notes to 'All I Want for Christmas Is You' before I had time to grab my phone and click skip). Yet it was bearable, because I could send a quick message to my friend, with a photo of the almost finished Shrek Santa waistcoat, or the massive piece of cheesecake I was about to eat, or Bob's smile when I tickled his tummy.

Monday lunchtime, when I had suddenly begun to cry, thinking about Shay's family, and wondering whether they'd have the Christmas Eve party without me, Sofia sent a photo of the snowmen her kids had made, ranging from a six-inch-high blob with one stick poking out of its head to a near-perfect replica of Jon Bon Jovi.

I was learning about being physically alone – devoid of adult company, at least – and yet not lonely.

I was starting to realise I would be okay.

Later that afternoon, before darkness fell, I bundled Bob into the papoose and went to investigate outside. The sun had made steady work on the snow, the patches on the lane now interspersed with puddles. I sent yet another photo to Beckett, with a big thumbs up, and spent the evening preparing for a day with Gramps tomorrow.

* * *

Beckett arrived at ten on Tuesday morning. He insisted upon shovelling the remaining traces of snow off my drive, clearing a neat track from my garden to the footpath leading to Hatherstone, before we headed over to his house.

'I am capable of handling a shovel,' I said, bringing him a coffee.

'As I'm capable of brewing coffee and sitting with Gramps. I thought you knew how friendship worked. Besides,' he grunted, heaving one last mound to the side before resting the shovel against the garden fence and accepting the drink, 'I'm a good foot taller than you. It's a matter of biology that I'll get it done faster, and more easily.'

He didn't need to add that he was also stronger. Having warmed up in the December sunshine, he'd taken off his coat and jumper, working in a torso-hugging top with the sleeves pushed up. I had no idea how Beckett maintained muscles like that, considering he had no time for a proper walk, let alone to go to the gym. Maybe he did workouts in his bedroom, or using a DVD, like Shay's mum bopping along to Davina McCall.

'Are things any better with Gramps?' I asked, taking a sip of my own coffee. I'd felt reassured enough by Marvin's demeanour to leave him in the living room with Bob, but there was a lingering frostiness between the grandfather and grandson that the sun would do nothing to dissipate.

'He's acting the same as normal.'

'And by normal, you mean grumpy and infuriating?'

Beckett nodded. 'Also, still worrying. He was up at four, making feeble attempts to sweep the last bits of snow off the patio with a dustpan and brush.'

'I'm glad I can give you a break today. Even if it is so you can work.'

Beckett smiled. 'I am going to do some work. Otherwise we'll be cancelling Christmas. But I'm also taking an hour to myself.'

'Doing what?'

His smile grew, lighting up his whole face. 'I'm taking Moses rowing.'

I felt so proud, I could have kissed him.

* * *

It took three 'I really need to get going's and me eventually leaving Beckett in his kitchen where we'd been chatting after lunch, shutting myself with Gramps in the living room, before he finally headed out in the taxi. I'd never had a friend who I could chat with seemingly endlessly and effortlessly. For a long time after Shay and Kieran decided I was one of them, they had taken the lead, the quick-fire words crowding in on top of each other, like popcorn in a pan. The kind of conversation that only kids who'd grown up together could have, when they already knew all the references and the subplots, the characters and locations. I often found it impossible to chip in until they asked me, or coincidentally both happened to pause to draw breath or take a synchronised swig of vanilla Coke. As the years went by, I never quite lost that sense of being allowed to eavesdrop in their conversation, and even when with only one of them, it had been easier to stick to my role as the 'quiet one'.

That was part of why I'd found Leo so impossible to resist. Our 'getting to know you' phase had been impassioned, fervent, as if we were being swept along in a fast-moving river, always slightly out of control, heads scrambling to catch up with the intensity of the emotions. We were consumed by each other.

With Beckett, it was more like a hike through the forest, where we varied the pace yet consistently came across something interesting, unexpected or beautiful where we needed to stop and take our time investigating, or merely allow our minds to boggle a little. Our backgrounds were different in so many practical ways. However, they had both led us to far more 'same here!' moments than I'd have thought possible.

Perhaps it helped that all the awkwardness had been got out of the way in that sweaty, groany, bloody first meeting, or that I'd left my old identity behind in Sheffield. Maybe it was inevitable after my months of isolation that the words would flow, but something about Beckett made it easy to open up to him.

I couldn't think of a better way to feel safe and seen than being genuinely interested in the details of each other's lives.

I ruminated on all this as I completed my secret task of the day. While Gramps explained sudoku to Bob, I hung up the decorations I'd cobbled together in between sewing sessions over the past two days. Beckett had told me Gramps waited until the twenty-first before putting up a tree, but he'd not said anything about a string of bunting, featuring random offcuts of fabric. He'd also not objected to the bin-bag of greenery I'd sneaked in Beckett's boot, pretending it was full of costumes awaiting construction. I hung swathes of holly, pine branches and ivy across the mantel, around the ceiling and in artistic arrangements on the other recently cleared surfaces, adding sprigs of red berries from a bush in the garden, and the odd ribbon or candle.

I wound more ivy up the stairs, and hung a giant paper star from the light fixture in the kitchen.

I then turned off the main lights, lit the candles, breathed in the scrumptious foresty smells and fed Bob while Gramps snoozed. By the time Beckett arrived home, I'd completed one seam of Original Santa's tunic.

'This is incredible.' Beckett took three slow steps into the living room. 'You're an artistic genius. I'm now utterly embarrassed by the hash job I made of your cottage.'

'Pah. I love what you did to my cottage. Especially once I'd rearranged a few things after you'd left.'

'Before you stepped foot through our front door, we were living in a dingy mess. I'd never even considered that how a place looked can change the whole way it feels.'

'And you're supposed to be the smart one.'

'Well, I did think your house would make anyone feel drab and miserable, so maybe that was my first clue.'

'Rude. But not wrong. Once the decorations are down, I might splash out on some homely touches.'

'So you've decided to stick around?'

I looked at him sharply. 'What made you think there was anything to decide about that?'

Beckett gave me a pointed look. 'Um, the drab, depressing house, for starters.'

'Which suited me perfectly, at the time.'

'But not any more?' He grinned.

'I was raised in a house where drab and miserable was the general style. I'm not doing that to my son.' I conceded a smile of my own. 'And, no. It doesn't suit me any more. I'd say... cautiously hopeful? Nervous yet optimistic? Petrified yet valiantly pressing on?'

Beckett nodded. 'I think John Lewis have a range called "stiff upper lip". You could check out their cushions.'

'Maybe I'll add it to my Father Christmas list.'

'Are you staying for a bit, or do you need to get back?'

'Well, I've only one nappy left, but I think I can chance some of whatever's in that box.'

Beckett held up the cardboard carton in his hand. 'Cranberry cookies. Sofia and the kids went on a baking spree while they were snowed in yesterday.'

'I'll put the kettle on.'

'I feel like I should protest after you've spent ages decorating my house, but I'm too knackered to be a decent host.'

Beckett groaned as he lowered himself gingerly into a kitchen chair.

'A good row?'

He rotated one arm, hand clutching his shoulder. 'Yes and no.'

I started making the drinks and waited for him to elaborate.

'Mentally, it was awesome, and Moses was a good partner. I'd forgotten how invigorating it is, skimming over the water, working in sync with someone. The smell of the river, wind at my back, ducks bobbing past. I felt fully alive for the first time in... so long it makes me want to cry thinking about it.'

'And the no?'

'I think I might have to sleep in this chair tonight. The exhilaration was dampened by how disgustingly out of shape I've become.'

I gave Beckett, still wearing his skin-tight rowing top and legging thingies, an indiscreet once-over. 'Looks like a perfectly good shape to me.'

'It's impressive what a six-foot-three frame can hide. I was so breathless I vomited.'

'Nice.'

'Not for Moses, sitting behind me. Every single muscle in my body is either screaming or playing dead in the hope I'll not try to move it.'

I brought over our tea. 'Proof that making the time to do something you love, to take care of yourself, was long overdue.'

'Thank you.' Beckett summoned up the energy to give me a faint smile. 'For making me realise how much I needed it, and for being with Gramps so I could go.'

'You're very welcome. Now, I'm going to order a taxi before you fall asleep in front of me. I'll leave the sewing machine here, if that's okay.'

Beckett rested his head on his arms. 'Could you do something, before you go?'

'Of course, but I'm drinking my tea and enjoying a cookie first, seeing as Bob's being quiet.'

'Make sure all the candles are blown out. If Gramps decides to start another fire, I'm not sure I'd be able to get out of here before the whole house goes up.'

I savoured my drink and the cookie, which was crumbly and

chewy with zingy lemon icing, kissed my friend on the head and left him to dream of water and wide open, winter skies.

* * *

I spent Wednesday at Beckett's house, sewing furiously while Beckett drove the taxi until his painkillers wore off and Gramps read Bob stories about various daring deeds throughout history. On Thursday, we brought some of the completed or mostly completed costumes to New Life Church. I invited those cast members who happened to be at the lunch club to try their outfits on, one at a time in Sofia's office.

'Are you okay?' Sofia peered at me. 'Is Bob letting you get any sleep? You look ready to drop.'

'She looks like she has a terminal disease,' Gramps announced, in case anyone needed clarity on the matter.

I felt as if dropping dead in the middle of the hall would be preferable to showing someone the costume they were going to wear on stage in front of hundreds of people.

Why did I volunteer for this? I asked my stomach as it churned like a washing machine.

I wasn't a designer, like Shay, or a creator, like Kieran. Did I honestly think that somehow their skills and talents would rub off on me? We'd all learned to sew together, as we'd customised bags and hats and scarves, even made jackets and T-shirts in those early days. There was a reason I'd swiftly retreated to the business side of things.

There was a reason they'd so easily let me go.

Here I was, a hanger-on in a fashion company, a second-hand seamstress, about to utterly humiliate myself. These people really cared about this concert. It was their big Christmas opportunity to bless the community, and Miss Ex-Director had gatecrashed a lunch meeting and inserted herself into none-of-her-business because she was trying to prove some stupid point about not being a useless waste of space to no one who cared.

I ran to the toilet, threw up my breakfast, splashed some cold water on my face, and tried to tell myself what Shay and Kieran would say.

Would have said. Before they stopped speaking to me.

'I can do this,' I whispered in the bathroom mirror, my voice quaking. 'Rosie loves the zebra bag. Beckett thought my decorations were incredible. What's the worst that can happen?' I stopped, a bubble of semi-hysterical laughter spurting out. 'Mary Whittington, you have faced far more difficult situations than the humiliation of letting an entire church and surrounding community down. Get some damn perspective. Princess Santa has seen your nether regions, for pity's sake.'

23

BECKETT

Mary's creations were spectacular. Seeing them draped over the kitchen chair or whizzing through the sewing machine, Beckett could tell they were works of art. When Angel Santa opened the door to the office and let him and Sofia have a look, Beckett could have burst with pride. He'd seen from the old costumes that the usual standard was, well, community carol service. The outfit would have befitted a West End show.

'She hates it.' Mary wrung her hands, face stricken as she cowered in the corner of the room. 'It's too flimsy, too plain. Too...' She glanced at Beckett, eyes frantic, voice lowering to a hoarse whisper. 'I thought it looked okay.'

'What?' Yara spun around. 'These are tears of wonder, Mary. This is the nicest thing I've worn since my wedding dress. If I ever get married again, I will literally wear this.'

'Really?'

'Wowsers!' Sofia gasped. 'This is what you call "not too bad at sewing"? I can't wait to see something you're actually good at.'

'It's been a while. I wasn't sure if I'd gone rusty.'

'How did you even come up with this whole layered effect? The way the skirt shimmers?'

'I did a whole *Midsummer Night's Dream* thing once...'

'What exactly was your job, before this?' Sofia asked, planting both hands on her pinafored hips.

'Didn't that ethical company who recycles everything do a *Midsummer Night's Dream* range?' Yara's eyes narrowed as she stroked the glitter on her bodice. 'The one whose floppy hats were at all the festivals a couple of years ago?'

'ShayKi?' Sofia asked.

'Yes! That's it. I bought my sister a Titania scarf. That's what this reminded me of. Oh, my goodness, Mary. Do you work for ShayKi? Do you get a discount?'

Mary looked like a cornered vole. 'No, I don't work for ShayKi or anywhere else at the moment. If I did, I'd have mentioned it when I offered to help with the concert. I spent a few years helping customise clothes for my friend's market stall back when I was at college. Should we get Bill in to try his costume? We haven't got loads of time.'

Sofia gave Mary a thoughtful glance before going to find Bill. Beckett waited in the foyer while Mary helped Yara back out of her costume. He'd bought Rebecca a ShayKi bag once. Mary might not work for them *at the moment*, but how many ethical accessory companies were there in the UK? If she'd founded a fashion business big enough for him to have heard of it, that explained the incredible designs.

* * *

'I kind of wish I'd not tried so hard now,' Mary said once she'd packed away Roman Santa's outfit and Beckett had driven them to Costa for lunch. 'I didn't expect it to generate all those questions.'

Yara hadn't been the only one grilling Mary about her dressmaking skills.

'It's a fairly obvious conversation, considering your level of talent. People are going to ask what you do for a living at some point. Will it really make that much of a difference once they know? Sofia doesn't strike me as the kind of person to judge someone by their job title.'

Mary took a desultory bite of her panini. 'I'm trying to move on from all that.'

'I'd noticed. This isn't just about them knowing you were a big boss, is it?'

She stared at her plate for a long moment. 'Once they know who I am, they can easily look online and find out other stuff. I'm not ready for people to know that yet.'

Mary glanced up at him, a fearful question in her eyes.

'I can't promise I'm not curious,' he said. 'But I'm not going to hunt down Mary Whittington, fashion company director, online. I'll wait until you're ready to tell me.'

She shook her head in disbelief. 'I think you might be the loveliest man I've ever met.'

The dopiest man, Beckett thought, cursing the sloppy grin he couldn't keep off his face.

'I'm serious. I hate secrets. I mean, absolutely *loathe* them. I know the kind of havoc they can cause. It's not like I've done anything awful, or shocking. I'm just not ready to talk about a really sad, painful time of my life. If I see the pity on people's faces, I'll be forced to remember. Right now, I need to focus on the here and now if I'm going to face whatever's next.'

'I understand.' Even as it killed him to know that something so painful had led Mary to here, it was hardly a surprise.

He finished his sandwich and checked the time. 'So, here and now. Do you fancy helping me choose Gramps a puzzle book for Christmas? There might be one in existence he's not already done.'

Mary's face lit up, and Beckett could breathe again.

'Or, now that you've turned all sociable these days, what about a board game?' she suggested. 'I could look for Li's secret Santa gift at the same time.'

They spent the hour before lunch club ended browsing through the shops in a nearby retail park. Beckett bought Gramps a murder puzzle book, and Mary got him a board game based on one of his favourite quiz shows. She didn't find anything for Li, but they had fun nominating the worst secret Santa present possible.

As Beckett drove her home afterwards, dropping off the sewing machine and other equipment, he couldn't help wondering why on earth he'd wasted six years persuading himself that friends were too much hassle.

Although, maybe that depended upon the friend.

* * *

On Friday, Beckett tried another shift with Gramps in the passenger seat. One woman asked him to turn off the podcast, as hearing about the American Revolution was disturbing her son. The boy, who had proudly announced he was turning ten in two weeks, spent the rest of the journey shouting, 'Liberty or Death!' and begging Beckett to turn it back on again, while Gramps recited quotes from other battles. Beckett got no tip for that fare.

When he stopped to pick up someone in the city centre, Gramps made a run for it. By the time it was safe for Beckett to follow, waiting to get out of the car on a busy main road, Gramps had made it inside the Victoria shopping centre, where he'd been swallowed up by the Christmas crowds. Beckett found him a maddening, nightmarish twenty minutes later, standing by one of those randomly placed pianos, tapping his toes along to a young man bashing out 'Winter Wonderland'.

'Why would you take off like that?' he asked, still breathless from fear as he dragged Gramps back towards the taxi stand, only to find he'd got a parking ticket. 'Why would you do that?'

Gramps creaked into the passenger seat. 'I wanted to buy my grandson a Christmas present,' he huffed, still clenching a plastic bag. 'Is that a crime?'

Beckett tried to steady himself, watching the mirrors for a gap in the traffic so he could get the hell out of there. 'Why didn't you tell me first?'

'You'd have said no.'

There wasn't a good reply to that, because it was true. 'I could have asked Mary to take you. Or Bill. They could have helped you order something online.'

He didn't add that if Gramps hadn't decided to start being racist, he'd have a new carer by now, and could have gone shopping with them.

'Perhaps I wanted to do something by my damn self for once,' Gramps snapped loudly. 'You treat me like I'm helpless. If you're not interfering, you're watching, waiting for an excuse to start fussing. Can't clear my throat without you making yet another appointment so more people can prod and poke and ask personal questions. Maybe I wanted fifteen minutes of not being scrutinised like I'm an imbecile.'

'I wouldn't have to watch you all the time if you didn't set fire to the garden, dismantle a perfectly good chest of drawers for no discernible reason or deliberately run off.' Beckett knew he sounded harsh, but he was too tired to hold it in any longer. Maybe this conversation had to happen.

'Run off?' Gramps scoffed. 'I wish.'

Beckett pulled over, signed out of the taxi app so he didn't get any more bookings, and took a few deliberate breaths before starting up again.

'I know this is hard for you.'

Gramps folded his arms, staring straight ahead.

'But things aren't exactly easy for me, either. I'm trying to earn a living here. We have bills to pay and food to buy, and you know I can't leave you alone for hours at a time. I don't know what else to do.'

'You shouldn't have messed things up with Tanya.'

'Is that what all this is about? You're angry with me about Tanya resigning?'

'I bought you a Christmas present, and you twist it into some sort of revenge!' Gramps yelled, before deliberately hunching against the passenger window and closing his eyes.

'I don't know what to do,' Beckett whispered once his grandfather began to snore a few minutes later. 'I'm scared, Gramps. Please tell me what to do.'

24

MARY

I had another cryptic message from Sofia, asking if I was around on Saturday, to which the answer was, unsurprisingly, yes.

> **SOFIA**
> Fab! We'll pick you up at ten x

> **MARY**
> Any hints? Dress code? Pushchair or papoose? Snacks?

> **SOFIA**
> Nope

Once Bob woke up, I had plenty of time to do a half-hearted tidy-up, shoving all the costume stuff in the dining room. While he enjoyed his morning snooze, I showered and dressed in my most versatile outfit, which was wide-legged jeans with a stretchy waist and a smart bottle green cashmere jumper that Shay had given me after deciding it was too baggy on her. I could fit into about half of my pre-pregnancy clothes now. While I loved having a change from leggings and joggers, it did feel daunting, as if this was another step out of my self-imposed hibernation.

I packed up a bag for Bob, checked I'd got my purse and a water bottle, and sat fretting until a car pulled up at ten past eleven, and the coffee mums tumbled out.

The moment I opened the door, they spilled inside, with various cries of greeting, hugs and smiles.

'Am I allowed to ask what this is yet?' I asked, the trepidation clear in my voice.

'Didn't Sofia tell you?' Rosie asked, shaking her head at her friend. 'What about the no secrets rule?'

'This isn't a secret. It's a fun surprise,' Sofia retorted.

'Look at the poor woman. Does she look like she's having fun?' Rina said, putting a sympathetic arm around my shoulder. 'Go on, Li. It was your idea. You tell her.'

'It's Li's birthday spa day!' Li held out her hands like an old-fashioned game show hostess showcasing a prize.

'I'm pretty sure babies still aren't allowed in spas,' I said.

'They are in Li's birthday spa,' Li said, beaming.

'Come on, the rest of us have got a child free day,' Rosie said. 'No offence, Mary, but I for one don't want to waste a minute.'

'I don't think I've got a swimming costume. Or a birthday present for Li.'

'Not a problem. We guessed as much,' Rina said. 'It's all sorted. Cossie, robe, slippers, and the present is your presence. Off we go.'

And then I was bundled out of the door and into Sofia's people carrier while still trying to get my second boot on.

Once Bob was strapped in beside me, and Rosie's DJ husband's 'Cracking Good Christmas Crackers' playlist was turned up high enough to drown out the caterwauling to 'One More Sleep', they confessed that the spa was back at Li's house.

She'd only come to pick me up because she wanted to see the look of joy on my face. I apologised for her wasted trip and tried to look suitably excited.

'Itinerary for the day,' Li announced after insisting the music was turned off so we could pay attention. 'Brunch upon arrival, followed by hot tub, then Ellie and Kendra will do treatments. We've a winter-themed afternoon tea and time for more hot-tubbing, Jacuzzi, nap room or gym. We're missing a pool, and the sauna and steam-room stuff, but you can always sit in the airing cupboard or turn the fire up until we start sweating, if it'll make more of an authentic spa experience.'

'Li, I have never been to a spa,' Sofia said. 'You could have stopped at brunch and I'd be happy. Mary, have you done a spa day before?'

I had. Our ShayKi directors' away days had often involved sipping prosecco in fluffy robes by the side of a pool while discussing five-year goals and brainstorming future plans. None of these future plans had featured an argument so ferocious that one director packed her bags and fled the company, her apartment and twenty years of friendship, never to be seen again.

The next six hours were as heavenly as any high-end luxury spa could be.

Even better, because we had the whole place to ourselves so didn't have to bother about things like overly hairy, overly friendly men climbing into the hot tub and interrupting our conversation, having to queue for fresh towels or feel guilty about bagsying the good loungers.

Li had arranged for a private caterer to serve us all brunch. We had pastries and coffee, followed by eggs and smoked salmon on sourdough and pots of berries with a bite-sized pancake on the side.

We then spent a long time sipping mocktails in the hot tub on

Li's patio, gazing at the fields stretching out across the valley beyond her garden, not another living soul in sight.

I had a massage and a facial with Kendra, and it felt as though, for the first time since discovering I was pregnant, every muscle in my body was able to breathe out and relax.

'I think my bones have turned into marshmallow.' I sighed, sinking into an orangery sofa and eyeing up the mugs of soup the caterer had just brought in to accompany the platter of warm cheese scones with lashings of butter.

Rina, cuddling Bob on the opposite chair, smiled. 'You look like a whole new woman.'

'I think I am one,' I replied ruefully. 'Or, at least, becoming her. It's as if I've been in a cocoon since moving to the forest. My old identity, all the things I thought were important about myself that gave me value, have dissolved into caterpillar mush. When Bob was born, I genuinely had no idea if anything in the mush was salvageable. I had no idea who I was now, let alone how to be her.'

'It's huge,' Li said, helping herself to a mug. 'Becoming a mum is taking on a whole new identity, but most of us get to keep enough of our old one to still hang on to our true selves, even as they inevitably change and grow. You were in a whole new place, with nothing and no one from before to anchor you. How *did* you not completely lose the plot?'

I gave a wry laugh. 'I'm not sure I didn't, for a few weeks there. But you, the Christmas Twins entrusting me with this new project—'

'Beckett,' Rosie chipped in with a smirk.

'Beckett,' I conceded. 'You all helped me realise that maybe I'm not a catastrophic failure, despite all the evidence.'

I took a thoughtful sip of tomato and lentil soup. 'I might even end up liking this version of myself more than before. I grew up being told constantly that I wasn't good enough, because I didn't care about the right things. I then spent my twenties trying to be this badass, ultra-successful businesswoman, so no one would notice I was a woefully unremarkable girl from Sheffield scrambling to keep up with her highly impressive friends. Then I met Bob's dad.'

Everyone suddenly leant forwards in their seats.

'And I tried being someone else again. Spontaneous, carefree. Adventurous.' I shook my head. 'Only that was worse. I felt as if I was playing a role that really didn't suit me. But when it all imploded, I got the chance to rebuild from scratch, to create whatever kind of life I want for me and Bob. I've decided I love the countryside. Hanging out with inspirational women who seem to be perfectly content with being themselves. I think I'd like to plant some vegetables. And make my own cushions. I still need loads more time and space to figure things out, but in my grotty little cottage, I've got that. So, in answer to your question, Li, I don't think I had a true self to hang on to. I'm finally starting to get to know her, and it feels pretty good.'

'That's wonderful,' Sofia said. 'I happen to think you're very impressive. I've never lived more than a few miles from my family, and have been with Moses since I was a teenager, so I can't imagine having to pick up all the pieces and start again. Also, please can I have a cushion? Your sewing is pure art.'

'When you've finished all that, you should consider your new life including politics,' Rosie said. 'Or working for MI5.'

'What?' Rina screwed up her nose in confusion. 'What do cushions have to do with politics?'

'Nothing,' Rosie replied. 'But giving a speech like that and still managing to reveal literally nothing whatsoever about your entire life, apart from that you lived in Sheffield, is what impressed me.'

'Maybe today isn't the day to be sharing all that,' Sofia said.

'However.' She paused to look at me. 'If and when you want to share anything, because you've obviously been through something significant this past year, please know that every woman here has faced situations that certainly felt catastrophic at the time.'

'I think we should share.' Li put up her hand. 'Coffee mums have no secrets, and it feels weird you all knowing and Mary not. I want her to feel like properly one of us, not a hanger-on. I mean, that's if you want to know, of course?'

Did I want the chance to feel like less of a hanger-on for once in my life?

Oh, my goodness. My lunch went cold while I cried.

'Right,' Li said once she'd finally given in and let Sofia reheat my soup, because it was Li's house but also her birthday, and these were the type of women who tussled over who got to be kindest. 'I'll go first.'

She took a deep breath.

'I do know what it's like to have to start again with nothing. I was raised in a community calling themselves the Pioneers of Perfect Peace. I call them a controlling, soul crushing cult. We lived in a huge farmhouse in Lincolnshire. I only learned to read through our daily "moral studies", and knew nothing whatsoever about the world beyond our chain-link fence. My work, from six years old, was washing dishes and keeping the floors clean. If I missed a crumb, or left a smear on a greasy pan, I had to complete my Penitence. Usually a night in the coal bunker, or maybe sitting through a day of communal meals but not being allowed anything to eat or drink. You can imagine.' She sighed. 'Well, I hope you can't, but there we go. Anyway, I'd resigned myself to being married off to one of the Grand Pioneers like the other girls, but when my father announced that Herman had selected me, something inside me died. They thought I'd be happy, because he had no other wife, unlike the others, but I was petrified of him. He hardly ever spoke, and slunk from room to room, so I would often turn around and he'd be standing there, watching me. His first wife, Catherine, had died a few years earlier. They'd told us she had an incurable sickness. I think the sickness was Herman.

'Anyway, I decided to run away. I was sixteen, and had never been more than a mile from the farm. I had no idea that if I went to a police station or a hospital, someone would help me. My indoctrination included everyone outside our community, especially authority, being out to destroy us. I had no clue how to survive or protect myself, and when my father found me a few weeks later, living in an abandoned warehouse with a group of crack addicts, I was relieved.

'I still have the scars from the Penitence that followed. The only good thing to come out of those hellish weeks was that Herman did not want a "wilful wife". I was nineteen before anyone else chose me, and so beaten down I felt grateful a man in his sixties with three other women and nine children wanted to make me his next unofficial slave. For three years I played by the moral rules, took the abuse and the punishments and had every micrometre of my life controlled by a despicable human being.'

'How did you get out?' I asked, understanding why Sofia had suggested this wasn't an ideal topic of conversation for a spa day, but needing to hear the ending so I could stop feeling so sick to my stomach.

'Wife number three almost died giving birth. Afterwards she told me that if it wasn't for her children, she'd have let herself die. I knew it was a miracle I hadn't got pregnant yet, and surely only a matter of time, even with an older husband. This time, I stole a shotgun from the stores and walked straight out of there, my head held high. I did for my future children what I was too cowardly to do for myself.

'I went straight to a police station that time, thinking they must be better than the commune or a crack house. Someone found me a place in a homeless shelter, and the police raided the Pioneers of Perfect Peace, so there were no more child brides. Eons of therapy, adult education classes and cramming in every TV show I could find to figure out how stuff in the real world worked, and here I am.'

'Here you are, with a genetics degree, a job as a research scientist, one of the world's best husbands and a gorgeous baby,' Rina added. 'Not to mention organising a killer spa day.'

'This could make a great business,' Rosie said, with a much-needed change of subject so we could all recover from Li's story. 'At-home spa days.'

'Ha!' Sofia laughed. 'Can you imagine a spa day at my house? Crammed into my bath, using Mimi's bubble machine to make it seem like a Jacuzzi. The dog nicking our scones. Mess everywhere, kids bursting in demanding I find their football boots. Not many women have a house like this one.'

'Is anyone else going to share, or are you leaving me hanging?' Li asked as we moved on to cake.

'Mary's heard enough about my divorce from hell,' Rina said. 'Rosie?'

Rosie shoved in a large chunk of brownie. 'Ugh. You know I don't want to be that poor young woman who had cancer. Wasn't she brave? Isn't she inspirational? She fought so valiantly and was determined not to let it beat her! As if my nan and my cousin, and anyone else whose cancer is terminal, haven't tried hard enough. I had enough of feeding the tragedy gossip at the time.'

'Yes, but the point is we're showing Mary our catastrophe scars, so she's in the coffee-mum loop. Otherwise, next time you make a callous joke about chemo she'll just think you're a bit nasty,' Li said.

'I am quite nasty.' Rosie sighed. 'But I can summarise, as long as you promise not to feel sorry for me, Mary, or think that me still being here is anything to do with how strong I am, rather than an early diagnosis, brilliant doctors and the cruel unpredictability of cancer.'

'Of course.'

'Okay, I had bone cancer. Diagnosed at twenty-one, a month after I met Jay. Surgery, chemo, radiotherapy, became a bald, withered-up skeleton that smelled of vomit for a while. Gradually, inch by inch, got better. Got married. Got over it. Sort of. The end. Sofia's turn.'

Sofia got up, gave Rosie a kiss on the head, offered her a tissue, wiped her own eyes and braced herself.

'We spent four years trying to get pregnant, including failed IVF that broke us financially and emotionally. Adopting all the kids was the best gift, and the biggest challenge. We deal with the after-effects of their trauma, every single day. From a teen who's discovered that vodka temporarily numbs the pain, to a toddler who deliberately hurts herself. It's hard, some days, not to feel sad or angry or hopeless. It's impossible not to worry. I mostly have no clue what I'm doing, and if I didn't have Jesus I'd have run for the hills by now. But I have five precious kids, so I'm only whinging a tiny bit.'

Whew.

'There's a reason we formed the coffee mums,' Rina said. 'Everyone goes through crap. Parenting is always a roller-coaster ride.'

'More like the ghost train,' Rosie muttered.

'Well, the ghost train is also a roller coaster, but thank you for that helpful interruption. Anyway, my point is we all bonded because we couldn't be doing with the droning on about ups and downs like potty training or whether we've got a place at the top nursery. On the flip side, we're all way past pretending things are fine when they're secretly falling apart.'

'Honestly, sometimes it's more like the big wheel,' Li mused. 'Round and round, dragging on unbearably slowly, every day the same, so boring but at the same time stressful because that creaky cable could snap at any moment.'

'I wish all I did was go round and round,' Sofia groaned. 'I feel more like we're on the bumper cars, getting knocked sideways every minute, my teeth rattling inside my skull.'

'Um.' I dared to pipe up, because this conversation was starting to undo all the lovely effects of the massage. 'Isn't one of the rules no wallowing?'

'Spoken like a true coffee mum!' Rosie exclaimed. 'Phew. The enforced sob-story sharing was supposed to make you feel better, not worse. I think Rina was trying to explain that none of us have much patience left for fakery or faffing about things that don't really matter. We've all learned the hard way that we need to be there for each other, but to do that we need to really be *there*, if you get what I mean.'

I did. I'd experienced how bad it could get when people tried to hide their problems.

We properly changed the topic after that, heading back to the hot tub via a stroll around the garden to admire the view from all angles. We talked about Christmas films, global politics and how Sofia handled her thirteen-year-old, Adina, wanting a phone for Christmas, potentially introducing her anxiety issues to the rampaging monster of social media.

I left feeling relaxed and invigorated in equal measure. When each of those women hugged me goodbye, I felt enveloped by authentic friendship.

I smiled all the way home. Even Bob crying for a solid twenty minutes for no discernible reason didn't knock me.

Then my phone pinged, notifying me of a Facebook message.

It was Shay.

My heart dropped through my pelvis and hit the ground with a jarring thud.

I'd blocked Shay and Kieran's phone numbers, binned my rarely used Instagram and, as Mum had discovered, my old email had been deactivated. It had been so long since I'd used my Facebook account, I'd not bothered to delete it.

I couldn't resist opening it.

SHAY

Can we talk? We miss you.

My finger hovered over the phone for a few seconds, a thousand thoughts and regrets zipping through my brain.

Deleted. Blocked. Done.

25

BECKETT

On Saturday, Beckett got a message from Moses inviting him to the Christmas trail at the Peace and Pigs, a campsite near Mary's house. It seemed a strange invite from one thirty-something male to another guy he didn't know all that well, and a quick look online revealed it to include a 'sleigh-ride', Santa's grotto and various food, drink and gift stalls.

He sent a quick reply.

BECKETT
> Are you asking me out on a date?

MOSES
> Sorry, bro, I'm a one-woman man. Sofia's having a day with her coffee mums, so the dads are taking the kids out. Mary's gone so we thought you might be at a loose end.

BECKETT
> You do know Mary and I are only friends?

MOSES
> Of course you are

Moses included a winking emoji.

MOSES

> We're meeting in the car park at 11. You in?

Beckett really needed to work. It was the busiest season, and his bank account was giving him nightmares. At the same time, he couldn't take Gramps out in the taxi again. He might have considered asking Moses to take Gramps to the Christmas thing, if small children weren't involved. Then again, if Gramps had a busy day, maybe Beckett could head out later, when he was asleep for the night? He'd been thinking about their argument, whether Gramps really did need watching every single minute. He didn't usually start night-time antics until at least two. If Beckett went out at nine, and was back for midnight, that would be something. And if it worked, he could make it a regular thing.

BECKETT

> I'll need to bring Marvin with me, but if that's okay then yes, count us in.

MOSES

> More the merrier!

It was an okay day. Disaster free, Gramps-wise, which was as good a bar as any. He met Jay, who had a baby a few months older than Bob, and was clearly struggling to reconcile his late-night event work with the responsibilities of fatherhood. There was also Angus, who'd been at the games night, with a one-year-old, Kimmy, who Beckett recognised as the daughter of Mary's new friend Li. Moses had all of his kids apart from Eli, the eldest.

They rode the sleigh, which was a cleverly decorated wagon pulled by horses wearing reindeer antlers, and the older kids ran about in the woods and found all the hidden candy canes that led them to Santa's grotto, where a band were playing jazzed-up carols. Beckett found he didn't hate his first ever family day out since he'd broken up with Rebecca. What he did miss was having his own family there. He couldn't help thinking about how, in future years, Bob would love seeing the animals and having hot chocolate and a hot dog before telling Santa Claus what he wanted for Christmas.

When Santa asked Beckett what he wanted, because apparently at this grotto no one was too old to sit in the special chair beside Santa and ask for a present, he knew without thinking about it.

This was what Beckett wanted. To get to do all this stuff with Bob and Mary. Christmas, spring, summer in the forest, bonfire parties. First day of school right through until graduation.

Bob might well have a dad who'd end up being part of his life. Beckett might never become more than a friend to Mary, because, despite how hard he couldn't help hoping for it, she'd never given the slightest indication that she felt anything for him beyond that. It didn't matter. He'd be Uncle Beckett, if he had to (*please, don't let him end up as Uncle Beckett*).

* * *

Once they got home, he kept Gramps awake with card games and an unhurried evening meal, then helped him up the stairs and ready for bed. At nine, heart hammering, he cracked open the bedroom door enough to confirm the snores, then left a note on the kitchen table, just in case, and sneaked out like a teenager off to an illicit party.

He did a full three hours of taxi driving, adrenaline pounding through his veins, then broke every speed limit to get home. All the lights were off as he hurried up the short driveway, but as soon as he opened the front door, Beckett could sense something was off.

He followed the draught to the door leading from the kitchen into the back garden, and, with a lurching stomach, spotted a shadow on the patio, up against the wall of the house.

Gramps was slumped on the ground, leaning back against the bricks, panting. When Beckett tried to remove the bread knife from his grandfather's clenched hand, the fingers were too stiff to open.

'What happened?' Beckett asked, slipping his thumb to Gramps' icy wrist to take his pulse. He'd managed to put on his dressing gown, but his feet were bare.

'I blummin' well slipped over in the frost. What does it look like?'

'Let's see if we can get you back in the warm.' Automatically switching to doctor mode, Beckett sounded calm, but a tornado of guilt and panic was tearing through his insides.

It took a gruelling effort, but, with lots of guidance and questions to ensure it was safe, he managed to hoist Gramps up and provide enough support to get him to the living-room sofa.

He made two mugs of sweet tea, decided against adding a splash of whisky, and made sure the combination of the fire, thick socks and a blanket were doing their job.

'Why were you outside?' he asked after an agonising wait while Gramps sipped his tea and slowly regained his normal complexion.

'I want to go to bed now.'

'Of course, I'll help you up in a minute. But why were you in the garden with a bread knife?'

Gramps stared at the fire, his careworn face scrunched in annoyance.

'I was making a sandwich. You always cut the bread too thin.'

There'd been no bread visible in the kitchen, or any other evidence of a sandwich being made.

'Okay.' Beckett kept his voice soft and steady, as if coaxing a mouse out of its hole. 'Why did you go into the garden?'

'Does it matter?' Gramps snapped. 'Am I the owner of this house, or its prisoner? I don't have to explain my every move to you.'

'No, you don't.' Beckett was too sad to feel irritated, or frustrated. He mostly felt defeated, alongside the lingering trickle of worry that Gramps had hypothermia or was hiding an injury. 'But I hope you can understand why I'm concerned about you going outside in the middle of the night in December with no shoes or coat on.'

If Beckett had learned anything in the past six years, it was patience. Eventually, Gramps slumped a little lower in his chair, handed Beckett the empty mug and closed his eyes.

'I didn't know where you were.'

Beckett's heart crumpled in on itself.

'I'd gone out in the taxi for a couple of hours,' he said gently, crouching beside Gramps and taking hold of his hand, which was still cool, but no longer stiff. 'I left a note in case you woke up.'

'Didn't see it.'

'I'm sorry.' Beckett's throat ached as he fought back the tears. He was sorry for more things than he could say. 'I'm so sorry you were frightened. I won't go out at night again.'

They sat for a while, staring at the fire until Gramps' hand was warm, his cheeks pink.

'Come on, let's get to bed. Maybe think about a lie-in in the morning, eh?'

As he helped his grandfather to his doddery feet, Beckett caught him mumbling something, but dismissed it as he must have heard him wrong. However, as Gramps allowed his grandson to tuck the duvet up around his chin, he said it again, and this time it was unmistakable.

'Put me in a home.'

'What?' Beckett froze. 'No. Gramps! I promised I'd never do that. *This* is your home, and you're staying right here. I'll figure it out, I promise.'

* * *

Gramps slept in for all of an extra fifteen minutes. It didn't matter, Beckett hadn't snatched more than a few restless minutes of sleep, anyway. He helped Gramps with his morning routine, checking for injuries as he dressed and mercifully only finding light bruising, although he was even more unsteady than usual.

'Be honest now,' he asked once they were both bolstered with coffee and plates of egg on toast. 'How are you feeling? Any aches or pains we need to worry about?'

Gramps chuckled grimly. 'Where do you want me to start?'

'Okay.' Beckett couldn't suppress a smile. 'Any new soreness or stiffness, relating to your midnight escapade?'

'I'll do.'

'We can take it easy today. There's a new film on Netflix I thought we might like.'

Gramps furrowed his brow. 'It's Sunday, isn't it?'

'Yes.' Beckett was piteously pleased that he'd remembered.

'I want to go to that funny church.'

'Funny as in amusing, or funny strange?'

Gramps quirked a bushy eyebrow, his eye twinkling as if to say, 'You tell me?' and for a rare, precious moment, Beckett had his grandfather back.

* * *

When he messaged Mary, she replied instantly to say that she'd come, as she had another three costumes ready for a fitting. Beckett was well aware she didn't need his invite or his offer of a lift, as if she couldn't find her way there herself. But, well, it was a thing now. Besides, he'd agreed to help her with the carol-concert project, and if she was bringing along costumes then that counted. He could hardly leave her to transport them and Bob on the bus.

This week the advent theme was apparently joy, and, boy, did New Life Community Church embrace it. Even Beckett couldn't resist tapping his toes to the exuberant rhythm of the songs. A trio of teenage boys playing brass instruments created an atmosphere more carnival than Christmas.

It felt good – great – being part of something lively and jubilant, going with the flow and rolling with the silly shepherd game everyone joined in with, the 'New Life News' accompanied by passionate prayers, the talk from Moses about joy-hunting in dark times.

He knew enough faces now to nod and smile at a few people, and afterwards at coffee time chatted with Jay and his wife, Rosie, while Mary was fitting three other Santas, and Gramps was having an unnervingly rational conversation with an older woman who had once upon a time worked in the same office as him.

'So, what's the deal with you and Mary?' Rosie asked. 'Whenever we drop hints, she changes the subject.'

'Drop hints?' Jay queried. 'Your hints are about as subtle as Cheris and Carolyn with a stack of concert tickets.'

'Okay, whenever we happen to politely enquire whether her and this one have graduated from the friend zone, she pretends to not know what we're talking about and changes the subject.'

Beckett took a gulp of coffee. It was still hot, and he had to cough several times before he could reply.

'No graduation. We're just friends.' At least he could blame sounding strained on the coffee.

'Maybe stop embarrassing him by asking about it, babe,' Jay added. 'Or her.'

'No offence, *babe*, but you can't censor coffee-mum conversation. We don't do shame or embarrassment. It's a safe place to share.'

'Isn't it also a safe place for people who've made it clear they don't want to share on a particular topic?'

'There's nothing to share about,' Beckett interjected, while very much 'doing embarrassment'.

'Why not?' Rosie said, turning to him, so matter-of-factly that for a second he was tempted to be honest.

Because she's clearly not interested. Because something big and awful happened, and she's not ready to talk about it. Because when the registrar assumed I was somehow involved, she sobbed her heart out.

Because she's the first proper friend I've had in six years. The best friend I've ever had, and I won't risk losing that.

'It... just isn't like that.'

'Puh-lease. We've all seen how you look at her.'

'Then you'll have noticed how she looks at me.'

'Yeah,' Rosie conceded with a nose wrinkle. 'She's kind of swamped with the whole new-mum thing, I suppose.'

She gave Beckett a firm poke in the chest with a pointy nail. 'Keep your eyes open, though. When she's ready for more, you want to be straight in there. Don't let some hot single dad or chatty charmer swoop in and gazump you.'

'Babe!' Jay took her hand before she could poke Beckett again. 'Back out. Reverse. Shut it down. Remember, we've talked about

The Most Wonderful Time of the Year 255

where the line is between friendly concern and interfering? And, gazumped? Mary is not a house.'

'I'm not a what?' Mary appeared next to Beckett, causing his face to flush horribly while Rosie grinned. 'A house? Sounds rude.' She glanced down at her wide-legged tweedy trousers and slim-knit jumper with a Christmassy pattern, showing that there was nothing house-like about her.

'I said you weren't a house,' Jay said, seeming as flustered as Beckett felt. 'It was nothing to do with your appearance. Rosie had been talking about...' He trailed off, glancing at Beckett in desperation.

'I'd been grilling Beckett about asking you out,' Rosie readily confessed. 'He quite rightly told me to butt out of none-of-my-business.'

'I never said that.' Beckett was starting to regret getting out of bed that morning. He didn't remember socialising as being this fraught.

Mary, to his astonishment, had dropped her gaze to the floor, eyes wide, mouth opening and closing. By the time her eyes darted up again, her face was scarlet.

'Interesting,' Rosie murmured.

'Okay, we're going to find Amber. Great to see you again, Beckett. Nice to meet you, Mary.' Jay, still holding his wife's hand, led her away.

The second they were gone, Beckett leaned in as close as he dared.

'I'm sorry, that was totally inappropriate. I shut her down straight away; told her we were nothing more than friends.'

Mary sucked in a deep breath and straightened up. His heart stuttered in his chest as her eyes met his, more blue than grey today, reflecting the colour of her jumper. 'Aren't we?'

It was said so softly, he had to read her lips.

Before Beckett could answer, which could have been anything from a microsecond to minutes, as he stood, dumbstruck, his brain in suspended animation, someone tapped him on the shoulder.

'I'm going out for lunch.'

Beckett jerked to attention.

'What?'

Gramps rocked back smugly on his heels, then almost toppled over before Beckett grabbed and steadied him.

'You can pick me up around three.'

Beckett shook his head, muttering, 'I have no idea what's happening any more.'

'Sandra and her friend Pauline have invited me to their monthly silver singles lunch. That's what's happening.'

'Who are Sandra and Pauline? Where is this lunch and, more to the point – what on earth, Gramps? A *singles lunch*?'

Gramps gave an airy shrug, as if he went to silver singles lunches all the time.

'Point them out to me.'

Gramps nodded to a suitably grey-haired woman chatting in a small group. Beckett wasted no time in striding over.

'Sandra?'

'Yes?'

'My grandfather tells me you've invited him for lunch?'

'Yes, isn't that lovely? We'd be delighted to have him join us.'

'Thank you for your kind invitation. Unfortunately, he won't be able to go.'

'Oh?' Sandra narrowed her eyes, behind fuchsia-rimmed bifocals. 'Marvin mentioned you might be snippy about it.'

'Me, snippy?' Beckett spluttered.

'He explained how you'd become somewhat co-dependent,

following a minor stroke several years ago. With all due respect, Mr Bywater—'

'Dr Bywater.' *Ugh*. That again.

'Do you think a doctor deserves more respect than any other human being?' she quickly replied, with a saccharine smile that made him want to argue back, even though he agreed with her completely. 'Does that automatically mean you know best? Is it time you allowed Marvin to reclaim some life of his own? One that isn't solely reliant on you and your "professional opinion"? A little distance is healthy.'

'We only came here today because he wanted to.' Beckett's nerves crackled with irritation. 'He was pretty reliant on me when I found him collapsed on the patio, in the middle of the night, half frozen to death.'

'Ah.' Sandra nodded sagely. 'May I suggest you don't allow your unresolved emotions about that to overrule your grandfather's desire to build alternative support networks? You can't protect him from every eventuality, Beckett. We're all going to die. He has the right to live freely until that happens.'

'Wow.' This morning really couldn't get any more surreal. 'Firstly, it wasn't a minor stroke. Gramps was in hospital and rehab for months. Six years later, he still has multiple complex needs requiring constant care. Given that you apparently now have a clearer picture of his life than I do, can I assume you're aware of the foods he can't eat, that he needs help cutting up meat and can't carry a plate of food safely? Oh, and I'm sure he's checked whether this lunch is somewhere with a downstairs toilet, one with a handrail, because otherwise someone from his alternative support network will have about twenty seconds' warning to lug him upstairs before incontinence strikes. You'll know about the lifesaving medications he needs, some before and others an hour after eating. He calls them his "control pills", so he'll refuse them, given much choice.'

Sandra blinked a few times behind her glasses. 'We have one or two other infirm attendees...'

'Perfect. I'll pick him up at three. You can message me the address, because Marvin doesn't have a phone.' Beckett gripped the back of his head. He really needed to calm down. Sandra wasn't wrong about last night having affected him. He sounded like an arrogant prig. 'Or shall we have a respectful, realistic conversation about how this would work?'

Fifteen minutes later, Bill had merrily agreed to tag along to the lunch as a one-off, on the basis none of the singles tried to flirt with him.

'And if it all gets too bawdy, I'm breaking us out of there,' he said to Gramps, tapping the side of his nose. 'I know what these lot are like. They'll be sneaking a peck on the cheek goodbye if we're not on our toes.'

There it was. Gramps was off again, in complete contrast to everything he'd insisted, refused and been stubborn about for six years.

And Beckett and Mary still hadn't made it past 'aren't we?' more than friends. With Bob whinging the whole way back to Mary's house in the car, there was no chance to answer. Even if Beckett did have the courage to reveal a hint of how he felt about that question.

When Mary declined his offer of lunch, or help with more costumes, with no explanation and a distressingly polite smile as he dropped her off, he accepted that Gramps' interruption was probably a blessing.

26

MARY

In fifteen years of being a badass businesswoman, I'd developed a pretty decent poker face. Apart from a momentary lapse when Rosie completely caught me off guard with her comment about Beckett asking me out, I thought I'd done a good job of concealing my escalating emotions since.

Too discombobulated to come up with a believable excuse for turning down lunch with Beckett while Grampa was elsewhere, I rudely rejected him outright, pretending not to notice the confusion and hurt flash across his features.

How could I eat lunch, drink tea, chat casually or even talk deep and meaningfully with this man, when I couldn't look at him without crumbling into a gibbering wreck?

I didn't know when or how the tug of attraction, the glimmer of possibility, the tiny spark of silliness had erupted into a full-on, all-consuming, what *had* to be a fantastical rebound crush on the man who'd turned up out of the blue like a white knight and changed everything.

We'd had our moments, absolutely.

When he'd shown me how to build a fire.

Speaking softly on the phone, curled up on the sofa watching the snow fall.

When the coffee mums had kept dropping it into the conversation at the spa day, as if it was an inevitability, my mind had started to wonder. To wander along trains of thought I'd not dared to consider.

Beckett was gorgeous, in every way. After Leo – especially now there was Bob – I needed trustworthy. For me, dependable was the new sexy. Leo's spontaneity and recklessness had initially felt compelling, as if it promised a life of thrills and excitement that would reveal me to be, for once, an exciting person, too. If I was honest with myself, and for hours that previous night I'd tried my hardest to be, I'd also found it quite stressful at times. Beckett was proof that safe didn't have to equal dull. He made me laugh, he challenged me and, however long we spent talking, I never grew bored or tired of hearing what he had to say. We agreed on the things that mattered – like, for example, what should matter – and yet were different enough to stimulate and interest each other.

Beckett was the first friend I'd had who made me feel like an equal. I never felt as if I had to try. He was only my third proper friend, but still. As part of ShayKi, I'd had a lot of acquaintances.

He was also the first person who'd made me feel as if I was enough, all the quiet, simple, straight edges of me. Even as, at the same time, he inspired me to keep clawing my way out of my lifelong slump.

My husband had certainly not made me feel that way.

Added to that, I kept circling back to the whole him-being-gorgeous thing.

I hadn't been sure I'd ever feel in a position to experience that kind of attraction again.

I'd done my best to shut it down, cram it in some dusty emotional corner behind my pain.

And then, last night, after thinking about Beckett before going to sleep, like the lost, lonely numpty I was, I'd dreamt about him.

We were back in the ShayKi offices, no doubt triggered by the message from Shay, and I'd been arguing with Kieran about something that made no sense, when I'd looked up and seen Beckett standing there. He'd walked over and enfolded my hand inside his huge one, towering above my old friends, and I'd leaned close enough for my arm to brush against his side.

I'd felt seen, and understood, and loved. What rocked me was that I'd known, subconsciously, that I was also desired.

This man would fight dragons, if I asked him to. While reassuring me that he absolutely believed I had what it took to conquer them myself.

I woke up, hot and flustered and feeling things I'd long forgotten about, and wondered how long it was appropriate for someone in my situation to wait before falling in love again.

I feared it was already too late.

* * *

Leo started working for ShayKi three weeks after the summer party. I hadn't been surprised when he'd got the job in the design team. What had rattled me was when Kieran invited me into his office and introduced me to his brother.

Leo smiled politely. 'We met briefly at the summer party, but I wouldn't expect you to remember.'

I gave a tight smile in return, making a sterling effort to retain my composure, while inwardly fuming that he'd omitted such pertinent information. 'Sorry, I met a lot of people that evening.'

His eyes remained brazenly on mine. 'Well, I'm a great

admirer of your work. I'm looking forward to seeing how things operate behind closed doors, as it were.'

'I wouldn't expect our paths to cross that often, but welcome to ShayKi. I wish you all the best.'

Did he have the audacity to try to *flirt* with me? In front of *Kieran*?

With a brief nod at no one in particular, I excused myself and marched back to my office, where I firmly closed the door, then leant against it, eyes closed and hand pressed against my chest until it stopped heaving, like a maiden in a Mills & Boon story.

After we'd kissed in the hotel garden that night, we'd done more talking and laughing and then kissed a whole lot more before I'd firmly sent Leo off in a taxi and crept up to bed, assuming that was that. I had noted the new follower 'LondonLeoDesign' on my neglected Instagram, but hadn't added anything apart from ShayKi posts since the party.

Of course, I'd spent the past few weeks thinking about him, replaying our conversations and blushing as I remembered our midnight kisses in the garden.

Now, he was working here. A one-time interaction with someone Shay went on to hire wouldn't be a major issue, if we both acted professionally from now on. However, snogging Kieran's brother was something I had no framework of reference for. He still had layers of issues surrounding his dad's other family, ones Shay had barely been able to uncover, let alone me. I could foresee only trouble and heartache, and angry firings leading to a nightmare lawsuit if anything happened between us again.

The problem was, there had been nothing professional in that stare. Or the way he'd held up his coffee mug as I'd glanced back and caught him still watching me through Kieran's open office door.

What scared me the most was how, underneath the annoyance and anxiety, that stare sparked a frisson of anticipation. The newly discovered rash part of me from the party was thrilled by the blatant hunger I'd seen burning in those electric-blue eyes.

* * *

I did half-heartedly discuss with my co-directors whether there could be any issue with employing a close relative. Shay confirmed that Leo had bags of talent and excellent experience, and while we'd worked hard to avoid nepotism since those early years in our attic workshop, we weren't going to reject an applicant on the basis that he shared Kieran's deadbeat dad.

It took three agonising days before Leo knocked on my office door.

'I was hoping to chat to you about one of the induction forms.'

I nodded to indicate he could come in. 'Oh? Which one?'

He closed the door and took a seat across from me. 'I don't mind. Any of them.'

I closed my laptop, hoping he couldn't hear my heart thudding beneath my dress. 'Excuse me?'

Leo grinned. 'It was the best reason I could come up with to come to your office.'

'Leo.' I sighed. 'You know we can't do this.'

'What, talk about induction forms?'

I did my best to sound stern. 'This is highly inappropriate.'

His voice softened. 'Tell me to get lost, and I'll go.'

He stayed.

* * *

We kept it secret for two months. Not easy, when both my office and bedroom were right next to his boss's. We met in random tiny restaurants on the other side of the city, went for long walks in the Peak District and spent a few weekends doing the kind of activities I'd never even considered before. We caught the Eurostar to Paris, a mini-cruise across to Rotterdam. We tried indoor skydiving, Leo talked our way into a celebrity party and we got up hideously early to drive to the coast and take a sunrise swim in the freezing North Sea. Everything felt wild and exhilarating. *I* felt a tiny bit wild. Our relationship was similar to a never-ending game of truth or dare.

We couldn't go to my apartment, so we were always at Leo's, which, along with my long-time habit of going with the flow, meant he set the tone and pace of our time together. Leo constantly encouraged me to give it a go, be brave, embrace the moment. I couldn't, however, quite find the courage to admit how it sometimes all left me longing for a chance to catch my breath.

Things rapidly intensified throughout the autumn. Leo constantly told me how much he loved me, how he'd never felt this way before, I was amazing, dazzling, beautiful. We were made to be together. After a lifetime of being slightly on the edge, feeling like the centre of someone's world was irresistible.

He did, however, seem to get a kick from growing increasingly reckless at work. He made comments in front of colleagues that were too personal, and the couple of times we were at the same meeting, he reached for my hand beneath the table and leaned in far too close. When I tried to half-heartedly confront him about it, he downplayed my concerns with jokes, and reassured me it was his job on the line, not mine, so I shouldn't worry about it.

Until, one afternoon in mid-November, Shay walked into my office the exact moment he pulled me into his lap.

'Right.' She pursed her lips. 'I'd thought as much.'

Then she walked straight out again. The door slammed so forcefully, Kieran came out of his office to ask if everything was okay.

'Ask her,' I heard Shay bark from the other side of my door. 'If she won't spill, then try your brother.'

* * *

We had a long, drawn-out, embarrassingly candid meeting that night, back at the apartment.

I told them everything, including that it wasn't an office fling. Leo and I were deeply in love.

'Darling, you don't know what love is,' Shay bit back, her hackles rising.

'No,' I retorted, which was uncharacteristic enough to get them listening properly. '*You* don't. Either of you. Neither of your failed attempts at relationships have even come close, so you've no right to preach at me.'

Now wasn't the time to add that if they had the first clue about love, they'd be married by now.

'You think skulking about the office having clandestine smooches in the stationery cupboard is any better?' She tossed her hair in disgust. 'That's not love, it's lust combined with the thrill of doing something forbidden. At least I'm under no illusions about the men I date.'

'If it was anyone else—' Kieran hadn't been able to look at me since he'd arrived '—we could figure something out.'

'No, we couldn't,' Shay snapped. 'No dating someone of a higher or lower position. It's plain and simple and we aren't making an exception for a director. Or a relative.'

'What about Lucy and Steven?' I threw back.

'That's not the same.' Kieran shook his head vigorously. 'They're married.'

'So, if you're married, it's fine?'

'You're the damn HR expert here. You know the protocols,' Kieran said. 'But you've known each other, what, two months? Marriage is hardly relevant to this situation.'

'Even if we didn't employ him,' Shay sneered. I was used to seeing her livid, shouting and swearing, throwing things – although never at me. This bitter contempt was withering. 'Why Leo, Mary? Knowing what Kieran went through? It's so wrong.'

'I don't know what Kieran went through!' I exclaimed, in full defensive mode. I'd finally found a good man, who was crazy enough about me to risk his dream job, and they couldn't even try to be happy for me. 'I wasn't part of the inner duo, so I didn't get to know that information.'

'You know he couldn't talk about it!' Shay finally lost her temper. 'You saw how he was whenever he came back from London. Are you so stupid, you couldn't figure out for yourself how this would hurt him? Or so spoiled and selfish, you don't care?'

'What?' All my bravado disintegrated, exposing the guilt-ridden mess cowering behind it.

'It's basic enough! You don't date your best friend's brother. Let alone *this* barely a brother. Who also happens to work for us. Honestly, Mary, could you have picked someone worse? If I didn't know you better, I'd think you were trying to cause trouble.'

'So, what now?' Kieran sounded numb. 'How do we fix this without it becoming a legal nightmare?'

Shay whipped her head around to look at him. 'Do you think that's why he did it? So he can sue us down the line? Screw you over?'

If you'd asked me up until this meeting, I'd have sworn that

Leo and I were two people in love who happened to have the misfortune of working for the same company. Leo not making a big deal out of it had meant I'd really not taken Kieran being his brother seriously enough.

Were they right, though? Was this all a scam to hurt Kieran? Was I the monumental fool who'd been so easily reeled in?

Even if it wasn't, I had no idea what to do about it.

Would I resign, if it meant Leo could keep his job, and I could keep Leo?

I'd known him for just over two months.

I couldn't breathe. My heart felt like a boulder sinking to the bottom of my chest.

'I'll sort it,' I said, voice strangled.

'How?' Shay demanded.

'I'm the HR expert. I'll come up with something.'

* * *

After three agonising days and sleepless nights, wracking my brains, scouring the company policies I'd helped write, I'd come up with nothing better than my first solution: to leave ShayKi. It took me another day of avoiding Leo's panicked messages before I plucked up the courage to fill him in. I was worried he'd insist on being the one to go. I was equally worried he wouldn't, because, although I was the person officially in the wrong, if he'd meant it about how much he loved me, he'd surely at least offer as a gesture.

His reaction floored me.

'So, we get married, then. Easy.'

I took a long moment before being able to reply.

'What?' It was all I could come up with.

'It's obvious, isn't it? I'm sort of offended you didn't suggest it already. Although I get you might have wanted me to be the one doing the asking. And I will, properly. I promise. If I'm honest, I've already started planning it.'

'What?'

'Mary Whittington, will you marry me?' Leo had dropped to one knee. He wiggled off the platinum ring he wore on his little finger and held it out to me. 'Come on. Don't make me sweat, here.'

'That's insane.'

Leo looked hurt. 'You think the idea of marrying me is insane? I thought it was inevitable. Sweet pea, the only insanity is how madly I'm in love with you.' He hesitated, dropping the ring slightly. 'I thought you felt the same.'

'I do! I do feel the same. You know I love you. But we've not been together that long. We haven't even met each other's parents.'

I hadn't even told my parents I was seeing anyone, and I suspected he hadn't either.

He shook that off. 'Do we really care what our parents think? It could take forever for us to get to the US with your work schedule. And from what you've said, they disapprove of everything else you do.'

'Well, yes...'

'It's you and me, Mary. We know how we feel. The only reason we risked all this is because we knew it was real. It's worth it because it's forever. You're my person. Why should either of us give up our jobs when we would have got married before long, anyway?'

He went on, reminding me how much he loved me, how he'd do anything to make me happy, how we should elope, the two of us, get away from all the haters and show them how serious we were about each other.

I'd spent my whole life desperate to belong, to come first. Now, the man I loved was asking me to do just that.

I had promised Shay and Kieran I'd fix it.

On Christmas Eve, I kept that promise.

I'd already spent the past few days hiding at Leo's house, avoiding the traditional Christmas activities with Shay and Kieran. Instead of helping Shay host the annual Christmas Eve bonfire party in our apartment block garden, I was getting married in the Sheffield Register Office, the only witnesses two strangers we'd found off the street, which Leo thought was romantic and I found cringy and awkward.

Determined to do the whole thing differently, to play down the magnitude of the moment, we bought each other the tackiest Christmas jumpers we could find, and wore those. Afterwards we went to a cosy pub we'd never visited before, and got drunk enough to sing 'Fairytale of New York' in the karaoke competition. When Leo announced we'd just got married, we were bought so many drinks I could barely stagger home. After sleeping our hangovers off for most of Christmas Day, we caught the first Boxing Day flight with free seats at Sherwood Forest airport, to a tiny island off the Welsh coast called Siskin.

A true Leo honeymoon ensued. All last-minute plans and spontaneous adventures.

Or, he proudly told me, a true Leo-and-Mary honeymoon.

He kept stopping to tell me how much he loved his wild-hearted wife.

His wife didn't tell him how much she wanted to get back to her job and a familiar routine.

Or how much she missed the friends she'd left behind there.

27

MARY

All of a sudden, it was the Monday before Friday's dress rehearsal, and I still had eight outfits to either finish off, adjust to fit, or, to my agitation, start from scratch.

Back when I'd volunteered for this enormous project, I hadn't quite accounted for how little time there was with a baby who wanted feeding, and keeping clean, and needed cuddles and smiles.

I'd never done this without Shay and Kieran to help with the trickier bits. I had brilliant ideas, but neither the time nor the skill to make them happen. Some parts just needed an extra pair of hands. Thankfully, these days, I was being offered several.

When I let Sofia know I couldn't make coffee morning, she somehow read between the innocuous lines of my message.

MARY

> Sorry, not going to make it today. I need to work on the costumes. Hope that's ok x

SOFIA

No it's not ok. Where are you on a scale of calmly working to a perfectly achievable schedule, that happens to allow no time to hang with your friends, and rampaging panic attacks because no way on earth will you be ready on time? And how can we help?

MARY

I'm somewhere between Officially Freaking Out and beating myself up for volunteering for something I should have known I couldn't handle. Had a brief moment of weakness and looked online for fancy-dress shops. I don't know how you can help – don't shun me when the NLCCCCC is a giant wardrobe malfunction?

SOFIA

Right. We're on our way.

Within the hour, I had four women, too many small children and two more sewing machines set up in my dining room. They'd brought cake, of course, as well as a tub from Rosie's freezer that she thought might be sausage casserole. Most importantly, they brought stories, jokes, unrelenting positivity and some much-needed perspective.

'I can promise you, Mary, you could throw together costumes that are ten times worse than the Princess Santa outfit you made me, and they'd still be the best we've ever had. We've barely made it past tea-towel and dressing-gown shepherds. One year, we had an angel wearing a white bin-bag, because they spilt Coke on their original robe at the last minute,' Rina reassured me as she glued tiny stars onto Star Santa's dress.

'Besides, while these costumes will blow people away, if the last few aren't that special, everyone will be far too distracted with the utter bonkersness of the script to notice,' Rosie added, adjusting the buttons on Shrek Santa's waistcoat.

'Don't forget the props,' Li said, eyes widening as she ironed the creases out of some stubborn velvet, assuring us that she'd be more help if she didn't sew. 'Cheris and Carolyn have asked to borrow our ride-on lawnmower.'

'They've convinced Moses to let them hire a snow machine,' Sofia said, shaking her head as she cut out a pattern for Joseph's tunic.

I couldn't help smiling. 'While on the one hand I wish it were another month away, at the same time I can't wait to see it. For many different reasons.'

Whether the concert turned out spectacularly, or turned into a spectacle, it would be a night to remember.

By the time they'd all left, just after two, the progress we'd made more than made up for the time spent clearing up the trail of destruction created by four small children left largely to their own devices for hours.

The women were all too busy to offer much time for the rest of the week, but they promised to drop in when they could, and at the very least bring more cake.

I looked at the pile of fabric, weighed it up against the finished costumes hanging up along the living-room curtain rail, listened to Bob starting to whimper and called the man I most wanted to see, who the very thought of also happened to put me in such a tizzy, my finger trembled as I pulled up his number.

'Hi.' Beckett sounded slightly breathless – *relieved?* – when he answered. 'Are you okay?'

'Yes. And no.'

I went on to stammer out the situation, and unsurprisingly he listened, took notes and made me feel reassured as no one else could have done.

'I'm sorry,' I said once we'd come up with an action plan.

'For what? We already agreed that I'd be your assistant. I hoped you'd be calling on me far more than this.'

'Hoped?' My heart leapt, lodging itself somewhere behind my voice box. I really needed to get a grip on whatever these feelings were.

It's called love, you numpty, Shay's amused voice replied inside my head. *This is what it feels like. Not a charming man duping you into believing your whirlwind affair was a lifelong passion.*

Beckett cleared his throat. 'I don't exactly dread hanging out with you, Mary. If you hadn't picked up on that by now.'

'Right. Okay.' Thank goodness we were on the phone so he couldn't see me swooning. He didn't dread hanging out with me! What more could a girl want?

'Anyway, that's not why I'm apologising. I'm sorry for being a bit off yesterday. I told you I didn't need any help and that wasn't true.'

I didn't know if I wanted him to ask me why or not. Then again, if he did ask, I'd not have the courage to answer honestly. Not when we'd just arranged for him to spend a considerable amount of time at my house over the next few days.

'That's okay. You don't have to explain.'

I breathed a mental sigh of relief. I didn't want to make up some excuse about being tired, feeling unwell or something else that would mean lying to my friend.

'Any of it. Until you want to.'

'What?'

'I mean...' Beckett broke off, paused, then carried on, his voice more resolute. 'I'd love to get to know you better. Your whole story. I won't push or pry. I won't ask uncomfortable questions. But when you're ready, if it would help to share it with someone, I'd love to be the person to listen.'

'Thank you.'

And then I was crying again, dammit. Because I was tired and overwhelmed and about ready to pack my bags, call a taxi and pretend I'd never set foot in New Life Community Church, yet this kind, patient, understanding man always – *always* – managed to make me feel better.

* * *

For the next three days, I sewed and snipped and stressed out, and Beckett made pots of tea and rounds of toasties, listened to my self-doubt-fuelled rantings, cooked, tidied up and did menial but vital tasks like donning wings so I could adjust the straps or picking up the giant pot of buttons I'd clumsily scattered across the floor. Gramps was there, too, of course, cuddling Bob, watching quiz shows and occasionally shuffling about, inspecting my dodgy wiring.

The coffee mums popped in sporadically and handed out cookies or mince-pie cheesecake, did some of the simpler stitching or passed me feathers, rubber tubing or whatever else I needed.

When my eyes grew so tired the stitches blurred together, Beckett would drive us all to his house and head back out taxiing, while I kept Gramps company and then helped him to bed. I'd never assisted an elderly man in getting undressed and into his thermal pyjamas before, but we managed it with humour and historical anecdotes if things got a bit awkward.

When Beckett came home, we ate a late supper of cheese on toast or cinnamon bagels, accompanied with a tonic and gin (that I suspected he'd bought especially for me) and easy conversation until I knew I'd fall asleep if I didn't call myself a taxi home.

Aside from all the anxiety, the frustration of a jammed sewing machine or swatch of netting that just wouldn't sit right, it was the best few days I'd had in a very long time.

It felt like home.

Beckett felt like home.

I couldn't help my antenna twitching for any sense that he might feel the same way about me. I must have been about as different from his ex-fiancée as you could get. Then again, he was nothing like the man I'd married, so I decided not to dwell too much on that.

On Friday, I spent the morning finishing off a few final touches, washed my hair for the first time all week, took Bob for a frosty walk in the forest and paced up and down the dining room, pausing to smooth a crease here, adjust a bow or a beak there, and waited for Beckett, my friend, hero and the man I'd pretty much fallen in love with, to take us to the dress rehearsal.

28

BECKETT

Beckett was exhausted, completely skint and happier than he'd ever been.

He'd spent the past few days with a warmth in his stomach that gently swirled like molten caramel. When Mary smiled, or her arm brushed his when working closely on a troublesome part of a design, or – if he was being honest – every time he thought about her, that warmth boiled over, spilling into every part of his body, making it hard to focus on anything else.

He'd been in love once before, but it was nothing like this. With Rebecca – even thinking about her made him feel like a traitor – he'd never experienced this combination of rightness, as if his world could be at rest now Mary was in it, alongside such keen anticipation, as if he was embarking on the adventure of a lifetime, one that would require him to be bold, gallant and true.

It took a Herculean effort at times to prevent the intensity of his emotions from showing on his face, leaching into the way he spoke or causing his touch to linger when he handed her a reel of cotton. Until either he knew more of Mary and Bob's story, or else she gave a clearer indication that she wanted more,

The Most Wonderful Time of the Year 277

he'd do the honourable thing and stay firmly as the friend she needed.

He'd been amazed at Mary's skill in coming up with designs for the motley crew of characters. Although she'd found executing some aspects challenging, rather than giving up, she'd taken the time to come up with alternative solutions, and had listened to advice as well as sticking to what she decided was best.

When he'd asked how she found the energy to work so hard on the costumes, alongside caring for Bob and helping out with Gramps, she'd told him that, if anything, the project had energised her.

'Doing something familiar, that you love, isn't really work, is it?' she'd mused, a row of pins in her teeth. 'Isn't there a quote about how when you find what you love, you never have to work another day in your life?'

'Which do you love most, the sewing or looking after your baby?'

'Shay would have said these costumes were her babies.'

'Shay?' Beckett looked up from where he'd been holding two pieces of silky fabric straight while Mary pinned them together.

She went still. Beckett held his breath, waiting for her to possibly offer a tiny morsel of her past.

'One of the other directors. We were best friends.'

'Were?' Beckett asked softly.

'I thought it was obvious when we met that I didn't have any friends left.' She jabbed in a final pin, moving away to squint at the fabric with a no-nonsense manner that made it clear the conversation was over. 'There. Time for a quick tea-break and then I'll tack it.'

He thought again about having a look online, for a director of an ethical fashion company called Shay, even though it didn't take a private detective to make the link between Shay and

ShayKi. But he'd made a promise. She'd tell him when she was ready. He could only hope that wasn't too long a wait.

* * *

When he arrived at the cottage on the afternoon of the dress rehearsal, Mary was almost as wound up as the first time he'd knocked on her door.

He was a few minutes late. It had taken longer than he'd expected to get a grouchy Gramps into the car. Usually, seeing Mary and Bob had him cooperating, but he'd been up since four that morning, insisting he needed a walk, despite the pavements being covered in thick frost and the air hovering around freezing. Gramps hadn't forgiven Beckett yet for locking the doors and hiding the keys. He probably never would, but he'd hopefully forget it ever happened soon enough.

'Wait, I have a tick list!' she called, making him stop at the front door so she could check off the armful of costumes he was carrying. After four trips to the car, two more to redirect Gramps back into the passenger seat and another to collect Bob's pram and his other stuff, Beckett found Mary still loitering in the hallway, practically wringing her hands with agitation.

'Hey,' he said, stopping right in front of her.

She squeezed her eyes shut, giving her head an irritated shake before opening them again. 'I can't seem to keep it together. After everything I've been through, a silly, small-time carol concert has me crumbling into pieces.'

'Because you know it's not silly or small time to Cheris, or Carolyn, the cast and crew or most of that church.'

'I know that.' Mary shook her head again, face screwing up. 'I know it's not silly. But the last time I did anything like this was

London Fashion Week. I felt excited, and eager and proud. Now, I'm scared witless.'

'What are you scared of?' Beckett asked softly.

'What *aren't* I scared of?' She gave a watery laugh. 'I'm terrified they won't like the costumes. They're too much, over the top, show-offy. Like wearing a fur coat and Prada heels to pick up a pint of milk from the corner shop. I'm *petrified* they'll not fit, or fall apart or unravel at a crucial moment, as I'm doing right now.' She sucked in a juddering breath, the rest of it coming out all in one go.

'I'm scared I'll fail at the first thing I've ever tried on my own, or taken responsibility for, without my friends to sort me out or tell me what I've done wrong or got right. I've never been enough, not really, not good or intelligent or brave enough, and for a while here I thought I could be. My dead end opened up to a new start, and I dared to hope this time it would be different. But what if I'm wrong? I've gone and ruined something really special and everyone will resent me, or, even worse, pity me while pretending it doesn't matter. They will be perfectly pleasant to my face, but we won't be proper friends, we won't be equals, because I let them all down.' She groaned. 'Why didn't I stick to my limits? What a selfish way to prove some petty point. All I can think about is racing to the fancy-dress shop in Nottingham and grabbing whatever they've got. I don't think I can do it, Beckett. I can't show up there with this. With my heart and soul and the best of me, and it not be good enough…'

'Mary.' Beckett placed his hands on her hitching shoulders, repeating her name firmly until she looked at him, as he'd learned back in medical school. 'Breathe with me.'

There was no point correcting her while she was in no state to listen. He swallowed back the surge of anger that she'd been made to believe total hogwash about not being good enough in the first place.

Growing impatient after a couple of shaky exhales, he simply dropped his arms and enfolded her into his chest.

'Remember what they said?' he murmured. 'Sofia. Bill and the others? Yara cried. She said she'd wear her dress to get married in. Everyone loved their costumes. Those Christmas Twins are nothing if not straight talkers. They'd have told you if they were too much, or in any way not good enough.'

Mary hiccupped a couple of times as Gramps wandered back in from the car for the third time, causing Beckett to marvel yet again at how his grandfather somehow managed to always find the dexterity to do what he wanted.

'They are incredible. Because *you* are incredible. Even if a bunch of clothes you had a month to make weren't good enough – which they are, I genuinely don't think anyone could have done better – even if they were load of rubbish, it doesn't mean *you* aren't enough. You are a good enough mother, with hardly anyone to help you—'

'You help me,' she whispered, to Beckett's relief, because it meant she was listening.

'A single mum, recovering from... from something catastrophic, and you've still got on with it and done an awesome job. You are good enough for Gramps, which only two other people have managed lately, his own grandson definitely not being one of them. You're a great friend to the coffee mums.'

'What if they only came and helped because they knew I couldn't do it by myself?'

'Of course you couldn't do it by yourself. If I've learned anything the past few weeks, it's that most things are far better done with someone else. But they helped because they love you, and had fun doing it.'

Beckett took in a deep breath, which was a mistake because his expanding chest felt every inch of Mary pressed against him.

His voice dropped to a whisper.

'You're too good for me, Mary. Far more than enough.'

She didn't say anything, but simply sighed into his sweater, as some of the tension left her body.

Beckett stood there, in heaven and hell at the same time.

Gramps appeared in the kitchen doorway, carrying a spanner that he'd picked up from somewhere.

'Aren't you done canoodling yet? I thought we were going back to the lunch place?'

Beckett dropped his arms, unable to resist placing a soft kiss on the top of Mary's head before he moved away.

It was only after she'd wiped her face, straightened her jumper embroidered with pine trees, and smoothed back her hair that she met his worried, lovelorn gaze.

'How come you always know exactly the right thing to say?' she said, managing a hint of a smile. 'Is it a Dr Bywater tactic?'

'Definitely not.' He ducked his head, trying to sound casually wry to negate the flush spreading up his neck. 'Come on, if you're all done fishing for compliments. Let's not keep them waiting. The show must go on.'

He picked up the car seat containing a snoozing Bob and started towards the front door, but Mary caught his hand, pulling him around to face her.

'Thank you,' she said.

He grinned, even as his heart burst. 'You're welcome.'

'Not only for today. For... For being my friend. When I needed one most.'

Beckett doffed an imaginary cap. It seemed he'd lost control of his faculties. 'I can promise you, the pleasure was all mine.'

***

New Life Community Church was abuzz with activity. In the centre of this circus were, of course, the two Christmas Ringmasters. Resplendent in their own Santa and Mrs Claus outfits, with red glittery fabric and silver trim, Cheris and Carolyn gripped A3 clipboards from which they merrily called out announcements in line with the schedules they'd handed out.

Mary and Beckett missed a lot of the rehearsal, being in a Sunday school room that had been commandeered as the dressing room. One after the other, cast members came to don their finished outfits, and each time Mary seemed to relax a little bit more as her creations were greeted with gasps, grins or stunned admiration.

She frequently would turn to Beckett, eyes wide with wonder. He'd smile back, give a nod of encouragement, or shake his head with a light-hearted eyeroll to say, 'See?'

When the last cast member had slid into their Slug Santa outfit, and slithered backstage ready for their big number with the Boyband Santas, Mary turned to Beckett, grabbing his hand.

'We did it,' she breathed, eyes shining into his. 'They were okay.'

Beckett gave her a sideways look. 'They were not even close to okay. Bill reckons they'll be the talk of the show. Moses is considering auctioning them off in the new year to raise money for the food bank.'

Mary grinned back at him, radiant, and Beckett wanted to pause this moment so he could imprint every detail in his mind forever.

'Shall we go and watch the last few minutes? Sofia said Bob's big break will come right at the end.'

They made their way around the side of the main hall, which

was gradually being transformed into a giant Santa's grotto by Moses' auntie and the stage crew. They were sticking pictures of elves at work on the walls, and underneath the huge tree was a growing pile of presents donated for vulnerable children. There was even an animatronic elf set up as if loading a present into a wooden sleigh.

'Is it me or does that elf look quite sinister?' Mary giggled as they found a spot to stand near the back wall.

'I wouldn't want to come across one in a dark alleyway on Christmas Eve,' Beckett said. 'Apparently it was donated by a journalist from the local news, Bea Armstrong, who always covers the carol concert on her feel-good slot.'

'Oh, they're starting up again!'

Beckett was trying to be casual about it, as if he'd barely even noticed, but he and Mary were still holding hands. In reality, it was just about all he could think about.

He'd not kept holding her hand, in line with the friend-zone boundary, but he hadn't let go, either, just sort of done nothing, and her fingers had definitely tightened around his as they'd weaved their way through the hustle and bustle.

Now, the lights dropped across the hall, leaving a single spotlight on a manger in the middle of the stage, where Beckett knew Bob was lying, even if all they could see from this distance was an occasional tiny arm waving about before disappearing again.

There was total hush for a few seconds, as everyone stopped what they were doing to watch, and then the voice of a small child drifted across the darkness.

'Every year, children like us write letters to Santa Claus, asking for toys and things. A puppy or a new bike. But the real gifts of Christmas can't be found in a stocking or under the tree. They're something even Santa can't bring down the chimney.'

Another child took over from the first one. They sounded

about five. 'The first ever Christmas presents were peace, hope and joy. Love like never did get seened before.'

'A miraculous mystery, where the giver became the gift.'

'And this gift is for all of us, for all time. Young, old, rich or poor…'

Gradually as the children carried on talking, more lights went up, revealing more people. They looked even better lit up on stage than they had in the dressing room.

'Everyone is welcome and all are invited.'

'Sounds like this place,' Mary muttered.

'But the gift doesn't stop there. All of us can bring these gifts, free of charge, to those around us. Peace, hope and joy. I hope I get an Xbox, because I've been wanting one for ages, but instead of thinking about what *you* want for Christmas, why don't *you* be a Santa?'

'If everyone was a Santa, bringing the true gifts of Christmas, then it really would be a merry Christmas.'

At that, the stage lit up, the band began to play, and the cast went wild, belting out Shakin' Stevens 'Merry Christmas Everyone'.

Every person in the room stopped what they were doing to dance, clap and sing along.

Mary sang, but she held tight to Beckett's hand as she swayed, so that their arms kept touching.

When the song reached its climactic finish, to enthusiastic cheers and applause, Mary turned to Beckett, a bashful smile on her face, and he needed no more confirmation that this was the sign he'd been hoping for.

He tugged Mary gently closer to him, and, moving slowly enough to spot the flash of horror should there be one, he bent down and kissed her.

* * *

The rest of the evening passed in a blur. After a brief, sweet kiss that sent Beckett's heart tumbling into freefall, they both ducked their heads, hands dropping and stepping quickly apart as the main lights came on in the room, highlighting the dozens of people scattered about.

'There you are!' Cheris appeared, throwing glittery arms around Mary, jigging up and down a few times before one final squeeze and letting go. 'The costumes are a triumph! If Santa Claus had delivered them direct from Christmas HQ, they couldn't have been better. You are a blessing sent from heaven. You have to stick around forever now, because nobody can come close to those, and I'm not sure we can come up with a plot including Racing Pigeon Santa and the Very Hungry Camel every year.'

'Maybe get the big night over with before we start talking about next year.' Mary laughed before her head tilted as she tuned in to a familiar wail. 'Oops – that's Bob. I'd better go and fetch him.'

She gave Beckett a shy smile, unable to meet his eyes, and slipped through the hubbub to the stage.

'Looks like all your Christmases came at once.' Cheris gave Beckett a wink and a hard jab with her elbow before bustling off on more Christmas Twins' business.

He fetched Gramps from where he was lecturing some teenage lads on how to saw MDF, and, once Mary had checked all the costumes were safely hanging on a rail in the dressing room, they headed out. It took a while to weave their way through a gauntlet of compliments and congratulations before finally reaching the car park.

The atmosphere in the car crackled like Christmas Eve.

Gramps and Bob both fell asleep before they'd reached the city boundary, but as they left the glow of multicoloured lights for the dark of the countryside, Beckett still had no idea what to say to the woman he'd just kissed.

'Well done,' he said, cringing as he made what was about the inanest comment possible, under the circumstances.

'Are you talking about the costumes or the kiss?' Mary teased, leaning against the back-seat window.

'Is it normal to give feedback on a first kiss?' Beckett asked, because his brain was still floating on a deliriously happy post-kiss cloud and incapable of coming up with anything better.

'Well, no. It isn't normal to kiss your best friend and then make no comment at all. Someone had to mention it.'

'Yeah. I was waiting until we were alone.'

Mary was quiet for a while before answering.

'Now all I can think about is whether the kiss was well done. Are you waiting to talk about it because it was terrible? I promise I won't make things awkward if you want to pretend it never happened.'

Beckett couldn't help a bark of laughter. 'Are you serious? Did you miss the tiny hearts flying around my head? Was it only me who heard the orchestra? At the very least, you must have seen my goofy grin.'

'So... you don't regret it?' she asked quietly.

'Um.' Beckett tried to come up with a response that didn't include blurting how he'd been wanting to do it for weeks. Recently, to the point where he'd barely been able to think about anything else. 'Only if you do. If I misread the situation, or *you* thought it was awful...'

Mary leaned forwards and gently poked his shoulder. 'Maybe I didn't see your grin because I was still dazzled by the fireworks. Or did you not spot those?'

Beckett's insides dissolved into mush.

'I haven't messed up our friendship?'

'You've totally messed it up. There's no way we can stay friends after a kiss like that,' Mary said, incredulous. 'If you've no intention of performing more non-friendly gestures, I'm going to be extremely cheesed off.'

He resisted the urge to pull over right there in the middle of the woods and perform a non-friendly gesture. A baby was present, after all.

He settled for a corny 'Duly noted', and they drove for a few minutes in silence, before resuming a conversation about the rehearsal, Beckett's half-hearted attempts to find an independent carer, and Gramps' more recent nightly escapades. Attraction hummed through every word.

They'd agreed that Beckett would drop Mary and Bob off and head straight home, but Beckett's heart began thumping wildly as they approached Mary's drive. He'd obviously be walking her to the door, carrying Bob inside. She'd been very clear how she felt about a kiss goodnight.

Only then, he saw another car parked in the driveway. A black Lexus.

He sensed Mary stiffen behind him. Glancing in the mirror as he slowed to a stop, he caught her mouth dropping open in shock, eyes fixed on the shadowy figure of a man leaning against the car.

'Are you okay?' he asked. 'Do you know this person?'

Mary was already clambering out of the door.

Beckett hastily unclipped Bob's seat and followed her over to the other car.

'What are you doing here?' Mary asked, her tone brittle.

'You blocked me. I was worried about you. We knew the baby

must be born by now. I had to know whether you were okay. Both of you.'

'Really?' Mary stuck her hands in the pockets of her fake-fur coat. 'You weren't that bothered back in April, when you called my son an irresponsible mistake.'

'You had a boy?' the man said, his voice full of emotion.

'Yes,' Mary snapped, but it was a half-hearted retort and Beckett could see her shoulders dropping as her initial anger drained away. 'He's got your eyes.'

The man jerked his head back. Mary couldn't look at him.

And then he stepped forwards, wrapped his arms around her and she fell against him, both of them sobbing how sorry they were.

Beckett carefully walked over to the cottage and placed the car seat containing Bob in the porch.

He had no idea how he got back to the car. It felt as though the earth had tilted on its side. Everything was wrong and he had no centre of gravity any more.

Mary had become his centre of gravity.

And now he'd lost her, a mere moment after they'd begun.

29

MARY

I led Kieran into the cottage. What else could I do?

Well, the part of me still bitter and broken from what had happened argued. *You could have told him to get lost, instead of embracing him as if all is forgiven.*

He could still head home and arrive well before midnight. He'd no doubt have some fun activity planned with Shay for tomorrow, the Saturday before Christmas.

But it was Kieran. Bob's uncle. The concerned crease below his white-blond fringe had triggered a response similar to stepping out of a storm into a warm house.

Beckett had slipped away, so I made two coffees, automatically adding loads of frothy milk and sugar, how Kieran liked it. After chopping two thick slices of a leftover yule log that Rina had brought, I took a seat at the table opposite Kieran. As always, I waited for my friend to take the lead.

'What's his name?' Kieran nodded at Bob, still asleep in his car seat.

'Robin Timothy, after my great-grandfather. I call him Bob.'

'And is he... Are you... Has it been okay?'

'What, giving birth and then figuring out how to look after a baby, by myself?' I shook off another boulder of hurt. 'It's the hardest thing I've ever been through, by a mile.'

Kieran started to reply, his face creased in sympathy, but I hadn't finished.

'But also the best. For the first time, as an adult at least, I've had to deal with it alone. Make my own decisions. Decide what to do and how to do it. Discover whether I could actually function without you two – or Leo – propping me up. And I'm doing it, Kieran. Or starting to. Some days, at least. I've bought a cot, learnt the mystery of how to fold a pram down one-handed. How to do almost anything while breastfeeding. He's put four pounds on, all down to nutrients from this slightly saggier body. I gave birth in a church. Made new friends who threw me a baby shower. This evening, I was at a dress rehearsal for a carol concert, which I created all the costumes for. It's been full of the challenges and heartbreaks that go with any adventure. The sleepless nights alone almost broke me. But they didn't. I feel like it might be the making of me. I'm a mum now. And even as some days I want to bury my head under the duvet until someone else handles my problems, mostly, I love it. I'm slowly, two millimetres forwards, one back, building a life here for myself, and for maybe the first time ever, I'm proud of who I am. Or, at least, who I'm becoming.'

'That's amazing.' Kieran wiped his eyes. 'I'm so made up that you're proud of yourself. I'm proud of you. Leo would be, too. Although this house is grim. You should let Shay work her magic, sort it for you.'

'Okay, firstly, we are nowhere near ready to be mentioning Leo. Secondly, Shay made her feelings on sorting anything out for me again quite clear.'

Kieran took a sip of coffee. 'We will have to talk about him at some point.'

'I know. I'll decide when that is.'

'And Shay would do anything to make things right with you. She's devastated.'

'Yeah, right. She looked positively bereft on that red-carpet thing she did a few weeks ago.'

'Well, she's hardly going to reveal her feelings in public, is she? She drove out to Chatsworth on your birthday and ordered a cream tea, in the vain hope you'd show up.'

It had become an annual tradition, a fancy cream tea in the stately home restaurant.

It was my turn to blink back tears.

'I ate a cheap supermarket scone here, followed by a prepacked sandwich and a dry fairy cake. Wearing my pyjamas.'

'Watching *Hamilton*?'

I nodded. We could sing every word off by heart.

'Did you tell her you were coming to see me?'

Kieran shook his head. 'She'd have been crushed if you turned me away.'

'And she'd never have let you come without her. You were worried that her tell-it-how-Shay sees it approach could have ruined any chance of me letting you meet your nephew. How did you know where I was, anyway?'

'You had to give your forwarding address to HR. I sneaked onto Naomi's computer when she was flirting with the DPS guy.'

'What, weird sideburns man?' I screwed up my face in disgust. Not because of the sideburns. The DPS guy gave every woman in the building the ick.

Kieran laughed. 'He was replaced months ago. The new one apparently looks like that actor from *The Bear*.'

'Fair enough.'

There was a brief silence – not awkward, exactly. Kieran and I went far too deep for that. Maybe, a charged silence? We were teetering out onto a frozen lake, the hidden depths of which included my marriage to his half-brother, and everything that came after. It could crack at any moment.

'I missed you, Mary.'

'Really?' It was a genuine question, with only a smidgin of self-pity. 'I always thought you and Shay were enough for each other.' I smiled. 'You, Shay and whatever random woman you happened to have picked up like a stray kitten that month.'

'Harsh.' Kieran winced. 'On both counts. We always needed you. How could you not know that? You balance us. Bring common sense and an aura of peace. We'd have murdered each other by now, without you.'

'So, you still haven't admitted you're madly in love?'

I had nothing to lose at this point with Kieran. I might as well say what I thought.

To my mild surprise, he didn't reel back in horror or get annoyed. He looked down for a long moment, released a slow sigh and then was honest about how he felt, for the first time in twenty years.

'Even if she did love me back, she'd rather stay alone forever than risk messing up ShayKi by acting on it. Our fights would only be ten times worse if we had the added complication of being together. Without you to steady us, it'd destroy everything.'

'Or, without the bubbling underlying tension of your forbidden feelings for each other, you might stop fighting all the time.' I sat back. 'I can't believe you just confessed you're in love with her.'

He shrugged. 'I'm getting tired of pretending it's not slowly killing me. Dating other people isn't so much of a useful distraction these days.'

'We should invite her down here.'

Wow. That popped out of my mouth without getting approval from my brain first.

'What?'

'Or were you fudging the truth when you said she missed me?'

'No, of course we miss you! We love you, Mary. I accept now isn't the time to talk about what happened, but I have to say that we are so sorry. We let you down in the worst way when you needed us the most. Nothing is the same without you. Christmas is a sloppy mess without your schedules and recipes and perfect presents.' He finished his cake. 'That's another reason I'm here. Obviously I was worried sick, and needed to see if you were okay. I was desperate to meet my niece or nephew. But as well as that, I wanted to ask you to come home.'

'Sheffield isn't my—'

'Not for good. I get you won't be ready for that. But for a few days? Show Bob a ShayKi family Christmas? Everyone will be thrilled to meet him.'

I shook my head. 'I don't think so.'

'What, you can't seriously want to miss the Christmas Eve party? Lori's nativity? To spend it alone, here?' He glanced around the dismal kitchen, and I felt a prickle of defensiveness.

'Who says I'm going to be alone?'

That made Kieran pause. 'The guy who dropped you off?' He raised one eyebrow. 'I'd say that was fast, but compared to Leo...'

'He's just a friend,' I protested, as if it were any of his business these days. As if there were anything 'just' about Beckett. 'A really good friend. Who was there for me when I needed him.'

Kieran nodded. 'He's not a bad-looking friend. Who looked about ready to throttle the man waiting outside your house. Maybe you should think about whether you could be interested in more than that.'

'Which brings us nicely back to you and Shay. I'm not going back to Sheffield any time soon, but I wouldn't object to her spending the day here tomorrow.'

'Really?' Kieran peered at me, a glint of hope in his eyes.

'We can have a ShayKi Christmas Day here. Heal some wounds. Get the band back together and find out if we can still be in the same room without screaming at one another or crying about what we've lost.'

'Who we've lost,' Kieran said, meeting my eyes.

I sighed. 'Nope. Still too soon.'

* * *

Kieran set off soon after that, arriving back at eleven the next day with Shay, and everything we needed for a traditional Christmas, our way.

I hovered in the doorway, Bob in my arms, while they hauled in a cool box each.

'Hey,' Shay said, uncharacteristically small-voiced, once we'd moved to the kitchen and I'd put Bob in his bouncy chair.

'Hi.'

'You blocked me,' she added, sounding full of hurt.

'You deserved it,' I replied, because it was true, and I wasn't intimidated by her any more. She was an awesome woman, but I'd learned recently that awesome came in all shapes and sizes.

'I'll get the rest of the food,' Kieran said, ducking back out of the door and leaving us to it.

'I did.' She gave a rueful smile. 'Can I have a hug anyway?'

'Yes. But it's a temporary truce, like that Christmas Day football match in World War One. I'm not pretending everything is all fine now.'

'Nothing is fine while you're here and we're there,' Shay said, squeezing me so hard my ribs creaked. 'I hate not talking to you every day. I hate you not telling me when I'm being a cow or my outfit doesn't work or how your day has been. I have 226 days to catch up on and I need to know everything.'

'You've been counting?' I asked. Shay still struggled to know what date it was half the time, let alone keeping track over months.

'I worked it out on the way here.' She sniffed, pressing her face against my hair. 'Okay, Kieran worked it out. But only because it's so many days no normal person could count that high.'

I pulled away. 'I missed you, too.'

'You're all different,' she said, tugging on my hair, which I'd not had cut now for almost a year.

'You mean an exhausted, frumpy wreck? It's how mums of tiny babies look.'

'No.' She narrowed one eye. 'It's not your appearance as such. Although those new curves are rocking that sweater.'

It was her old sweater. All my jumpers were.

'You seem... self assured. That hunchy slump in your shoulders has gone. Your chin is higher. Like, you've stopped feeling embarrassed about taking up space on planet Earth.'

'Hunchy slump? I thought we weren't making digs or criticising each other today.'

'I thought we were acting as if the past twelve months never happened. If you'd grown yourself some swagger last Christmas, I'd have mentioned it.' Her face clouded over. 'Sorry. I know we aren't talking about then, either.'

We weren't, and for most of the day, we didn't. But the three of us did talk about everything else. ShayKi's new Antarctic-themed collection, how the manager who took on my role never had a pen on her, and always turned up irritatingly early. What Shay's nieces and nephews were getting up to, her grandma's hip replacement. We discussed films and TV shows that we knew the other two would have loved – or loathed. We ranted about politics and gossiped about celebrities, some of whom we'd met and even had dinner with. I gave the briefest of updates about my family, and then told them a sanitised version of the past few months. They didn't need to know how badly I'd crashed and burned, spending my pregnancy wallowing in despair. They did get to hear about how I was currently rising from the ashes, making friends and costumes and generally doing okay.

'Tell me about the man,' Shay ordered as we feasted on beef and roast potatoes that evening. There were also masses of Yorkshire puddings, obviously, because we were Sheffield born and bred, alongside festive trimmings courtesy of M&S food hall.

'The man who gave me a lift home, which really isn't that outrageous given that he's a taxi driver?'

'Yes, the tall, dark, brooding man who looked as if he was fighting the urge to punch Kieran in the face.'

So, I told them. About how we met, how kind he'd been since. How he'd maybe not saved me, but helped me save myself. After a moment's deliberation and a swig of red wine, I also told them about the kiss.

'You love him.' Shay's eyes shone as she pushed her chair back from the table and stood up, brandishing her glass like a toast. 'You have actually managed to finally fall in love.'

'Careful,' Kieran warned, aware she was skirting dangerously towards the thinner conversational ice.

'Tsk,' Shay tutted, tossing back her braids, which clicked with gold and silver beads. 'I don't see Mary disagreeing with me.'

I put down my fork. I was stuffed anyway, and maybe this, at least, needed to be said.

'I loved Leo. As much of him as he allowed me to know, I loved. However—'

'We knew there was a however!' Shay exclaimed, causing Kieran to chuck a Christmas cracker at her.

'I may have developed feelings for Beckett that are... different from how things were with Leo. It's only been a few weeks, but I'm comfortable enough to completely be myself. At the same time, he makes me feel like I'm the most fascinating person on the planet.'

'He loves you back!' Shay crowed, bouncing up and down on her toes.

'I think he might.'

'Why isn't he here?'

'Because this is our day. I'm not doing a Kieran and gate-crashing it with a man I kissed for the first time yesterday.'

Shay grabbed her phone and ran around the table to take a snap of the three of us, all rosy cheeked, skewed party hats and satisfied smiles.

'Send him this, with our very best Christmassy wishes, and that we insist upon meeting him soon.'

'He doesn't even know who you are yet,' I said, sliding lower in my seat.

'What? We're the most important people in your life.'

'You *were* the most important people in my life. If I told him about you, I'd have to explain about Leo, and ShayKi and the rest of it, and I didn't want all that contaminating a new friendship.'

'Contaminating?' Kieran furrowed his brow. 'Is that how you see my brother? As a contaminant?'

'No. I saw him as my beautiful husband, who ended up the most painful, horrific, awful thing to happen to me, that I couldn't face going over again when I had to cope with a baby and everything else. Obviously, now we've kissed I'll tell him.' I frowned. 'If we're going to be dating or whatever, he needs to know.'

Shay forwarded me the photo and when I dug my phone out of a coat pocket to send Beckett a message about how my old friends were visiting and wanted to say hi, I found two missed calls from him, the first around four-thirty that morning. I'd left my phone in my bag, still on silent after the rehearsal, last night. After the shock of Kieran turning up, and the full-on day, I'd completely forgotten to look at it.

'Call him back!' Shay insisted. 'A post-kiss follow-up call the next day is a good sign.'

I tried, but there was no answer, so I put my phone away and we got on with exchanging gifts. Mine were hastily bought from Hatherstone market that morning, but I knew they'd appreciate the Major Oak T-shirt and silver arrow earrings I'd found on one of the touristy stalls.

They had bought me a gorgeous pair of Grace Tyndale walking boots. She was a shoe designer local to Hatherstone, and had a range of Sherwood Forest-themed boots. This pair were covered in mushrooms and beetles and I loved them. They had bought a whole sack-load of gifts for Bob, including a ShayKi hat and gloves from the baby range, and a pile of toys he wouldn't be interested in for months.

We spent the rest of the evening belting out our favourite karaoke classics and stuffing in cheese and crisps on top of our monster dinner.

Somewhere in those hazy hours around midnight, I blabbed to Shay about Kieran. Kieran knew I would; that was one reason he'd told me.

'You know, if you two want kids, you really need to stop faffing about,' I said when Kieran had nipped out to grab their overnight bags from the car.

'Who said I want kids?' Shay drawled back, lolling on the opposite end of the sofa to me, her feet in my lap.

'You did, many times. What's new is that you haven't denied that all those previous denials were denying the truth.'

'I don't know what you're talking about.' She couldn't have sounded more half-hearted if she'd tried. Quarter-hearted, maybe?

I sat up. 'I'm talking about accepting that he's completely in love with you.'

She pursed her lips, picking at a stray thread on the throw Beckett had bought.

Beckett – why hadn't he messaged me yet?

'There's been times when I've wondered whether he might be. I mean, the string of terrible girlfriends is a classic giveaway. And I know he's not in love with you. No offence.'

'Yuck. None taken.' I leaned over and took hold of her hand. 'He's your person, isn't he?'

Shay spoke slowly, as if working it out as she went. 'I honestly never thought so. Or at least, I knew he was my person, but dismissed the feelings as nothing more than friendship. You know how much it aggravated me when people assumed we were together, or should be together. Why can't a boy and girl simply be close, without needing to make it romantic? I didn't want to kiss Kieran. I wanted to hang out with him. Every day, more than anyone else. And then, the business, and working, and the odd time there was a flash of maybe attraction or our gaze lingered a few seconds too long... it was easy to push to one side, and pretend it was a silly moment.'

'You always hated his girlfriends. That's the other half of the secretly-in-love-with-my-best-friend cliché.'

'You hated his girlfriends!'

'I knew he was with them for the wrong reasons, so they wouldn't last. I wasn't jealous like you were.'

'Of course I was jealous, he was choosing to hang out with boring, fluffy women he had nothing in common with instead of me. The difference was, I had no desire to paw him all the time, unlike the girlfriends.'

'You've been talking in the past tense. What changed?'

Shay sighed, dropping her back against the sofa.

'After you left, he was so upset about Leo – and you, of course – then he started dating this woman, Eva, and she wasn't like the others. I actually liked her. She wouldn't put up with crap, so he stopped being crappy. It was the stupidest thing. We went out to a burger place, the three of us, and when the waiter asked if we wanted any sauces, he asked for mayo like he always does, and blue cheese for her, without even asking. Then he turned to me, as if waiting for me to say what I wanted.'

'Barbecue.'

'Well, obviously. The whole meal was full of these tiny, natural interactions between them, like he knew this woman, and she knew him. He noticed her. He cared about what she wanted. It made me so scared I actually threw up after the taxi dropped me home and they carried on back to his place together. It was as if whenever he topped up her water glass or she helped herself to a spoonful of his fudge cake, my eyes opened a little wider. I didn't feel ill because I had to share my friend, or even because he might be starting to care for someone more than me. It was like a horror show unfolding, and I was realising that all the irritating comments and jokes about us were right. I am totally in love with this man. Of course, like all emotionally stunted dopes, I only realised when it was too late.'

'Why didn't you tell him? Even if you didn't want to cause trouble with Eva, he's not still with her, is he?'

She shrugged. 'Why does anyone hide how they feel about their lifelong best friend? After seeing him with Eva, I properly doubted whether he felt the same, in which case me saying something would ruin everything. It might ruin everything, even if he does. What if he is just a commitment-phobe who can't handle a serious relationship? Eva was great, and still only lasted four months. We go at least one day a week not being able to stand each other. What if, once we got together, it ended up being every day?'

'He's handled a serious relationship with you since primary school. He told me this evening that being in love with you is killing him.'

'What's killing him?' Kieran asked, appearing in the doorway with a bag in each hand. 'And who's him?'

'You,' I said, pointedly, before getting up to pull him over to the sofa. 'I'm going to check on Bob and make us all a Baileys hot chocolate while you two finally talk about how you're in love with each other, and what you're going to do about it.'

I gave them a good twenty minutes, and when I got back I still had to cough several times and lob a reindeer cushion at them before they noticed me and stopped snogging.

I crawled into bed another hour or so later, my voice hoarse from all the singing, talking and laughing. I'd shown Shay and Kieran the spare bedroom and left them making up for lost time.

I sent Beckett one message.

MARY

All okay?

After our kiss, I'd been expecting a trickle of funny, sweet, flirty messages throughout the day, although perhaps the missed calls indicated that Beckett wanted to talk to me in person rather than send a WhatsApp.

When Bob woke me up the next morning, the day of the NLCCCCC, I still hadn't got a reply.

30

MARY

I didn't know how long a honeymoon period was supposed to last. Leo and I spent two and a half months in a post-marriage bubble, partly down to Kieran and Shay's bruising reaction to hearing I was now Leo's wife.

I expected them to be surprised, maybe upset that we'd denied them the opportunity for a hen-do, being bridesmaid or best man, and a celebration. But given how unenthusiastic they'd been about the relationship, knowing how I shied away from being the centre of attention, I hoped they'd at least try to understand why I'd done it.

They were irate. Coming up with all sorts of arguments about how we hardly knew each other; I'd been reckless and irresponsible. As they'd insisted earlier, I was fooling myself. I couldn't possibly love Leo, and it was bound to end badly.

'I thought you'd be pleased about having your tricky HR problem solved,' I snapped, after Shay made a pointed comment during a directors' meeting.

She glared at me. 'You honestly think I care more about that than I do about my friend making the stupidest decision of her life?'

'Why are you so determined to believe it's a bad idea? We've been together for months now and there's not a single red flag. You and Kieran can't come up with one solid reason for why this is a mistake. All you can say is that it's too soon. I'm thirty-two years old. I don't even buy a new kettle or book a haircut without thinking it through. It's beyond insulting that you of all people, who know me so well, can't accept that I know what I'm doing. Leo is Kieran's brother, not some random stranger I met on a dating app. What are you so worried about?'

'I just don't think he's the best match for you,' she mumbled. 'You aren't yourself when you're with him.'

'Maybe that is me being myself. The me when you and Kieran aren't constantly dominating and deciding everything. Maybe this is the me who was hiding behind you all along.'

I felt hurt and betrayed. They were acting like my parents – as if I were irresponsible, thoughtless and shallow. The one time I had made a proper decision alone, the people who had always accepted me disapproved. The only way I could cope with it was to pull away, even as it sliced through me like dressmaking scissors to not have them involved in every microscopic detail of my life.

However, while I hated their disappointment, the way they completely froze out Leo shocked me. When I tried to talk to him about it, he shrugged it off.

'Don't worry about it. They're having a tantrum because you've got your own life that doesn't include them, for once.'

Wow. That stung. And I didn't want my life with Leo not to include Shay and Kieran. There wasn't a lot I could do about it though, so I simply got on with my job, went home to my husband and kept on missing them.

Leo continued cramming in day trips and evenings out into our time together, which was fine on the one hand, but I was starting to fantasise about a day pottering about at home. Leo didn't understand why I didn't want to potter about in the Cotswolds or Lisbon. He was baffled when I tried to explain it was because my favourite blanket wasn't there, or my Hattie Hood cappuccino mug. I simply didn't find a swish hotel as relaxing as my own house. It was enough adjusting to Leo's semi-detached rental, after so many years living with Shay. It turned out I was a woman who liked a place for everything, and everything in its place. Including me.

This, alongside the continuing tension with my co-directors about the marriage, meant that I'd initially been less than enthusiastic when Leo said he'd booked us a surprise mini-break in Edinburgh for Valentine's Day, requiring me to take two days off. But after a brief internal whinge, I ordered myself to buck the hell up, because it was my first Valentine's Day with my brand-new husband and he wanted to treat us to a gorgeous break. Last year I'd gorged on takeaway pizza, then fallen asleep while watching the newest *Top Gun* movie with Shay.

Edinburgh was delightful. After driving up in the morning, we wandered along the Royal Mile and stopped for afternoon tea before visiting the castle, then headed back to the hotel where we'd booked dinner.

It was only much later, when brushing my teeth before bed, that I realised I'd forgotten my contraceptive pills.

I was on the wrong side of tipsy and after a wonderful evening, heady with the promise of twelve luxurious hours in our upgraded room, I couldn't face telling Leo that our early night was not going to be as anticipated.

And then, my foolish, drunken brain thought, *Do I really need to mention it? What's the worst that can happen?*

According to an article I'd read recently, my thirty-two-year-old eggs would need more than one pill-free night to spring into action. Other women my age were doing everything they could to get pregnant. And the unexpected flash of disappointment this produced made it easy to make up my mind. Perhaps I'd ask Leo how he felt about me forgetting to take a few more... Reluctant to put a dampener on our plans with a badly timed discussion about children, I said nothing.

Three weeks later, still sceptical that skipping one pill could have resulted in ovulation, let alone conception, I bought myself a pregnancy test. Away from the romance of Valentine's, snowed under with paperwork as we headed towards the end of the financial year, I had complicated feelings about the potential result. Despite working hard to convince myself that a late period was probably down to stress, I had an inkling. A gut feeling – or, more accurately perhaps, a uterine feeling – that this was going to be Big News. Leo had been fighting a nasty flu virus so I decided not to bother him until I was sure, taking the test in the bathroom at work.

It was with a mixture of astonishment (because despite the inkling, things like this didn't happen to people like me), panic and excitement that the fattest, bluest of blue lines appeared on the stick within seconds.

I sat on the toilet lid for the whole two minutes, in case the line disappeared again, and then several more, while every connection in my nervous system went haywire.

When our head of accounts messaged for the third time asking if I was going to make the scheduled meeting, I wrapped the stick in toilet paper and stuffed it in my bag, slapped some life into my ghostly cheeks and stepped back into a world that had changed completely.

I had no idea how Leo would feel. We'd talked about having

children one day, but only in a light-hearted 'what name would we call them? Boy or girl?' type way. While he was always up for a challenge, a baby would put a serious spanner in his free-range lifestyle.

If I was honest, that might be a bonus.

An image flashed into my head of me, clad in my pyjamas, cuddling a baby while watching *Anne with an E*, and it felt like bliss.

So, mind made up that this was brilliant news, I stopped off on the way home to get Leo's favourite Mexican takeaway, a bottle of non-alcoholic champagne, and a box to put the pregnancy test in, so I could hand it to him like a gift.

It didn't stop my hand trembling with nerves as I unlocked the front door and called hello. Hearing no reply, I made my way around the living room and kitchen-diner, but he wasn't there. His phone was on the worktop, so I left the takeaway bag and bottle on the side and went to look upstairs.

I found my husband unconscious on the bathroom floor.

w w w

Three hours later, as I sat hunched on the most uncomfortable chair ever invented, my predominant thought was, *Why am I the only person here who doesn't know what the hell has happened to my husband?*

The ambulance had arrived after a merciful twenty minutes. Kieran and Shay were there seconds later, Shay helping me out of the way and into the kitchen where she made me a mug of tea that was still on the side when I arrived back, an eon later.

Kieran stayed with the paramedics because, a) he wasn't freaking out, crying and wailing and generally being a nuisance, and, b) the sobering truth was he knew more about Leo's medical history than his wife did.

I felt as though my skull was stuffed with cotton wool, my thoughts sluggish and nonsensical as I allowed myself to be bundled into Shay's car and driven to the hospital. We ended up in one of the private relatives' waiting rooms, which, even in my hazy fuzz, I knew was the place they sent you when someone was dying.

Phrases like *'As you will know, this was always a potential risk... his situation means that it isn't as straightforward... due to his history, we will need to monitor extra closely...'* echoed off the walls, causing a wave of anger to build alongside my unbridled fear and confusion.

'I don't know,' I blurted as soon as the doctor had left. 'I don't know anything. I don't know what's happened, or why it's happened or why everyone, including that stuffy, pompous cardiologist, knows more about what the hell is going on with my husband than I do!'

After an ominous silence, Kieran came to sit beside me, taking hold of my hand. His face was grey, a sheen of sweat on his forehead. He looked at me, and what I saw in his eyes made my own heart shrink away in dismay.

'Leo has endocarditis,' Kieran said.

'I don't know what that is,' I sobbed. 'Am I supposed to? What is this, Kieran?'

'It's a bacterial infection in his heart.' He paused, swallowing hard. 'In the prosthetic heart valve.'

'The *what*?'

Kieran told me that when my husband was nineteen, he'd collapsed playing football. It turned out to be a heart-valve defect. After a few years of increasing breathlessness, tiredness and other symptoms, he'd ended up having a replacement valve.

Open-heart surgery.

He'd told me the scar on his chest was from a car accident when he was very young. I'd not wondered why the line was so straight. He'd said he didn't like talking about it, so I'd moved on.

Him not talking about it also meant that he'd not explained how he was now at increased risk of endocarditis, a heart infection that was serious if left untreated.

If left ignored, while pretending to your wife you have the flu, it could be fatal.

For the next thirty-six hours, they pumped Leo full of antibiotics. I spent most of that time drifting from his bedside to home and back like a zombie. My friends forced the odd cereal bar or piece of toast in my hand. I would stare at the food, wondering how on earth I was supposed to eat when everything turned to dirt in my mouth, until I remembered that it wasn't just me now, and I'd try to swallow it past the block of concrete lodged in my chest.

I finally fell asleep on the sofa, the morning of the second day, only to be roused by Shay a few hours later.

'He's awake.'

It was another two days before we were able to talk about it.

I sat beside Leo, his face shadowed with hollows, skin tone how I imagined a corpse would appear before the funeral make-up, an IV drip in his hand, surrounded by machines and monitors, the smell of sickness ripe in the air, and I tried not to throttle him. Needless to say, I was an emotional shambles.

'Why didn't you tell me?'

He slowly, painfully, twisted his head to look at me. 'I couldn't bear to spoil it all. The chances were it wouldn't become a thing. I was going to tell you. Of course I would have.' He had to stop to catch his breath before continuing. 'I just kept convincing myself to enjoy one more day without it being tainted by something that would probably never be an issue.'

'You lied to me,' I said, doing my best to sound supportive and sympathetic, while simultaneously wanting to stab him with the thermometer. 'Can you imagine how I felt when the doctor told me those vitamin supplements you take are warfarin? And when I asked him whether the injuries from the car crash would have any impact... I'm your wife, Leo. This is absolutely all about you right now, but if I'd known, I could have taken you to the doctor a week ago. You almost died.'

You still could, I thought, but knew it wouldn't do any good to say it out loud. 'I almost lost you because you kept this a secret.'

'I'm sorry,' he rasped. 'I'm a selfish coward. After getting diagnosed, I had so many years of being treated as weak, pathetic. I couldn't bear to be pitied by you as well.'

'That's why the rushed wedding. The grand gestures, the need to cram in as many "moments" as possible. Because you knew we might not have forever.'

'No one has forever, Mary. I'm just more aware of it than most.' He shifted on the bed, wincing. 'Aren't you glad you got all that time free from this hanging over us? I was jealous at how you enjoyed being in love like a normal person, with no reason to worry that it might all disappear far too soon.'

'No, Leo. No part of me is glad. When I married you, I married all of you. Not only the fun parts, or the easy bits. Even if your heart never got any worse, or needed further treatment, this is a hugely significant part of you. It dominated your entire twenties. It must have impacted how you think or act. Who you are. How could you not tell me? I feel like I never really knew you. I decided to marry you, without knowing the most important thing!'

'You're the most important thing to ever happen to me. And

this is why I couldn't tell you. Because if I had, every time you'd looked at me, or we made plans, every time I coughed or felt tired or had a quiet day, you'd have been thinking about it. Worrying. Watching. Waiting. Would you have even married me, if you'd known?'

'If you thought for one second that I might not have, then it's even worse you didn't tell me.' I was slowly losing the battle to remain calm and compassionate. 'At least I would have been a tiny bit more prepared to find my husband collapsed on the bathroom floor. I would have understood what was happening, rather than feeling like the only person in the room who didn't know why the man I share my life with is on first-name terms with a cardiologist.'

I shook my head in frustration. 'Of course I'd still have married you. You're still Leo. I don't know what to do with knowing you thought it would make a difference. Except remind myself you went through a horrible thing, and the trauma means you're not always rational about it.'

He was still for a long time. 'How about if I'd told you there's a 20 per cent chance I would pass this on to our children?'

What?

Those words jammed into my heart like a shard of ice, causing my whole body to break out in chills.

He struggled to pull himself up as I swayed dangerously on the chair. 'It's okay, there are tests they can do... They offer really good genetic counselling. Different options, if we ever decide to think about kids.'

I couldn't speak. Could this nightmare get any worse?

'And whatever happens now, I'm so glad we had this time together. These have been the best six months of—'

'I'm pregnant.'

The nurse found us, hours later, squished up in the bed

together, a damp circle of tears staining the hospital gown where it covered his scarred chest.

* * *

Three days later, Leo went into cardiac arrest. The surgeons did all they could. His heart was besieged by bacteria. The long-term damage caused by his congenital heart defect made any attempt at repair like patching up a wet tissue.

Leo died on 16 March. I was five weeks pregnant.

When Kieran and Shay came to collect me from the hospital, my shock and grief erupted in a torrent of red-hot rage.

Suddenly it made sense, why they'd been so blinkered about me rushing into things, so negative about the relationship in the first place. They'd known our marriage contained a secret that turned out to be deadly.

All I could think of when I looked at them was that if my ShayKi brother and sister had told me – or at least told me enough, so that I asked Leo for the rest – my husband would not have died. My baby would have had a chance to meet their father.

I left them at the hospital entrance and went back to my new home, alone.

31

BECKETT

Beckett was a mess. He'd faced worse, obviously. Turning up at the hospital to find Gramps in Intensive Care, barely alive after the stroke. Overhearing the phone call that ended his engagement to Rebecca. But the way Mary had stepped into that man's arms, as though coming back home, had felt like watching all his tender hopes and dreams crash and burn.

Bob had this man's eyes.

Mary's reaction at the register office had convinced him there'd been a husband.

Now, here he was to claim his wife and son, and Mary had embraced him as though the past few months had never happened.

As though that kiss had never happened.

Of course she did, you clown.

Beckett berated himself for being selfish enough to feel so aggravated as he drove home and spent a painstaking hour getting Gramps into bed. His grandfather was hard work that evening, belligerent and rude, fussing and griping. When Beckett allowed a shred of exasperation to leach into his tone, as Gramps tried to insist upon looking for a pair of socks that Beckett repeatedly assured him were halfway through a washing-machine cycle, Gramps stared defiantly at the floor and barked, 'Stick me in a home where I belong. Why force both of us to endure this misery?'

Beckett breathed deeply, counted to five and reminded them both that he'd made a promise not to do that, and nothing would make him break it. They'd have help again soon enough.

The endless Mary loop continued, as soon as he'd left Gramps in bed. *He's her husband. You're a guy she met at a vulnerable moment a few weeks ago, who she happened to kiss, once. A part-time taxi driver. With no money, and no life outside your job and taking care of your ailing grandfather.*

Ugh. The man had been driving a Lexus.

Still, he'd better have a heck of an excuse for abandoning his pregnant wife. It was clear there'd been zero contact since.

Beckett poured himself a whisky and turned his phone off, the urge to search for answers online stronger than ever.

* * *

After tossing and turning for hours, eventually drowning out with another large whisky the tormenting thoughts about what Mary and her probably-no-longer-ex were doing right then, Beckett snapped awake at four. Instinctively, he sensed something had woken him up. The kind of thing that always meant trouble. With a weary groan, he hauled himself out of bed and pulled on jeans and the Grinch jumper he'd worn to the rehearsal. Heart sinking, but not yet alarmed, he found Gramps' bed empty, along with the rest of the house. His pulse picked up when he found the back door locked, the front one not quite closed properly.

Wrenching it open, he sprinted down the path and scanned

the street in both directions, looking for huddled shapes, misplaced shadows, an old man who could barely walk stumbling along in the freezing darkness.

His curses barely squeezing past the tension in his throat, he threw on his coat, grabbed his phone and Gramps' parka, still hanging on the rack by the door, and raced back out.

He managed the first few minutes without descending into complete panic, expecting to spot his grandfather any second, already anticipating the flood of relief when he found him.

As more seconds ticked by, the sense of dread suddenly grew overwhelming. Beckett tried to force himself into doctor mode, removing any emotion from the situation and thinking logically. Easier said than done, when it was his only relative and not a random patient.

'Where the hell have you gone, Gramps?' he mumbled to the empty street, turning his phone back on. He called Mary. Yes, she had bigger things going on, but she also loved Gramps, and would have as good an idea as anyone where he might have wandered off to.

Who was he kidding? The truth was, her voice was about the only thing that would keep him from completely losing it right now.

No answer.

He carried on pacing along the road, searching frantically as he dialled a different number.

'What's up, my friend?' Moses sounded wide awake. 'Just trying to get Tabitha to accept Santa isn't coming for four more sleeps, so it couldn't have been reindeer she heard on the roof.' He paused for a second. 'Nope. *Or* sleigh bells. Sorry, sweetie.'

'Gramps is missing.'

Moses instantly switched tones. 'Fill me in.'

Within half an hour, the police had been informed and there

were five men – *five!* Beckett hadn't even met Clive before, but he was a retired police officer, so had offered to help – scouring the Bigley streets in a systematic grid formation that allowed Beckett to hold on to a paltry shred of hope that they'd find Marvin before he froze to death.

He'd cried, great, big, gasping gulps that had almost brought him to his literal knees, when the two cars had pulled up, and Moses, Bill and the other guys had sprung out, bearing huge torches, blankets and serious expressions.

Not for the first time in the past few weeks, Beckett appreciated afresh the monumental difference it made when heading into a storm with good people either side of you.

He barely felt the biting wind and icy drizzle, mind as numb as his fingers as he set his face like flint and doggedly followed the route assigned to him by Clive. Bill's wife, Susanne, was waiting at the house in case by some miracle Gramps found his way home.

Beckett had accepted that Gramps wouldn't live forever. But for him to go like this, alone and lost on a cold, dark street. Spreadeagled in some alleyway or sprawled in a gutter. Especially when, after the despair of the past few years, Gramps had finally started to find some enjoyment in life again. Beckett's head might be frozen, but his heart ached with a ferocity that put his earlier anguish about Mary to shame.

He couldn't even speak when he answered Sam's call, thirty minutes later.

'Found him curled up on a bench in that tiny park behind the school.'

Beckett sank to the wet ground. That park was a five-minute walk from their house. Fifteen, maybe, for Gramps. A good ten from where he was now.

'He's got a pulse. Breathing shallow, but steady. His extremities are ice, but his dressing gown and hat probably saved him.'

'Conscious?' Beckett was already lurching to his feet, gearing up for the sprint.

'For a few seconds, then drifted out again. Ambulance is on its way.'

Six minutes later, Beckett cradled his grandfather against his chest, as the worst of the fear seeped slowly into the night. Gramps had cried out when Beckett ran a hand down his left leg, the doctor pulling down the thick socks that had previously been in the washing machine with a grim shake of his head to find a purple, swollen ankle.

'Cancel the ambulance,' he told Sam. 'It'll be quicker if we go in a car. I can take care of him.'

Moses drove the two of them to the hospital. Gramps was drowsy, but lucid enough when he did stir.

'I told you,' he growled as Beckett strapped him in, after moving a booster seat and mountain of kid's clutter. 'Put me in a damn home.'

* * *

Beckett called Mary again once Gramps was finally settled on a ward. Still no answer, despite it being late morning. An X-ray had showed up a nasty fractured ankle, but mercifully minimal signs of hypothermia (the socks had helped, a nurse cheerfully informed them). Beckett related some of the other worrying behaviour and symptoms that had developed recently, and the doctor assured him that they'd refer Mr Bywater on to the help he needed.

Beckett felt like a deflated balloon. He'd sent Moses home at some point in the hours spent waiting for assessments and tests and then finally a free bed, then, much later, got a lift home with Jakob from Sherwood Taxis. It felt almost eerie to be entering an empty house.

He debated sending Mary a message, but he fell asleep on the sofa before he'd come up with something to say. After waking up in the late afternoon, he showered and changed, grabbed a banana and raced back to the hospital, not bothering to charge his dead phone. Gramps stayed awake for maybe ten minutes, during which he had the energy to grumble about half a dozen words, so, after watching him sleep for a couple of hours, Beckett chose the sensible option and left him to rest.

Instead of turning off to Bigley, he instead found himself heading along the smaller road towards Hatherstone. Beckett promised himself he'd no intention of causing trouble; he would pretend the kiss never happened, simply fill Mary in and be clear that, no matter what she'd said about ruining their friendship, he would make it work.

His foot rammed on the brake when he reached the cottage. The Lexus still squatted like a giant flea on the driveway.

All the hopes he'd dared not admit, that maybe Mary would have had an official goodbye conversation, agreed to work out some arrangement for letting this man see his son from time to time, and sent him on his way, collapsed along with his resolve to act like the better man.

Still reeling from the night before, unable to face putting on a polite mask when inside was a devastated wasteland, he turned the car around and headed back to his empty house, wondering what on earth he was going to do now.

32

MARY

Kieran and Shay crawled out of bed just before lunchtime. We made Christmas leftovers sandwiches and I told them I was ready to talk about Leo. Waking up that morning, I knew I needed to open this door, deal with what I found on the other side, then properly close it before I spoke to Beckett.

We went over everything. How Leo and I had fallen for each other. The glorious and the bumpier side to our relationship. How he'd almost, sort of, steamrollered me into a wedding, but that, without Shay and Kieran on my side, I'd felt as if, without Leo, I'd have no one. Besides, I'd been desperate to prove that I could be my own woman, for once. Make my own decisions and control my own life.

They shared their anguish at whether to tell me about Leo's heart problem. They knew it wasn't their place, but since when did the three of us have those kinds of boundaries?

Instead, Kieran had repeatedly pushed Leo to tell me himself, praying that, after years of difficulties and family issues, he'd not have to betray his brother's confidence.

Once I was married, they'd felt even worse. I'd emphatically pulled away, and shut them out, and they felt I'd removed their right to stage an intervention.

'We were petrified of losing you altogether. We knew you'd find it too hard to be angry at Leo. While our bridges were burning, you needed him, so instead you'd be upset at us for meddling,' Shay tried to explain.

'And we could see how important it was that you made a success of this,' Kieran added. 'We'd honestly never realised how you'd been feeling all these years, like a tag-along or afterthought. We never saw you like that, Mary. You're our sister.'

'If you were a third wheel, then ShayKi is a tricycle.'

'So, the more we interfered, the more you resented us.'

'You could have taken me out for a drink and broken it to me gently, instead of having a go at me all the time,' I said, feeling slightly bamboozled by their different perspective.

Shay sat back, counting off her fingers as she answered that. 'Bar Humbug. The Frog and Fly. That spa day, when I brought it up you stalked off and sat in the sauna with the scary man.'

I sighed. 'Okay. Maybe I didn't give you much chance. But this wasn't a fallout over my choice of partner. Leo died. I lost my husband. Bob's dad.'

'My brother,' Kieran said, with a sharpness that jolted me. 'I love you, Mary, but in the aftermath, you seemed to forget that. You'd known him six months. I'd helped him take his first steps. Sat with him in the wreckage of his diagnosis. Kissed him goodbye as they wheeled him to open-heart surgery. We might have had our issues over the years. But I lost my brother. We can all grow bitter about what if one of us had done things differently.'

'You think it's my fault?' I sat back, stunned.

'No more than mine, or Shay's, or our deadbeat dad's. No more than Leo's, for being so blummin' stubborn. The doctor for waiting almost a week before operating. Blind, cruel chance that he was the one to inherit the gene, not me or any of the others.'

We talked about afterwards. About why I had to leave. ShayKi had become a brutal reminder. Leo's designs were a major feature of the autumn collection, and every meeting, every decision, was like a knife thrust into my wound. It felt wrong, living in what I still considered to be Leo's house, but how could I move back in with Shay, when I couldn't bear to look at her? I wasn't strong enough to begin putting it right between us, and I would end up hating both of them if I stayed.

At that point I was also afraid that the baby would be a constant reminder. I was terrified that Leo's child had inherited the heart defect. I'd had no idea that a child could produce enough joy, and hope and wonder, to help heal my own damaged heart. Bob would have been a new bridge between us, but I couldn't see that then.

'Is Bob...?' Shay asked, taking Kieran's hand as his eyes filled with fear.

'He's fine,' I said. 'We got the all-clear while I was still pregnant.'

They asked what my plans were now, after eventually accepting that they wouldn't include ShayKi.

'I don't know. I'm giving myself a year of maternity leave, so can start deciding that in the spring. I think it's here, though. I'm wondering if it might include making things. A small business. I know it will be something simple, that allows me as much time as I want to be with Bob.'

'I think you should come back with us, just to double check,' Shay said. 'You can live with us and still do your own thing.'

They both knew that wasn't true, so instead simply begged me to come back for a visit.

'Just for Christmas! We've got the worst panto in the world

this evening, then carols at the pub with a brass band tomorrow. At the very least, we'll come and get you on Christmas Eve for the party.'

I held my ground. There was no way on earth I'd miss the carol concert that evening, I'd been invited to a festive fuddle at Li's on Christmas Eve, and felt sure I'd be spending Christmas Day with Beckett and Gramps. Hopefully a whole lot of days after that, too.

'You know I need to have a conversation with Beckett,' I said, manhandling Shay in the direction of the front door. 'Go and enjoy being all nauseatingly loved up, and I'll maybe visit in the new year.'

'With your gorgeous boyfriend?'

'He's not my boyfriend.'

'Yet,' Shay said, making me grin, because we both knew he soon would be.

'It's not too soon?' I asked, suddenly gripped with doubt and regret.

'Uncle Danny always said it's not about the right time, it's the right person that matters,' Shay said, her frivolity evaporating. 'You loved Leo, but you've admitted he wasn't necessarily right for you. You've found a man who brings out the best of who you are, instead of making you try to be who he thinks you are. Personally, I've recently concluded that waiting around when you've found your person is a stupid waste of precious time.'

'Do as I say, not as I do?' I asked, laughing.

'Do as I say, and as I'm doing as of now.' She grinned back, before hugging me with the force of all those missed months, and left me to it.

* * *

By the time I needed to leave for the NLCCCCC, I had given up waiting for Beckett to reply to any of my messages, and accepted Rina's offer to pick me up. Apart from the two missed calls, there'd been nothing. I refused to consider the possibility that, after our kiss, Beckett would suddenly ghost me. Even if it had prompted a minor freak-out, or what he'd said in the car was a lie to protect my feelings, he wouldn't be so ignorant as to flat out ignore me. These past two days were the longest we'd been without contacting each other in ages. I was genuinely worried, and when the reserved seat beside mine in the New Life hall remained empty, I couldn't quench the jitters. Either he genuinely couldn't bear to be in the same room as me, even for something as significant as this – and if so, I hadn't the faintest clue why – or something awful had happened.

A couple of minutes before the concert was due to start, I ducked outside to try calling again.

As I did, a message pinged through.

My initial relief, however, died with a splutter.

BECKETT

> Hi, Mary. I've been thinking a lot about what happened on Friday evening, and I wanted to apologise for letting the emotion of the moment take over. Kissing you was wrong.

What? It wasn't wrong! Beckett kissing me had been one of the rightest things to ever happen!

BECKETT

> You said you couldn't be friends with me now, but I sincerely hope we can both move past this rash mistake. It's probably best to take a bit of time apart, given the situation, but I would hate to lose your friendship altogether. Best wishes, Beckett.

A rash mistake? Time apart? Best wishes?!?

Was he serious?

Wow. How could two people experience the same two-second kiss and come up with such completely different conclusions about it?

I slunk back to my seat, huddled over with humiliation, hurt, and a growing flicker of anger.

How dare he act all pompous and rational, after flipping everything upside down, making me believe I could find love again after the crappiest year ever?

How could he do this to me, three days before Christmas? What was I meant to do now? Spend the day alone, me and Bob? Crawl back to Sheffield, my miserable face gatecrashing my sickeningly in love friends' first Christmas as a couple?

Beckett could take his perfectly punctuated brush-off and stick it up his stocking.

Thankfully, at that moment the house lights dropped, so no one could spot the tears about to pour down my face.

After the wackiest, wildest, most wonderful carol concert that surely ever graced a community church stage, while the crowd whooped and clapped their approval and Cheris and Carolyn burst out of a giant Christmas cracker to yet more rapturous applause, I slipped out of the audience. Collecting Bob from where he slept as peacefully as the baby Jesus in his makeshift manger, I mumbled some incomprehensible excuse about having to get straight off and practically ran to the bus stop, Bob bouncing against my broken heart.

* * *

The next day, Monday, I woke up feeling as if I'd slid back three months. As if all the worst things I'd ever wondered about myself were true after all. The urge to hide under the duvet was overwhelming.

I had to get up, though. After I'd fed Bob in bed, he produced the kind of stink that needed a changing mat and a bath, if not a hazmat suit or breathing apparatus, and by the time I'd sorted that, I decided I might as well decamp to the sofa. At least there was a TV there, and leftover crisps and mince pies from Saturday.

There I stayed, until, when I was thoroughly lost in a haze of cheesy Wotsits dust, foil wrappers, damp tissues and *The Holiday*, someone knocked on the door.

Clambering off the sofa, the blanket slipping to the floor, I scrambled to answer it, knocking over a tub of Quality Street as I went, only one person on my mind.

Surely he'd realised that the message was the mistake, not the kiss or the conversation?

Or not.

Standing there, with the biggest, fakest grins on their faces, were the absolute last two people I expected to see.

'What?' I blurted, before seeing the smiles freeze and realising that this probably wasn't the way to greet the parents I'd not seen in eighteen months.

'I mean, hi. Hello. I mean, sorry, this is a surprise.'

When she'd asked for my address I'd assumed it was to send me a Christmas card.

'Can we come in?' Mum asked. 'We've travelled rather a long way. It would be a shame if you're busy.'

She gave one of her quick full-body scans, and I automatically shrivelled a little. I was still in my pyjamas, which weren't exactly clean, my hair a mass of tangles, the effort I'd put into yesterday's make-up now smeared around my eyes.

'Obviously not busy,' I said, trying to sound more humorous than horrified as I stepped back to make room. 'It's great to see you.'

Mum left her coat on the banister and vigorously wiped crumbs off the sofa before sitting down, smoothing out the charcoal Hobbs dress bought from a charity shop several years ago.

Dad went to give me a stiff hug, angling his jacket to avoid the hot-chocolate stain on my pyjama top.

I ran upstairs to throw on jeans and a jumper, made us all drinks, then fetched Bob from where he'd been napping in his pram. Mum gingerly cradled him, eyes solemn.

'My first grandchild,' she announced. 'Welcome, Robin. Welcome to the Whittington family. I am your grandmother. But you can call me... Veronica.'

'Seriously?' I asked, rolling my eyes a little. 'Are you sure you wouldn't prefer Mrs Whittington?'

Mum squirmed. 'Grandma Veronica, then.'

She lasted about three minutes then passed him on to Dad, who looked as if he were holding a sleeping alligator.

'Now, I'd ask how you're coping, but I think that's all too apparent,' Mum said.

'I'm coping fine,' I said, more defensively than I intended, considering they'd traversed the Atlantic Ocean to visit us, no doubt cancelling numerous good works to be here. 'I had a busy week, so was taking things easy today. Bob had a restless night.'

Bob woke up once in the night for a feed and went straight back to sleep. His mother, on the other hand...

'Busy doing what, hosting a party for pre-schoolers?' Dad scanned the food wrappers and other debris.

'Shay and Kieran came down for a couple of days.'

'Of course they did,' Mum said grimly, as if that explained everything.

'I also designed and created eighteen costumes for a community carol concert,' I ploughed on, ignoring her. 'The show was last night, but it was pretty hectic the week before, so I was planning on catching up with cleaning and everything today.'

At least, I'd planned on putting all the sewing equipment away at some point, because the sight of it made my chest ache.

'A community venture?' Dad asked, raising his eyebrows.

I showed them a few photos of the cast in costume.

'Well, I'm pleased to see you using your talents to bless other people, for once,' Mum said, handing me the phone back after a cursory glance.

I swallowed back all the comments about bursaries, scholarships, fair trade, sustainability, apprenticeships... then changed the subject quick before I vomited them up again.

'What happened to your plans with the charity? The beach house?'

'We told them they could do without us for a couple of days,' Dad replied. 'Cameron is doing a live podcast on "Why it's your fault Christmas is a catastrophe", so couldn't take the time off to visit.'

'You know that staying somewhere so huge by ourselves doesn't align with our values,' Mum added.

'Besides, we wanted to meet our grandson,' Dad said, voice gruff. 'And check how you are. We interpreted your comment about the care package as a request for help. Sometimes it's our own family in need, and we know you don't find it easy to admit when you're struggling.'

I had made a point of ensuring I would never need to admit that, under any circumstances.

'Having a baby isn't easy. Especially if doing it on your own…' Mum glanced around, as if expecting a father to waltz in at that precise moment.

There was a long silence, interrupted by Bob's alarmingly vigorous hiccups. I gently lifted him out of Dad's arms and cuddled him against my chest, a mini human shield to deflect their reaction to what I was about to say.

And then I told them everything.

Well, the bits not including lies, betrayal, broken friendships, secret office romances and eight months drowning in despair, anyway.

* * *

'Please come home for Christmas,' Mum asked, for the fourth time, after I'd opened the presents they'd bought for Bob, all ethical, natural fibre, educational gifts. They gave me a pair of wool socks knitted by men enrolled in one of Dad's programmes, which went perfectly with the boots Shay and Kieran had got me, and was one pair of socks more than I'd bought them.

We were now eating the organic Christmas fruit cake they'd brought accompanied by chunks of extra-strong cheddar cheese, as dictated by Yorkshire tradition.

'This is my home,' I repeated, as I had the previous three times.

'Oh, you know what I mean. Our new tenants don't move in until the end of January, so you could linger on once we've headed back to Chicago.'

Her eyes swept up from the shabby carpet to the patch of damp in one corner of the ceiling, via the cracked fireplace, and I took the hint.

'I think it's probably best if you go now,' I said, standing up to make a hint of my own. 'Like I said, I've got a fair bit to do this afternoon and am pretty busy over the next few days.'

'Busy?'

'I'm going to a party at a house so posh you'd be guaranteed to disapprove, and hanging out with my friends. Some of whom have given their lives to noble endeavours like adopting traumatised children and running food banks, others who enjoy doing equally acceptable things like writing books or driving a taxi.'

'Right.' She started looking for her bag in amongst the pile of Bob's presents. 'Well, as long as people are at peace with their choices, and can look back without regret at the impact they had on the world—'

'Mum, it's Christmas. I've not seen you in forever. I heard a perfectly good sermon at the carol concert yesterday. Can you please spare me another one?'

She paused for a moment, before straightening up. 'I can, yes. But if you don't mind, I must say this.'

I braced myself, already dismissing whatever advice or passive-aggressive critique she was about to thrust upon me.

'Honestly, Mary, you're doing tremendously well, after a hellish start to motherhood. To begin again, alone, in a new place, and manage the sleepless nights and feeding and the mountain of stuff parents are expected to buy these days...'

I could literally not remember Mum praising me like this without adding some kind of judgemental dig on the end.

'You're resisting the pressure to bother with superficialities like your appearance, or your house, or pretending you're a superwoman needing to ace every facet of motherhood...'

There it was.

'Well. I'm proud of you.'

I nearly fell back onto the sofa.

'Thank you,' I stammered. 'I... I appreciate you saying that.'

I thought about it as I cleaned and tidied up once they'd gone. Reflecting on the past few weeks, where I'd been, and where I was as we headed into a new year, I had to conclude that, despite the sting of Beckett's rejection, I was proud of myself, too.

33

MARY

I did my best to focus on the positive, getting my house in order, having a long bath before distracting myself with two Hallmark Christmas movies back-to-back (in neither of which did the handsome love interest message the main character to say kissing her was a rash mistake) and dragging my sleep-deprived bones up to bed.

When I woke up on Tuesday morning, however, the space in my heart and mind where Beckett should have been felt crammed with jagged rocks.

I was so grateful for all the lovely messages and photos I'd had from people at New Life, thanking me for the costumes. I was also cheered up by watching the coffee mums WhatsApp group descend into frazzled hilarity as the women dealt with prissy relatives, a little boy who'd discovered the present stash and decided Christmas had come early, plus a dog who'd snarfed a tray of pigs in blankets.

ROSIE

I honestly think I might slip some of that super-strong bleach into Nadia's low-cal mimosa.

Rosie's sister-in-law had announced she was giving Rosie's bathroom a 'quick once-over', producing her own cleaning products and spending nearly an hour scrubbing before informing her eight- and ten-year-old girls that they could now 'pee-pee' without worrying about 'boy tinkles all over the place'.

RINA

How did we end up here? Christmas is supposed to be time off for fun and festivities. Joy to the world and peace to all men!

ROSIE

That's it. To all MEN. For us women, it's usually more work, more stress, more demands on us to attain the impossible Insta-Mum heights of perfection as we collapse under the pressure to make sure everyone has the Most Wonderful Time of the Year.

SOFIA

Preach it, sister. Add to that, any time we do anything that goes well, we're expected to reproduce it faultlessly, endlessly, every Christmas until the end of time. The list of 'family traditions' in our house has become a monster threatening to consume the last crumbs of my sanity. If I'm not buried alive in Amazon orders, vegetable peelings and board-game tantrums first.

LI

You should try sharing the tasks out more! Angus always wraps presents while I write the tags and we have a great time cooking together

The Most Wonderful Time of the Year

ROSIE

> We love you, Li, but we're not coming to your party, which no doubt Angus will have co-organised and prepared in a perfect fifty-fifty split with you, if you don't stop showing off.

Rosie added a kissing emoji as if that took the snark out of her comment.

RINA

> What say you, Mary? Is Christmas a patriarchy-driven scourge on women?

MARY

> Maybe it's up to us to draw the line? My mum has never cooked a Christmas dinner in her life. We had one present each, a few paper chains made from old Socialist Lawyer magazines, and the closest we got to celebrating as a family was someone asking for a hand with a crossword clue.

> Personally, I'm looking forward to me and Bob creating some Christmas memories to treasure. I want him to look back and remember that we both enjoyed a magical time together. I guess it'll take a while to figure out what that looks like for us. Do what brings happiness, to you as much as everyone else. If that's a five-course banquet, hand-printed wrapping paper and carols around the piano, go for it. If it's a takeaway pizza in non-Christmas pjs and a bunch of gift vouchers, then all power to you.

LI

> If ever we doubted Mary was a true coffee mum…

SOFIA

> Even if I am now craving a large pepperoni.

> What are you having for Christmas dinner, Mary? I hope Beckett is doing his share!

And there it was, jabbing at me like a reindeer headbutting my chest. I was so sick and tired of missing people. Leo and my friends had been too much – raw, painful, paralysing. This time, I felt as though every vital organ had been bruised and battered. Whenever I thought about Beckett – which, let's be honest, was at least once a minute; his kindness and generosity were scattered in every corner of my home – it made me sad, of course, but, more than that, 'taking a bit of time apart' simply felt wrong.

I typed out a dozen messages, ranging from jokey:

MARY

> Is this enough time apart? Because I spent ages choosing your Christmas present and can't be bothered to return it

To heartfelt and rambling:

MARY

> Can we talk? Because I don't think the kiss was rash, or a mistake. I miss you, Beckett. If you can't be more than friends, I understand, and I will never cross that line again, but it would really help if you could explain why, because I'm miserable without you.

I deleted every single one.

* * *

Li's gathering started at three, so I arrived at half past, hoping it would be busy enough for me and Bob to blend into the crowd. Her home had been transformed yet again. I'd have predicted tasteful decorations in silver or gold, but instead every room was now a multichromatic riot. Coloured lights hung around the edge of the ceilings, paper baubles the size of footballs dangled above our heads in a random mix of red, orange, teal and sunshine yellow. Sofas and chairs were covered in spotty, stripy or swirly blankets while wreaths, stockings and various other shimmering, glittery or light-up ornaments hung on every bare patch of wall. Every surface was laden with canapés and miniature festive treats. Tiny Christmas puddings, smoked salmon and cream cheese bagels that could be eaten in one mouthful, cocktail sausages, Brie and cranberries on postage-stamp squares of toast. Li was wearing a dress covered in rainbow sequins with silver tights, and I felt positively dull in my dark red jumpsuit, even with a gold belt.

Glancing around the room, I had to smile as I compared it to the Christmas Eve bonfire party, which was amateur chaos in comparison. Nevertheless, the sudden pang for a bowl of lamb curry, a sparkler and people who'd known me forever made my breath catch in my chest.

And then, a deeper longing. I'd guessed that Beckett wouldn't be there, given that he'd know I would be. I still couldn't help scanning the clusters of people, in case he'd decided he could handle being in a crowded room with me, after all.

The room felt somehow empty without him. I felt like a clumsy, miserable stranger. The effort of walking up to people and inserting myself into their conversation demanded energy and confidence I simply didn't possess right then. I decided instead to find a seat in a corner, preferably next to a person I'd never met before, so if they insisted on chatting I could keep it to vague trivialities.

I should have known better. After Sofia immediately came and asked for a cuddle with Bob, I spent the next hour or so nodding uncomfortably and saying awkward thank yous as at least half of the party guests came to congratulate me on the carol-concert costumes, wonder where I'd learned to sew like that, or suggest I set up a business.

'I have,' I said, eventually running out of polite responses.

'You have?' Sofia asked, breaking off her chat with someone else to spin around and stare at me. Bob was now fast asleep on someone else. 'What business? You said you'd helped out friends on a market stall.'

'I did. But then those friends happened to be fashion wizards who were hugely successful, and we set up a company together.'

'Which company?' Rina asked, eyes wide.

I glanced at the ShayKi changing bag she'd been showing off at the coffee morning a while ago, now sitting beside a recliner.

'ShayKi!' Rosie gasped, because at this point half the room was listening in.

'My friends are Shay and Kieran.'

'No wa-a-a-ay!' There was a sudden flurry of movement as people shamelessly whipped out their phones and started searching.

'Mary Whittington?' someone breathed.

'Does Beckett know?' Sofia asked quietly.

I shook my head. 'I was going to tell him, but then...'

'Yeah, he's got other things on his mind right now. Have you been to see Marvin today? Moses popped in this morning, but Marvin was asleep most of the time so he ended up taking Beckett to get some food. Are visiting hours the same over Christmas?'

'Visiting hours? Where?'

She looked confused. 'Isn't he still in King's Mill?'

'The hospital?'

Sofia stared at me. 'Have you not spoken to Beckett?'

The Most Wonderful Time of the Year

I shook my head, the dread rippling over my skin standing my hairs on end.

'Marvin wandered off in the early hours of Saturday morning. Moses and a few others helped Beckett find him. He'd fallen and knocked himself out, has a nasty broken ankle and other bumps and scrapes. After briefly coming round, he'd managed to clamber onto a bench, which helped avoid hypothermia, at least. Mary, why didn't you know this?'

'He phoned me, about four-thirty in the morning, and again later on but I'd left my phone in the bottom of my bag so I missed the calls.'

My synapses had shot into overdrive, propelled by the need to do something, to get to Gramps, to see Beckett, to crank back time and answer those damn calls. To ignore his stupid request for time apart and tell him that of course it wasn't a mistake. We loved each other.

I love him.

Beckett didn't have nobody else to help him any longer. He had Moses and Sofia, and whoever had joined in the search for Gramps. But I was more than that. I'd never met anyone who I fitted alongside so well as Beckett.

'Mary, what's happened? It's been three days. Why hasn't Beckett told you this?'

'I... I have to go.' I frantically looked about for Bob, grabbing his changing bag. 'Can you explain to Li that I need to see Gramps?'

'She'll completely understand. I mean, apart from how come you didn't already know, of course.' Sofia pulled me in for a fortifying hug. 'I'll be praying you can both work it out, whatever it is, and you know we're here if you need us. I'll message you Gramps' ward number, because I couldn't remember that kind of information even if it weren't the most wonderfully busy and stressful time of the year.'

'Thank you.'

I had Bob in his car seat and was halfway to the front door before I realised I had no way to get to Mansfield. It was Christmas Eve – what were the chances of booking a taxi on the fly?

'This is Eric,' Li said, appearing at my shoulder. 'He's happy to drive you to King's Mill.'

'What?' I turned to find a rotund man with a white beard who, I supposed in the spirit of the season, wore a red padded jacket and a matching woolly hat with fur trim. 'No, I couldn't possibly ask you to do that.'

'You didn't. My niece did, and I'd do anything for that lass.'

'Rina,' Li explained.

How could I not know about Gramps after three days, and yet everyone here knew that I didn't know within seconds?

'Besides, I hate parties. Only came to stop Rina and her mother whittling about me being alone on Christmas Eve. I live around the corner from the hospital. It's the perfect excuse to skedaddle without offending Li and Angus.'

'No offence taken.' Li beamed. If he'd told Li her party sucked, her decorations were ugly and the food tasted like cardboard, I didn't think she would have minded.

As weird as it was to be driven in Eric's ancient Ford Escort, the entire dashboard vibrating in time to his Neil Diamond cassette tape, he was the perfect chauffeur. He drove as swiftly as my galloping heart while remaining entirely silent until parking up outside the hospital entrance twenty minutes later.

'Thank you so much,' I said, fumbling to unstrap Bob's car seat. 'Hope you have a lovely Christmas.'

'Sooner it's over with, the better,' he grumbled, before giving a mischievous wink. 'Get in there and snag your man.'

Pausing only to follow the signs, I hurried through the hospital, which thankfully was relatively small considering I was also lugging Bob in his seat. Still, it felt far too long until I arrived, breathless for so many reasons, at the entrance to the geriatric ward.

Here I forced myself to stop, steady myself, plaster on my attempt at a cheery yet concerned expression, and entered the room at a more inconspicuous speed.

Gramps was in one corner, the bed next to him empty, which seemed miraculous given the busy time of year. His eyes were closed, but as I approached, he slowly opened them to wrinkled slits.

Oh my.

He had a dressing on the side of his head. One cheek was a shocking mix of grey and purple bruises, and his whole demeanour was terribly old and horribly frail.

'Wondered when you'd finally show up.'

I hastily sat down, undoing Bob's straps and lifting him up so Gramps could see.

'Bob missed you.'

Bob was currently fast asleep.

'Bob could have come to see me yesterday. Or however long I've been here.'

'Bob didn't know,' I said, feeling another flood of guilt. 'I didn't know. I missed Beckett's calls on Saturday morning, and then he must have been too busy here to see my messages since. He... We...'

Gramps grunted. 'That explains why he's been so miserable, then. If you two have had a tiff.'

'No, we haven't... I don't think.'

He narrowed one eye even further, if that was possible. 'He tells you all my other business. Can't think of another reason he'd not be pestering you about this.'

I sighed. 'I don't honestly know what happened.'

'Best try asking him, then.'

'I will.' I gave a firm nod. 'I will. Is he here?'

'Out working. Might as well earn some money while I can't get into any mischief.'

'Right. Well, I didn't come here to see him, anyway. I came to see you. What happened, Gramps?' I dared take hold of his spindly hand. 'Why were you out in the middle of the night? Didn't you consider it could be dangerous?'

He glanced at me, before staring stubbornly at the sheet for a long moment.

'I knew it was dangerous. That's why I was out there.'

I tried not to tighten my grip.

'You were trying to hurt yourself?'

Or worse? I thought, with a jolt of horror.

He gave a barely perceptible shrug.

'It's not right. A grandson being chained to his grandad all the time. Worse than prison. Buttoning my trousers, cutting my dinosaur-claw toenails. I didn't mind so much him being shot of that woman. She wasn't right for him anyway. But he let go of everything else. Himself included. Beckett used to laugh. It was infectious. All my doubts and guilt about everything, losing his mother for starters, would disappear when I heard that laugh.

'It was bad enough being saddled with me when the only diagnosis was being a chronically grumpy old fart. Now, though. Now...' He broke off, voice cracking.

I waited until he could speak again.

'He should be free to make his own choices, get on with his life.'

'He is,' I said, gently. 'He chose to take care of you.'

Gramps shook his head in frustration. 'I liked Tanya well enough. Even if she is an old battleaxe. But he works all day, comes home to me night after night. I've told him. It's not right. And it's not like I'm getting any better,' he added, as an aside.

'So why the night-time wanderings? Why make it harder for him?'

'So hard he has to make the right choice. Either that or I freeze quietly to death in a doorway, spare the both of us any more misery.'

'Is that really something you want?' My voice was little more than a whisper. I knew what it felt like to fall asleep not particularly caring whether you woke up.

He sighed. 'No. I want to be somewhere where the sorry folk stuck with changing my dressings get to go home at the end of the day to their own families. Where they get paid, so I don't feel terrible every time they chop up my meat as if I'm a toddler. Trained professionals, so I don't shrivel in shame when I make a mess of myself. Somewhere with other people I can moan at and gripe about, or thrash at *Countdown*. I like having lunch with other people my own age. Who talk sense. I might even want to try a hobby, or an old geezers' trip to the seaside.'

'You want to go in a care home?'

'I want my grandson's face to light up when he sees me. For us to hug when he says goodbye like when he'd head back to university. For us to have something to talk about. News to share. Our time together should be precious, not a prison sentence.' Gramps finally looked at me, his eyes swimming with tears. 'I want him to miss me when I'm gone, not feel relieved.'

'Oh, Gramps.'

'I might even find myself a lady friend.'

'Why haven't you told him?'

'I tried!' he said, voice switching to irritation. 'He keeps going on about how he made a promise, he's never putting me in a home. Won't listen when I tell him that's what I want.'

'So you decided to make it so hard, Beckett would have to break his promise?' I tugged on his hand. 'Did you forget in your old age that he's just as stubborn as his grandfather? He'd run himself into the ground before going back on a promise.'

'It was all going to plan until you turned up,' he snapped, but there was affection behind the grumble. 'Offering to babysit me, make it easier.'

'Well, if you'd told me all this earlier, I could have helped!' I retorted, smiling. 'Saved you a broken ankle and some nasty bruises.'

'Humph.'

'Have you told him now?'

Gramps shook his head. 'They keep talking about what to do with me when they think I'm asleep, like I'm a child. I'm not so doolally I can't make my own decisions.'

'I'll talk to him. Help him understand.'

He managed a feeble nod before slipping into sleep.

I stayed for another hour or so, hoping Beckett would turn up, while at the same time scared about what would happen if he did. At one point, a nurse with tinsel in her hair bustled over and informed me that children under five were only allowed on the ward under special circumstances. Then Bob gave her the biggest of baby smiles, and her sternness melted.

'Ah well, so,' she cooed in a strong Belfast accent. 'It's Christmas. It doesn't get much more special than that, I suppose. We'll let you visit Great-Grandaddy, as long as you keep it down. Don't disturb the other patients. Deal?'

Then she shook Bob's tiny fist, discreetly drew the curtain far enough to hide us both, and left us to it.

'Hey.'

I'd almost dozed off myself, when the familiar voice jolted me upright in the chair.

I twisted around. Bob was back snoozing in his seat, and suddenly I had no idea what to do with my arms. 'Hi.'

Beckett looked like a total wreck. His hair was an unruly mop. His bloodshot eyes were ringed with dark shadows, the rest of his face wan. He had a splodge of something – barbecue sauce? – on his bobbly jumper.

For some reason he was also wearing a headband with Santa on a bouncy spring.

'Everyone's a Santa?' I asked, unable to think of anything else to say.

'Something like that.'

'You look how Santa Claus must feel on Christmas morning.'

He gave a rueful smile, dragging up another chair and sinking into it. 'You look incredible.'

'Why didn't you tell me?' I whispered.

He leant forwards, dropping his head into his hands. 'I did call.'

'You should have left a message. Texted. Called round and cried on my sofa! I know you said about needing time apart, but I'm a grown-up, Beckett. This is way more important than feeling awkward about a kiss. I could have got over it.'

'You had more important things going on.' He peered up at me, face squashed against his fingers.

'What?' I sat back, confused. 'Like the carol concert? That was one evening. Oh, and my parents called in. I'd have infinitely preferred to have been here with you and Gramps than tolerating their Christmas anti-cheer.'

'I meant your husband.'

Now I was really flummoxed.

'Bob's dad?' Beckett mumbled.

There was a horrible silence.

'What are you talking about?'

'He was there, after the rehearsal.'

Oh! *Oh.*

'That was Bob's uncle. My husband's brother.'

Beckett sat up.

'Um. What?' It was his turn to look bewildered.

'My husband died in March. His brother, Kieran, was one of my best friends and fellow founder of our company, ShayKi.'

Beckett went so pale I feared he might slide off the chair into a dead faint.

Instead, he swore under his breath, dark eyes not leaving mine.

'But that explains your weird rejection,' I added, voice wobbly as the pain of Beckett's message hit me all over again.

He swore more loudly this time.

I reached down and covered Bob's ears. 'Maybe we should talk about this somewhere else?'

Beckett shook his head, as if coming back to himself. 'Yeah. Yes. Visiting time is nearly over anyway. We could go back to yours. I mean, if there's no one else...'

'There's no one else,' I said, firmly enough to convey that I was talking about a whole lot more than my cottage.

We both gave Gramps a soft kiss. Then, in a move bolder than I'd have believed possible coming from me, I took hold of Beckett's hand as he carried the car seat to his taxi.

34

BECKETT

Beckett had never felt so deliriously happy and such a complete numbskull at the same time.

He was her *brother-in-law*.

Bob's uncle.

Beckett felt genuinely distraught that Mary's husband had died. He couldn't imagine what that must have been like, but he guessed a whole lot worse than finding out your fiancée is a callous cow.

However, the abject misery that had been plaguing him since seeing the Lexus had evaporated. He would still have felt an undercurrent of panic that he'd completely messed things up with that cowardly message and the silence since. But she'd held his hand all the way to the car, and had smiled at him as he'd started the engine in a way that made it impossible to feel scared.

It was basically impossible to be scared when he was with her.

They waited until they were home before resuming the conversation, instead chatting about the carol concert, Li's party, Mary's parents. The trauma of Gramps going missing.

Mary told him about her conversation with Gramps in the hospital, and even as Beckett veered between disbelieving, irritated, furious and to some degree relieved, knowing Gramps, it did make sense.

'It's typical of the stubborn old goat not to simply admit he's changed his mind.'

'How do you feel about him being in a home?'

Beckett thought about this. He had so many feelings it was hard to distinguish them.

'If it's what he wants, then of course I'll support it. It'll be so strange him not being around all the time, but, like he said, if we can go back to being more like grandfather and grandson – father and son, really – rather than carer and patient, how can that not be a good thing?' He smiled. 'And I won't be complaining about no more interviews with home-care managers.'

'You didn't fail him.' Mary reached over and took his hand where it rested near the gear stick.

It was all Beckett could do to nod. He wasn't sure he quite believed that, yet, but he would try.

* * *

Once Mary had put Bob in his cot, she made omelettes using the leftovers from a Christmas dinner she'd eaten with her friends.

They lit the Christmas candles Beckett had brought around, and with them combined with a fire in the hearth and the Christmas tree lights, the room flickered with a cosy – dared he imagine romantic? – glow. They sat either end of the sofa, plates balanced on their knees, and he waited for her to talk.

The fire was mostly embers by the time she'd described meeting Leo, their secret romance and rushed wedding. His heart ached as she wept while sharing how, after discovering she was pregnant, she'd found her husband unconscious, and a week later she'd lost him.

After he'd made a pot of tea and brought through slices of cake, she explained how she'd tried going back to work, but could barely make it past the entrance. How her relationship with her friends had disintegrated, leaving her lost and alone. She couldn't bear to stay in Leo's house, surrounded by his things, and had fought so badly with Kieran over what happened to the possessions, she'd simply packed her bags and left.

'How did you cope, being here, after all that?'

Mary shrugged. 'I didn't. Remember the state of this place when you turned up? I hadn't even bought a pack of nappies.'

'You coped, Mary. In your own way. Maybe the best way. You needed time, so you allowed yourself to take it. You needed to rest and recover. To grieve and to get over losing your business and your friends as well as your husband. Your whole life. But you did it.'

'I did wonder if this cottage had been like my cocoon.'

'You were a caterpillar?' He considered that. 'But now you're a butterfly. I'd agree with that.'

She screwed up her face. 'Maybe one of those dull, browny-grey moths.'

Beckett put his mug on the table. 'I've always loved moths.'

She gave him a sideways look, eyes shining in the candlelight. 'Is that the first time you've lied to me, Beckett Bywater?'

'Nope.'

She widened her eyes in surprise.

'The first time was when I said kissing you was wrong.'

'Ah.'

'And the second was that it was a rash mistake.'

'Any more, while you're on a confessional roll?'

He edged closer to her on the sofa, emboldened by her putting her own mug down.

'The third lie was that I thought we should take some time apart. And the moths. I haven't always loved moths. But if that's what you are, I absolutely love them now.'

'You love moths?' she breathed.

'I love you, Mary.' He slowly reached up and cradled her cheek with his hand. 'The truth is, I am absolutely, agonisingly, irrepressibly in love with you.'

'I love you, too,' she said, smiling so hard he didn't know how he would manage to kiss her.

They figured it out.

35

MARY

After more talking, more kissing, more smiling like a pair of lovesick teenagers, then feeding and settling a baby before more conversation and crying about all the things we'd left unsaid, I ended up falling asleep in Beckett's arms. He nudged me awake enough to drag myself up to bed and change into pyjamas before immediately collapsing back into oblivion the second I crawled under the duvet.

After Bob woke me up with an urgent request for breakfast, I changed into leggings and an oversized hoodie and went downstairs, expecting to find Beckett under a blanket on the sofa.

The living room was empty. To my dismay, the rest of the house was, too.

That was fine – it was only six and still dark outside, but maybe Beckett had headed home to change before going back to the hospital. Perhaps he was working an early shift.

Except that he would have told me, wouldn't he? Or at the very least left a note, or sent me a message.

By the time I'd made coffee, I was debating whether it was

within my rights to feel upset that he'd disappeared on me when the front door opened and he hurried inside, closing the door against a gust of wintry wind.

'Are you okay?' he asked, coming to find me in the kitchen, his eyes flickering with doubt.

'I thought I must have scared you off,' I said, managing a hesitant smile.

His brow furrowed, head shaking as if the very idea was preposterous. 'Not possible.'

I leant against the table, the rush of relief followed by a swift surge of joy.

'So, where did you go?'

'To get this.' He disappeared, then came back carrying a large box wrapped in glittery paper. 'Happy Christmas, Mary. In the spirit of being a Santa, I thought I'd be able to bring it over before you woke up.'

'It's Christmas Day!' What with everything else going on, I'd completely forgotten.

'I also got us breakfast, but that's still in the car. I wasn't sure which you'd like first.'

I thought about that. My stomach was more than ready for breakfast, but I was beyond eager to know what was in that box.

'Both at the same time?'

He grinned. 'That's why you're the clever one.'

* * *

It was a sewing machine. Second-hand, because he'd rightly deduced I'd rather a reconditioned better-quality machine than a cheaper new one. There was also a beautiful velvet box containing all the essential sewing kit, including threads, pins, scissors and a tape measure.

He gave me an envelope with Bob's name on it, inside of which was a photograph of a brown and white cocker spaniel puppy.

'I haven't confirmed it yet. But I thought, with Bob growing up out here with no neighbours close by, he might like a friend to play with. It's a good reason to get out on walks, and might help you feel safer when strange men come wandering into your back garden, rapping on your windows.'

'I've never had a dog before.'

'I have. I can show you what to do, what they need. Like I said, if it's not what you want, I can cancel. Or keep him myself. He's already house-trained. One of my regular clients bought him and then got a job overseas. He's called Hudson.'

I took a moment to picture it. Me and Bob, walking through the trees with a spaniel scampering alongside us. Hudson curling up in front of the fire, playing fetch with Bob once he grew older. A best friend who'd love him unconditionally. A long-term commitment, not to living in a penthouse apartment in the middle of a city, but to this new life, here in the forest.

'It's perfect.'

Cue more crying into my bacon butty.

My present for him was a three-month membership of a local rowing club. A bit presumptuous, but not even close to buying someone a pet.

He promised to accept the gift on one condition.

'You have to try it with me some time.'

I squinted at him over my coffee mug. 'What, with Bob as our cox?'

He grinned. 'I'm sure one of those coffee mums would love to have him for a couple of hours.'

'Okay. But not until it's warmer. Pick a date sometime in the spring.'

'A date?'

We both exchanged soppy smiles at the confirmation that we'd still be hanging out together in the spring. That we so casually arranged a date that both of us knew would be 100 per cent a romantic one.

'This is the best Christmas present,' I said once we'd finished eating. My heart felt swollen with happiness at the simple act of clearing up breakfast together. I hadn't been alone for that long, compared to some, nothing compared to Beckett, but we had both felt very, *very* alone, given how insular and empty our lives had become.

'Okay, that's not true. The puppy is better. But having you here is... more than I could have ever dreamed of.'

'Is that how it's going to be?' Beckett raised one eyebrow, tugging me gently until I bumped up against him, having to crane my neck to meet his sparkling eyes. 'Me coming second to the dog? The dog who will chew your furniture, steal your socks and never once bring you breakfast?'

'The dog who'll never say he wants "time apart", or that kissing me was a "rash mistake"?'

'Ouch. How long is it going to be before I'm allowed to forget that?'

I grabbed his woolly jumper with both fists. 'I don't know. How long are you planning on sticking around for?'

He replied with a slow, sexy smile that flipped my insides upside down. 'I'm here as long as you'll have me.' He bent to give me a soft kiss. 'Well, I actually need to see Gramps at some point, but I was hoping you might want to come along too.'

He kissed me again. 'To see Gramps, and wherever else we decide to go.'

'Are you talking about the New Life Christmas Day Lunch? Because I promised Sofia I'd bring custard.'

'I'm talking about the lunch. Dinner. Breakfast. A billion mugs of tea, pieces of cake and tonic and gins. Hot chocolates at the Winter Wonderland. Ice-cold beers in the summer. Wherever. Forever. Sticking around, hanging around. I'm not sure how else to say that I'm yours now. If you'd like.'

'I would like. A lot.' I rested my head against his firm chest that had always felt like the safest place on earth, adding a whisper. 'Almost as much as a puppy.'

* * *

We drove to the church, where Yara had invited us both (separately, the night before, presumably in some obvious attempt to get us talking again) to a lunch for people who would otherwise be spending the day alone.

I was nervous about eating Christmas dinner with the kind of people who had no friends or family to be with, while at the same time chastising myself for being judgy, given that up until very recently, I was one of those people.

I should have known my fears would be totally unfounded. As well as Sofia, Moses and all their children dropping in on their way to Sofia's enormous half-Irish, half-Italian family Christmas, there were the Christmas Twins, Patty and a whole bunch that together were lively, lovely and the exact opposite of my actual family, in all the best ways.

'Are you sure you two qualify to be at a lunch for lonely losers?' Yara asked with a knowing smirk.

We both made no effort to hide our grins, Beckett squeezing my hand underneath the table.

* * *

'Did you still want to come with me to see Gramps?' Beckett asked as we headed home after helping clear up, stomachs almost as full as our hearts.

'Yes. Absolutely.'

'You don't sound very sure.'

'I just... I don't want to give him the wrong impression.'

Beckett gave me a sharp glance as he stopped at the last set of traffic lights before leaving Nottingham. 'Which is what? I thought I made my feelings about that very clear.'

'Well. Yes. But feelings are one thing. You haven't actually asked me anything... specific.'

He drove for a minute in silence, while the insecure, never good enough, unimpressive part of me wondered again whether I'd pushed things too far, even as the new, improved Mary had no doubts about the man sitting beside me, and where I stood with him.

'Are you asking me to ask you to be my girlfriend?'

'I'd really prefer not to have to ask you to ask.'

He did a sudden sharp turn, pulling into a track by the side of the road and bumping along for about twenty metres until coming to a stop surrounded by woodland. Turning off the engine, he got out of the car, strode around to the passenger side and opened my door.

'Come on.'

'Is this where you finally murder me and leave me in the woods?'

He gave a frustrated-crossed-with-amused eyeroll, then took my hand and pulled me out.

After staring at me for a few seconds, he dropped to one knee.

'Beckett! Stop! What are you doing?'

'Mary.'

'No. This is not the time for a proposal. Please don't make me have to turn you down.'

'It's not a proposal. Although I mean it just as much, so it might as well be. But it isn't! You wanted a formal ask, so this is me showing you I mean it. Mary Whittington, will you be my proper, monogamous, committed, romantic, in-love-with-me girlfriend?'

I took in a deep breath. Thought about Bob. About Leo. Shay and Kieran and the life I'd lost, and the one I now wanted more than anything. The one where every day I got to share it with Beckett Bywater.

Still, I had to ask.

'Are you sure? Because I can't take another broken heart just yet.'

'Are *you* sure? I'm never going to offer you grand gestures, wild adventures, everything Leo gave you. I'm really a very boring man. With an elderly, grumpy Gramps as baggage.'

'Then I love boring. I don't want all that faff and forced fun. I never did. But are *you* sure? Talk about baggage. I'm a woman with a baby, a dead husband, no job and a whole load of family issues. I'm honestly still quite a wreck.'

'I love your baby. As if he were my own.' Beckett stood up, pressing his forehead against mine, his voice dropping. 'One day, I would love to call him my son.'

'Shucks, Beckett.' I had to pull back to wipe my face. 'Asking someone to be your girlfriend shouldn't be this emotional.'

'Let's try again, then. Hey, Mary, do you fancy being my girlfriend? No pressure or anything.'

'Go on, then.' I laughed through my tears. 'I've no better offers right now, so might as well give it a go.'

* * *

Given the rule about children, Gramps was allowed to be pushed in a wheelchair to the café for a mince pie and a cup of tea, but wasn't well enough to linger for much longer than the time needed to give us a present. He had somehow got someone to buy us theatre tickets for the spring, offering to keep Bob company while we enjoyed a night out alone.

'You think they'd allow you out of a care home to do babysitting?' Beckett asked.

Gramps looked affronted. 'You're finding me a retirement home, not shipping me off to prison.'

Making a mental note to ask Sofia or Li if they'd be free on that date, I gave him the super-warm coat I'd bought, with a promise to take him out in it often, and then Beckett and Gramps discussed the future plans to find him somewhere 'not full of morons or zombies' to live, until Gramps told us to wheel him back to the ward and leave him in blessed peace.

We drove back to my cottage as the sun set behind the oak trees, the Christmas stars already twinkling above our heads. I had no idea what the new year would hold for me. This time last year I was founding director of a brilliant company, living in Sheffield and zipping between business meetings and trips abroad with my brand-new husband. Now, here I was. A mother, living in a ramshackle cottage in the middle of a forest. I had new friends, new hopes and dreams starting to emerge. A boyfriend who I felt completely myself with.

For the first time, I genuinely knew who that was. Curled up on my shabby sofa with Beckett as he cuddled Bob, the fire crackling, an extra-gooey pizza in the oven, I wouldn't have chosen to be anyone else.

* * *

MORE FROM BETH MORAN

Another book from Beth Moran, *Have I Told You Lately*, is available to order now here:

https://mybook.to/HaveIToldYouLately

ACKNOWLEDGEMENTS

As always, an enormous thank you to the fabulous Boldwood Books, and all those who have helped turn my shaky first draft into a book that I'm really proud of. I'm especially grateful to Emily Yau. Your kind words have alleviated any trace of nerves I had at the prospect of working with a new editor.

Thanks as always to my agent Kiran Kataria, for her continued enthusiasm, as well as all the detailed input behind the scenes.

Back in 2024, at my million books party, I had a quiz, with the prize of having a name featured in my next book. I'm delighted that my cousin, Carolyn, who has read every one of my books, and my Auntie Cheris (who had just celebrated her 90th birthday at the time!) have lent their names to the Christmas Twins. I hope it goes without saying that there is absolutely no resemblance when it comes to personality!

Huge thanks as always to everyone who has read, bought, borrowed or shared about my books. I wouldn't get to do this wonderful job without you. I love reading your messages – do keep getting in touch!

For Ciara, Joe and Dom, who always make Christmas one of my Most Wonderful Times of the Year, I love you. For Asher and Bella – being part of your story continues to be a joy and a privilege. George – thank you for all the nights you stayed up with a crying baby so I could have enough energy to get this book written (and for everything else!).

ABOUT THE AUTHOR

Beth Moran is the award winning author of ten contemporary fiction novels, including the number one bestselling *Let It Snow*. Her books are set in and around Sherwood Forest, where she can be found most mornings walking with her spaniel Murphy.

Sign up to Beth Moran's mailing list for news, competitions and updates on future books.

Visit Beth's website: https://bethmoranauthor.com/

Follow Beth on social media here:

facebook.com/bethmoranauthor
instagram.com/bethmoranauthor
bookbub.com/authors/beth-moran

ALSO BY BETH MORAN

Christmas Every Day

A Day That Changed Everything

Take a Chance on Me

We Belong Together

Just The Way You Are

Let It Snow

Because You Loved Me

Always On My Mind

We Are Family

Take Me Home

Lean On Me

It Had to Be You

Have I Told You Lately

The Most Wonderful Time of the Year

BECOME A MEMBER OF

THE SHELF CARE CLUB

The home of Boldwood's
book club reads.

Find uplifting reads,
sunny escapes, cosy romances,
family dramas and more!

Sign up to the newsletter
https://bit.ly/theshelfcareclub

Boldwood

Boldwood Books is an award-winning fiction publishing company seeking out the best stories from around the world.

Find out more at www.boldwoodbooks.com

Join our reader community for brilliant books, competitions and offers!

Follow us
@BoldwoodBooks
@TheBoldBookClub

Sign up to our weekly deals newsletter

https://bit.ly/BoldwoodBNewsletter

Printed in Dunstable, United Kingdom